WITHOUT GOOD REASON

COLETTE LEWIS

CRANTHORPE
MILLNER
PUBLISHERS

Copyright © Colette Lewis (2025)

The right of Colette Lewis to be identified as author of this work has been asserted by them in accordance with section 77 and 78 of the Copyright, Designs and Patents Act 1988.

All rights reserved. No part of this publication may be reproduced, stored in a retrieval system, or transmitted in any form or by any means, electronic, mechanical, photocopying, recording, or otherwise, without the prior permission of the publishers.

Any person who commits any unauthorised act in relation to this publication may be liable to criminal prosecution and civil claims for damages.

This book is a work of fiction. Names, characters, places and incidents are either products of the author's imagination or are used fictitiously. Any resemblance to actual events or locales or persons, living or dead, is entirely coincidental.

First published by Cranthorpe Millner Publishers (2025)

ISBN 978-1-80378-315-4 (Paperback)

www.cranthorpemillner.com

Cranthorpe Millner Publishers

Printed and bound by CPI Group (UK) Ltd
Croydon, CR0 4YY

For Chris, with love

CHAPTER 1
CORINE

It's freezing outside, the farm cocooned in a shroud of darkness as absolute and endless as the early morning sky. If she could, Corine would crawl back into bed, retreat beneath the womb-like warmth of her duvet, and sleep. All that tethers her to the outside world is a small herd of Highland cows, fifty sheep, and a scattering of goats and chickens. Even in sleep, she hears them—primitive sounds that echo like the fragile cries of newborns, calling out to be fed.

A coffee pot rattles on the Aga. Corine lifts it from the heat, startled when she catches sight of Joe asleep in his chair. For a moment, her heart plummets—imagining she'd left her husband in the new kitchen extension all night. He's facing the large window that, in a few hours, will frame the best view of the farm and the North Sea beyond. His head lolls to one side, the tartan rug she'd placed over him pulled tight across his arms and chest, as though comfort had been the least of her intentions. A scar runs the length of his scalp, raw and angry-looking, slicing through his unruly grey hair.

Corine averts her eyes and pours herself a coffee, noting the tremble in her hands: a warning sign that she is failing to take care of herself. Not that she needs reminding. The empty bottles stacked by the kitchen door say enough.

A border collie appears from under the table and sniffs

at the empty food bowl in the corner of the room. She looks back at her owner accusingly.

'What?' Corine snaps.

The dog stares intently at the bowl, as if willing Corine to hear her thoughts.

With a sigh, Corine shuffles over to the fridge in her too-big suede slippers. 'Fill the damn bowl—right? Isn't that what you'd say to me if you could?'

There's a note stuck to the fridge door that catches her eye. It's from Cathy, the community nurse, telling her she will be back in a few days to pick up the remaining bits and pieces.

Corine laughs bitterly. 'That's all we are in the end, Betty, a few worthless fragments.'

Betty whines and backs away, her claws scratching on the stone floor. Corine takes an opened tin of dog food from the fridge and shakes what remains into the bowl, watching as it's quickly devoured.

Leaning with her back against the cluttered work surface, she closes her eyes and raises the cup of steaming coffee to her lips, hoping it will help ease her morning grogginess. It tastes bitter, and in sheer frustration, she thrusts the cup down amongst the squalor of the kitchen table. Coffee spills everywhere, seeping into a pile of unopened mail.

'Fuck!' She grabs a handful of envelopes, mopping the spilled coffee with her sleeve. 'Go, lie down,' she growls, as Betty emerges from beneath the table, gazing up at her.

The dog whimpers, turns, and pads off toward the extension, curling up beside Joe's chair.

Most of the envelopes are official-looking—bills and bank statements—except for one: a small, cream envelope, handwritten and addressed to Dr Corine Alexander.

Corine tears it open, hoping the coffee hasn't sunk through. The card inside is an invitation to a baby shower; it's simple, floral, and there's not a baby or stork in sight. It makes Corine smile, despite her mood.

Join us for our Baby Shower, from mummy-to-be Lisa Thompson.

Lisa has written on the back, "*Miss you. Would love to see you. Love, your favourite niece*". Corine's smile broadens. Lisa is her only niece.

She checks her watch: five-thirty. Perfect—no one else will be awake yet. Corine dials the number she knows by heart and waits for the voicemail to kick in. She forces a smile, lifts her chin and keeps her tone light—the exact opposite of how she feels.

'Hi Lisa, it's Corine. I'm so sorry, but I won't be able to make the baby shower next week. It's the farm—you know how it is. The animals won't feed themselves, and, well... it's not exactly a quick trip from up here.' Her throat tightens, the dryness making it difficult to swallow. Her voice sounds unfamiliar, strained. 'If things were different, you know I'd be there in a heartbeat. But—'

Before she finishes speaking, the phone clicks, and she hears the muffled voice of her niece, still thick with sleep.

'Aunty Corine?' There's a slight pause while she listens. 'Is that you?'

Corine closes her eyes, wincing. 'I'm so sorry, did I wake you?'

'Oh, I'm not sleeping anyway; the bump's way too big. Is everything alright?'

'Yes, yes, it's just, well, you know how early things start here, and I wanted to leave you a message about the baby shower before I got caught up with work.'

'Can you come?' Lisa sounds hopeful.

'No, I'm sorry, darling, I can't get anyone to look after things at such short notice.'

'That's why I sent the invite early.' Lisa's tone is playful, but the reprimand hits home loud and clear; the invitation had been sat on the table for over a month. 'It's not until the end of next week.'

'What with everything, you know I… I just can't.' Corine closes her eyes tighter, hating herself.

'Sure, I understand. It's still so soon.' Lisa pauses. 'Since Uncle Joe's—'

'I would if I could, but I don't have time with the farm. That'll be you in a few months, when you have a little one crawling about everywhere,' Corine says, quickly changing the subject and keeping the conversation light.

Lisa's laugh sounds throaty. She was at that uncomfortable stage, Corine recalled, when birth is close and excitement and fear co-exist in every breath.

'How are you feeling?' she asks.

'Nervous. Missing Mum. I wish…' Her voice trails off. 'You know.'

'I do know, my love. Me too.'

'Oh, I'm sorry Aunty Corine, just ignore me. I haven't spoken to you in ages and I'm getting all maudlin.'

'It's only natural, she was a good mum—the best.' Corine's

older sister, Mary, had been gone for over a year now, but hearing the emotion in Lisa's voice, it was clear she hadn't yet made peace with her loss. When Lisa announced her pregnancy, Corine had hoped a baby might give her the focus she needed—but, as she well knew, even that could go either way.

Birth and death were all too common on the twelve acres Corine called home. It wasn't unusual for calves or lambs to be stillborn or deformed and, quite often, the smaller, weaker ones didn't survive a season—especially if the weather was as harsh as it was now, or when born to neglectful mothers.

She hears Lisa telling her husband, Peter, to go back to sleep, and the rustle of a duvet. Most likely Lisa shifting position, getting comfortable, ready to talk.

'Listen,' Corine says. 'I'll have to call you back. I'm sorry, but I really do need to feed the hairy beasts, otherwise they'll get all moo-dy on me.'

Lisa laughs politely as they say their goodbyes, failing to acknowledge the source of the familiar joke. Before the accident, and for the entire twenty-eight years of their married life together, Joe had offered up corny jokes, like how a cat might deliver a mouse to its owner's doorstep. He had wanted to please her; to see her looking happy, and she hadn't always appreciated the effort that took. Even the kitchen extension, vaulted and magnificent—he'd been an architect for most of his working life—had been to please her, to expand her view so she wouldn't get bored and turn inwards, regretting their move to a place they had once considered paradise.

Corine *had* regretted it, though. The croft and Joe hadn't been enough, and she had made that clear to him when she scurried back to London after her sister died.

She hears Joe coughing in the other room—deep, wrenching coughs, as if something is lodged in his throat. She squeezes her eyes shut and presses her hands over her ears, but the coughing persists, ragged and insistent. Unable to bear it a moment longer, she stands abruptly and slips through a side door, into a small porch. Removing her frayed housecoat, she pulls on her boots, waterproof trousers, and a heavy, padded coat. Betty is already beside her, eager to go outside.

A powerful wind lashes Corine's face, whipping her hair into her eyes as she strides towards the fields, where sixteen cows cluster by the gate, waiting to be fed. She tugs her woollen hat down over her ears, stuffing stray strands of greying hair beneath it. Head lowered, she leans into the wind, making her way towards a circular steel feed rack that's been toppled and now rests against a drystone wall. Gripping the cold metal, she hauls the rack upright. It towers above her, heavy and awkward, and she braces herself before slowly rolling it forward.

'Away, stupid dog!' Corine yells as Betty gets too close.

The border collie drops back obediently, weaving left and right as she trails behind. With considerable effort, Corine wrestles the rack further away from the wall, but the ferocity of the wind makes it almost impossible to control. She should call her neighbour for help, but instead, she presses on alone, straining every muscle until a violent gust sends the rack hurtling back towards her, slamming into the side of her face. Adrenaline surges. Gasping, she shoves the rack away, sending it clattering to the ground. A warm trickle of blood slides down her cheek.

Instinctively, Corine looks to the big window, but there's no sign of Joe, just the outline of dark clouds reflected in the tinted glass.

After filling the rack with hay and checking on the cows, Corine heads back inside to clean her wound. As she watches Betty run on ahead towards the house, she knows she's been lucky this time. And reckless.

†

Inside, Corine relishes the warmth from the Aga, stripping off her outer layers and boots. Underneath, she's wearing the same top she's slept in for the past week—stained and slack-looking. She sniffs her armpits and wrinkles her nose.

'You could have been killed.'

Corine hears Joe's voice, slurred and slower than it was before the accident, and her heart surges. Pulse quickening, she walks over to the extension and sees him back in his chair, steadfastly facing the view, refusing to meet her eyes.

'Yeah, well, I wouldn't be missed.' Corine knows she sounds petulant, like the teenager they never had, but she isn't in control of her emotions.

Betty whines and shoots past her, circling a spot in front of Joe's chair and settling down on the rug, her head resting on her front paws, ears and eyes alert.

'Says the man who went out on his own in a storm—on a quad bike,' Corine grumbles; she can't help herself. 'What did you think I was going to do, Joe? Abandon you? Go back to London and start a new life? Lisa had just lost her mother—my *sister*—for Christ's sake! I had to go to her. I'm all the family she has left!'

It was out of her mouth before she could stop herself—not that she wanted to. Something perverse within her was enjoying twisting the knife, pushing it deeper into already spoiled flesh, reopening old wounds, conflating one trauma with the other.

'You told me I had my chance to have a family and threw it away, or don't you remember saying that?'

Betty's low growl, like a warning, stops Corine, and she checks herself.

'Okay, okay, I'm sorry. Come on, come here, good girl.' Reluctantly, the dog inches forward as Corine bends down and offers her upturned palm. 'Loyal to the end, so you are, you big softie.' Her voice is quiet now, lilting—not her natural accent. 'And who is it that let you finish off my plate last night, hm?'

Corine often thinks they'd have been like this—competing for their son's attention, had he lived. Yet she was certain that, no matter what, when it came to their child's wellbeing, they would have been on the same team.

Tears surprise her, spilling silently down her face. *This won't do,* she tells herself, brushing them away. Yanking open a cupboard, she roots behind rows of tins, eventually pulling out a new bottle of single malt. Without hesitation, she opens it, pours a generous glass, and downs it effortlessly.

The side of her face throbs as she glances at her reflection in the small mirror above the sink. A welt is already forming around the cut.

'Just a scratch this time,' she mumbles, dabbing a little antiseptic over the area. She pours her second coffee of the morning and sips. 'Cold, like everything in this frozen place.'

Still shaken from the near miss with the feeding rack, and with her resolve to keep running the farm all but gone, Corine moves to the table and sifts purposefully through the mess of papers. She pulls out a folder. Inside is a letter addressed to her from Richard Forbes, Senior Psychiatrist at The Orchard Clinic. She dials his number and waits for the voicemail to kick in.

'Hello, Richard. It's Corine. Look—I've changed my mind.' Her fingers drift to the cut on her face. 'I've decided to come to London as soon as I can organise cover for the farm.' She hesitates. 'That's assuming you still want me to be Mae's psychiatrist? And just to be clear, it's not just that Mae asked for me, which is still…' she searches for the right word '… irregular. But if she's finally willing to meet her mother after four years of refusing, then there's a slight chance she'll admit moral culpability. Forgiveness from Dr Bailey, though… that's an entirely different matter. And if I'm being honest, I don't know who could forgive an attack like that—not from your own child.'

CHAPTER 2
MAE

Mae is already awake when she hears the usual warning to be up and washed for breakfast at seven-thirty. Normally, she stays in bed for five minutes longer each morning—an indulgence that allows her to feel in control of a tiny portion of her day.

Her eyes follow the direction of the sunlight filtering through the faded lilac curtains, coming to rest on the top of the bookshelf—lined with awards and certificates from her time at The Orchard. Beside them is a row of books by an American author, each set in the same neglected neighbourhood on the East Coast. The characters are, for the most part, ordinary people living ordinary lives—but it's their flaws that make them stand out, make them relatable. At least, to her they do.

She likes to imagine herself part of their quirky families, endlessly intrigued by the inner lives of such decent people—lives that feel impossibly distant.

Mae reaches under her pillow and pulls out a book. On the front cover a couple and a young man sit on a bench at a train station. There's something about the young man's stance that makes him look nervous. Perhaps he's worried about the journey he's about to make? Or the person due to arrive on the next train? As Mae stares, the confusion of imagined possibilities darkens her mood. To make matters worse, she hears, for the second day in a row, the undulating moans of the new girl in the room next door.

Disgusted, Mae throws off her duvet and strides across the room to the small sink in the corner. She turns on the tap, letting the running water drown out the unwelcome noise. Without glancing at the mirror above the sink, she ties her hair back and splashes her face, then brushes her teeth and hair—both with brisk, almost aggressive strokes. Finally, she pulls on clean joggers, a T-shirt, and an oversized sweatshirt that hangs just above her knees. Her androgynous style makes her seem younger than eighteen. Younger, and much easier to overlook.

The corridors and social areas are filling up with noise and conversation as patients and staff move towards the breakfast area. It's the usual fare: toast, a choice of cereals, fruit, milk or juice, tea or coffee, and for the several patients with eating disorders on top of their other problems, the steely eyes of staff recording what's chosen and eaten. Not always the same thing.

Mae nearly skips her usual Cheerios and juice. Someone, no doubt well-meaning, has taped a handwritten note to the cereal container: *Positive thoughts create positive feelings.* Another, stuck to the juice jug, reads: *Hope is seeing the light despite the darkness.* Mae tears the second note to shreds and drops it in the bin. It's far too early to deal with the Sunshine-and-Lithium brigade.

Carrying her breakfast on a tray, she makes her way slowly to the back of the room and sits next to a beautiful dark-skinned girl, who shifts over wordlessly, without glancing up from her food.

Malika has been Mae's only friend and ally for the last four years. Both were admitted on the same day, young and in shock, equally terrified by the reality of their sentences and the crazy people they now shared a living space with. Facing their own and other people's mental illnesses close-up every single day was frightening, especially at so young an age.

Mal's method of coping had been to allow her emotions—all manner of anger and hurt—to pour forth, reacting to whatever real or imagined slight she heard, regardless of whether it was directed at her or not. It took several months and various interventions before she finally settled down and accepted her situation, but not before upsetting staff and patients alike. Only Mae seemed unaffected by the force of Mal's personality. She had been immune, somehow, as though she had mentally drawn a veil over herself, blocking out the sounds she heard, protecting herself from Mal and anyone else's intrusive behaviour. To some patients, it made her look even more insane than Mal. To others, and there were one or two who had taken a dislike to her in the early days, Mae's silence was proof that she thought herself better than everyone else. Being well-spoken, along with her fondness for books, was simply further evidence of her aloofness.

It took several months following her sentence before Mal was allowed to attend group therapy. Mae had been going since her fourth week, contributing nothing to the conversation and showing no interest in the other patients. Sixteen-year-old Mal, on the other hand, when asked at her first session if she could pinpoint when things started to go wrong for her, had spoken openly and confidently about her past.

'I was nine when my family emigrated from Mauritius. Always buy a guidebook, people!' A chorus of sniggering followed. 'Mum and Dad worked different jobs. Shift work mainly, so they were never home, and my fifteen-year-old brother was put in charge.' Mal laughed. 'Total fucking oik! Meanwhile, he gets talent spotted by'—she made air quotes with her fingers—'the estate's *entertainment committee*. Fast forward six months, my boy's in serious debt with a developing crack habit, and to save his skinny arse, I start selling to pay off his debt. After that, there's drink, the occasional weed, but I'm a fast learner, what can I say.' Mal shrugged. 'By the time I was twelve, I was dealing in class A drugs and services, if you know what I mean. It's your classic fairy story. A rags to riches tale for people like us.'

The therapist, guard, and four of the five other patients had all nodded along with the familiar account, except for Mae, who had been rubbing at a spot on her hand.

'Was he worth it?' Mae had asked then, looking up and staring intently at Mal.

Everyone's eyes had widened.

'No way!' Mal had exclaimed. 'I sacrificed myself for a total fucking dickwad!'

To the rest of the group's surprise, Mae had begun to laugh. Quietly at first, then louder. Mal joined in too, though her eyes had given away her uncertainty. One or two of the others had voiced their disgust at Mae's response; at her disrespect and blatant disregard for the rules of group therapy, but Maria, a large, docile girl who brought out the maternal side in everyone, swiftly moved the conversation along, asking Malika if she'd ever taken any of the hard drugs that she sold.

Mal had shaken her head. 'Apart from the time I was found wandering on the M6 naked and covered in my drug dealer's blood, with no fucking recollection about what happened.' She shrugged. 'The judge said drugs contributed, but they weren't why I was arrested. Truth is, it's only since I got locked up in here that I became dependent. Man do they push them antipsychotics!' Her laugh was loud, from somewhere deep down inside, and Mae had loved it.

After that first group session, the girls became inseparable. Opposite in every way, except one—they both feared being labelled "psychotic".

Mae watches as Mal spoons in the last mouthfuls of porridge from her bowl before moving on to her toast, which she barely chews, gulping it down with milky tea. She wipes her mouth and only then looks up at Mae, watching her slow, steady chewing with growing impatience.

'For God's sake, Mae, be careful. You almost got four Cheerios on that spoon!'

'Mal!' Mae snaps, her eyes darting around sharply to check if any staff are watching. She waves at Judy, a stout matronly type from Woking, who's giving a pep talk to one of the new patients. 'I'm never hungry of a morning,' she murmurs.

'What's going on with you?' Mal follows her every move with her eyes. 'You need to eat, or you'll be dead before we get outta here. That's hopefully soon, babe. Soon!' She closes her eyes and crosses her fingers.

Mae nods, but knows she doesn't look convinced. She slowly places her spoon into her bowl without finishing.

'If you don't feel like eating nothing, imagine you're doing something else.' Malika picks up a banana, opens it delicately and pretends to fellate it.

Both girls laugh, unnoticed by the tables of patients and staff, who continue eating and chatting. If it wasn't for the bars on the windows and locks on the doors, the dining hall could be a normal cafeteria at a typical college.

'That's about all you *could* do with the drugs we're on.'

'My libido's just fine, girl. Speak for yourself.' Mal wafts her hand as if batting the thought away.

They both laugh, their heads close together like conspirators sharing secrets.

Just as Mae and Malika take their dishes to the kitchen hatch, a crash of plates has everyone jumping back, alert to the sound of trouble. The atmosphere shifts in an instant, staff spring into action, quickly surrounding a patient who hammers her fists against a table in the far corner of the room.

'Say it again, go on, I dare you!' she screams.

'Nothin', I didn't say nothin'!'

Mae and Mal watch as another inmate backs away from the larger woman, looking confused and terrified in equal measure.

'You were talking about me!'

'She wasn't talking about you, Shana,' says one of the nurses, moving between the two patients. 'Remember what we discussed? It's just the voices you're hearing. You know this, Shana, they're not real.'

'Look, there, it's there.' Shana points to an empty space on the floor. 'It's following me, her shadow! Look!' Her eyes are wild as she points randomly at the floor, then beside her, before lurching towards another group of inmates.

Guards and nurses close in, forming a circle around her.

Shana leaps back, agitated, bouncing on her tiptoes like she's about to spring forward at any moment.

'Stop following me. Shut up, tell her to shut up!' she says to no one.

Three guards edge closer still as one of the nurses tries to calm her.

'Try to ignore the voices, Shana. Come with me to your room and I'll give you something to calm you. You'll feel better then, you know that.'

'Stay away from me. I don't need none of your fucking pills. It's not me, it's her!' she shouts, banging her hands on the metal tabletop.

Mae watches plates and cutlery fly everywhere as, within seconds, the situation escalates. Shana shoots away from the far side of the room, dodging guards and knocking chairs and tables out of the way with such force they might as well be cardboard props. Mae sees her rushing straight towards Mal as though in slow motion, Shana's dark eyes bulging; fear-filled and unseeing.

Mae looks at Mal, but she doesn't react, seemingly rooted to the spot. Strips of sunlight stretch across the room, bouncing light off an object—a sliver of silver in Shana's grasp. Realising the terrible inevitability of the situation, a darkness seizes hold of Mae, empties her of thought, fear, and instinct, and she steps in front of Shana, shoving Mal out of harm's way.

Somehow, guards manage to restrain Shana moments before she collides with Mae and a knife is wrestled from her hand. Another guard quickly takes control, clearing the kitchen of patients. Malika clings tightly to Mae's arm, the pair walking in stunned silence towards their bedrooms.

†

Once out of earshot of staff, Malika turns to Mae. 'Why would you do that? Push me out of the way like that?' She scrutinizes Mae's face, like a sculptor looking for signs of imbalance.

'She was coming straight at you,' Mae replies defensively. 'I don't know, I saw the knife and…' She smiles, unsure. Her shoulders curl up as she retreats inside herself.

'I don't need you to go putting yourself in danger for me. I mean, what's wrong with you? Don't you care what happens to you?'

'She could have killed you.' Mae shakes her head, unsure of what else to say.

'That's crazy, Mae. I'm telling you now… crazy.'

'Maybe we should try that.'

They both spin round in the direction of the voice. Angela, another inmate, approaches the room next to Mae's.

'What?' Mae asks, confused.

'Anything to get out of group therapy. All that ball rolling is fucked, man. We're locked up in here, without access to relief, and they're making us roll giant red balls at each other? Come on, I mean, it's no wonder she's climbing the walls. That girl is sexually frustrated.'

'Yeah,' Mal says, a smirk spreading across her face. 'And it's not just her from what I hear.' She saunters past Angela slowly, heading to her room. 'I'm only a few doors down, babe.'

There's a pause before Angela realises what Mal is referring to. Her chubby face crumples.

Too distraught to laugh, Mae lowers her head and slips into her room. Once inside, she stops, trying to digest Mal's harsh words. She can't help but feel aware of a rising sense of shame at her own naivety, at mistakenly believing Mal cared for her in the same way.

'Idiot!' she shouts, balling her fists. The space around her seems to shrink. Mae kicks the door shut and starts to perform squats to distract herself. If she's caught, she knows it won't go down well.

At forty-eight kilogrammes, Mae's underweight. Not dangerously, but enough to make the staff notice. After thirty squats, she sits slowly on her bed and lays her head on the pillow, curling into a foetal position.

'She wouldn't have done the same for me. No one would,' she whispers. She hears Malika's voice taunting her, *"That's crazy, Mae, crazy",* and it quickly triggers a memory of her seven-year-old self.

"It's all in your head, Mae." Her mum is sitting on the sofa, not looking at her. *"He wouldn't do anything like that. It's a misunderstanding, that's all it is."* She stops. *"Is this because I took your sister out without you? Don't do this to me, Mae, I can't cope with the two of you playing up."* She's shaking her head so much it looks like it might spin off. *"You had a dream, that's all. Get back to bed and stop this nonsense."*

"I can't sleep."

"Pretend!" her mum snaps, and gulps back a half-filled glass

of red wine. *"As if I haven't got enough on my plate without you starting too. Go! Back to bed!"* As Mae turns away, she hears, *"Happy fucking Mother's Day."*

'I wish I'd never been born,' Mae whispers as the pain of the past collides with the present and the raw feeling of worthlessness begins to take hold. She slides her hand under her pillow and pulls out a book. Taking the bookmark out, she prises open a seam and shudders. A razor blade drops into her lap. Just as she takes it between her thumb and forefinger, a bell sounds outside her room and Mae hears the noise of thirty or so women moving to their nine o'clock appointment. Someone knocks on her door.

'Group therapy in two minutes.'

'Wouldn't miss it!' she shouts with forced joviality, pushing aside the voice in her head telling her that not only is she alone, but also crazy, unstable, and unbalanced.

As the sting of the razor cuts through her inner thigh, her thoughts blur.

CHAPTER 3
CORINE

A week later, Corine boards a train bound for London, carrying only a small suitcase and an oversized tote bag. Her gruff but straight-talking neighbour, Callum McBride, had agreed to look after the farm while she's away—it would be four weeks at most.

She hadn't slept at all the night before, tossing and turning into the early hours until anxiety about not sleeping drove her from her bed. One small nightcap had led to another increasingly generous helping, and soon it hadn't been worth going back to bed and risking sleeping through her five o'clock alarm.

Almost as soon as the train pulls out of the station, Corine takes a manila folder from her bag and slips on a pair of tortoiseshell reading glasses. They slide down to rest on the tip of her nose. A white label on the folder reads: Mae Bailey, followed by a prison number. Beneath that: *The Orchard Clinic, Secure Unit*.

She sits upright in her seat and draws a steadying breath before opening it. Clipped inside is a photo of Mae at fourteen. But she doesn't need the picture to remember. Mae is etched into her memory—scalp raw and bloodied from tearing out her own hair, and those doleful eyes. More victim than perpetrator. Why would a child do that to herself? Why attack her own mother?

On the top are the original court papers. Corine sifts through them, then pauses to read. Mae was tried at Kingston Magistrates Court in September 2012, aged fourteen, where she pleaded guilty to, and was convicted of, unlawful wounding. No history of physical or emotional abuse was recorded.

The victim, Kate Bailey—Mae's mother—had written to the court asking for her daughter not to be given a prison sentence, stating that she and her family had already suffered enough. But in his summation, the judge had noted that it was a minor miracle that Mae wasn't facing murder charges, given the violent and senseless nature of the knife attack. The injuries were described as life-altering, and due to the severity of the crime and Mae's lack of remorse, the victim's wishes could not be considered.

Mae was sentenced to six years, with a parole review set for two. Following sentencing, she was transferred to The Orchard Clinic, a medium to high security prison facility, where she was placed in the assessment ward.

Corine pauses. That was four years ago. As a senior psychiatrist, she had been responsible for writing one of the initial assessments and, from what she remembered, Mae had barely spoken then. Even if she *had* talked, would it have been the truth? Most likely, Mae's new willingness to speak was prompted by her imminent second parole hearing. Yet the idea that Mae's mother would forgive such a terrible attack, and was presumably prepared to support her daughter, intrigued her.

After a while, Corine's eyes start to feel heavy. She closes the file, slips it into her bag, and lays her head back against the headrest. Within moments she falls into a fitful sleep, waking briefly to see Durham Cathedral bathed in a glorious yellow light, followed by glimpses of tired towns, soulless industrial estates, and vast swathes of chequered farmland. She misses York altogether, waking somewhere before Doncaster with a start. Judging by the amused smile on the face of the man sitting diagonal to her, she's been snoring. Corine pulls the neck of her jumper higher and turns her face towards the window, thankful that the seats beside and opposite her are empty.

She'd dreamt of Joe. His face twisted with anger, rasping the word "*selfish*" over and over. In the dream—she often had strange ones—Corine had turned into a hare. Confused by his accusation, by the rattle in his throat, she'd bolted, gaining speed, putting distance between herself and her accuser.

She'd woken with a question fully formed in her mind: Was it selfish to want to be a parent above all else?

Perhaps, she concedes, thinking of the many failed attempts they'd endured. But didn't most people want that? Had Mae's mother? Surely she'd felt that same need?

If the desire to reproduce was selfish, then Corine wasn't alone in it.

A headache throbs behind her eyes and along the left side of her head. She roots through her bag, pulls out a box of paracetamol and a water bottle, and swallows two tablets with a gulp of tepid liquid. The train had grown busier at the Durham and York stops, but everyone, without exception, is glued to their phone. A young woman in her early twenties enters the carriage carrying two coffees. She sets one in front of an older woman, her mother, Corine assumes, noting the resemblance.

'It's very hot,' the younger woman warns. They whisper conspiratorially, cupping their mouths as they speak, their eyes eventually resting on Corine.

She looks away, pretending to rummage in her bag, then remembers her niece is expecting a call. She dials Lisa's number, but it goes to voicemail.

'Hi Lisa, it's Corine. I'm due in London at midday, but I have a work meeting, so I'll call you once I settle in at the hotel… or tonight, if I don't get a chance. Looking forward to seeing you.' She ends the call and stares out of the window, trying to ignore the sharp burst of laughter coming from the mother and daughter as they share a private joke. *Some people never grow up*, she thinks bitterly—but in the same instant, she acknowledges the real source of her annoyance and shuts her eyes tightly, trying to block out the pain.

The chatter of cleaning staff wakes her at King's Cross Station. Still half-asleep, Corine looks around her—and sure enough, she is the last remaining passenger. She pulls her suitcase down from the overhead rack and quickly makes her way off the train, swept along in the flow of people heading toward the ticket barriers.

Beyond the barrier, the station itself is no less fraught with people converging from every direction, never seeming to look, yet somehow avoiding one another. Corine's shoulder collides with a woman holding the hand of a small child; she murmurs an apology, but the woman doesn't look back. Her limbs feel blurred at the edges, unmoored in space and time, as if her proprioception has gone awry.

To her relief, Corine spots a cab right away but struggles to find the hotel address she'd scribbled on the back of Lisa's baby shower invitation. The young driver watches her with a blank expression and it's not hard to imagine what he's thinking. When she finally locates it tucked inside a notebook, she feels foolish. She sinks back into the seat, staring out of the window, a million negative thoughts racing around her mind.

'First time in London?' the cab driver asks.

'No,' she replies frostily. 'I lived here for most of my life… until I escaped.'

'It's not for everyone.' He smiles at her through the rear-view mirror and remains quiet for the rest of the journey. Just how she prefers.

†

Her hotel room is barely three metres by four, with an open wardrobe by the door, a small double bed, and a tiny desk beneath a mirror and wall-mounted TV. The institutional feel continues in the bathroom—marble-effect surfaces, no frills, and the same neat, confined space. Corine places her suitcase on the bed, pulls out her toiletry bag and hangs up a few items of clothing. The rest she leaves packed.

Her phone pings—a reminder flashing on screen: meeting with Dr Richard Forbes in thirty minutes at The Orchard.

It strikes her as faintly ridiculous that she, at her stage in life, has dropped all her commitments at the whim of a girl she barely knows.

'What are you hiding, Mae Bailey?' she murmurs.

In the bathroom, the harsh light above the mirror casts

unforgiving shadows across her greying hairline. She fluffs the front, trying to add volume. Her face looks tired, older, with a bluish tinge under her eyes, made worse by the weight she's recently lost.

I look like my mother, she realises, and her heart sinks.

With little finesse, she applies a touch of blush and lipstick, then twists her hair up, clipping it loosely at the back of her head. Finally ready to face the world, Corine picks up her bag and heads out.

The receptionist smiles as she steps out of the lift, but she offers only a brisk nod in return, avoiding conversation. Moments later, she's outside. Sunlight floods the street, and she squints against the glare, already wishing she'd made time to change out of the black jumper and trousers.

She arrives at the hospital grounds with five minutes to spare. Nothing has changed in almost four years; if she didn't know The Orchard was a medium secure unit for women, she might assume it was an extension of the hospital itself. The same yellow brick, cream-painted render and dark-framed windows carry through seamlessly.

Inside, the space is bright and airy, built around a large central atrium. Corine knows, that beyond that are rooms for individual and group therapy, a gym, a wellbeing centre, and even a hairdressing salon. Staff bases overlook the open-plan living area and bedrooms. It's only the airlocked security door at the visitor's entrance that hints at the building's true purpose.

Once inside, Corine is taken to the staff entrance via a set of secure revolving doors, where she is processed. Her phone, keys, cards, and purse are stored in a zip bag, which she signs over before being escorted to a small waiting area. A sign on the door opposite reads: *Dr Richard Forbes, Lead Consultant Psychiatrist.*

He's done well for himself, she thinks. Positions like that are hard-won. In another life, it might have been her name on that door. Almost immediately, Corine scolds herself. This is not her world anymore, it's a temporary diversion to tie up some loose ends—a favour to Richard.

In truth, though, Mae's case was more than that. She had somehow, during a handful of meetings, lodged herself under Corine's skin and remained there, like one of the slender chips inserted in the ears of cattle, to track them when they wander off.

An image of Mae from before the trial plays in Corine's mind—back when she was being held at a high-security youth detention centre and Corine had been called in to assess her. She'd been painfully thin, refusing food and obsessively rubbing a raw patch of skin between her thumb and index finger. Her head had been shaved to stop her tearing out chunks of hair during the night. She looked like a wounded animal—anxious, afraid—and Corine had to fight the overwhelming urge to wrap her in a blanket and carry her out of that cold, sterile interview room.

It should have surprised her, but it hadn't, that there had been nothing in her clinical records about self-harm, or thoughts of self-harm, despite the scars on her skin suggesting otherwise.

"Tell me about when you started cutting yourself, Mae."
She hadn't answered.
"Some of those scars are old, from before you came here. Can

you explain why you do it?"

Ever so slightly, Mae had shaken her head.

All the while, her thumb kept working the raw spot, digging deeper, going back and forth, until a smear of blood appeared. Even then, Corine knew she wasn't going to get anywhere. Everything about Mae had been defensive and closed off. She was most likely still reeling from the trauma of her sentence, or her containment. The hours spent in isolation, ruminating, reliving whatever had brought her there. It wasn't natural. It wasn't healthy. Not for anyone—especially not for a young child.

"Don't worry, I've seen enough to write my report." Corine had smiled and reached out towards Mae, stopping just short of touching her. *"That looks painful. Is it?"*

Mae had shaken her head.

Corine had been about to leave when something about Mae's fragility, her brokenness, made her stop. In a soothing voice, her hand reaching for Mae's shoulder, she had tried to offer a spark of hope. *"When you're ready… if you feel able to talk, ask for me. For now, I'm going to make sure the staff keep you safe and you get some medical attention for that wound there. Are you okay with that? You do understand what I'm saying, don't you?"*

Mae had nodded. In that moment, Corine thought she'd never seen anyone look so broken.

"You're not alone, remember that."

As Mae had been led away, flanked by two prison guards, she'd looked back at Corine, the flicker of a smile on her lips.

It would shock those outside the prison system to know what fell through the cracks, but Corine had seen it all before. In her report, she'd recorded evidence of depression and self-harm—cutting and refusing to eat—with possible psychosis and a potential anxiety disorder. She'd seen enough to recommend Mae be transferred to an appropriate mental health provision and flagged her as a likely suicide risk.

After the trial, when Mae was first admitted to The Orchard, her condition had deteriorated. The early weeks focused more on stabilising her food intake than beginning any real therapy. Mae hadn't seemed to realise it, but she was one of the lucky ones. At least here, she would have access to regular therapeutic treatment—essential if she were to have any chance of rehabilitation.

Her refusal to talk had been a concern. She hadn't explained, apologised for, or even attempted to defended the attack on her mother. Silence, for a therapist, was a hurdle that couldn't be underestimated—though, looking back, Corine feared she had.

The sharp sound of shoes on tiled flooring jolts her back into the present. She sees Richard striding towards her and rises to greet him. He stops a little too close.

She takes a step back and extends her hand.

'Corine, it's so good to see you,' he says, shaking it. Her formality seems to catch him off guard. 'How are you?'

His bright eyes are fixed on hers, smiling, but Corine senses the awkwardness she's created—the hesitation that's kept him from hugging her. She hadn't meant to offend him; it had simply been a while since she'd felt the warmth of another's touch.

'Honestly, I'm exhausted, hot, and annoyed at myself for not saying no.'

'You did, remember, but I persuaded you.' Richard gestures towards his office, looking pleased with himself and making no attempt to hide it.

'It had nothing to do with you, Richard. Don't flatter yourself.'

He laughs.

'Do I address you as Dr Forbes now? Lead consultant no less, congratulations,' she adds, redirecting the conversation.

He dismisses his promotion with a shrug, gesturing to the chair beside Corine. 'Coffee?' he asks, without taking his eyes of her.

She shakes her head.

'How've you been? How's Joe?'

'Fine.' She nods. 'Well, I will be if you could crack open a bloody window. I'd forgotten how stuffy these offices can be.'

Corine scans the airless room; she feels as though she's suffocating, like she's being forced down a dark rabbit hole despite the windows. Suddenly aware of Richard studying her, her hand shoots to her chin, brushing her jawline for stray hairs. It feels like he's scrutinising her.

Richard laughs warmly as he reaches to open a window. 'You haven't changed much.'

'Careful,' she replies, surprised by how sharp her voice sounds. 'I know the last few years haven't been kind, but you needn't gloat.'

'I meant you're still barking orders.' Richard laughs again, though there's a flicker of confusion in his smile.

'Oh… right,' Corine says, feeling embarrassed. It felt strange being the focus of his attention, but she knew if she didn't reign in her insecurities, she might damage a friendship she'd once genuinely cherished.

Thankfully, Richard is too polite to dwell on any awkwardness but Corine can sense his uncertainty—unsure of his footing, of how the meeting will unfold. Physically, he hasn't changed much in the thirty years she's known him. His hairline has retreated a little further back on his forehead, and his shoulders appear less straight, but he still makes quite the impression in his expensive suit.

When Richard takes his seat at the desk across from her, he hesitates, stumbling over his words. 'It's... well, we really appreciate you stepping in. It was a big ask, and I know you have your own commitments. It can't have been easy finding someone to cover for you—'

'Tell me about Mae,' Corine interrupts, her voice noticeably softer this time. She reaches across the table, and he takes her hand—a conciliatory gesture between old friends.

'She's never asked for anything before, and like I said, it surprised everyone when she asked for you specifically. No one was aware that she'd formed any attachments here, aside from one friendship with another patient. We still haven't had her version of what happened that night, or seen any real signs of her showing remorse for what she did. Apart from that, she's a model patient. She probably would have been paroled two years ago, had she agreed to talk to her mother back then.'

'And her mother's still okay to meet me?'

'Yes. Tomorrow.'

'Good. So, when can I meet Mae?'

'Now, if you'd like? She's expecting you, but be warned, Mae isn't a big talker. Keeps things bottled up inside. We're all amazed she agreed to meet her mother this time round. Though I'm not ruling out that she won't back out at the last minute. I reckon she's only talking now because she didn't get parole last time, and she realises she needs to show remorse to the victim as well as for her crime.'

Although hearing this should make Corine cautious, for some reason, it galvanizes her. Whilst some offenders—or patients, as they were referred to at The Orchard—played the system to their benefit, Mae obviously had some integrity. That was a start. It gave Corine hope—something positive to latch on to. She would help this young woman face the truth, no matter how dark it got. Even if Mae showed little remorse, Corine hoped the journey itself might, in some small way, transform her.

CHAPTER 4
CORINE

A narrow window casts vertical strips of light and dark across the walls of the small therapy room where Corine waits for Mae. Not for the first time, she is reminded of what it means to lose one's liberty; of the quiet, persistent tension that comes with working among volatile, dangerous patients.

Opposite her is a flesh-coloured bucket chair identical to the one she's sitting in. In the middle of the room, a small coffee table offers a neutral distance between patient and therapist. Corine gives the table a little kick. It doesn't move. Nailed down, she supposes, like most throwable items. It's plastic too—less chance of it being used as a weapon. A framed poster of a green meadow dotted with wildflowers adorns one wall, an empty beach with lone footprints in the sand on another. She frowns, acutely aware of how a change in season could dramatically alter both scenes.

Many a time in Scotland she had watched a fast-moving weather front quickly turn a calm day into a scene of destruction. She'd learnt to be cautious. Back in her early career, Corine had thought herself a stenographer, watching and listening for clues and insights that might enable her to understand her patients. But patients weren't always forthcoming about their past, or their feelings, for that matter, and for incarcerated patients, revelations could expose them, revealing weaknesses. Knowing who to trust was a minefield within a prison environment. The truth had to be earned.

Most of the young people she had seen over the years had been injured or abused by people who were supposed to love and protect them—parents, siblings, relatives, family friends, neighbours, coaches, teachers. The list was endless. It was practically unheard of in Corine's line of work for a patient to come from a comfortable family home like the one Mae had been born into.

Corine hears muffled voices, followed by footsteps on the tiled floor of the corridor. She places her notepad and pen onto the table, then has second thoughts and slides the pen into her trouser pocket just as the door opens. Mae enters, followed by a female prison guard. The guard nods at Corine.

'I'll be back in forty minutes,' she says, smiling broadly at Mae.

'Thank you.' Corine gestures to the empty chair. 'Please, Mae, take a seat.'

Mae sits slowly, folding her legs beneath her, the expression on her face inscrutable. The whole time her eyes are fixed on Corine, as though expecting her to do something.

She looks like any other teenage girl in her joggers and T-shirt, perhaps a little young for her age. She's thin still, but no longer dangerously so. Her blonde hair has grown back thick, and now comes to her shoulders, but it's her face that draws Corine's attention. She's beautiful. Pale, fine features, with full lips and green eyes that only reveal their colour when she moves her face into the light. A stray section of hair falls across her cheek, which Mae brushes away, tucking it back behind her ear. It's then that Corine sees the scars—intricate white lines, like raised tattoos of empty blood vessels—running the length of her inner arms, turning her skin to parchment with every turn of her wrist. More scar tissue than healthy skin.

Mae clocks the focus of Corine's gaze and folds her arms. 'I haven't cut my arms in nearly three years.'

'Good. It's good to see you looking so well, Mae.' Internally, Corine adds a silent caveat—well, considering Mae had been locked up as a child and imprisoned for four years. 'It's been a long time.'

Mae nods. She laces her hands in her lap and rocks slightly, elbows drawn in tight. Corine waits, giving her space to speak, but she says nothing—just stares at the floor in silence.

'How have you been?' Corine asks finally, conscious of slipping into her therapist's voice again.

She hopes she doesn't sound too patronising; Joe often accused her of that, especially during arguments. Once or twice, he'd snapped, calling her a patronising bitch before storming off as if it had been his feelings that had been hurt. Inwardly, she'd laughed. She still did whenever she thought about it. He'd shocked himself more than her. Working in the prison system, she'd been called far worse. Sticks and stones, she'd yell after him, certain he'd heard the stifled laughter in her voice.

'Oh, you know… I'm okay, I suppose.' Mae sniffs and slowly sinks into her chair, without looking at Corine.

'Good, that's really great to hear. I've been told that you're a model patient.'

They sit in silence again, Corine wondering whether Richard had exaggerated the progress that he claimed Mae had made. She wants to ask why Mae chose her, but her instinct tells her it's too soon.

'I've been told you would like me to join you when you meet with your mother. Your first meeting in over three years.'

Mae nods her head and sits forward.

'Your notes say that you only saw her a handful of times in the first six months after your sentence. It was your choice not to see her.'

Mae's eyes flick sharply towards Corine. She holds her gaze, her face tilted slightly, as if about to ask a question. 'Yes, I suppose it was my choice not to see her. But now I'd like to… with you beside me.' She hesitates. 'If that's okay?'

'Sure. And how are you feeling about meeting her?'

'Feeling? Well, I'm not really sure.'

Corine waits, allowing space for Mae's emotions to reveal themselves. 'Are you excited or nervous at all?'

'No.' Mae pouts and shakes her head.

Again, Corine waits for her to say more. Mae doesn't oblige, so she probes a little further, all the while conscious that Mae's silence will help no one, least of all herself.

'Have you given any thought to how your mother might feel about meeting?'

Mae seems unsure of what to say. She looks past Corine, as though trying to find answers on the bland walls. Her hesitancy makes Corine uneasy—four years out of the job is a long time, and she feels like a novice, learning all over again. The stakes are high too. She's known colleagues whose reports helped clear prisoners for parole, only to have them commit the most heinous crimes once released.

'Okay, well, what do you think my impression of her

might be?' Corine pushes.

Mae nods and mindlessly traces the cluster of scars up her arm. 'You'll think she's normal.'

Corine smiles. 'Normal. Anything else?'

'She'll seem friendly, sociable… the injured party, I suppose.' Mae shrugs. 'Nothing to suggest she deserved what happened to her—if that's what you're looking for.'

'Did she deserve what you did to her?' Corine knows this is a risky approach, but a meeting has been scheduled between Mae and her mother in two days' time. She has no choice but to push, to make sure Mae is ready to face her actions—to be held accountable for her crime.

'I know what I did was wrong… despicable, and I deserved to be punished for it. Violence is never the answer.' Mae leans forward. 'But that doesn't mean she wasn't culpable in some way.'

A warning bell sounds in Corine's mind. Mae had deflected the blame in an instant, giving no sign of any real remorse. It was a known fact that inmates who felt guilt were less likely to reoffend. Shame, on the other hand, was a more complex emotion.

'You're aware that these meetings—and those with your mother—will feed into your parole hearing, yes? Questions will be asked about the safety of your mother and the general public should you be granted parole. That's the reason for these meetings, Mae. You do understand that, don't you?'

'Yes.'

'And what are your feelings towards your mother now?' Corine asks, gently. 'Are you still angry with her?'

'I would never hurt her—or anyone else. I'm a different

person now. I'm in control of my emotions. With all the therapy, I'm probably more emotionally aware than most people my age.' Mae gives Corine a slight smile and continues. 'Besides, I'm eighteen now. If I get out, I'll have my own place. Hopefully, it'll be a fresh start—away from London.'

It often took time for patients to open up—but time wasn't on their side. Still, Corine could tell that Mae needed to be eased in; despite all her talk of emotional confidence, she wasn't ready to talk about that day.

Instead, they chatted about her plans to go back to college, what her first job might be, and her time at The Orchard, which seemed—on balance—to have been more positive than negative. Mae had taken A-Levels in English Literature and Maths and had been pleasantly surprised by her results.

She spoke about the therapy sessions—how she'd hated them at first, especially group therapy—but had grown to like them. They helped her process what had happened to her, and why. It was helpful to listen to the other girls' problems, to put hers in context. She'd even discovered she was good at giving advice—on the odd occasion.

'Like mother, like daughter, I suppose,' she said, without a hint of humour. 'One thing I know for sure—she'll bring her job up in the first five minutes of meeting you. You'll see.'

'Why do you think she does that?'

'Kudos,' Mae replies. 'It works, too. You know, the whole noble profession crap. No offence.'

Corine chuckles.

'Don't ask any medical questions or she'll bore you to death. If you didn't know she was a doctor, and you kept the conversation general, you'd think she was a different person—less capable. Her title implies everything. The word *doctor* carries all sorts of positive connotations, and in my experience, very little of it is true.' Mae laughs, bullish now. 'I read somewhere that there is a higher incidence of psychopathy in surgeons than in the general population—something to do with stress immunity.' She watches Corine with an amused smile.

Corine shrugs and smiles back.

'But you can make your own judgement. See her tomorrow—with totally unbiased eyes.'

'How do you see her?' Corine nudges.

'I'll let you know once we meet. It's been a while. I'm hoping to see her differently.' Mae brushes her hair behind her ears. 'More objectively, like you.'

Corine nods. 'You must have met a number of psychologists and psychiatrists over the years. Why ask for me?'

Mae leans forward. 'Can I ask you a question?'

'Go ahead.'

'Is it difficult to remain detached from your patients? I mean, especially when they're telling you some pretty traumatic stuff?'

'It can be,' Corine admits. 'But I've had years of training and experience. I help no one if I become so emotionally involved that I lose sight of the bigger picture—the truth.'

'Okay… but I was emotionally involved with my mother. I couldn't see the bigger picture—that's why I'm here.'

'Are you worried I'll get the wrong impression of your mother?'

'No, it's more that I don't want to influence your impression of her. It might sound a bit odd, but I really would value your opinion. I know you're seeing her tomorrow, so I don't want to tell you what I think. That way, if we come to the same conclusion about her, I'll know I'm not imagining things.'

'Well, I suppose it makes any judgement more credible if two people come to the same conclusion separately. But lots of factors can influence opinion: things said in earlier discussions, or reports that you may have read. You can never really rule out external influence completely, you've just got to be aware of it.'

Mae giggles.

'Sorry, did I say something funny?' Corine can feel the mood shift. Mae's face is shadowed; her eyes look dark now, like storm clouds closing in too fast.

'I just remembered our first meeting at the remand centre. Your shirt was buttoned all wrong—one side was hanging lower than the other.'

'I'm afraid I don't recall.'

Mae laughs again. Corine wonders whether she has already lost her respect, assuming she ever had it in the first place.

'When you mention influence, do you mean the sort of influence a mother has over her daughter?' Mae asks, suddenly picking up the previous thread of their conversation.

'Well, yes,' Corine replies, taking note of Mae's fast-changing emotions. 'Any close relationships, but particularly with family members, can influence how you see the world. The mother-daughter relationship is usually pretty crucial.'

They sit in silence for a while.

Mae is the first to speak. 'I never felt like a checklist of conditions to be ticked off with you.' She smiles, twisting a stray strand of hair. 'I got the impression you cared—I mean, beyond the job title. Obviously, there were things you had to tick off to do your job properly, but...'

She had started off complimentary but ended somewhere else. Corine smiles anyway.

'Psychosis, though? Really?' Mae continues. 'I mean, I know people with psychosis can't help it, but it's a huge label to be given aged fourteen.'

Corine wasn't expecting the conversation to turn in this direction. Had Mae read her report? She'd almost certainly heard the evidence at her hearing. Surely that was all it was?

She takes a deep breath and keeps her voice steady. 'At the time, that was what I believed. Someone as young as you, who's been through such a traumatic event, is often experiencing psychosis. The signs were all there.'

'Do I still show signs of psychosis, Dr Alexander?'

'Not according to all of your psychiatric and therapy reports, no. I'll put my observations and recommendations in my report and, if used, they'll feed into your parole hearing.'

Mae leans across the table, her hand reaching towards Corine's face. Corine shoots back, wincing.

'Sorry, Dr Alexander, you've something on your face.'

Corine feels the redness spreading upwards from her neck and curses her thin skin. She knows she's overreacted; her heart shouldn't be thudding in her chest like this. Running a hand over her cheek, she pulls a small black thread from her face—it must have come loose from her jumper.

'It's fine, I just wasn't expecting you to... to—'

'Reach out? Yeah, sorry, it's probably against the rules—a sanctionable violation or something. I should really know better.'

Corine knew Mae was toying with her—making a point. Mae understood all too well how being labelled *psychotic* would shape the way others saw her. Was this her way of blaming Corine for the final sentence? After all, it'd been Corine who recommended The Orchard. The outcomes were better there; she'd genuinely had Mae's best interests in mind when writing the report. But Corine's own life had been strained back then. Had she missed something? Misread the signs? Seen what she wanted to see?

Pretending to brush fluff from the sleeve of her jumper, Corine exposes her watch. 'Right, well... we'd best move on. Mae, this next question will be a difficult one, but I'm told you've discussed the attack openly on a number of occasions over the years. Can you tell me what you remember about that day? I need to ask this because your mum will most likely bring it up—and I have to be sure you're prepared.'

Mae looks directly at her. 'I understand,' she says, without a trace of objection in her voice. 'I'm prepared—for her, for talking about the attack. It's all in here.' She taps the side of her head, then slides her fingers down her face. 'My memory's good—there's nothing wrong with *that* part of my brain. But like I've said before, my mind seems to have blanked out the actual attack... and when I do have flashbacks, it feels like someone else was doing it.' She sits back, folding her hands across her knees.

Such small hands, Corine thinks. Smaller still when she picked up a knife and repeatedly slashed her mother.

CHAPTER 5
CORINE

The following morning, Corine stands outside The National Gallery, where a small queue has already started to form. She waits off to the side and checks her watch—it's barely ten, yet the streets are already alive with noise and movement. Everything feels intense, frenetic. People stride past with a sense of purpose she no longer recognises, a certainty she lacks. A sudden sense of dislocation washes over her, and she finds herself craving something familiar—the moss-covered hills of the farm, the crisp, salt-tinged air on a windy day. An image of Joe, before the accident, walking alongside Betty, flashes through her mind. Without thinking, she reaches into her coat pocket for her phone.

She hesitates. 'Don't be stupid, he can't answer the damn phone.'

Still, she calls. The line rings a few times before she hears her own voice play back at her. *"We're not available just now, please leave a message."* Corine waits impatiently for the beep.

'I know this is silly, but I wanted to share something. Something I know you'd laugh to hear me say. There is something worse than our shitty single-track roads. It took me half an hour to get a couple of miles in a cab just now, so I got out and walked. Now, if I have to wait ten times at ten passing places, ten times over, I promise—I won't moan.'

Corine spots her niece walking towards her and waves. 'I miss you,' she whispers. 'Don't be mad, but I'm meeting Lisa.' She ends the call abruptly, imagining Joe's voice, warning her not to tell Lisa anything.

'Aunty Corine!' Lisa cries, throwing open her arms and wrapping them tightly around her. 'It's so good to see you.'

'Let me look at you,' Corine says, drawing back. 'You're the definition of blooming, you look beautiful!' She reaches out to stroke Lisa's distinctive mane of strawberry curls.

'I'm a double decker bus and you know it.' Lisa laughs. 'You never were very good at lying, it's written all over your face.'

'You look like how a mother-to-be is supposed to look—glowing and lovely. I put on three stone with mine.' The words are out of Corine's mouth before she can stop herself, and she instantly regrets them. Bringing up death—a baby's death, no less—in front of a mother-to-be wasn't just inconsiderate; it was downright stupid. 'Are you sure you're up to walking round the gallery? We could just go for a coffee instead?'

Lisa's face is smooth and impossibly youthful—much younger than her twenty-eight years. 'Of course I want to. I also want an enormous slice of cake, but only after I've earned it.'

Corine laughs. 'You make it sound like a chore. We can do something else. I don't want to force you to do this for my sake.'

'I suggested it, remember? Besides, it was always our thing. It's just a Pavlovian response. When I see a gallery, my mouth waters. I expect cake, and I entirely blame you for over-indulging me as a child.'

Corine threads her arm through Lisa's and the pair join the now slightly larger queue.

Inside, they wander through the various rooms, chatting and pausing occasionally when a painting catches their eye. Lisa stops before a portrait of a man holding the hand of a heavily pregnant woman in a sumptuous green dress. She reads the description next to it.

'Well, I wonder how Van Eyck's Mrs Anolfini's birth went? She doesn't look happy, does she? I hope for the child's sake it took after her and not the father,' Lisa says.

'I read somewhere that it's the dress that makes her look pregnant. A sort of good omen on their wedding day.'

'Their wedding day, really?' Lisa frowns. 'Nothing like a bit of pressure. She was probably terrified he'd go all Henry the Eighth on her if she didn't produce a son—a male heir to secure the family line. No wonder she looks miserable.'

Corine links arms with Lisa and guides her out of the room towards the café. She didn't mention the other theory—that the woman in Van Eyck's painting had died in childbirth; that the painting was likely her husband's way of remembering a wife he had loved, captured at the start of their life together, a few years before hope had vanished.

†

The café is busy, but a waitress notices the swell of Lisa's stomach and discreetly leads them to a corner table. They both order immediately, without looking at the menu, and another waitress promptly brings over a tray with breakfast tea, sourdough toast, and jam for Corine, along with a hot chocolate and apple cake for Lisa. The waitress holds out the slice of apple cake.

'Who is for, please?' she asks in a heavy Polish accent.

'Me, thanks. Got to get my five a day in for this little one,' Lisa says, patting her stomach. The waitress gives a half smile and leaves without comment. 'Everyone's a judge.'

'I remember when I was pregnant, Joe and I were in Sienna at a restaurant. I'd ordered sorbet, but the lady who owned the place brought me over a plate of the most delicious strawberries I'd ever tasted. "*Instead,*" she'd said. "*For the baby*". I was way too happy to be offended that my choice had been dismissed. Moments later, I felt my mouth and throat start to itch. I'd never had an allergic reaction before, and as mad as it sounds, I castigated myself for eating those strawberries. What if I unintentionally harmed Michael in the womb?'

Lisa looks serious again. 'How old would he have been?'

'Eighteen,' Corine says without hesitating. *The same age as Mae.* 'Probably would've been costing us a fortune at university.' She laughs, but her eyes are cast down at the table.

'Does it ever get easier, do you think?'

Not with your child, Corine wants to say. Grief was patient; it bided its time, waiting to surprise you—to take you under with the sheer force of its destructiveness. 'Time softens the edges,' she offers instead. 'But you've got to work at it too—talk about them, celebrate them, miss them. You focus on that baby of yours. He or she will need you to be one hundred percent present. That's what your mum would have wanted.'

'I just hope I'm half the mum she was,' Lisa says, slicing her cake in half, then into quarters. The knife cuts through the layers without resistance, collecting a residue of crumbs along the edge of the blade—like tiny pieces of flesh.

Without warning, Corine has a sudden vision of Mae attacking her mother: a knife slashing skin over and over again; a bloodied face. The violence of the attack takes her breath away, and for a moment, she can't hear what Lisa is saying. The intrusive image, she knows, is a warning from somewhere in the darkest corner of her mind, reminding her to tread carefully.

Just as quickly, Corine is back in the moment—aware of all the sounds of the busy café and her niece's concerned voice.

'I mean, I still think about her every single day. We'd argued the day before, about the long hours I was working,' Lisa says.

Corine's hand trembles as she reaches for her glass of water—but accidentally knocks it over. Water spills across the table and drips off the edge. Lisa picks up the glass and soaks up some of the water with her napkin.

'You've gone pale—are you okay?'

Corine swallows hard, her mouth dry. She stands. 'Sorry—I felt a bit queasy then. I'm just going to nip to the bathroom.'

'Shall I come with you?'

She holds up a hand and shakes her head. 'I'll be fine.'

In the bathroom, she closes the cubicle door and sits on the toilet, her heart fluttering. The space feels reassuringly dark. She opens her bag and takes out a half bottle of vodka. With unsteady hands, she twists off the lid and drinks.

CHAPTER 6
CORINE

Every house looks the same on the neat, tree-lined street of solid Edwardian homes. Lisa's house, Corine realises, is only a short walk away, hidden somewhere in the network of identical streets. She checks the house number of Mae's mother—Kate Bailey—on her phone: thirty-five. Crossing the road, she walks a few houses down and pauses before a large, double-fronted house with a formal knot garden and an intricately tiled path. Even the bins are concealed in a neat wooden box, freshly painted black—the same colour as the front door.

It takes a few knocks and rings of the bell before the door finally opens. Dr Bailey appears—smiling, apologetic—explaining that she'd been working at the back of the house. She isn't the middle-aged woman ravaged by tragedy that Corine had expected, though her face still bears the scars of her daughter's attack. Several narrow lesions mark both sides of her face. They're pink still, which surprises Corine. She immediately thinks of Joe—and has to shake off the guilt that follows.

Kate leads Corine through the house, down a long corridor lined with closed doors, and into a spacious, open-plan kitchen.

'Forgive the mess—this is where we spend most of our

time. Please, take a seat.' Kate gestures to one of the stools at the kitchen island.

Corine can't see any mess. The house is pristine. If anything, she's grateful that Kate will never see how she lives—though it wasn't always that way.

She says yes to tea, using the moment to take in her surroundings while Kate boils the kettle. The room wouldn't look out of place in one of those glossy home magazines she occasionally flicks through at the supermarket. She takes a seat at the long kitchen island, running her fingers across the pale marble worktop—cool to the touch. An industrial-sized stainless-steel cooker and double sink fitted with an oversized chef's tap remind her—uneasily—of a mortuary prep station.

It's hard to find anything out of place, but eventually she does: a small pile of toys scattered in the far corner of the room, two mugs left on the windowsill by the door to the garden, and breakfast dishes still sitting in the sink despite it being midday. Those few small oversights, reassuring as they are, simply give the place a lived-in feel, a stark contrast to her own indifference.

At the thought of the farmhouse and the months of neglect, Corine feels her stomach dip. *Don't compare*, she chides herself, as though that was the source of all her troubles.

'How long have you lived here?' she asks.

'Since just before Mae was born. We moved in when I was eight months pregnant—a month before Christmas. Eighteen years. Milk? Sugar?' Kate asks.

Corine shakes her head and smiles, waiting for her to take a seat. Kate sits opposite, with her feet crossed beneath her. She leans forward, cupping her mug, but doesn't drink. Both her hands are badly scarred, front and back, and up close it becomes obvious that the heavy make-up Dr Bailey wears is a camouflage of sorts. Corine wonders how to put Kate at ease as she watches the poor woman tease the front of her hair forwards, over her scarred cheeks. Making people comfortable used to come naturally to Corine, but she'd been living in the wilderness for too long—tending worms and foot rot with patients who didn't answer back.

'Are you still practising, Doctor?' Corine immediately regrets the question. She should have waited for Kate to bring it up, just as Mae had said she would.

'Part-time now. It's one of the benefits of having set up my own GP practice.'

'Still, it must be demanding.'

'It's pretty much babies, bunions and a heap load of admin thrown in for good measure. I only work two days, the rest of the week I mostly look after my grandchildren.'

The revelation shocks Corine—though it shouldn't. After all, Kate is old enough to have grandchildren. She thinks about what she will never have, then just as quickly pushes the thought aside.

'Mae's sister's children?' she asks.

'Lyndsey... yes. She has two gorgeous girls, Beth and Zizi—my little angels. Beth's almost four and Zizi's coming up to eight months.' Kate jumps up and takes a photo-frame off the shelf behind her and hands it to Corine, looking every bit the proud grandma. Two little cherubic faces stare blankly at the camera. 'They're my world, these two. Into everything, but I suppose that's just kids for you.'

'They're beautiful,' Corine says. 'Lyndsey's lucky to have

you around to help out. Only yesterday my niece was telling me about the cost of childcare, especially in London.'

Kate laughs. 'Yeah, it's insane. I'm lucky I can afford to help her. Otherwise, it doesn't pay to have kids.'

'It would be good if I could meet Lyndsey sometime.'

'She's away at the moment, I'm afraid… working.'

Corine waits for her to continue, but she doesn't say anything more. Instead, Kate sits with a half-smile on her face, waiting for the next question.

'Still, that's a big commitment on your part, especially given how young they are.' She wonders how a part-time GP's salary can pay for such a beautiful house.

'That's just what us mothers do, hey? The kids always come first.'

Corine nods. It happens all the time—people see her age and make assumptions. Hadn't she herself expected to be a mother three or four times over by now? Besides, it would be rude to correct her, and a distraction from the real purpose of her visit: to determine whether it was safe for Kate to visit Mae under supervised conditions. If Kate was willing and able to cope without undue concern or trauma, then the meetings could go ahead.

'Do you know why I'm here, Dr Bailey?'

'Yes.'

'Do you mind if I record our conversation and take a few notes?'

'That's fine.' Kate folds the cuff of her white linen shirt as though readying herself.

Corine takes out a note pad and pen from her bag, then activates a voice recording app on her mobile. Kate watches, her eyes dark and unreadable.

'Kate, you've said you're happy to meet Mae. Is that still the case?'

'Yes.' She leaves a slight pause. 'But my understanding is that I won't be alone?'

'That's right, though it sounds as if you may have some concerns about meeting Mae?' *You should have*, Corine thinks, trying not to focus on the scars.

Kate leans her head on one hand and clasps the other between her knees. 'No... she's my daughter, and I've been told all along that she's a model patient.'

'She also served four years for assaulting you.'

Kate sits up straight, her posture stiffening. 'I never wanted that.' She sighs and lowers her gaze, looking away.

She reminds Corine of the black-and-white photograph in her spare bedroom—a framed image of a statue of the Roman empress Livia, symbol of *univira,* the one-man woman. Poised, elegant, and quietly powerful.

'How have you been coping over the last four years?'

Kate laughs theatrically. 'Me? Well, as you can see, I'm fine. Life goes on. I've got my job, my granddaughters to look after, friends... I do a bit of volunteering when I can. I don't have time to dwell. I like keeping busy.' Her answers feel evasive to Corine—focused on what she *does*, rather than what she *feels*.

'Are you comfortable talking about the attack?'

'Yes,' she says, then draws in a sharp breath.

It can't be easy remembering the worst day of your life.

'What is it that you want to know?' Kate's voice is clipped now, defensive. The earlier playfulness has vanished from her demeanour.

'Just take your time. In your own words, if you could describe what you remember to me.'

Dr Bailey exhales, her voice edged with fatigue. 'It was an ordinary Sunday evening. We'd finished dinner. Lyndsey had gone upstairs to her room with her boyfriend, Stuart—they're married now.'

'Lyndsey is how old?'

'She'll be twenty-three soon.' Kate's phone buzzes. She pulls it from her pocket, glances at the screen, then lays it face down on the worktop. 'Please, go on,' she says, tapping it lightly with her nails.

Corine smiles. 'You were talking about the day of the attack.'

'Of course—yes, sorry. Mae and I were talking about her homework. An essay she had to write—history, I think. Anyway, she didn't want to do it, and I told her it wasn't up for negotiation. Those were the rules. I asked her to tidy away the dinner things while I finished some paperwork. She complained… got angry—the way teenagers can be suddenly enraged by some perceived injustice. I don't remember exactly, but I think she said I expected too much—homework and the fucking dishes. Then she threw a plate across the room.'

Kate raises her eyes to the ceiling and shrugs. 'I told her she'd just have to get over it and got up to leave. That's when she attacked me. It was unexpected. Sudden. She had a knife. I tripped, fell on my side, and banged my head. I don't remember everything—just trying to stop her, trying to grab the knife. I didn't really feel these,' she says, touching her face. 'Adrenaline, I suppose.'

Corine waits, but Kate looks spent. Her eyes, unfocused, flick back and forth between her scarred hands, which she now holds out towards Corine.

'Thank you, that must have been difficult.'

Kate shrugs again, but recalling the attack is clearly distressing for her. She reaches across the worktop and yanks two tissues from a wooden box decorated with gold hearts and dabs her eyes. It's hard for Corine to imagine such a frenzied attack happening within this perfect, orderly home. Harder still to imagine it happening for the reasons given.

'Sorry—I haven't thought about it in a while. I don't usually cry like this.' Kate dabs at her eyes again, then blows her nose loudly into the tissues.

'I'm sure you're aware that seeing and speaking with Mae may bring these emotions back more strongly. Do you feel ready for that?'

'Ha, well, there's a question,' Kate says wearily, laughing sadly. 'Like I tell my patients who self-medicate with alcohol or other crutches—you've got to face your demons sooner or later.' She waves her hand dismissively. 'I didn't mean that Mae is… well, I just meant that I'm ready to face her. I know it'll be hard, but she's my daughter, no matter what she did to me, and I'm more than ready to see her. I still love her… and I always will.'

There it was—a mother's refusal to reject her child, even after suffering at their hands. Kate looks so certain that Corine will understand her declaration that, once again, her heart sinks. Most of the parents she'd met over the years who'd been assaulted by their children attributed the abuse to drugs or other substances. Having an external factor to blame gave them something to hold on to—something that made it possible to begin repairing the damage done to the parent-child bond.

Mae, though, had never been a drug user. She wondered how Kate had processed the attack. How she'd rationalised it—if at all. It was human nature to want answers; reasons for bad things that had happened.

'Mae still hasn't formally apologised to you or said why she attacked you. This is just hypothetical, but how do you think you'll feel if she blames you in some way?'

'Well, she must have blamed me for something; otherwise she wouldn't have attacked me in the first place,' Kate replies, unable to hide her irritation. 'I know what she did was unjustified. I didn't do anything to deserve it—I was just being a good mother, worrying about her… her future. This isn't about me. It never was. I hope Mae knows that.'

'So, how do you explain the attack?' Corine asks gently, meeting Kate's gaze. She's curious how Kate will respond, especially after four years—plenty of time to apply some retrospective logic.

'A moment of madness. Hormones can turn even the most placid children into teenage nightmares almost overnight. I see it all the time in my practice. Some have psychotic episodes out of the blue—they hear voices, see things that aren't there. For the vast majority, though, things return to normal and they never have another episode. Others, unfortunately, suffer lifelong mental illness and spend much of their lives in and out of hospital. Thankfully, that's not Mae.' She pauses, taking a deep breath. 'I wouldn't wish that on anyone.'

Kate had come up with a diagnosis that would release her,

and to some extent Mae, from the burden of guilt. Powerful feelings like shame, Corine well knew, could destroy a person's will to go on.

She glances at her notepad. 'Babies and bunions, and everything in between,' she says. 'Life, death, and all manner of human frailty.'

Kate stares blankly across at her. 'Sorry?' she asks, narrowing her eyes, then lets out a small, dry laugh. 'Oh, yes.' Her scarred hand reaches up to her divided face and Corine wonders what unimaginable traumas lie hidden behind her mask of normality. She worries Kate's difficulty in collecting her thoughts may be a consequence of being asked to revisit such trauma. Has avoidance been her defence these past few years, she wonders? She writes in her notes: *possible avoidance*—and *talk to Richard*.

'You know, I've had colleagues treat menopausal women for psychotic episodes,' Kate says dryly. 'Menopausal schizophrenia is more common than you'd think.'

'I imagine they had pre-existing conditions?'

'Not always,' she replies pointedly, crossing her legs and keeping her gaze fixed firmly on her guest.

Corine nods, doing her best not to take it personally. It was true—she'd reached another definable stage of life, one where the gains steadily shrank in proportion to the losses, hormonal or otherwise. And it wasn't as if she had a brood of doting children or grandchildren to take care of her if she failed to grow wiser—or worse, went completely bonkers. That would be just her luck. Might Callum, or his children, look after her as well as her animals? Hard to imagine.

Corine shifts on the stool, feeling uncomfortable. 'So,

you're saying there were no obvious signs of psychosis or extreme stress at any point before the attack?'

'That's right. I mean, Mae may have been stressed, but she never told me. Things were difficult around here… my marriage was breaking down.'

Corine nods sympathetically. 'Can you tell me about Mae's self-harm? Do you know when it started, or what prompted it? I know it started prior to the attack.'

Kate closes her eyes and sighs heavily. 'Her father,' she says. When she reopens them, Corine notices her entire demeanour has shifted. 'It was never made official… social services weren't involved… but Lyndsey accused him of sexual abuse. I often wondered if he did anything to Mae, but Mae being Mae, she wouldn't talk—not to me, not to her sister, or the counsellor I arranged. She must have been about eleven or twelve when Lyndsey spoke up.' Kate's voice is so quiet that Corine has to strain to hear her from across the worktop.

'Do you have that counsellor's number?' Corine asks, surprised Richard never mentioned Mae receiving counselling prior to the attack. She couldn't recall seeing it in any of the official reports.

'I'm afraid I'll have to dig it out. She only saw him once and refused to go back. I'll email you.' Kate's gaze drifts to a laptop perched on a side table, her eyes lingering there.

'Were there any signs of abuse? I'm assuming Lyndsey exhibited some—withdrawal, depression, anger, risky behaviour?'

Kate shook her head, her eyes still resting on the laptop.

'Everything okay?' Corine asks.

Kate slides off the stool to retrieve the laptop. 'I was

watching this before you arrived,' she says, turning the screen to face Corine and clicking on a file. The video shows a child's birthday party taking place outside, in a garden.

Is it this garden? Corine wonders. Laughter and noise fill the scene as the camera moves a little too quickly, catching children mid-chase or batting balloons, lingering briefly on a chaotic bouncy castle. Adult guests stand in groups, talking and drinking.

The camera eventually settles on a little girl in a pink tutu, sitting on a bench in a quiet corner of the garden, reading.

'That's Mae. It was her ninth birthday. She was always a bit… not different, but quieter than most—withdrawn at times.' Kate hesitates, biting her bottom lip. 'I never noticed any changes in her behaviour, or expected things to turn out the way they did.'

'She doesn't look happy,' Corine says, as she watches a younger Kate take hold of Mae's hand, leading her somewhere.

'There's me trying to include her. I know parties can be overwhelming for children—all that attention, too much sugar and excitement, you know what they're like, but…'

Corine continues watching as a man approaches, holding up a bear onesie. He hands it to Mae, who immediately pulls it on over her tutu.

'Who was that?'

'Her father. Always on hand to do the wrong thing.'

'She seems happy with the bear outfit.'

'Hm. Frank spoiled her—gave in to keep her quiet. Not exactly a parenting technique I'd recommend, would you?'

Corine smiles, careful to keep her expression neutral.

'Mae could be wilful when she wanted. Don't let the

butter-wouldn't-melt look fool you. All children know how to manipulate their parents, it's human nature.'

In the video, Mae storms off, followed by the camera, until she disappears inside.

'But their father was more giving with his girls than most.' Kate raises her eyebrows in a knowing way and uncrosses her legs.

'She didn't want to be filmed,' Corine says, trying not to sound judgmental.

'She was so rude that day… right in front of everyone. The person filming was an old university friend of mine, Martin. He'd bought Mae the tutu she didn't want to wear. She sulked until her father gave in and brought her that ridiculous bear onesie.'

CHAPTER 7
CORINE

It's almost six o'clock when Richard knocks on her office door. Corine is so absorbed in writing up her meeting notes that she doesn't notice. He tiptoes in, careful not to disturb her, but she catches sight of him and shakes her head.

'Idiot,' she mutters, trying not to smile—and failing.

'We were always sneaking into lectures late,' he says, one eyebrow raised expectantly as he takes a seat. 'Hungover and ill-prepared.'

'No, that was you. You were a bad influence.' Corine continues typing. 'You didn't care who saw you creeping in; you liked the notoriety.'

'You've just reminded me, one of my patient's complained this morning of feeling invisible. I said I couldn't see them right now, but—'

Corine shakes her head, a faint smile still lingering on her lips.

'What?' he chuckles.

'Mae's mother… did she seem vulnerable in any way to you?' she asks, changing the subject.

He frowns, puzzled. 'No, not particularly. I've only ever exchanged emails and a phone call, but she seemed solid. She's a GP, runs her own practice, came across as well-adjusted given everything that happened to her. Why?'

'Oh, I'm not sure, but I don't think she's prepared for Mae's release.'

'Prepared? In what way?'

'I think there's a lot of unspoken anxiety.'

'What, that Mae will attack her again?'

'No, not that. It's just... I don't think she's processed what Mae's release will mean—practically and emotionally.'

'That's not really our concern,' Richard replies, wrinkling his nose. 'We think Mae is ready for parole, but we need her to—'

'I know, you don't have to say it. Admit responsibility, show remorse, ask for forgiveness, promise she'll never do it again.' Corine stops typing and, for the first time since he entered the room, she looks at him directly.

Richard leans back in his chair, crossing his legs, a playful glint in his eyes as he watches her.

She looks away, suddenly embarrassed.

He smiles. 'We already know Mae won't do *all* of that,' he continues. 'If she were to apologise to her mother, that would be a great help. I'll happily take even a half-hearted apology.'

'Did Mae ever mention sexual abuse?' Corine asks bluntly.

Richard sits bolt upright. 'What? Against her?'

Corine nods.

'No. Never. Why?' he asks, his voice defensive.

He's expecting me to accuse someone at The Orchard. She lets him stew for a few moments, aware of the power she holds over him. It's unkind. Maybe tinged with a bit of jealousy over his position, after all? If only she hadn't left work, moved to Scotland, made the choices she did so long ago...

Richard looks so deflated that her own self-pity quickly

turns to shame.

'Not anyone at your precious hospital,' she says. 'Her father.'

'Ah.' He sounds relieved. 'No, that would have come out in one of her sessions. Did Mae say something?'

'No, her mother did.'

'Oh.' Richard purses his lips, rubbing his fingertips against the smooth skin around his mouth.

She can tell his mind is racing—every thought plays out on his expressive face. *He's the complete opposite of Joe.* All those years ago, she'd been drawn to her husband's silence. When he finally spoke, after months of her serving him in the pub where she worked, his few words had felt meaningful— which was ridiculous really, since he'd only offered to buy her a drink.

'Well, I must say, I'm surprised it never came up in one of her weekly sessions.'

Corine shrugs. 'Kate suspects her husband might have abused her. Apparently, Mae's older sister, Lyndsey, accused her father, but nothing was made official.'

'Right, well, that would make sense, of course, with all the self-harming, not eating, withdrawal, anger—'

'But not the ferocity of the attack on her mother. Or the refusal to speak.'

'No,' he concedes. 'You're not wrong.'

'Which is your way of saying I'm not right either,' Corine retorts, snorting dismissively. 'Mae was a mess when I first met her: unstable, suicidal. I'd never seen someone so vulnerable. I couldn't imagine her being capable of attacking her mother unless she was suffering from psychosis. Did I get that wrong?'

'How about we discuss this over a glass of wine? My shout.'

Corine's tempted by the idea of a few drinks in a cosy bar with an old work colleague and friend, but she knows how it will end—with regrets—and she's not prepared to do that to Joe.

'I can't, sorry. I promised my niece I'd buy her dinner.'

'Your niece,' Richard repeats, nodding. 'Another time, then.'

For once, he seems stuck for words.

†

Later, in the hotel, Corine pours over Mae's file and the notes from her meeting with Kate, pausing at a random remark in the margin of her notepad—*perfectionist*. She looks up and, with a sinking feeling, takes in the chaos of the tiny room. In less than a week, she has destroyed the place. Empty miniature vodka bottles are scattered about her on the bed; the minibar, she knows, is almost empty. Worn clothes, underwear, and tights are discarded over chairs and the wardrobe door. An empty pizza box and paper coffee cups litter the desk. Even the receptionist has started to give her disapproving looks. It crosses her mind that, whatever situation she found herself in—even if everything had turned out very differently— her chaotic side—that part within herself that lets go, that abdicates responsibility—would have found a foothold in her life. Even if she hadn't suffered losses that changed the course of her future, she had always been aware of a self-destructive streak; a finger hovering over the trigger. *Boom*.

Corine bats at the mess, sending a couple of miniatures

flying across the room. No one could accuse *her* of being a perfectionist—that was for sure. She'd met mothers like Kate before—women juggling high-stress careers and plagued by feelings of inadequacy; never quite giving enough to either their job or their child. She'd struggled managing just herself and Joe, never mind the needs and demands of multiple children. She wonders if Kate had been a super-mum, pushing herself to be everything to everyone, or if she had simply given up, overwhelmed by an impossible ideal? It certainly seemed like the former.

Corine sighed. If anyone had given up, it had been *her*—not just on herself, but on Joe and on their life together. Would she have been any different if she'd been someone's mum? She'd always believed she would. Not least because children were supposed to give you a reason to fight on, no matter how difficult life got or how meaningless it sometimes seemed.

In Scotland, during those few years before Joe's accident, she had felt liberated by the changes they'd made to their lives and the freedoms that remote living had brought. Managing the day to day running of the farm had taken up all their time. It was a steep but rewarding learning curve that left them both exhausted at the end of each day. The farm had thrived, the livestock had been healthy, and even the weather had seemed to be on their side with early springs and the relief of a good lambing season. It had been the diversion they had both needed.

She'd been glad to say goodbye to the packed trains, heavy traffic, pollution, and infuriating weekend wake-up calls of delivery vans. Even more so, she had felt freed from constantly witnessing neighbouring families caught up in the mundanities of daily life—taking everything for granted: school runs, playdates, football practice, swim club, gymnastics, ballet, music lessons, parties, sleepovers. The tantrums, slammed doors, loud music, first boyfriends, first girlfriends, cars, jobs. All that forward momentum, that constant change. How she had envied it.

'I almost had it all… a family, but I got distracted. Is that why I was punished?' She looks upwards, her hands clasped together. At what point had she crossed the line and allowed chaos to take over? 'If only we could warn ourselves against the stupidity of what we're about to do.'

She closes her eyes and pictures Kate's house—the polished parquet floor stretching down the hallway as she walks through it. Was it a show home that Mae had grown up in? Sterile and polished… more a theatrical backdrop than a real home?

Corine kicks the remaining empty miniatures off the bed, pushes papers and a file to one side, and curls up, praying for sleep to wash over her.

For her brain to finally switch off.

†

Corine is woken in the early hours by the muffled ringing of a mobile phone beneath her pillow. She is still wearing yesterday's clothes, rumpled and twisted about her now. The inside of her mouth feels like parchment.

She sits up, her face creased from the pillow, and pulls her skirt out from under her. 'Yes?' she answers, her voice hoarse.

'Hello, Callum here, sorry to be the bearer of bad news.' Immediately, Corine thinks of Joe, and her chest thuds. 'There's a problem with that pregnant cow of yours. The vet suspects Johne's Disease, but he's about to do some tests.'

'Fuck!'

'I'm sorry. I know it's not the news you wanted to be woken with this morning.'

'I should have called the vet in myself, earlier.' Callum says nothing, which to her feels like confirmation of her neglect. She looks at her watch—it's just gone five. 'I should come back. Shit! Callum, I know I should be there, but I can't see me getting back this weekend. Or the next. Could you...?'

'Aye, I promised I would and nothing's changed, for the next few weeks at any rate. Hopefully it can be contained. I'll let you know as soon as the vet has all the facts. Keep yer heid.'

'I will,' she says, ending the call. An outbreak of illness amongst the herd is all she needs. Was she even cut out for this life? A weariness descends. Still, Corine is touched by Callum's concern. 'Keep your head,' she repeats—a warning to herself.

Once again, she pictures Joe—he's younger, in his mid-forties, and still handsome. They'd been on a walking break in Perthshire, Joe's idea—always an advocate for fresh air and exercise as a cure for all ills. They'd just reached the top of Ben Chonzie, an easy Munro, according to Joe, which might have been true if Corine had been fit. They had paused to admire the views across Glen Turret and the Loch Turret: expansive and beautiful, yet to Corine, achingly desolate; a scene that stirred raw, primal emotions. She had fought the urge to scream.

"You see, it's the perfect spot," Joe said, but it had sounded more like a question.

Corine had nodded, her heart thudding against her ribcage until she felt it might burst. A tear had trickled down her face, left to fall unwiped.

Joe had opened his rucksack, taking out a small silver pot. *"Ready?"* Unscrewing the lid, he'd offered the pot to her, but Corine had backed away, as though touching it might burn her.

Then, in one quick movement—perhaps afraid she would change her mind again—Joe had lifted the pot in the air, gently shaking out the contents. The precious grey ashes had plumed upwards and away, carried by the wind.

Corine feels bereft all over again at the memory—empty, stricken. Loss hits her like a speeding train. Her broken heart thuds inside her chest, even as she wills it to stop, to end the pain.

She feels Joe's arms around her. Perhaps he'd held her up—she wasn't sure—but she remembers feeling as though he anchored her; that without him she would have blown away on the breeze, disappearing along with the ashes.

That was when she'd seen the hare, sitting amongst the heather, its white and brown fur blending into the rocks. It seemed aware of them, just a few metres away, and yet the reclusive creature had looked as relaxed as if it were a domestic pet waiting to be fed.

The hare had edged closer, sitting tall on its powerful hind legs and stretching its full length, long ears flicking back— one, then the other—while its nose sniffed the air. Slowly, it turned, and they had watched, entranced, as it picked up speed, heading across the mountain in the same direction as their son's ashes.

"Michael would have loved that," Joe had said. *"It feels like a sign."* He wasn't usually one to believe in such things, but grief was speaking now. *"It's a long road that's not got a turning."*

In that instant, Corine had hated him and his empty platitudes. She'd wanted to say, *I carried him for nine-months, gave birth to him, felt the warmth from his tiny body flood my heart from the moment he was placed in my eager arms. One brief, blissful year was all I had. And now he's gone.* The hare hadn't represented a turning point. If anything, it had marked Corine's realisation that she was alone—that Joe could not make life feel worth living again. Nothing and no one could fill such an emptiness.

Now, laying in her own mess, she could see how selfish she had been. How unfair it was to rely so heavily, so completely, upon Joe. Expecting him to have all the answers; to mend her when he had been suffering under the weight of his own quiet grief. No, it had been her who had chosen the wrong path, Corine could see that now. Her who had, even then, pointed them firmly in the direction of failure.

Corine rang Joe and waited for the answer machine to kick in.

'I never apologised to you for Michael, and I should have. It might have helped.'

CHAPTER 8
CORINE

A door slams in the corridor outside her room, jolting Corine awake. She turns instinctively, reaching for Joe's familiar presence—only to find the empty space beside her and the relentless coldness she's come to dread. Glancing at her phone, she sees it's just gone six-twenty, and pale morning light is already filtering through the ill-fitting curtains. Any hope of returning to sleep feels lost.

Corine's body feels heavy and sluggish. Her throat is so dry that a slice of toast might finish her off. She craves water, but the glass next to her is empty, and the bathroom feels like the other side of the world.

She had fallen into a deep sleep sometime after Callum's call—dreaming of things she'd rather not remember. In those dreams, she did and said things she would never dare express aloud—not to Joe, her sister, or, more recently, her own mother. Things that were years, decades, even a lifetime beyond saying.

Had Joe been beside her, they might have discussed her dream. He'd learnt to do that for her over the years—to indulge her—but any deeper self-analysis, for that was what he'd considered a discussion about dreams to be, would be fleeting and over with as soon as emotions seeped in. Joe was a firm believer that people should live in the present, but try as Corine might, and despite all her training, it was the past that kept drawing her back.

She takes a cool shower and gets dressed quickly. Before leaving, she opens the mini-bar and lets out a small tut—all the vodka and gin had gone, likely drunk by her the night before, though she can't remember a thing. She grabs three whisky miniatures and tosses them into her bag.

When she arrives at The Orchard, Kate Bailey is already there. Corine watches her laugh easily with one of the prison guards as she is shown through the security doors. A thought pops into her head before she can censor it—*having a damaged child is better than having no child*. Corine immediately scolds herself. Had Mae's knife been an inch in the wrong direction… she shivers at the thought. Her mind is all over the place. What that woman suffered at the hands of her daughter must be the worst kind of agony.

Corine passes through security without saying a word and makes a beeline for the toilets. All three cubicles are empty. Relieved, she slips into the farthest one, locks the door behind her, and pulls out a whisky miniature from her bag. As she takes a sip, a slow warmth unfurls through her body. *Just one*, she tells herself.

†

Corine is already in the therapy room when the guard enters with Mae. It's important she prepares Mae—ensures she knows what's expected of her. She asks the guard to wait outside and to warn her when Kate arrives. The guard nods and leaves without speaking.

Once the door clicks shut, Mae goes to take the seat closest to the door, but Corine stops her. 'Not that one... Here, please, on this side.'

She smiles, hoping that Mae won't pick her up on her reasoning. Corine wants to be able to contain her, should she need to, and provide Kate with a means of escape. Nothing should obstruct access to the door and the guard outside.

Mae does as she's told and saunters over to the chair on the far side of Corine. She looks bleary eyed; disengaged.

'Your mother's here, but I wanted to check that you're ready before I ask her to join us. It may feel traumatic—'

Mae snorts and shifts in her seat. Her eyes remain downcast as she picks at the torn cuticles around her nails.

'Especially for your mother,' Corine adds, pointedly. Mae didn't seem capable of seeing things from her mother's perspective. Corine pauses, irritated by Mae's silence. 'It's you who's facing parole. I'd caution you to remember that. If you're feeling any anger towards your mother, I suggest we stop right now. It won't help your case—not to mention that poor woman out there who's come to hear what you have to say. Have you *thought* about what you're going to say?'

Mae's eyes flick up. 'No, Dr Alexander, but if I'm right, I won't need to say much.' She looks pleased with herself, smug.

Foolish child, Corine thinks, feeling the familiar taste of acid at the back of her throat. She picks up a plastic cup of water and sips.

'Of course, I'll direct the questions, but this is an opportunity for you both to speak openly. When I say openly, I mean be mindful of your mother's feelings as the victim here. She'll be feeling nervous.' Corine wonders if she's being too harsh, endangering their relationship, but she sees Mae smirk and it angers her all over again. She wants to grab hold of her and shake her to establish her authority.

'Sorry,' Mae says, covering her mouth with her hand.

'Let me be clear, a parole board will expect you to admit responsibility *and* apologise. This is your chance to make amends, to show remorse.' Corine stares at Mae, but she won't meet her eyes. 'Not taking this meeting seriously could damage your future, and for someone who's been rejected for parole, locked up for four years, you need to show you've learnt your lesson.'

There's a knock as Corine finishes speaking and the guard peers in from behind the door.

'Dr Bailey is here.'

'Thanks, please send her in.' She turns to Mae and whispers. 'Remember, you control your destiny.'

The second it's out of her mouth, she regrets it. She sounds like a cheap fortune cookie.

As Corine watches Mae slumped in her chair, picking her cuticles raw, it crosses her mind that today could mark the end of her professional reputation—or worse still, the delivery of an already-traumatised mother into the hands of her unstable daughter. Mae glances up at Corine with shaded eyes, as though reading her mind. She smiles, but Mae's focus has already shifted back, intent on drawing blood.

Perhaps Richard had been too dismissive of her concerns about Mae and Kate's readiness for this meeting. He had ranted on about rehabilitation and the principles of restorative justice as though giving a speech to potential funders. Then he'd said something curious—that Mae *valued* Corine's detachment. When pushed, he qualified it in terms of objectivity—professional distance—but it struck her that she might come across as cold or emotionally detached. Perhaps she was? Is? It *was* Joe who had softened her personality over the years they'd been together. He'd allowed her to see that she didn't always need to be in control.

With a heavy heart, Corine reminds herself to stay focused, to be in the moment, not only for Mae's sake but also for Kate's.

'That looks sore,' she says.

Mae shrugs, digging her thumbnail even harder into the soft tissue.

Corine winces.

A loud knock puts an end to her questions. She springs up, relieved to be active, and when she opens the door, Kate stands demurely beside the guard, dressed in pale jeans and a beige woollen jumper.

She seems smaller than the last time they met. Her scars, though, are less subdued—raw and vivid, they almost look fresh. It's obvious that Kate has made no attempt to conceal them. *Good for her*, Corine thinks. She wonders how Mae will react to seeing the destruction she caused all those years ago. Hopefully it will help her locate her guilt, or at least soften her a little.

Corine ushers Kate in. 'Stay inside,' she whispers to the guard, who throws Mae a confused glance before taking up a position adjacent to the door.

Corine gestures to the chair next to her and Kate sits down. Dr Bailey looks nervous, her eyes flicking from Corine to Mae repeatedly as she perches at the edge of the seat and places her jacket and bag behind her.

Mae doesn't acknowledge her.

Crossing her legs, Corine smiles, trying to remain upbeat. 'Right, well, this meeting has been a long time coming and I'm hoping it will be a positive, therapeutic experience for both of you. I know we're doing things a little differently from what you may have discussed with your Victim Liaison Officer in terms of restorative justice.' She meets Kate's eyes and gives her a look that she hopes conveys reassurance. 'I need to ask you both some difficult questions and get your answers on record, but I'm happy for that discussion to come about a little more organically over the coming weeks. We should look at today as a step towards the process of reconciling what happened to you, Kate.'

Corine looks over at Mae, to find her still focused on her nails. *Great.*

'I know this isn't easy for either of you,' she continues, 'but I hope it will allow you to move beyond the assault. I'm here to help facilitate your conversation, but Mae, ultimately, these meetings are a chance for you to understand the impact of your crime on your mother—to apologise—and for you, Kate, to work towards acceptance.' Corine can't bring herself to say forgiveness. Or, given the way Mae had been behaving, hope for a healthier relationship. She isn't sure she believes either are possible.

'Could you pass me a tissue, please.' Mae holds her finger up and a thin line of blood trickles down it, splashing onto the laminate floor.

Once again, Corine pictures a knife slashing through soft

skin. Flustered, she reaches for the tissues, her hand shaking, but Kate gets there first. She passes a fistful of tissues to Mae.

'They'll become infected if you're not careful,' she says.

'Like the rest of me,' Mae mumbles, just loud enough to be heard. She turns her head to one side and aims a syrupy-sweet smile at Kate, the blood-soaked tissues still clutched in her hand.

'You always were your own worst enemy,' Kate says, her brow furrowed in concern. 'You look well, though.'

Corine takes a deep breath, relieved that Kate's being the adult in this situation and not allowing Mae to goad her.

'I am, as a matter of fact. Turns out routine, stability, and boundaries suit me. Who would've thought?'

Kate ignores her daughter. 'The reports might have stopped once you turned eighteen, but I never stopped worrying about you—not for one moment. I'd call sometimes. They said you were studying… responding to treatment, behaving. They couldn't tell me much.'

'What can I say, you raised a model inmate. I follow the rules, but then I always did, didn't I?'

Mother and daughter hold each other's gaze, and Corine imagines a whole world of shared experiences that she will never be privy to. Somehow, she had to put a stop to Mae's nonsense, and quickly.

'Let's talk for a moment about happier times. Mae, I read in your notes that a family Christmas was always important to you. Something you've missed whilst serving your sentence. Would you like to talk about that?'

'Yes, I would like that very much, thank you, Corine.'

Corine knows she's mocking her, but she keeps her face

deliberately expressionless and waits for Mae to continue.

'But I think it's only polite to ask my mother for her positive memories first.' Under her breath, she whispers, 'It shouldn't take long.'

Corine shoots her a warning glance, which Mae duly ignores.

If Kate hears her daughter, she has the good grace not to react. She runs a hand over her scraped-back hair and sits higher in her chair. 'Mae's father and I split up on Christmas day, 2011,' she says, through pursed lips. 'Well, that's the sanitised version. He walked out on me. Christmas was, and still is, a time of mixed emotions. For me, anyway. But children… they have a way of getting over things, don't they? They move on, focus on their own lives, their futures. It's only natural, I suppose.'

Corine's heart sinks. Was Mae going to sabotage her plans every step of the way? She glances down at the form she asked Mae to complete in preparation for today's meeting. Her neat blue handwriting, listing Christmas as her number one happy memory. Then Mother's Day, then June twenty-third, followed by a question mark. These were supposed to be happy memories—safe topics to discuss—but obviously Mae had other ideas. She was damaging her chances of parole from the offset.

'And then, almost a year later, I was sentenced and had my first ever Christmas in a psych ward. That, as they say, was merry and bright… what with the suicide watch and the strip lights.' Mae flippantly wafts her hands in the direction of Kate's scarred face. 'For doing *that*.' She smiles, as though enjoying the memory of her cruelty.

Corine glares at her, but Mae's attention is directed at her mother. Kate looks stricken. She bites down on her lower lip and looks across at the picture of an empty beach. Corine imagines that Kate would like to disappear into it, allowing the sound of the waves crashing against the curve of rocks to drown everything out.

'Parental separation is difficult for children to come to terms with at any age, and it's usually difficult for the adults involved too,' Corine says diplomatically, though the tone of her voice is meant as a warning for Mae. 'Did you find your parents separation difficult, Mae?'

'Seriously?' Mae glares at Corine. She looks like she's about to say something else, but then seems to think better of it and looks away.

'It was an awful time,' Kate concedes. 'For all of us, for different reasons. We all struggled to make sense of things. One minute you're a family, the next you're… well, I guess you're a broken home.'

'That'll be it, then. Job done. That's why I did, you know, what I did.' Mae shakes her head, her face screwed up as though recalling a distasteful memory.

Does her future have so little value to her? Corine wonders, shocked and frustrated by Mae's attitude.

'It might surprise you, but most young people, even those from the most difficult backgrounds, where violence is commonplace, don't end up attacking their mother the way you did,' Corine says, keeping her tone neutral.

She can feel the tension in the room immediately shift up a gear as Mae turns to face her, the teenager's anger unmistakable now. Blood pools in the tissue she holds as she digs her nails into her cuticles. Corine wonders if this was how she looked the day she lashed out.

'I know,' Mae says, leaning forward. 'Like I've said, I regret that ever happened.' She looks directly at Kate. 'It should never have happened.'

'Oh, Mae!' Kate looks like she's about to cry. 'Thank you. Thank you for saying that. It means so much to me.'

There's little evidence of the regret Mae claims to feel in her cold, immobile stare. *She's ticking boxes*, Corine thinks, *saying what's expected to secure parole.* This little performance is all about her and her needs, and Kate seems to be blind to it; she smiles at Mae, blissfully clueless, dabbing her eyes with a scrunched-up tissue. Corine feels a surge of pity for her. *She's like a neglected dog, grateful for any morsel of kindness.*

Twenty years of experience in the prison system, and Corine had never treated a daughter who'd attacked her own mother in such an horrific way. It was usually boys who carried out parental attacks. Boys or young men who'd been left to grow from children to young adults with untreated behaviours. Sometimes those behaviours escalated in a small number of cases but, even then, assaults didn't usually involve knives. It was rarer still for parents to press charges. Shame prevented them. That, and not wanting their children to end up in the criminal system.

'You decided not to prosecute, Kate. Then, in court, you did everything to prevent a custodial sentence.'

Kate nods, reaching for a fresh tissue, but the box is empty, and a tear slowly trickles down and around the scars on her face. Corine searches in her jacket pocket and pulls out a small packet. She hands the tissues to Kate, who smiles gratefully, the skin puckering on her cheeks like poorly sewn fabric.

'Why was that?' Corine continues.

'That wasn't my Mae that day. The person who attacked me wasn't the child I'd raised. Oh, I know people say it was as though a switch had been flicked, but it's true, that's how it was.' Kate's voice wavers as she struggles to fight back tears. 'Sorry.'

'That's okay—whenever you're ready.' Corine's voice is low, purposefully soothing.

'She came flying at me with such unexpected rage.' Kate's eyes are wet now as she struggles to remain in control. She doesn't take her eyes off Mae. 'It wasn't you. You were always such a good girl—clever and quiet. A bit too quiet at times, but what happened—it was completely out of character.' She pauses to gather her thoughts. 'And just like that, my world changed.'

Mae doesn't answer. It's as though she's watching a film; one she'd seen countless times before. *There's a barrier in her*, Corine thinks, and nothing Kate says seems to penetrate it.

'Is that how you see it, Mae? Was it as though a switch had flicked for you?'

Again, Corine is met with silence. It crosses her mind that it wasn't only Kate's world that changed in those terrible moments, but she chooses a less confrontational approach. Kate appears fragile, and she doesn't want her to feel in any way judged. She turns the conversation to Frank, Mae's absent father, in the hope that it might help Mae understand her mother's situation around the time of the attack a little better.

'Okay then, Kate, I wonder if you could tell me about your

relationship with Mae's father before the split. I know there was tension, but was there much arguing around the time of your separation? Verbal or physical aggression?' Corine hopes Kate's response will encourage Mae to open up.

'No. As I've said in the past, there was never any aggression between us. We argued, like all couples, but he was never physically abusive to me, or me to him. Mae didn't grow up in a household where violence was used.'

'How about you, Mae? Is that how you recall it?'

'Only idiots use violence.' She looks straight at her mother.

Was this finally an apology? Corine waits, hoping for more.

Eventually, Mae adds, 'A switch flipping isn't how I see that day, more like a light being switched on, and not just for me.'

'Can you explain what you mean?' Corine asks, though she isn't sure she wants to hear the answer.

'No.'

'Okay then,' Corine says, glancing down at her notes. 'From how your mother describes you, you must have been close.'

'I thought so.'

'My girls were… are… everything to me,' Kate interrupts. She takes another tissue from the packet and wipes her eyes. 'Then and now, I'd still do anything for either of you. Once you're a mother, everything changes… your life… priorities. Your world shifts on its axis and you're no longer the person on top. Your children come first.'

A heavy silence follows.

Corine turns to Mae. 'Did you ever feel like a lot was

expected of you?'

Mae sits upright and hugs her ribs. 'Not at the time.'

The implication hangs in the air. Corine shifts her gaze purposefully to Kate, but she looks down. Getting these two to open up, to agree on anything, wasn't going to be easy. *What I wouldn't give for a shot of vodka right now.*

Corine notices a slight tremor in her hands. She twists her wedding band as a distraction. That's when she hears Joe's voice, warning her not to make matters worse. It unnerves her, and for a moment, she struggles to focus. In the silence, she can hear footsteps walking past the room; muffled voices talking, whispering.

'I wanted them to do well at school, is that a crime?' Kate asks, shrugging dismissively. 'Mae was always bright—top of her class. Not like Lyndsey, bless her, she struggled with school. I pushed them both, of course I did. I wanted them to get the best out of life. I'm not sure kids appreciate it, not when they grow up comfortable. Not like me. My life growing up was very different. My parents were always scraping by, struggling to pay the bills. Mum gave up her chance at university when I came along, and never failed to remind me. Dad, well, he nurtured a very healthy, lifelong gambling addiction.'

Mae rolls her eyes. 'Unlike Dad's cushy upbringing?'

Kate drew a sharp breath. 'Oh, he liked to think he was different. Always made out that his father was this successful property developer.' She laughs bitterly. 'In reality he had a few dives he rented to students. His mum—good old Iris—never worked a day in her life. Five boys she had, all altar boys, three of whom went on to have affairs.' She sneers, not taking her eyes off Mae, who offers nothing in return—not even a flicker. 'Well done, Iris! Anyway, Frank will be her third son to be divorcing.'

'What?' Mae sits up, alert now. 'You and Dad are divorcing?'

'You must know we've lived apart since he walked out?'

Mae nods.

'Well, I've finally made the decision to get on with the rest of my life.' Kate smiles and looks to Corine. 'I'm not getting any younger, and I need to live the life I have left.'

'You sounded surprised just then, Mae, about the divorce,' Corine says. 'Are you?'

'Only that she's allowing it.' Mae glares at Kate.

Kate laughs. 'Foolishly, I believe in commitment, so hang me, but your father is what he is… a cold, selfish bastard, and that will never change. I have to be realistic and move on.'

Good luck with that, Corine thinks. If only moving on was easy.

It's Mae's turn to look at the pictures on the wall. Without taking her eyes off the seascape, she laughs. 'I can't see what difference a divorce will make for you. I mean, you got everything anyway… the house and everything in it. Aren't you satisfied with that?' She looks at Kate, puzzled. 'Then again, you also got Lyndsey, and it's no secret she's damaged goods.'

'Not helpful,' Kate hisses.

Mother and daughter scowl at each other.

'Tell me why you feel that way about your sister?' Corine presses.

'Because she's a fucking idiot.' All traces of calm are gone in a single moment, like a fast-moving storm. Mae scrapes her fingernails up her arm, leaving white indentations that quickly turn red.

'Alright, Mae,' Corine says, her voice soothing. 'It's understandable to feel upset hearing that your parents are divorcing each other, but they're not divorcing their children.'

Mae snorts in disgust and looks away.

Corine turns to Kate, hoping that she might help explain Mae's reaction, but she simply shrugs and looks at the ground, deflated. Corine assumes Mae's referencing the accusations of child abuse. It was possible that she blamed Lyndsey for not speaking up sooner and saving her, and Kate for not protecting her. Corine makes a mental note to speak with Lyndsey. Perhaps she could shed some light on the attack.

'Can you talk a little more about Lyndsey and why you referred to her as damaged goods, Mae?' Corine doesn't look at Kate; she knows this could easily become an upsetting conversation.

'It's no secret that Lyndsey's father crossed a boundary,' Kate interjects. 'He's no longer in her life. Thankfully, she's moved on, and bringing that up again would be devastating, especially when she's already got enough on her plate with a young family to care for.'

'Poor Lyndsey—well and truly sucked into the hive.'

'She's done well, despite everything. Got on with her life, has a lovely little family of her own.' Kate ignores Mae's jibe, redirecting the conversation like a seasoned politician. 'She's happy, and that's all that matters to me,' she says, looking at Mae. 'It's all any mother wants.'

Mae doesn't respond, her body language is closed off, defensive.

'Actually, Beth—Lyndsey's eldest—reminds me of you.' She pauses, waiting for Mae to look over. When she doesn't, she adds, 'Always eager to please.'

Mae shoots forward, like a sprung coil. Even the guard shifts position. 'Perhaps she should have got rid of it, saved herself a lifetime of disappointment.' She shifts position in the chair, her rigid mouth and red face betraying the anger she's struggling to hold back.

'They're hard work; into everything,' Kate continues, seemingly oblivious to the surge in tension. 'I guess I'm lucky to be able to help her that way.' She hesitates. 'When it could have been so different.'

Mae stands abruptly and rushes past Corine. 'I need to get out of here.'

Corine looks to the guard and nods, apologising to Kate as soon as they leave. She asks if Kate has any idea what just happened.

'She's always been jealous of her sister's relationship with me. Lyndsey is just easier, and that's the truth of it. I've always loved Mae, but at times she's difficult to like. She can be cold—superior.' Kate gives a small laugh. 'I suppose that makes me sound like an awful mother, doesn't it?'

Corine shakes her head.

'I forgot how she can be,' Kate adds, shivering. 'I felt like I was back walking on eggshells, afraid to say the wrong thing. Christ, I'm the victim here, but you would have thought it was me who held the knife. I don't even have to do this.'

The last thing Corine wants is for Kate's anger to escalate and for her to openly oppose probation—Richard would never forgive her if everyone's efforts were derailed—but the meeting had thrown up more questions than answers about Mae's father and sister; about the pent-up anger she refused to voice; about her lack of empathy towards her mother, despite what she might say to tick boxes.

'Let me have a chat with Mae and I'll call you tomorrow. I know this is difficult for you, but she's been locked up for four years. It often takes a few sessions before we see progress.'

Kate nods, but her mouth is drawn tight.

'I'd like to talk with Lyndsey and Mae's father before we meet next.'

'He won't talk to you,' she says, a new sharpness in her voice.

'Oh. Why not?'

'He's terrified Mae will accuse him of something, like Lyndsey did.'

'There was no mention of that in any of Mae's records,' Corine reminds her. 'It seems strange.'

Kate studies Corine for a while. 'When Lyndsey was seventeen, she told me he'd come into her room one night… she'd been about eight years old at the time. A baby. I wasn't at home. He'd climbed into bed with her, touched her. Just the once, but…'

'Does he still see Lyndsey?'

'No. She wouldn't… doesn't want anything to do with him. She must have repressed the memory for years, God love her. It was never mentioned because it was never officially reported. I didn't want the girls to go through a court case, I know what that would entail. How difficult it would be to prove anything without physical evidence. It's his new partner I worry about. I mean, I've never seen the girl, but I've heard rumours from friends we still have in common. She's barely out of nappies.' Kate wrinkles her nose. 'A twenty-eight-year-old fucking teaching assistant.'

Before Corine can ask another question, Kate stands.

'I don't consider myself a pushover, but if Frank can destroy *my* life, I'd hate to think what he could do to a young girl like that.'

CHAPTER 9
CORINE

It's warm in the bar, and the whisky Corine has just knocked back is beginning to take the edge off things. Her left shoulder burns, as it always does when she's overtired or stressed. She rolls each shoulder back slowly, trying to ease the tension, then tilts her neck from side to side. She's no longer used to spending hours stuck at her desk; she misses the fresh air and open space she once took for granted. Even the sometimes-gruelling physicality of farm life doesn't seem so bad with a bit of distance.

Just as she is about to call Callum for an update on her sickly cow, Richard slides into the seat next to her.

'Isn't six o'clock a bit early for you?' he asks, eyeing her empty glass. 'Meeting someone, are we?'

'No, we are not.' She sniffs and rubs her shoulder. 'At least, I hadn't intended to. I had half an hour to kill, that's all.'

'Another?' he asks. Before she can answer, the barman appears, and he orders two more of the same.

They watch in silence as the drinks are poured, waiting until the barman moves down the bar to serve someone else before speaking.

'So, you really didn't know anything about the accusations against Mae's father?' Corine asks, shaking her head in disbelief.

Richard watches Corine down her drink and signals to the barman to refill their empty glasses. 'No. Poor form, I know, but if patients, their families, the authorities don't reveal it, I can't do anything. I'm not going to lose any sleep over it, but it would explain a lot.'

He's gotten harder, Corine thinks. She sighs, turning her glass in her hands. 'I'll talk to her tomorrow.'

'Never take it home with you, remember that. You never were very good at letting things go. With clients, I mean, not colleagues.' Richard glances sideways at her, a single eyebrow raised.

'Colleagues?' She laughs, insulted. 'We used to be friends.'

'Do you even know what you leaving did to me?' His tone is uncharacteristically serious. 'You'd been a part of my life since that first term at Edinburgh. Most *marriages* don't last that long.'

Corine takes a while to answer. 'I should never have taken this job on. I'm not good at it anymore. And Mae…'

Richard reaches out and holds her hand in his. 'She's acting up in front of her mother, that's all. Make sure she doesn't say or do anything stupid. Be there for her.'

'Christ!' Corine laughs, withdrawing her hand. 'Now I know you're having a laugh. You want me, with my track record, to be there for her?'

Richard lowers his glass, his eyes searching her face. He's careful around her; afraid she might run away, disappear back to Scotland, and refuse to answer his calls again. 'You didn't cause the accident. Even if you'd been at the farm, it wouldn't have made any difference. We've all had those moments of anger, pure rage, when you could drive a car into a wall, but the majority of us don't act on those impulses.'

'Joe didn't crash the quad bike on purpose.'

'No, but he went out in a storm, pissed off at you for being in London. He'd been drinking… was, very likely, drunk.'

'He thought I was leaving him—moving back to London—using my niece… my sister's funeral, as an excuse. Even before that, I suppose I was struggling with Scotland—how remote we were from family… friends. It was no secret that I needed to sort my head out, but I should never have told him I was leaving over the damn phone.' Corine's face crumples, but she manages to hold it together. Exhausted, she props her head up with her hand.

'No one could fault you; the way you look after him. Tell me the man is at least grateful for that?'

'Can I get you folks anything else?' the barman asks.

Richard looks at Corine. She shakes her head.

'Just shout if you change your mind.' The barman wanders off to the far side of the bar to serve another customer.

'Do we ever really know what someone else is thinking?' Corine asks. 'Twenty-eight years of marriage and sometimes I feel like I never really knew him.' Even before the accident, Joe was a closed book most of the time.

'Joe only thinks about himself. I would have thought that was obvious. He went ahead with his dream of retirement without your complete consent. He put your house on the market, for crying out loud. You should have been the angry one, Corine. I don't know why you stick by him.'

Corine stands abruptly, sweeping up her coat and bag.

Richard reaches for her wrist, then releases it almost immediately. 'Stay. I'm sorry—I shouldn't have said all that.

Let me buy you dinner. I won't mention him, or the past, or work… or how good you look.' He watches her closely, and she can see how much he's hoping she'll change her mind.

It's been a long time since anyone has complimented her. It feels good. 'Another time,' she says, quietly.

Richard doesn't push. 'Right. Get some rest, and if you need me.' He mimes a phone call.

Corine smiles.

Reluctantly, she heads for the door.

†

It's grown dark outside, and Corine fumbles with the buttons of her coat. She walks briskly, passing shuttered shop fronts and tall grey blocks of flats crammed between older Georgian buildings—gutted inside and repurposed as offices or small hotels. All around her, curtains are being drawn and blinds lowered as soft yellow lights glow in the windows. On the third floor of a modern complex, she watches a young girl roughly towel-dry her hair. A few flats along, a man stands on a narrow balcony blowing plumes of white smoke into the night.

The sky looms dark against the buildings. It edges everything before her, even the twisted skeletons of trees that line the road. There's an absence of stars, a lack of moonlight, and as Corine walks, she realises how much she misses them.

Crossing the road outside of the hotel entrance, she sees a silver Range Rover with darkened windows pull away. She has the strangest feeling that someone is watching her. *Don't be insane,* she tells herself.

Inside the hotel, Corine rushes past the receptionist, who's too busy with a booking to look up at her. It takes her three attempts to get her key card to work, and once she's successful, she flings her coat and bag on the bed and goes straight to the minibar. She pours herself a whisky and downs it in one gulp, then opens another. Stripping off her clothes, she steps into the shower, moving quickly, without thinking.

After drying off, Corine checks her phone: five texts from Richard, and two missed calls.

'Fuck,' she mutters, slumping down on the bed. She sips at her whisky and adjusts the towel she's wrapped around herself. The phone rings again. Richard's name pops up on the screen. She answers.

'I wanted to make sure you were okay, you seemed upset.'

'Where are you?' she interrupts.

'Reception.'

She hesitates. 'Room 202.'

Corine puts the phone down and goes straight to the bathroom. *Don't overthink it*, she tells herself. In the steamed-up mirror, she brushes her hair and ruffles it with her fingers. She looks for her perfume, but can't remember packing it, so picks up a small bottle of hotel body lotion instead and rubs it over her arms, legs, and chest. It smells cheap and floral, but when she tries to rub some of it off, she realises it's already absorbed. Quickly, she brushes her teeth, leaning under the tap to rinse. Moments later, she hears Richard knock at the door.

Corine closes her eyes. 'You want this,' she whispers.

When she opens the door and sees Richard's pale face and blue, hopeful eyes, she smiles. They close the door behind them and kiss in the small entryway. She feels his cool lips, tentative, and the coldness of his clothes from being outside.

'Are you sure?' he asks.

'No. You?'

Richard laughs.

She steps back, pulling him towards the bed and the comfort and oblivion her body craves.

CHAPTER 10
CORINE

Mae hides her face behind her hands in a childishly uncooperative manner. What began as a simple conversation about her two nieces being cared for by her mother had quickly grown tense. But Mae's real anger seemed aimed at her sister, Lyndsey, though she refused to explain why. They had been in the therapy room for nearly half an hour, with Mae offering the same vague, increasingly defensive answers to every question.

'You need to talk to me, Mae,' Corine says, finally showing her frustration. 'If we keep going round in circles, I won't be able to help you. You've got two weeks until your parole hearing. Refusing to speak when your mother's here is a waste of everyone's time. The only one who'll suffer is you.'

'I've said I'm sorry, haven't I?' Mae replies brazenly. 'What more do you expect?'

'You and I both know that saying sorry isn't the same as meaning it.' Corine sighs. It was going to be a long session and she didn't want things to become tense between them—that would help no one. Her eyes flick over to the picture of the seascape, and she pauses. 'Those images mean well, but—'

'Fucking cruel, if you ask me.'

They both laugh, and briefly, Corine sees the beauty of

Mae's animated face. A wide, perfectly straight, white smile, seen only for a second, until Mae remembers who she is and where they are. The shutters come down again.

'Okay, well, tell me about your father then,' Corine pushes as gently as she can. 'Did you two have a good relationship?'

'I suppose. He worked a lot. After Lyndsey said he'd done things to her, we didn't see him again. Mum kept him away; threatened to report him to the police.'

'Did he ever touch you inappropriately?'

'No.' Mae shakes her head. 'I couldn't believe he'd done what Lyndsey said, but Mum said there was evidence. Medical. So…'

'Yet she didn't press charges. Do you know why?' If it had been her child, Corine is certain she would have demanded an investigation.

'You'd have to ask her, but imagine the embarrassment if that got out. Dr Kate Bailey: perfect wife, mother, GP, pillar of the community, and all-round good egg, yet she didn't know her husband was a paedo.' Mae scoffs. 'It'd be the end of her fragile utopia.'

'It must have been difficult fitting into that world.'

Mae shakes her head. 'I didn't realise back then that it was all about her… that she was the sun and we all pivoted about her. It was all I knew.'

'Can you explain a little more?'

Mae stops and thinks for a moment. 'Have you ever been to London Zoo?' she asks, rocking forward in her chair.

Corine shakes her head, painfully aware of her childless state; how different her life would have been had she been a parent. Corine had avoided those places—anywhere that might remind her of what she had lost.

'It doesn't matter, any zoo will do,' Mae tells her. 'They keep the big cats in small enclosures; they're supposed to replicate their perfect environment. They're well fed, given little activities to keep them occupied, but they're there to fill a need in somebody else's life. They're contained.'

'So, you felt caged-in at home?'

'No—the opposite. I felt like she kept me outside, at arm's-length. Like I was only let in when I served a purpose. If I ever said or did something she didn't like, she'd say, "*That's him talking*" or "*You're just like him.*" And just like that, I'd be shut outside again, watching her and Lyndsey cosying up from behind an invisible screen.

When Dad left—or when she kicked him out—it only got worse. It was always Mum and Lyndsey cuddled up on the sofa, giggling about something. And if I asked what was so funny, she'd brush it off: "*Your sister*", she'd say. Then, completely out of nowhere, she'd ask, "*Why don't you ever give Mummy cuddles?*" *And* before I could even answer, she'd say, "*I love you, sweetie, you're such a comfort to me*". Meaning Lyndsey, obviously. Then she'd look at me and pause—before she'd add, "*Love you too, sweetheart*".'

'You felt she played you off against each other.'

'Yeah. But then she'd say stuff like, "*What would I do without my girls?*" and suddenly I was back on the inside. Then the tears would come, and we'd both hug her and cry. Only, I never cried. I think she took that as me being heartless. Ungrateful. But honestly, I just didn't know what she wanted from me. Mum was unhappy with Dad; they argued constantly, always sniping at each other—and then suddenly I was supposed to cry because he'd gone.'

'That's hard.'

Mae gives a short, mirthless laugh, then takes a breath. 'One time, I said maybe it was a good thing he'd left. A friend at school was happy when her parents split up, and I thought Mum might feel the same. But she went ballistic. Called me ungrateful. Said I wasn't a real daughter, that I didn't love her back, didn't understand what she was going through, didn't appreciate what she did for us.'

'Was that the day you attacked her?'

Mae shook her head, her lips shut tight, pale.

'I'm trying to help you, Mae, I really am. Please try to trust me,' Corine urges, sensing her growing reluctance.

'Dad had been gone for months by then. He'd called round, asking to see us, but Mum would never let him in. I wanted to talk to him about what he'd been accused of, so one day, I opened the door and let him in. My God, the way she reacted. Wailing and screeching, accusing Dad of doing all sorts to Lyndsey. Dad left—he literally ran out—and Mum didn't speak to me for two weeks. I was thirteen, almost fourteen. We didn't see him after that. Not for months.'

'Do you think he abused your sister?' Corine's voice is quiet, barely above a whisper, as she leans forward, listening intently.

'They say he did, but...' Mae shrugs. 'He left, didn't put up a fight. Now all I can remember are the vile things she said he did to Lyndsey. I wish I'd never heard any of it.'

'It was more than once?' Kate had implied it was a one-off when Corine had spoken to her. What else wasn't she saying?

Mae shrugs. 'We didn't speak about it. I felt devastated.

I wanted to know the truth, but I was scared to mention his name. It only led to tears or screaming arguments.'

Corine nods, all too aware of how quickly one angry word could lead to another and, before you knew it, the thing you never meant to say was out there, never to be unsaid.

She suddenly pictures herself with Joe, walking out of a bar in Soho.

"What are you saying? We've been talking about moving to Scotland for the last fifteen years. How's that a surprise?"

Corine had been conscious of Joe's voice getting louder, and of her work colleagues still inside.

"Well, I'm not gonna count down my days living in a mausoleum, being reminded of what might have been every time you see your sister and Lisa together. No wonder Mary's avoiding you. Fuck it! I'm going whether you come or not." His face had been red; fuming.

"Well, I'm not," Corine had said, aware they were drawing amused glances from the crowds milling outside the late-night bars and restaurants.

"Stay here then, keep your precious job. But we both know that's not the reason you're staying. Why aren't you ever honest with yourself, Corine?" Joe had bumped into a young woman and her boyfriend, throwing up his arms in annoyance, waiting for an apology.

"You're embarrassing," she'd hissed, catching him up. *"I'm trying to be a good wife, here, but "*

"Yeah, well, you failed."

Mae coughs and Corine is suddenly back in the present, aware of Mae staring at her.

'Did you say something?' she asks.

'No… you did,' Mae replies, looking amused.

'Sorry, I'm not sleeping very well.' A surge of heat courses up Corine's back and explodes across her face. 'Hotel beds,' she explains. It's a poor excuse and she knows it.

Stay in the moment, she warns herself, but the memory still feels real, like a fresh wound that won't be ignored. It was true, for Corine anyway, that over time, the painful memories were the ones that cut through most vividly.

'Earlier you mentioned accommodation,' Corine says, changing the subject and giving herself a moment to recover. 'Don't you have any family you could stay with?'

Mae shakes her head. She tugs the sleeves of her sweatshirt and grips the hem—for comfort, Corine assumes. Her fingers work at the frayed edges, twisting the loose strands, lost in thought.

We all have ways of dealing with stress, whether consciously or not, she thinks. Mae's approach was definitely avoidance—but Corine knew from experience how flawed that could be. Refusing to face a trauma didn't make it disappear, it simply lingered backstage. No matter how polished your performance, it would eventually step into the spotlight and demand your full attention.

'I'm seeing your mother first thing tomorrow. Is there anything you'd like me to say to her, or ask her on your behalf?'

'Anything?' Mae smirks, not looking up.

'Stop making this hard on yourself, Mae.'

'You could tell her my life has value now. And if I ever have children—which I probably won't, because I understand that having them isn't the same as wanting them—I won't expect anything from them in return.'

'I'm pleased you feel your life has value, but why do you think your mother didn't want you?'

Mae ignores the question. 'On second thoughts, maybe you should just ask her about Mother's Day. Why she seems to hate it so much.'

Corine sighs. Mae was back to the riddles and sabotaging her own freedom. 'So, the cage you spoke about, the big cat enclosure—do you feel pushed out of the cage, left unprotected? Are you worried about being released? Where you'll live?' It crosses Corine's mind that, at this age, Michael would have flown the nest. Most likely, he'd be at university, and she would have encouraged it. Like most parents, she would have wanted the best for her son, even if that meant losing him to the world.

Mae smiles. 'Something like that.' She clasps her hands together, fingers interlaced. 'I was watching a wildlife documentary the other day, about a pride of lions. A new dominant male came in and killed several of the younger males—cubs, really.' She pauses. 'Babies. What shocked me was how the lionesses let it happen. Yeah, they bared their teeth and roared, but then later, when given the chance, they mated with him.' Her brow furrows, eyes narrowing.

'I suppose the young males would have become a threat eventually,' Corine says. 'It's all about self-preservation—having cubs with the dominant male.'

'There's that.' Mae glances at her watch. 'Self-preservation, and then... what you desire more.' She stands, pushing her hands into her trouser pockets, and gives Corine a resigned smile. 'People are selfish, they think of themselves, their needs. We're all just animals really, aren't we?'

A knock at the door signals the end of their session and Corine sighs in frustration. They were *finally* getting somewhere.

As Mae stands to go, Corine remembers something from a conversation with Kate. 'Your mother mentioned she'd arranged for you to see a counsellor in the past. Do you recall why, or what you discussed?'

'Counsellor?' Mae looks confused for a moment. 'Oh, yeah, vaguely. He was a family friend. I refused to talk to him, I think. Don't remember anything else, except he had a jar full of sweets on his desk. Well, not after I'd left.' She laughs.

'Look, don't worry about your release. I'll have a word… see how the plans are going.' Corine smiles, trying to look hopeful. They're standing close enough for her to see the tiny blonde hairs on Mae's face and the thin, dark rim around her irises that makes them pop. She has eyes that remind her of Michael's.

'I'll try my best.'

When Mae leaves, Corine is left wondering if a day, hour, minute or second will ever come when she won't think of her son—his loss. Who is she to expect a young girl to face her darkest trauma and move on when she is stuck forever contemplating an empty space where Michael should have been?

Corine heads straight for her office.

With the door closed, she takes out a bottle of vodka that she'd bought on route to work and drinks. She closes her eyes, welcoming the soothing numbness.

CHAPTER 11
CORINE

The blinds are drawn against the glare of the afternoon sun, the air stuffy with recycled breath. Corine shifts in her seat, trying to maintain her focus. The weekly Multi-Disciplinary Team meeting—the second she'd attended—is already running over, with several agenda points still to go. Though better organised than some she remembers, the issues are all too familiar: lack of funding and inadequate support for service users returning to the community. Listening, Corine can't help but worry about Mae's future. Securing the right support upon release is critical to successful reintegration—and right now, nothing about Mae's situation looks straightforward.

Much of the past hour had been given over to discussing a patient in crisis—Shana—who isn't responding to treatment and recently injured a junior nurse. Tension is rising between the nursing staff and Simon, the young psychiatrist overseeing her care, and the conversation is going round in circles. With his prematurely receding hairline and heavy glasses, Simon appears older than he is, and for reasons she can't explain, Corine feels sorry for him. His pretence at being nonplussed by the nurses' pointed questions is painful to watch. In Corine's day, such an open challenge to senior clinical staff wouldn't have happened. There had been a natural hierarchy, a fixed order no one—herself included—ever openly questioned.

Perhaps change was a good thing?

'Still, don't you think it would be helpful if her meds were reviewed sooner rather than later?' asks Caitriona, a red-haired senior nurse.

'Someone should first and foremost be checking she's keeping her medication down and not disposing of it in the bathroom,' Simon retorts, his anger finally showing itself.

'Well, of course we check that,' snaps Caitriona, rolling her eyes.

'This only works if we operate as a team,' Corine finds herself saying.

She raises her eyebrows at Richard, but he looks away, and she wishes she'd kept her mouth shut. It wasn't her meeting to run or her place to defend a junior colleague. Her position was only ever temporary.

'I'll reassess her medication with Simon,' Richard says. 'But it's important that all safety protocols are followed by all staff, and that includes junior nurses not being left alone with a patient in crisis. As her Care Plan states, Shana is a risk to everyone, including herself, and she should be with two members of staff at all times.'

'Like I said, we had an incident kicking off in the art room, and she was only left for a matter of seconds.' Caitriona's face and body language remains defensive. 'We were already two nurses down and security staff need to be aware of who takes the lead on any decision to restrain.'

'Well, I think we're all agreed then,' Richard continues, cutting short any further discussion. 'We can see how Shana settles with the new meds by end of play tomorrow.' He turns to Simon, addressing him directly. 'You and I should have a quick chat after this.'

Simon nods, clearly unhappy.

Corine looks at the ten other people sitting around the large conference table: psychologists, occupational therapists, mental health nurses, psychiatrists, a social worker, and Bridget from administration, taking notes. All well intentioned, hoping to make a difference—within the ever-tightening confines of their roles.

'Right, item six. Gemma, would you like to update everyone on Malika?' Richard asks. 'Sorry for taking over, Bridget, I've got to leave in ten minutes.'

Bridget nods and shuffles the papers in front of her. 'Actually, if we're all in agreement, we could leave items seven to nine until Friday's meeting?'

Everyone voices their support. Corine is secretly relieved—she isn't sure she has anything positive to contribute to Mae's situation. Given that everyone else in the room is juggling multiple cases, she feels slightly indulged—present more because of her friendship with Richard than any particular expertise or qualification. Not that Richard would give anything away about their friendship in front of colleagues. He was too professional.

'Well, it's good news,' beams Gemma, a slender woman with thin, mousy hair and sharp features. 'We've finally secured a place for Malika at Willow Mount. It's a relatively new low-secure unit with twelve beds, and one's just come free. There's an amazing kitchen-café setup, so she'll get to continue with her work training, and she'll get community release days too. Better still, they have good links with possible work placements where Mal hopes to settle down once she leaves low security.'

'That's fantastic news. How has Malika responded?' asks Richard.

'You know Mal, she'll be keen. I'm going to talk to her after this—the placement becomes available from the twelfth, so a week's time.'

'Have you told her about her mum yet?' Simon asks.

Gemma shifts in her seat and pulls a face. 'No, her father wants to tell her in his own time, but he's stalling—and I'm not sure it's the right decision. They'll have to tell her soon, though, it's only fair. Willow Mount have already said it's possible to have someone with her at the funeral.'

'Okay, good, thank you,' says Richard. 'What's next, Bridget?'

'We have Annalise to discuss, Mae, and an update on the equine therapy programme.'

'Okay, well, unless anyone has anything urgent to add, we can discuss the rest at Friday's meeting.' He scans the table. 'All agreed?'

'Richard, is there any chance that I can speak to whoever is running the equine therapy programme?' Corine asks. 'I think it would benefit Mae.'

'That'll be Krissy, she's running the research with a team from London University. Should be on her way back from the stables any time now, so you can certainly speak to her, but the programme's full, and they're already three-quarters of the way through the trial period. Mae's progressing well, isn't she? She was never flagged as someone who would particularly benefit from this type of therapy. And all being well, she'll be paroled soon—placement permitting.'

'It's not that I want her to join the programme, exactly. Temper and conduct aren't really the issue—but she still has a significant problem with trust. From what I've read, working with horses, even for a day or two over a couple of weeks, might help her open up to me.'

Richard nods. 'I'll put in a call to Krissy. I happen to know Charles and Fiona from the Equine Therapy Trust, so I could put in a word… see if there's any spare funding going.'

Corine smiles and nods her assent. It's the first time in two weeks that she has felt a part of the wider team.

CHAPTER 12
CORINE

'I don't have any expectations of her, I gave up on those a long time ago,' Kate says with a laugh, spooning orange gloop into her youngest granddaughter's mouth. 'There you go, good girl. You'll grow up to be big and strong eating up all your food.'

The little girl shrieks with delight, banging her chubby fists on the highchair. Her mouth open again, expectant, like a hapless chick.

'Not like *someone else* I know who *isn't* eating the lovely lunch Grandma made especially for her. *She* doesn't deserve any pudding, does she Zizi?'

Zizi squeals and shoves a fist into her wet mouth, while Beth continues to steadfastly ignore Kate. She sits at the kitchen table, a barely touched sandwich in front of her, entirely absorbed in the tiny plastic toys clutched in her hands.

'It must be hard for her,' Corine says, nodding in Beth's direction. 'She's old enough to miss her mum while she's away working.'

'Mummy's in hospital,' Beth informs her.

Kate laughs. 'No, sweetheart, she's working.'

'Daddy says she can't come home until she's better.'

'Okay, go and play.' Kate shoos Beth towards the seating

area on the far side of the room.

Corine watches, once again struck by how perfectly arranged everything is: the surfaces gleam, each cushion is immaculately plumped, and a citrusy hemp smell lingers in the air, reminding her of the spa day her sister had bought for her after her second miscarriage. A wooden dollhouse sits on the coffee table, ready to be played with.

'You get nothing else until dinnertime, mind.' Kate takes a baby-wipe and cleans her youngest granddaughter's hands and face.

Zizi tries her best to snatch the cloth, crying out in frustration when she misses.

Corine looks on, mesmerised by the ordinary domestic scene unfolding before her, until the familiar feeling of loss rises to the surface.

She pushes it aside.

'She's adorable,' she tells Kate.

'Down you go,' Kate says, freeing Zizi from her highchair and placing her beside her sister.

The child immediately launches herself at the dollhouse, grabbing hold and shaking it with both hands. Corine wonders how long it will take before Beth protests, but the older girl calmy offers her sister a small baby doll and toy pushchair. Zizi is instantly absorbed, placing the toys in and taking them out on repeat.

'She makes things up, that one,' says Kate, gesturing towards Beth. 'Overactive imagination, bless her. Gets it from her father's side.' She laughs. 'Lyndsey's fine, but like most young mothers, she could do with a couple of days off to recharge and feel human again. Children can be so draining.'

Corine nods. 'They're very well behaved.'

Kate smiles, then glances up at the large silver clock on the wall behind Corine's head. The gesture isn't lost on her.

'Are you still okay to see Mae this Friday? It'll be the penultimate meeting, so it's important you've had the chance to ask everything you need to—that you're comfortable with her apology... and with her release.'

'Actually, I'm not sure I can make it.'

'Oh.' Corine struggles to contain her surprise.

Corine had planned to be back at the farm in three or four weeks—or at least, that's the impression Richard had given her when they first discussed Mae's case. The sudden change is disappointing, especially given how carefully she'd noted the scheduled meetings with Kate when she arrived at The Orchard. How would Mae take the news? *Not well*, Corine imagined.

'I've just got so much on, especially with Lyndsey being away. Work mostly... nothing I could have foreseen,' Kate explains.

Corine picks up her phone and opens her calendar. 'That would mean we meet for the final time next Tuesday, as agreed. Until Mae's parole hearing, of course.'

'That's fine.' Kate moves over to the sink and wipes the already clean worktop. She picks up a bowl and puts it straight back down.

Was the tension Corine could suddenly feel a sign that Kate was having doubts about Mae's release?

'Mae could be out quickly after that,' Corine warns, 'unless concerns are raised.'

Kate shrugs. 'Well, I'm certainly not going to raise any

objections. I never wanted her to go to jail in the first place. Anyway, Mae's made it clear she wants nothing to do with me. I suppose she'll just get on with her life. Maybe one day I'll suddenly hear from her—most likely when she's had children of her own and realises how hard it is to care for someone so difficult.' Her eyes flick to the clock again.

"Difficult" felt like a colossal understatement, and Corine didn't entirely blame Kate for struggling to stay engaged in the conversation—not with two young children to look after. They were her priority. Still, it niggled her that Kate was willing to cancel such an important meeting. If Mae were her daughter, Corine knew she'd be doing everything in her power to…

She caught herself, sensing it was time to bring the conversation to a close.

'Is there anything you would like to talk about, or for me to ask Mae—in advance of our next meeting?'

Kate shakes her head and stoops to pick up something from the floor—another distraction. It didn't make any sense to Corine. None of it did. She still didn't know why Mae had attacked her mother; why she still felt such animosity towards her. And now, Kate was acting like she was discussing a cancelled dinner date—not the potential loss of her youngest daughter.

'I still don't know why Mae attacked you,' Corine blurts out, seizing the moment as Kate finally stops fussing about the kitchen.

Kate turns to face the sink, her back to Corine. 'I've explained what happened so many times. I've got my hands full—these two, work, Lyndsey, I don't have the energy to dig around, looking for meaning where none exists. It happened. She's served her time.'

Censoring her response, Corine makes one final attempt to appeal to Kate's softer side. 'I wouldn't usually push, but… Mae's clearly anxious about her release. If I could better understand her mindset at the time—why she—'

Kate turns, sharply. 'I don't know why she attacked me. Maybe it was teenage hormones. Maybe a psychotic episode. There isn't always an obvious answer. You've seen how she cuts herself—thirty years ago, that sort of self-harm was unheard of. Now it's practically a rite of passage.'

Corine nods. Sadly, it was true.

'Distress, attention—I don't know why she does it,' Kate continues, her lips flecked with spittle. 'That's your job isn't it? To understand those things? And if she hasn't told you by now, she probably never will.' She gives a bitter laugh. 'Yes, I'm a GP—I see patients every day for depression and self-harm. But the truth is, our understanding of mental illness is still shockingly poor. In the ten minutes I get with someone, I can suggest CBT—if they're happy to wait a year—or hand out pills with side-effects as long as my arm. Holistic care? Don't get me started. It's nothing but a—'

An almighty crash from the other side of the room. The dollhouse lies on its side, its contents strewn across the floor. Beth is struggling to stop her sister from climbing onto the glass coffee table to retrieve her toys.

Kate rushes over. 'Beth! Don't drag Zizi like that—you're hurting her!'

Beth releases Zizi, who immediately clambers onto the table.

Corine watches as the older sister stares through sullen, half-closed eyes, while Kate scoops Zizi into her arms and smothers her with kisses. Before her grandmother can turn her disapproving gaze her way, Beth clutches her two tiny toys and makes to leave the room, head bowed.

'And where do you think you're going, madam?'

'Toilet.' Beth doesn't look up.

'Come straight back, and don't forget to wash those hands. I'll know if you haven't.' Kate glances at Corine, and it's obvious she wants her gone. With a swift, darting movement, she sets the dollhouse back on the table.

'Just one more question and I'll be out of your hair.'

'Right.' Zizi squirms in Kate's arms as she shifts to maintain her hold.

'Mother's Day—what does it mean to you?'

'Probably the same as it does to any mother: a day that forces you to reflect on just how unrewarding motherhood can be.' She gives a dry laugh, but there's no real humour in it.

'Right.'

'Ah, please don't judge me. It's the one day when shops pass off cheap tat so our grateful little darlings can *show their appreciation*. As if cheap body lotion, garishly dyed flowers, and inedible chocolate hearts can ever make up for the stretch marks, incontinence, and years of broken sleep. And as you know—it only gets worse.' Kate laughs again, but there's a steeliness there that unnerves Corine.

'I wouldn't know.'

'You're lucky, then. Most women get at least two of those battle scars.'

'No, I meant, I don't have children.'

'Oh! But, I thought I saw you with your daughter?'

'Sorry?' Corine looks at Kate blankly.

'Outside the National Gallery.'

It takes Corine a moment to absorb what Kate has said. When she finally responds, her voice is tight. 'That was my niece.'

'I was in Trafalgar Square, checking out the Fourth Plinth installation. Don't you just love it?'

'It's not really my thing. Sorry, I didn't see you. Were you—'

'*Pooh…* Zizi, stinky girl!' Kate immediately puts an end to any further discussion. 'I'm gonna have to change this one. Do you mind? Can you show yourself out?'

Corine nods.

She hears Kate thudding up the stairs and is left feeling curiously violated. So accustomed to being the watcher herself—scrutinizing and interpreting the behaviour of others—it feels strange to be on the receiving end.

Collecting her things, she heads towards the front door, only remembering Beth when she spots the little girl standing at the window.

'When's Daddy coming?' she asks Corine.

'I'm not sure, lovely. When did he say he would come?'

'He's taking me and Zizi for ice cream. Then we can visit Mummy.'

'At the hospital?'

Beth nods.

CHAPTER 13
CORINE

Lisa's voice rises above the female chatter that fills the small but elegant sitting room. 'Aunty Corine! Aunty Corine! Can you come here for a family photo?'

Relieved to escape a conversation with one of Lisa's earnest teacher friends about the lack of counselling services for vulnerable children—fearing tears were imminent—Corine makes her way across the room toward her niece.

Everywhere is decked with pale pink and blue balloons, and there's a giant cut-out stork carrying a baby in a blanket in the corner that Lisa's mother-in-law had delivered, along with an apology note for not being able to make it to the baby shower. Boxes and wrapping paper in every shade of pastel litter the table and floor as the roomful of women sip prosecco, chatting and nibbling on delicate, pale-toned macarons late into the afternoon.

Corine feels out of place among the crowd of young women in their mid to late twenties, most of them focused on building careers, buying homes, or planning weddings. Thoughts of babies are some years off yet, or so one or two of them have already exclaimed a little too dramatically. Corine would confidently bet that one of them is already pregnant, judging by the flushed glow and untouched glass of prosecco, though she suspects the woman is holding back, reluctant to steal Lisa's thunder. It warms Corine to see Lisa surrounded by such good friends; a strong female support network, should she ever need it.

A flash of light goes off as someone snaps Corine and Lisa. The photographer has been drifting through the room, capturing people mid-conversation, all very natural and unposed. *It's all so Lisa*, Corine thinks, everything operating smoothly, chilled and relaxed. *Not like Mary.*

The thought surprises her.

Her sister had been a fan of a checklist from an early age, never leaving anything to chance. Whereas Corine had always preferred to let fate decide. *Look how that turned out.*

'Having you here has made all the difference,' Lisa says, giving her hand a squeeze and pulling Corine gently out of her thoughts. 'It doesn't feel like I'm doing this alone anymore.'

'You've got such lovely friends, though. And Peter.'

'I know, I'm lucky, but still… it's so reassuring, you being nearby, in London. You're family.'

Lisa throws her arms around Corine, the feel of her niece's hard, swollen stomach against her own setting off a complex mix of emotions that Corine has to fight to suppress. She feels like a fraud.

'You'll have all the family you need when this little one arrives.'

'Promise me you're not going to go radio silent on me again when you go back. In fact, won't you stay?' Her eyes are wide, questioning and hopeful.

Mary had always been better at expressing her feelings—which was ironic, really, given Corine's chosen profession.

'I'd love you to help me with this little one,' Lisa continues. 'Peter's mum's a nightmare. Thank God she lives in France.'

Lisa smiles sheepishly.

'She's certainly made her presence known.' They both glance towards the stork and laugh. 'You know I wish I could be here,' Corine adds, and for a moment, she lets herself imagine it—helping Lisa raise her child, offering support, being needed. A substitute grandparent, stepping in where Mary couldn't. She smiles, a little sadly, at the foolishness of it.

'Isn't it lonely,' Lisa presses, 'living on the edge of the world with cows for neighbours?'

Corine chuckles. 'It's not just the cows. There are sheep, goats, Joe's dog—Betty—and the occasional human neighbour.' She grins. 'We're not entirely off the map.'

'Come and be busy here, with your family,' Lisa pleads.

Corine feels her heart swell. The words stir something in her—longing, maybe, or guilt.

'Mum hated that you two weren't talking,' Lisa continues. She said you always had each other's backs growing up.' She pauses, studying Corine's face. 'You've got your job back, too.'

'No, that's just a one-off—a favour I'm doing,' Corine corrects, shaking her head. Still, she isn't sure Mae would see it that way.

'Well, we'll figure something out,' Lisa says, laying her head on Corine's shoulder—just as a photograph is taken.

'You two look so alike!' The photographer—a pretty woman with cropped hair—calls over. 'You could be sisters.'

Corine laughs, quietly flattered by the compliment. People outside the family had remarked on their likeness before, though it had been a while. Mary, for her part, had always seemed reluctant to draw attention to their resemblance.

Outside the window, the afternoon sun slips behind a

slow build-up of cloud. Someone switches on the lamps, and a warm yellow glow fills the corners of the room, softening the space from the edges inwards.

'I wish we lived closer, too,' Corine says, returning to their conversation. 'I promise to keep in touch, and I want regular pictures of this little one.' She touches the curve of Lisa's stomach. 'I regret what happened between your mum and me, too. Refusing to speak was juvenile—wrong of both of us.'

Lisa looks thoughtful. 'Mum said you left because of Uncle Joe. That he found himself a remote hole and buried himself in it.'

Corine shakes her head, slowly. 'He put up with so much—for my sake.' She falters, the sudden rush of emotion catching her of guard.

Lisa nods gently and squeezes Corine's hand. 'You know, Mum felt like she'd let you down, in the end.'

'She did?' Corine frowned. 'Gosh, what are we like, dragging up the past at your lovely baby shower. Come on, let's talk about happy things. Though I might add—I'm not sure the proud folk of Caithness would appreciate their beautiful landscape being likened to a hole.'

Lisa giggles, her hand held coyly to her lips.

Another habit of Mary's, Corine recalls.

†

After the last guest leaves, Corine persuades Lisa to take a nap while she helps Peter clear up. They work side by side in comfortable silence, first tidying the living room, then moving onto the kitchen. Corine washes the delicate champagne flutes; Peter dries them—exchanging the occasional shy smile when their rhythm falls out of sync and he's left waiting for her to catch up.

She feels almost miniaturised standing next to him. He's a giant of a man, his hands as broad as the dinner plates she's just washed, yet he's softly spoken and quick to laugh.

A casual mention of the baby's due date leads him to admit he never expected to be a father at twenty-six. Corine is struck by the realisation that he's two years younger than Lisa. And just like that, the thought surfaces—*Peter isn't much older than Michael would have been.*

'She's missing her mum,' he says. 'I guess she's about to become one herself and feels a little overwhelmed. It's only natural she'd turn to her mum at a time like this.'

Corine nods sympathetically. 'It's an emotional time.'

She does her best to keep her therapist voice in check, knowing there's nothing more off-putting than unsolicited advice. Mary had often called her a *know-all* growing up—and with good reason. She had been insufferable, especially in her early twenties: newly graduated, convinced she had life all figured out. *It's easy to feel in control when nothing has ever gone wrong.*

'It means a lot to Lisa, having you here,' Peter says quietly. 'To me, too.'

Corine brushes her hair back, a little flustered by the compliment. 'She'll be fine once the baby arrives. And you'll take good care of her—I can see that.'

'I'll do my best,' he replies. 'But it's not the same as having your mum. And with her dad gone so long ago, I guess she sort of feels like an orphan.'

Corine smiles sadly and sighs, her thoughts shifting

quickly from Lisa to Mae—one craving her mother's love, the other pushing her away. To feel such absence of connection towards a mother who, on the surface, seems perfectly reasonable made no sense to her. Kate's support had been steadfast and accepting, despite everything. Something must have happened between mother and daughter. There had to be a concrete reason for the self-harm, the temper, Mae's insistence on distancing herself from her entire family. What was she hiding?

Determined, Corine resolves to speak with Mae's sister and father, even if it meant showing up unannounced, since neither had responded to her emails or calls. What did she have to lose? This was her last chance.

†

Neither Corine nor Peter have the heart to wake Lisa, leaving her to sleep on into the early evening. After clearing everything away, they sit with a glass of red that Peter insists Corine tries—the irony is not lost on her. She should know better than to accept. Rather than drowning in self-pity, she should act on her own advice and face her problems—talk them through with another professional. It's not like she doesn't know any.

Their chat turns to the topic of Peter's family—his parents, both of whom he is clearly fond of. His father had been a wine buyer for various supermarkets over the years, while his mother—whom Corine is especially keen to hear about, given Lisa's earlier comment—had worked in PR or advertising; Peter wasn't quite sure which. They'd had him late in life, and once he'd started university, they retired to France, eager to embrace a new chapter in their lives.

Wasn't that what her and Joe had done? Except Scotland hadn't been so much a new challenge as a new distraction—a rational reappraisal when the pretence of careers being everything stopped working. Corine had never thought of herself as suffering from empty nest syndrome, though perhaps her and Joe had. And weren't those feelings of loss only magnified by their circumstances? By getting old. Her body slowly divesting itself of the hormones needed to produce eggs, until her dream of motherhood had become just that—a dream.

Peter joked about being abandoned, though he sounded as pleased as punch that his parents had fulfilled a lifelong dream of owning their own vineyard in Provence.

By the time they were on their second glass, the conversation had turned to politics.

'I know highland farming will suffer,' Corine says, 'but I'll share why that is another time. It's getting late. Shall we move the presents into the nursery, before we ruin this lovely wine with politics?'

'I'll drink to that.' They raise their glasses. 'You really like it?' Peter asks.

'It's delicious.'

'It's from my parent's vineyard,' he says, grinning.

'Oh, thank God I said I liked it.' Corine threw a tea towel at him. 'That was very, very naughty of you!'

While Peter is downstairs getting the last few presents, Corine allows herself a moment to admire the nursery. It's calm and cosy, with white furniture, buttery walls, and floor-to-ceiling bookshelves already filled with well-known children's classics and the Beatrix Potter figurines Corine remembers buying for Lisa as a baby. Seeing them pleases her more than it should. In one corner of the room, a beautiful sheepskin chair beckons to be touched. She lowers herself into the curved seat, visualising the mother and baby bonding that will take place here in the months and years to come. She can't help but smile.

Her expression shifts as her mind drifts to another nursery—the one she and Joe had prepared for their baby, Michael. The sound of his weak cry still makes her heart race as she recalls her failed attempts to comfort him.

"He's not feeding properly; we should call the doctor," she'd said to Joe, lifting Michael's small body towards him like a precious offering.

"He'll be fine. It's just sod's law, that's all. He's probably feeding off your anxiety about going back to work tomorrow."

'Join me for one more drink?' Peter's voice pulls her back from her memories.

'Oh, go on then, twist my arm.' Corine replies, with a forced laugh, standing up from the chair. 'I'll have to make myself one of these; it's so comfortable I almost dozed off!'

As she follows Peter downstairs—past photographs of the couple on various holidays, their wedding day, and Mary, looking lovely as mother-of-the-bride in a lemon two-piece—Corine once again registers that her past holds more for her than her future does. It's a reality she doesn't care to face.

Peter offers for her to stay the night, but she refuses, claiming she has notes to read over before the morning. Truthfully, she doesn't want any fuss. She calls a cab and finishes off a glass of white burgundy while listening to Peter recount the mistakes his parents made when they first took over the vineyard. There were many, but they survived with their sense of humour and drive intact.

Corine decides Peter is good company. She likes how comfortable he is in his own skin, and realises he has the ability to make even the weightiest topics feel lighter. It makes her happy, for Lisa's sake.

Peter stifles a yawn, just as her phone pings to tell her the cab is outside.

'Get some sleep… while you can,' Corine jokes at the front door.

Peter leans forward and kisses her goodbye. She's not expecting it, but for the second time that evening, she finds herself ridiculously pleased.

'Tell Lisa I'll pop round in a few days,' she calls from the cab.

He continues waving until the cab turns into the next street.

The cab driver zigzags through a maze of back roads, speeding down one-way streets packed with cars. After a while, the heavily spiced aftershave he's wearing starts to cloy, and Corine opens a window. She lifts her face towards the cool air, taking long, deep breaths. They pass a development of modern flats, all floor-to-ceiling glass, built too close to the road, as if privacy had been overlooked by the architect, or simply no longer valued by this next generation of homeowners. Corine feels like an observer again, forced to watch snippets of other people's lives on giant screens she can't control.

What would people have seen if they'd looked in on her

talking to Peter? Mother and son, no doubt. Sharing a glass of wine—discussing hopes, dreams, a little politics. If that was what families with grown children even discussed these days? Corine smiles to herself, feeling a little giddy; it had been a wonderful evening, filled with excellent conversation and unexpected moments of warmth.

When she checks her phone, she has four missed calls. All from Richard. *It wouldn't be fair to call him now*, Corine tells herself. Not when she isn't sure how she feels about him.

Immediately, she thinks of Joe. She whispers his name, her breath catching at the thought of him. If they'd had children together—a child who'd lived—she is sure their marriage would have been a happy one. But it wasn't to be, and, like a building imploding, she had surrendered to her grief—lashing out, pushing him away. The need to blame someone else had been overwhelming.

'Selfish,' she mutters.

She catches the driver watching her in the rear-view mirror and digs her nails into the palm of her hand, fighting the urge to cry. A strangled sound slips from her throat, and again their eyes meet. Quickly, she looks away, forcing her thoughts elsewhere—imagining herself walking along a beach, her feet sinking into soft, wet sand. With each step, she sinks deeper, but when she turns to look behind her, the footsteps are gone. She closes her eyes and focuses on the sensation—pressing her toes harder into the cold dampness, determined to leave a mark. Anything to stop herself from spiralling into grief.

Just as the shifting sand begins to lull her, the cabbie speaks, and she realises they've arrived at the hotel. Corine pays the fare and dashes inside, escaping the heavy downpour that had loomed all evening. The hotel lobby is busy with a group of Japanese tourists, who step aside when she walks in and bow politely. She nods back and waves to the receptionist, who manages a flustered flap in return.

Once safely inside her room, she takes a handful of whisky bottles from the mini-bar and collapses on the bed. She kicks of her shoes of and peels off her trousers before slipping beneath the covers. Unscrewing the cap from the first bottle, she takes a slow sip, enjoying the burning sensation in her throat. Then she picks up her phone and dials home.

When the voicemail clicks, she closes her eyes, listening to the silence before her own recorded greeting. When it ends, she speaks softly into the phone. 'You were right—I'm torturing myself being here, but seeing Lisa pregnant...' She sighs heavily. 'She's so lovely, and her partner, Peter—you'd get on with him. You'd have been proud of me, Joe. Lisa mentioned Mary and me not talking, but I didn't go there. It wasn't the right time.'

CHAPTER 14
CORINE

After leaving multiple messages with no response from Mae's father or sister, Corine is well aware that she is taking a risk turning up unannounced at Frank's home. But time was running out for Mae, and it had become increasingly clear that she wasn't going to help herself. If Corine was going to secure Mae's probation, she'd have to do it despite Mae's resistance. That meant digging deeper, and fast.

Had Mae been abused by her father? If so, it might be enough reason for a traumatised child to blame her mother.

The substantial Victorian house had been converted into several flats. Some windows were newly painted, framed by colourful window boxes and internal shutters; others were cracked and peeling, showing clear signs of neglect.

Corine checks her phone for the umpteenth time—still no messages. She knocks at the front door of the ground floor flat and glances around her. The communal hallway has seen better days too, despite someone's attempt to brighten it up with a stunted bay tree crammed into an undersized pot.

As she waits, an elderly man with weathered skin and sparce white hair walks gingerly down the steps to the ground floor.

'Who are you looking for?'

It sounds like a demand.

'Mr Bailey—flat 1A,' she replies, glancing back at the door.

'So that's his name? Right, well, he's in,' the man says loudly. 'I'm the flat above. Heard them yelling a few minutes ago. May look solid, but the floors are as thin as banknotes. People should think twice about raising their voices in here, never mind children and pets.'

Corine nods politely. 'Right, well, thanks.'

The man peers at the door of 1A, a sour smell—his, presumably, hangs in the air around them. Then, with his face set to a grimace, he turns and walks away.

Corine knocks again, louder this time. When no one answers, she lifts the letter box and listens. She can hear someone whispering inside.

'Mr Bailey—I'm here about Mae. If I could just talk to you for five minutes, ask you a couple of questions. It could help your daughter.'

There's no answer.

'I'm from The Orchard Clinic. You might be able to help with her release.'

Moments later, the door partially opens and a slender, bespectacled man in a fitted shirt and worn looking chinos peers out.

'What about her?' He forces the words out through strained lips, holding the door open just enough for her to see him but nothing of the flat.

He has Mae's eyes, Corine notes.

'She has a parole hearing very soon and I'm helping to write a report that will go to the parole board, but there are a few unanswered questions.'

'And you are?'

'I'm Dr Corine Alexander, your daughter's psychiatrist.'

Mr Bailey looks behind him nervously.

'I left several messages,' she adds.

'Are you in favour of her getting parole or not?'

Corine hadn't expected such a direct question, nor the intensity of his gaze.

'It's not as simple as that, I'm afraid. I've met your daughter a number of times in the last two weeks and, to be honest, I'm not sure she wants parole.'

Frank hesitates. 'I wouldn't blame her. I mean, what would she be coming out to? That psycho masquerading as a mother?'

'Can we talk somewhere?'

'Not really.' He looks back inside the flat, his movements quick, jerky, as though he's hiding something. 'Not here.'

'Please,' Corine implores. 'It could help your daughter. Mae doesn't seem very capable of helping herself... quite the opposite, actually.'

Mr Bailey is silent for a while, his hands gripping the front door. 'Just give me a minute,' he finally says, before disappearing inside.

Corine can hear him speaking to a woman she presumes is his new partner. Things escalate quickly, and soon, every word of their conversation can be heard in the hallway.

'If you'd told me, I would have asked Mama to fly over earlier so she could go with me! Save you the bother!'

'Calm down, Irene! I'll be quick. We've got plenty of time to get there.' The door swings open and Frank rushes past Corine. 'I've got ten minutes—let's walk,' he calls over his shoulder.

For a man of average height, he covers ground quickly. She practically has to jog to keep up with him.

'Thank you for this, I really do appreciate your time,' she says, trying to match his pace. A sour taste hits the back of her throat. She swallows hard, regretting her lack of self-control last night—along with the liquid breakfast that morning. 'You're still a GP, aren't you?'

'Why wouldn't I be?' Frank asks, meeting her eyes.

Best get to the point, and quickly, she thinks. But just as she's about to explain her involvement with Mae, Frank speaks.

'Not that *Kate* helped as far as my career is concerned. My *wife*.' He spits the word out. 'She turned my girls against me. Got Lyndsey to make up some sick story about what I'd supposedly done to her—all because I'd threatened a divorce. It's all part of Kate's twisted power play. Her way of saying "look what I can do if you leave". She's a selfish, conniving *bitch* who is only interested in herself—*her* needs, *her* reputation… *her* life.'

Corine watches as anger contorts his face.

'Did Mae ever tell you why she attacked her mother? Or anything else about that day?'

'No.' Frank speeds up, his shoulders hunched forward defensively. 'Kate didn't allow them to see me after Lyndsey's accusations.'

'You didn't fight that?'

'I probably sound like a coward, but I didn't want my name dragged through the newspapers. I'm sure you know what I was accused of.'

Corine nods.

'You're tarnished for life with something like that. She's clever, Kate—knows how to get everyone on her side. She plants an idea here, a thought there—cries a few crocodile tears. Still, I never expected her to get my own daughter to accuse me of such fucking depravity.' His face and neck are red now, his eyes full of rage. It's hard to imagine him parenting anyone.

'I kept thinking Kate would stop lying, that Lyndsey would step up and tell the truth, but now… honestly, I think the girls are brainwashed.' He slows his pace a little and looks at Corine. 'Lyndsey, in particular, was very impressionable—Mae less so—but they both followed her around like puppies, always ready to perform.'

'Mae mentioned that Kate sometimes plays the victim.'

Frank nods. 'Yeah, when it suits her. It depends on who's listening and what the motivation is. Her own gain, mostly.'

'Where you in a relationship with someone else at the time of your split?' Corine tenses, expecting Frank to react badly, but he doesn't.

'I met someone a few months before, but believe me, our marriage was well and truly over. Kate probably told everyone I was having an affair, but that wasn't true. It was a new relationship—it didn't survive the accusations. We hadn't known each other long enough.'

Long enough to tell the truth? Looking back on her own relationships, Corine had been no different. Even with Joe, she'd buried certain truths, telling herself she was protecting him.

'Does your current partner know about the accusations?'

He stops, studying her with a guarded expression. 'Not

everything,' he says slowly. 'I don't think she needs to know every sordid detail. Let's just say she knows enough—why Mae ended up in prison, the bitter split before that, how it wasn't exactly amicable, and that the girls chose to stay with their mother.' He pauses, a flicker of regret crossing his face. 'I didn't do what Lyndsey accused me of, but I'm ashamed to admit I resented her for those accusations at first.'

'Something changed?'

'Not when it comes to Kate—she's poison.' Frank says bitterly. 'But the girls... well, as Irene—my partner—pointed out, they were still just children when we split. Of course they sided with their mother.' He keeps walking, his face tightening with the weight of his memories. 'Kate got pregnant with Lyndsey while she was supposedly on the pill. We were travelling at the time. I'd just graduated as a medic, a year behind her, and I wanted to see a bit of the world before settling down. I fell in love with Australia, made friends there, but for some reason, she struggled. I wanted to stay, maybe even start practicing over there, but after four months, Kate flew back. Said she wanted to have the baby here. And... well, I did the right thing. I followed. She was seven months pregnant with Lyndsey when we married.'

'You think she got pregnant on purpose?'

'I could never prove it. Just like I could never prove I didn't molest my own daughter. It will always be her word against mine, and even if it wasn't proven, the charge itself would ruin my reputation if it came out. It was horrendous.' He pauses, running his hands through his hair repeatedly. 'I want to protect Irene from all of that poison.'

Corine could see his dilemma. Reputations were easily

destroyed by rumour, never to be recovered, but still... she couldn't for the life of her imagine walking away from her own children. Not like that.

Though... wasn't that exactly what she'd done? In her own way?

'Did you ever try to contact Mae or Lyndsey?' she asks.

'A few times, but they didn't reply. Actually, I went over there once, not long after Lyndsey's accused me. Kate went ballistic. Screaming—pulling her own hair. She looked demented. The girls were terrified. I left before someone called the police.' Frank keeps shaking his head, reliving every painful moment.

'Mae mentioned that to me as well.'

'Did she?' He looks shocked. 'God knows what she must have thought; she was about twelve or thirteen at the time. Quiet as a mouse. Always with a book in her hand.' Frank smiles to himself.

Corine imagines him picturing Mae—pleased he has some pleasant memories to draw upon.

'Kate used to joke that she'd destroy me if I ever left her.' He holds his hand over his eyes to shield them from the sun. 'She really fucking meant it.'

'You think she's that calculating? That she'd involve her own daughters in that way?'

They slow to a stop a few feet from an inviting Arts and Crafts pub. It's a family-friendly place, with a well-worn climbing frame beside an empty seating area. Frank turns to face her again. 'I was with her for eighteen years—seventeen of them difficult. I know for a fact she's *that calculating*. If she can convince her own daughter to lie the way Lyndsey did, or if she's somehow managed to convince Lyndsey I actually did those things…' His voice trails off, his gaze drifting to the climbing frame, worn and rotten in places. 'I'm not sure which is worse.'

'You think she manipulated Lyndsey? Got her to fabricate the allegations against you?'

'I know she did,' he doesn't hesitate. Frank's pace picks up again, forcing Corine to trail after him. 'But that's small fry compared to what she did to Mae. Kate's a fucking scary woman. Mae will have had good cause to do what she did, I have no doubt.'

'Do you have any idea what that might be?'

'I don't know, but Mae wouldn't attack anyone unless pushed. Even then, I find it difficult to believe.'

'Yet Kate appealed against Mae's conviction.'

'At the end, she did. In court, when it was too late—the scarred, traumatised mother appealing for her psychotic daughter to be released.'

It seemed that the closer Corine got to this family, the more unclear the truth became. For all she knew, Kate, or Frank, or both, were lying. Mae too. But who did *that* benefit? Certainly not Mae.

Corine feels like a plaything being toyed with, unable to shake the feeling that everything she feels certain about could turn out to be a lie.

Just ahead of them, two cyclists dismount from their bikes and push on towards a gate. They'd arrived, without her realising, at one of the entrances to Richmond Park. In the distance, Corine spots a small herd of deer grazing beside the road, unphased by the steady stream of cars and cyclists passing a few feet away.

She hasn't been here in years. It used to be Lisa's favourite place when she was little. On warm days, Mary would pack a picnic and the three of them would eat ice cream under the shade of the large oaks. She pictures Lisa playing with her hair, feels her small, delicate fingers attempting to plait her curls. She shivers, still feeling her touch.

"I'd like to be a psychiatrist like you, Aunty Corine," Lisa had said. *"Mummy, why don't you do anything good like that?"*

"I do, I look after you. I waited such a long time to have you. I want to spend every minute with you." Mary had laughed at her daughter's comment, but Corine had known from the sound of her voice that her sister was hurt. Shamefully, an inner part of herself had been pleased.

'I suppose,' Corine falters, trying to pick up where Frank had left off. 'After an attack like that, Kate wouldn't have been in a good place mentally. Maybe that's the reason she appealed on Mae's behalf.'

'God knows.'

'Mae suggested I speak to Kate about Mother's Day, for some reason. Do you know why that could be?'

'I'm not sure, but Kate could turn any special occasion into a bad memory.'

'Did anything specific happen on Mother's Day that you can recall?'

Frank shakes his head. 'No, but Mother's Day was supposed to be all about her and, well, kids… they don't care about that, do they? Once they've handed over the box of chocolates and a soppy card, that's it, job done.'

Corine nodded.

'The only good thing about my relationship with Kate was that she taught me that some people are takers. It's their nature. As time went on, it became obvious that she would never be satisfied with her lot, no matter how good it was.'

I guess we're all selfish creatures at heart, Corine muses to herself, thinking of the two daughters that Frank had sidelined in his life. Besides, didn't everyone imagine how their life could have been had they made different choices?

'Did you know that Kate looks after her... after your grandchildren while Lyndsey works?'

Frank's body tenses. 'Good for Lyndsey for working, but I can't say I know anything about my grandchildren, for obvious reasons. Again, what more can I say... I'm a coward. I've moved on. That life was a disaster and I'm trying to get on with living a better one.'

Frank's final assessment of his marriage, his children—their broken relationships—seems more than a little cold to Corine, but she understands the threat of a prison sentence lies behind it.

She is about to push her questioning a little further when she hears the toot of a car horn and a woman's voice calling Frank. A dark Mini pulls up in front of the wrought iron entrance to the park, and a woman in her late twenties—pale, with dark blonde hair—leans out of the driver's side window.

'I can't be late for my appointment!' she yells to Frank without smiling.

Corine recognises the voice from the flat and notes the redness around her eyes.

'I have to go,' Frank says.

'Of course.' Corine nods. Frank turns to go, but she calls

him back 'Does June twenty-third mean anything to you?'

Frank's expression darkens, his face and body fully alert. 'What?' He turns his back on the car, as though shielding it from what he's about to say. 'Why don't *you* tell me what that date means and stop playing games? Or ask Mae. She seems to know a damn sight more than she's letting on.' He turns abruptly, strides to the Mini, and slams the door behind him.

As the car pulls away, Corine is left standing in silence, wondering whether Mae would be better off on her own after all—starting afresh, free from all the complications of this angry, dysfunctional family. A family where father and mother are pitted against each other, each claiming to be the injured party. Both daughters pulled into the conflict: one accusing her father, the other blaming her mother.

Whatever the truth, Corine could see that the Bailey home hadn't been a healthy environment, no matter what the records failed to reveal. If she couldn't make sense of the situation, how could a timid, young girl be expected to?

†

Corine walks a few steps, then pauses to check her phone. A message from Lisa—but still nothing from Mae's sister. Maybe Lyndsey was the missing piece of the puzzle? If Corine could just speak to her, perhaps things would finally begin to make sense. Even if Lyndsey proved as evasive as the rest of the Bailey family, a meeting might at least confirm what Corine had come to suspect: that the only thing holding this family together was the secrets they kept.

She checks her notebook and dials Lyndsey's mobile.

The phone rings, unanswered—just as it had with all of her previous attempts. On a whim, she dials Richard. He picks up immediately.

Kate launches straight in. 'Mae and her family are hiding so many secrets, none of them dare say a word.'

'Mae just has to say sorry, Corine—and sound like she means it.' Richard's voice is tired, flat. She must have caught him at a bad time.

'I'd like to know the truth, though—wouldn't you? Why Mae did what she did.' She can hear Richard breathing, but he says nothing. 'Richard?'

'Depends on what's at stake. There's always something at stake when a secret's being protected. Perhaps they're all protecting someone? Might it reflect worse on Mae if the truth were to get out?'

'Well, if it's to avoid punishment, it seems to me they've all been punished for what Mae did. And if the father really *did* molest his own daughter, why doesn't Lyndsey come out and say it? I need to speak to her.'

'That makes sense.' Richard pauses. 'You seem a little agitated. Everything good with you?'

Corine felt a twinge of guilt. Richard had sounded low, and yet here he was, asking about her. The answer, of course, was no—she wasn't fine. She was worried she wasn't up to the job, that she would let Richard down. And now, the losses that had consumed her thoughts for months suddenly felt even more palpable. If anything, Mae's case—and Corine's proximity to Lisa—brought her own sense of loss into sharper focus.

'It's nothing that a glass of wine won't fix,' she lies.

'You asking?' Richard sounds suddenly perkier.

'Meet me at The Swan, by the river in Twickenham,' she blurts out.

'I know it, but why there?'

'Because it's a beautiful day and I fancy sitting by the river, enjoying a drink with one of my oldest and dearest friends.'

Richard laughs. 'Flattery will get you everywhere.'

'And I've got something I need to say,' she adds. 'And I think a pleasant scene might help.'

'Oh Lord—if the murky water of the Thames is the distraction, I dread to think what you're reluctant to divulge. I'll meet you at six—The Swan.'

She hears the phone click and laughs to herself.

†

They sit on the decked area outside the pub, each with a glass of red wine, watching the brown, chocolatey flow of the river. Two teenage boys race past in kayaks, whooping and hollering as they slice through the water. Their excitement is contagious, and Corine smiles at their exuberance—at the memory of her own youth, so full of hope and expectations; the longed-for adventure of university tantalisingly close. She sniffs the warm air; a gentle breeze carries the scent of water mint and a hint of something else she can't put her finger on.

Richard has been talking about an inter-departmental planning meeting for the last ten minutes, but Corine is struggling to concentrate. He mentions budget cuts and an all-level salary freeze, which caused a junior consultant to storm out of a meeting in tears.

'There's a huge culture shift happening,' he says. 'I'm seeing young doctors and newly appointed consultants going private sooner than they normally would. Some are even going abroad—or leaving the profession altogether.'

'You can't live on idealism,' Corine says, though she knows how hard it is to walk away from a profession that's taken up such a large part of your life.

'This incessant drive to cut budgets, pay, and staffing... it undermines everything. Then there's the poorly defined roles, responsibility without authority, limited resources, crowded wards, and patient self-harm... suicide rates have never been higher. I don't know how we're meant to retain staff—and we're one of the better funded units.'

'It's been going on for years and it will continue long after you've retired. You've got to stop taking on so much, Richard—worrying about everything. You never used to. Remember—there's a direct correlation between stress and premature death.' Corine clears her throat. 'Sorry, that was cheery.'

'Someone once compared our profession to parenting. You give everything you've got, work ridiculous hours through eighteen of your best years, get little to nothing back and then just when you think it's safe to sit down and catch your breath, it all kicks off again. You're back to being the unpaid intern, babysitting grandkids.' Richard takes a sip of his wine. 'It's never been about the money for me. I mean, it's not as if I've got kids to support.'

'You don't have to be a martyr, Richard—attending every planning meeting, sitting on every panel you're invited to. Let the youngsters in your team to take on a bit more—they'd bite your hand off for the opportunity.' Corine smiles lazily, the wine calming her thoughts. 'But while we're on the subject of stress versus satisfaction—'

'Please don't tell me that you called me all the way out here to quit?' He pretends to take notes. 'So, tell me—are you experiencing feelings of incompetency having been thrown in at the deep end? If you are, then it's my fault. That's why I've been rambling on about all the bloody things I have to deal with every day—to gain a little empathy. If not for me, then for my situation.'

'No, I'm not quitting,' Corine laughs. 'And I already felt incompetent—and much, much worse—long before I came to your department. Truthfully, though, I think working with Mae and delving into another family situation is helping.'

'Thank Christ for that,' Richard laughs, mock-wiping his brow. 'I didn't mean that you are… that there are any signs of incompetency.'

Corine waves her hand dismissively and laughs into her glass as Richard fumbles his words.

'More to the point—when the fuck did it become acceptable to show your emotions at work? I mean, crying and storming off?'

'Yeah, that's fucked up.'

They both chuckle.

'You never show your emotions,' he notes, pointing a dramatic finger at Corine. 'You're practically—'

'Spock, yeah, I know. Dead on the inside,' she says flatly. 'Holding it together at all costs is my poison of choice.'

Richard raises his glass. 'To smothering it down!'

They both drink.

The boys in the kayaks shout to each other, but they're too far away for either of them to make out their words. Richard watches them for a moment, then turns his gaze back to Corine, his smile is tinged red with wine.

'Did you manage to get anything useful from Mae's father earlier? A confession, hint... flavour of anything we can use to understand Mae's silence?'

'He hates the mother, denied abusing Mae's sister, and said there would definitely have been a valid reason as to why Mae attacked Kate.'

Richard looks upwards and rolls his eyes. 'Oh, Lord.' He sighs. 'And did he have a hypothesis as to what that might be?'

Corine smiles faintly and lifts her hands in a shrug. 'Nothing solid.' She leans back slightly, eyes narrowing as she gathers her thoughts. 'Both parents say Mae was a quiet child, withdrawn, but fast forward... how that leads to a full-blown psychotic episode? I'm no clearer. There's no indication of drug use or any underlying conditions apart from anorexia and anxiety.' She shrugs again. 'From the way Kate describes the events leading up to the attack, hormones or not, there's just not enough there to justify something that extreme.' Corine pauses, her eyebrows raised. 'And Mae herself? She feels let down by her father, but not abused. She's dismissive—almost resentful—of her mother's job as a GP, and she still seems jealous of Kate's relationship with her sister. I get the sense Kate pitted them against each other.'

She takes a slow drink, licks her top lip, and continues. 'Mae claims her mother is self-centred... but this same mother spends all day caring for her grandchildren and didn't want to testify against Mae in court.' She shifts in her seat and lets out a sigh. 'Maybe Mae had unrealistic expectations of her mother and Kate just couldn't live up to them.' Another shrug. 'I'm hoping a conversation with her sister might shed a bit more light.'

'Here's to clarity.'

They clink glasses and drink.

'So, go on, fess up to why you got me to travel all the way out here,' Richard probes, changing the subject.

'Actually, I used to serve here before I went to university, and whenever I came back.'

'You were a barmaid here?' He sounds surprised.

She nods. 'It's where I met Joe.'

'Oh! Really? Here?' He's smiling, looking about as if he might find evidence of her former self in the space around him.

Corine is sure that Richard thinks it was Joe who stood in the way of him having a relationship with her, perhaps even now. She knows he deserves her honesty. He's been a good friend—reliable, honest, as sharp as anyone she's ever known—and for any one of those qualities alone, she values him.

'I served him here… for months. You know, he was never much of a talker.'

'And there's you, a professional listener.'

She laughs. Then Corine braces herself to tell the truth. 'The night Joe had his accident… he thought I was with you.'

Richard sits up. 'What? Why?'

'I told him I was staying at your flat rather than at my sister's house. I'd travelled up for her funeral, I don't know whether you remember?'

He nods. 'But why say you were staying at mine?'

'Oh, well, there were reasons why I shouldn't have stayed at my sister's, which was what I'd intended to do.'

Corine pauses, expecting him to ask what those reasons were. He doesn't. She'd known Richard for decades; he was the epitome of discretion, the one friend who always listened without judgement. Still, she had never been comfortable exposing the true root of her sadness. It was too tangled, too layered. And after years of sidestepping it, offering a partial truth had become easier.

Once again, Corine hears herself telling Richard a version of the truth. It's honest, and connected, but still not the real reason why Joe had begged her not to go to Mary's house. 'I wasn't in great spirits at the time, and the house where my sister lived—originally my family home—it wasn't a happy place for me. It was always perfectly clean and tidy, we all got three square meals a day, but they were served by a mother who quietly resented her lot in life and never really loved my father. As soon as I hit sixteen, she was off with her new man—they'd met at my parent's tennis club—and twelve months later, they had a child. Dad died when I was twenty-three, having never recovered from the shock of her leaving. I think he blamed himself.'

'Bloody hell. Do you see your mother—half sibling?'

'No, she died in childbirth. And from what I've heard, the boy emigrated with his father to Australia.'

'God, that's awful. I'm so sorry.'

Corine shrugs. 'None of that's important now. I wanted to apologise for dragging you into the difficulties Joe and I were having. I know he called you. I saw your number when I paid his phone bill. It was the last call he made.'

For a few moments Richard says nothing, watching her with his kind eyes. 'He did call me. He'd been drinking, heavily by the sound of it. Kept saying that you'd told him you weren't coming back. He accused me of stealing you when you were vulnerable. I'm sorry to say I could have handled it better.' Richard shifts position and smiles apologetically. 'In the end, I told him to sober up and to start appreciating what he had—getting you to give everything up and move to the middle of nowhere at the height of your career. I'm sorry, I should have said something, but then he had the accident and…'

'He kept calling me that night too. It kills me to say it, but I stopped picking up.'

That night—the night before Mary's funeral—Corine had stayed in a cheap hotel near Euston Station. She emptied the minibar and steadfastly ignored Joe's pleas to talk. Using Richard to make Joe jealous had been impulsive and ill-conceived; she could see that now. But back then, she just wanted him to feel some of the pain and anger she'd carried. She hadn't thought about the consequences.

'People argue, you can't keep blaming yourself for his accident. It was his jealousy that drove him to drink, to get on that bike and go out in the storm. He knew the risks.' Richard's face is a little flushed as he leans towards her.

She picks up her glass and sips. 'I told him I'd decided to stay in London. Indefinitely.' A tear slips Corine's cheek, and she wipes it. 'That Lisa needed me.'

'Were you considering leaving him?'

'No.' She shakes her head. 'It was complicated.'

'Joe could have moved back. You'd given Scotland a go by then.'

'He put up with a lot from me over the years. The struggle to have a baby; losing Michael; the endless rounds of IVF. We never had any money despite both of us being on decent salaries.'

'I'm sorry, it must have been hard.'

'It was... for him, too. I was so focused on becoming a mum from my thirties onwards that I neglected him, our marriage. I neglected everything. As the years passed, when things should have gotten easier, when I should have finally come to terms with being childless, nothing changed. I felt like I'd been cursed somehow by life, fate, God... anyone and everyone.'

Corine makes a face across the table at Richard.

He smiles, waiting for her to continue.

'I was a nightmare to live with. And though I didn't blame Joe outright for our lack of children, I wondered—if I'd married someone else, would I be surrounded by children.'

'Was it Joe who couldn't have them?'

'No, we never found out why we struggled. I mean, by the time we tried IVF, ageing was certainly a factor, but...' Corine sighs. 'Nothing ever showed up in the tests we did.'

Why is she telling him this? He hasn't probed for details, certainly not gynaecological ones. Back when they'd been trying to conceive, Corine could provide detailed reports on her ovulation cycle; her thyroid; her hormone levels. They'd had every test available, both of them—all inconclusive. The results of Joe's semen analysis were still in a folder at the bottom of her wardrobe, along with all the other reminders of their failed attempts to be a normal family.

'Was that what prompted the move to Scotland?'

'It wasn't just that.' Corine's eyes prick with tears. She blinks to control them, but feels the tell-tale warmth on her cheeks.

'Jesus, is he still giving you grief? I know he has his problems now, but you've dedicated yourself to him. Tell me he's at least grateful for that?'

'He was. I mean, he would be…' She hesitates, the words sticking in her throat like a physical obstruction. 'Joe's dead.'

Corine registers the fast-changing expressions on Richard's face. Confusion, disbelief, followed by more confusion.

'What? He's… He's *dead*?' Richard shakes his head. '*When*?'

'Almost seven months ago. A stroke, linked to his head injury. The damage from the accident weakened blood vessels in his brain or, at least, that's what the doctors suspect. I found him in his chair.' She sighs quietly. 'He looked asleep, his blanket tucked all around him, facing his beloved view.'

Richard moves towards her, but Corine holds up her hand. If she starts crying now, she won't stop.

'I'm so sorry.'

She shrugs.

He looks horrified, Corine thinks.

'Why didn't you say anything?'

'The thing I'd dreaded most had finally happened.' She forces a smile. 'I didn't want to face it.'

'Are you sure you should be working? I mean… I'm sorry, I didn't—'

'Yes. I'm fine, honestly. It's been good for me getting

back to work. Besides, it gave me the chance to sort a few family matters here in London. Things to do with my sister's property.' The lie comes easily.

'Why tonight?' he asks, frowning. 'What made it possible to talk?'

'Uncovering all the secrets and lies in the Bailey family made me confront things I've been avoiding. I'm sorry, Richard—I should have been honest from the start. But sometimes, if you let that moment for honesty slip by, it feels wrong to go back.' She pauses, searching his face before continuing. 'We'd just started at university when we met. I wanted to have fun, reinvent myself a little… not burden you with the whole "*Hey, I never told you, but I fucking hated my mother for leaving me*" thing. And then, somehow, it was never the right time. I'd already lied once, and the guilt crept in. You know the drill.'

He squeezes her hand. 'I'm a fairly good listener and, hopefully, I've improved with age, unlike this fucking awful wine.' He pulls a face.

Corine laughs, grateful for his humour. 'I'm not quite ready for full disclosure, but I'll bare that in mind. Another?' she asks, standing. 'I'll check out the bar. See if it's changed.'

CHAPTER 15
MAE

Encouraging a horse to step into a small corral within a wide, open field—without the aid of food, a lead rope, or any previous training—is a difficult task. After thirty minutes of trying, Mae can't hide her frustration. Maisie, the little chestnut mare, has turned her back and resumed grazing, her tail flicking lazily at the occasional fly.

Mae tries everything she can think of—clicking her fingers whilst walking backwards towards the corral, altering the pitch of her voice, stroking and cajoling—but nothing works. Finally, she shouts at Maisie in exasperation. The mare remains unmoved. From across the field, the instructor, Fiona, calls Mae over.

Mae walks towards Fiona and Corine, her shoulders slumped, looking every bit defeated by the first task.

'How did you find that?' Fiona asks in a bright, cheery voice, her hands buried deep in the pockets of her khaki quilted coat. Rosy cheeks give her a youthful look, despite the lines on her weathered face and dry, unkempt hair.

'Hopeless.' Mae's eyes flit between Fiona and Corine. A guard stands a few metres away. 'She either stood still and ignored me or walked away. Apparently, I just don't speak horse.'

Corine laughs at her response.

'It wasn't hopeless,' Fiona assures her. 'Far from it. Yes, you didn't manage to get her to listen to you, but I knew that would happen because she doesn't know you and needs time to suss you out. It's predictable horse behaviour. They need to know who the boss is, and they need to trust you. Trust is everything. Maisie's a real softy; she'll do anything for a treat, or when she's following a routine or a known instruction, as long as she trusts you. That being said, there's a big fat caveat.' Fiona pauses for emphasis. 'All animals can be unpredictable, remember that. But once trust is established, well, she'll love you and follow you anywhere, especially if you've got a treat. So, what if you haven't got a treat? Or you don't know the instructions that she's used to following? What then?'

'I've tried everything... she's bigger than me, so it's not as if I can force her to follow. And she's got those hooves and big teeth, so...'

Fiona laughs. 'She does, and it's good to always be mindful of where you're standing with a horse. Over time, a rider usually gets to know a horse's mood through its body language. Trust me, Mae, I wouldn't put you in a field with any old horse. We use Maisie to work with young people with special needs, and I can assure you she has patience by the bucket load.' Fiona smiles, pushing a wisp of hair off her face. 'You're right, though, this isn't about forcing anyone to do anything, it's about gaining Maisie's trust. So, what might you do next? I'm not expecting an answer, just go on back over: think of her as a young child and what you might do to encourage her to follow you.'

Mae nods and starts back towards the still grazing Maisie, who doesn't so much as flick an ear in her direction. She edges closer—one step, then another—but the moment she's within reaching distance, the mare drifts away. Mae tries again, and again, each approach ending the same way with Maisie wandering off. Before long, their slow-motion dance has carried them some distance from Corine and Fiona.

'Okay, Maisie, I can see you like your space, so I'll just stand here. I promise I won't come any closer if you're not comfortable.' Mae keeps her voice low and calm in an attempt to soothe the animal. 'I'm sorry I don't have a treat for you, but if I could give you something tasty, I'd probably give you an apple or carrot, or maybe a sugar cube. Horses like sugar cubes, don't they?'

Maisie's ears prick up, as though she recognises the names of the various treats.

They remain like this for a while, with Mae talking as the mare grazes. Mae's attention drifts to the surrounding fields and she breathes deeply, enjoying the fresh air—a not-unpleasant mix of horse manure and damp vegetation. To her left, a large metal building—Fiona had called it a manége— glints in the light, flanked by a cluster of official-looking buildings. Fiona had mentioned they were part of the police's equine training facilities, though Mae hasn't seen anyone about.

The sun comes out and a warm breeze picks up, lightly caressing her cheeks and lifting her hair. It feels wonderful. She closes her eyes, enjoying the sensation, experiencing a sudden surge of gratitude that she'd been allowed this day. Later, when she's back in her room, she will draw upon this feeling; use it to help her feel positive about her release.

When Mae opens her eyes, Maisie is a little closer, but

sideways on now, and still grazing.

'You don't want to talk to me, and that's okay,' Mae says quietly. 'No offence taken. I've been ignored by people who had a reason to be interested. My own mother would lock herself away in her bedroom for hours, sometimes days. Fuck, how irritating must I have been?' She laughs without smiling. 'Pleading only irritated her—crying, more so. In fact, it would just make her determined to stay there for longer.' Mae bends down absentmindedly and scoops up a handful of grass, rubbing it between her palms. 'When Dad left, she never actually said he'd gone, or why. She didn't even tell us that Grandma had died—that's Dad's mum, not hers. If she mentioned her parents, it was only to criticise them. They were small people with narrow minds who held her back, apparently. Mum would fire that information at you like a gunshot—BAM—and while you were still trying to take it in, she would say "*and now I have to deal with your dramatics too*".' Mae pauses, looking into the distance. 'I think she resented us the whole time.'

Feeling warmth on the side of her face, Mae stops talking. To her surprise, Maisie is standing beside her, head lowered, ears forward and alert.

'Well, hello there,' Mae whispers.

The horse snorts and nuzzles against her shoulder. Trying not to frighten her, Mae turns slowly, keeping her hand flat like Fiona had shown her, and offers the handful of torn grass she'd been clutching in her hand. At the feeling of Maisie's warm mouth on her hand, a smile spreads across Mae's face.

'There you go, Maisie, thank you for listening. How about you follow me over to the corral area over there so I can pass today's task?'

Mae scoops up another handful of long grass and offers it, all the while moving backwards in the direction of the corral. Maisie, though, has other ideas. She flicks her tail and heads in the opposite direction.

†

CORINE

Back at The Orchard, Corine and Mae sit in the quiet, empty canteen, two half-finished mugs of coffee before them.

'I can't believe she ate the grass from my hand!' Mae laughs, still buzzing from the morning activity.

'You should be proud of yourself. Like Fiona said, it takes time to build trust. You stayed calm, spoke in a soothing voice, and responded to the horse's body language. We were impressed.'

'If we're being honest, though, I did bribe her with food. Could that be seen as cheating?'

Corine laughs. 'You used whatever means were available. I'd call that smart.'

With her hands held together in front of her, a pleading expression on her face, Mae looks at Corine. 'Could I do it again? Please!'

'Oh, I should think so. Fiona's agreed to one—maybe two—more sessions. I just need to figure out which days work best for everyone, and I'll let you know.'

'Thank you, Corine, thank you so much.' Mae suddenly leans forward, arms open wide, and pulls her into an embrace.

Later, whilst typing up her notes in the hotel room, Corine replays the moment in her mind. It was the first time Mae had truly let her guard down, and it felt like a breakthrough. Something had shifted between them, a subtle loosening, as if a small space had opened for a relationship to take root. Corine knew from experience that animals could help people step outside themselves. She'd read various animal therapy studies citing improvements in mood, anxiety, stress levels, and even pain tolerance—but witnessing Mae's genuine happiness had been an unexpected gift. Perhaps, at last, Mae was beginning to trust her.

Corine looks up from her laptop and rubs her eyes. Catching her reflection in the mirror above the desk, she frowns. 'Don't get carried away,' she cautions. 'Afterall, what teenage girl wouldn't enjoy a bit of pony time?'

Gaining the trust of someone as closed off as Mae would be far less straightforward than winning over a docile horse. And without trust, she could forget any real therapy taking place, let alone a truthful account of the attack. She lifts her glass to her lips and drains the last of the wine in one swift gulp.

'And a dog's tail can still be wagging when it bites.'

CHAPTER 16
KATE

Kate is sliding a stuffed chicken from the oven when the doorbell rings. She leaves the baking tray on top of the cooker, whips off her apron, and hurries to the door. As she goes, she smooths the folds of her cinnamon-coloured dress and checks her hair—swept to one side and held in place with a matching jewelled clip that catches the light. When she opens the door, she puckers her heavily glossed lips.

'What the fuck, Martin, you're an hour and a half late. You said you'd be here to help at six-thirty.'

Martin, Kate's old university friend, stands on the doorstep in baggy corduroys, a flannel shirt, and an ill-matched bow tie. 'Look who I bumped into,' he replies brightly, waving his plump hand.

A chorus of hellos and giggles rise from behind a laurel hedge and three heads pop up one by one.

Embarrassed but brazen, Kate beams as she ushers everyone inside. 'Niamh, I can't believe you're on time! You must have heard that I just got a wine delivery in.'

'You ran out last time, so I brought my own,' says Niamh, a slender, freckly Irish woman with short, dark hair. She narrows her eyes and holds up two bottles of red, then air-kisses Kate as she walks through the door.

'You're on drinks duty,' Kate grumbles at Martin.

'I'd better get pouring,' he replies jovially, then lowers his voice. 'Got us a nice little pick-me-up. That's why I was a bit delayed.'

'Behind the mirror, upstairs loo,' she murmurs, giving him a peck on the cheek. 'You're the best kind of therapist, Martin.'

'Don't!' he says. 'Only this afternoon I had to remind the headmaster that I joined the school to be Head of History, not to take on pastoral responsibilities for sixty horny little fuckers.'

'Oh, come on, you love it really. Surely you can relate? You were a horny little fucker once.'

Martin laughs and follows Kate to the kitchen, where she rips open two bags of salad and tips them into a wooden bowl. She carries the salad and a jug of dressing to the table, which is already set for five people.

'Jake, do me a favour and sort out the ambiance in here, would you?'

'Ellie tells me you're on duty tonight,' Jake replies. He strides over to a side-table and picks up a remote control.

'I am, but they're sleeping like little angels for their grandma, so I can't complain.'

'Did anyone ever tell you that you're an absolute saint, Kate?' says Ellie, resting a hand on Kate's arm.

'Yeah, back in '82, and he'd just failed to get into my knickers. If I'd allowed him, I'd have been a whore five minutes later. In fact, I *was* a whore five minutes later… just not with him!'

They all laugh.

'I'm pretty sure you wouldn't be such a saint now given the

chance.' Martin winks, lifting his glass towards Jake.

Kate raises her eyes towards the ceiling. 'Change the record, Martin.'

'We might be middle-aged, but we're not fecking desperate,' Niamh remarks, sniffing a fragranced candle on the breakfast bar. 'Lush,' she announces to herself.

'Easy to say when you've got Jake pandering to your every need,' Kate jokes.

'I bloody wish.' Niamh teases the ends of her hair behind her ears, revealing an emerald ear cuff that matches her eyes.

'Are you sure about the music?' Jake asks, seemingly oblivious to the current conversation. He points upstairs. 'Won't it wake the girls?'

Kate scoffs. 'Is this a fucking party or not? Besides, they're conked out on Calpol… lots of nasty viruses going around.'

Martin nods in understanding as Jake gets the music going, his choice sparking a lively conversation about Bowie.

'*Ziggy Stardust* is the first vinyl album I ever bought,' he tells them.

'Well, I saw him in Holland, '76, I think.' Kate holds her glass of wine up for Martin to refill.

'Always a competition with you, Kate,' Ellie chimes in. 'New York; I was about twenty-five. The ticket was a freebie from a sales rep, I don't remember his name. Bowie, though…'

Dinner is a noisy but friendly affair, with idle chit chat and in-jokes flowing freely. Children and home life are, largely, avoided. Wine is poured and topped up on repeat.

Between the main course and dessert, Kate slips upstairs to check on the girls. Both are fast asleep: Zizi curled in a portable cot that's way too small for her, Beth's tiny frame barely denting the double bed. Satisfied they're sleeping, Kate steps into the bathroom. She opens the mirrored cabinet and takes out a small clear packet of white powder. On the washbasin, she tips out a little and smooths it into four lines with a credit card pulled from her pocket. Then she leans down and snorts two.

Back downstairs, she nods to Martin, who excuses himself and disappears upstairs.

'I don't know about you lot, but I feel like dancing,' Kate announces. 'Anyone wants any pudding, help yourself. There's vanilla pannacotta and frangipane tart in the fridge.'

A chorus of appreciative noise follows, but no one gets up.

'This takes me back,' Martin says as he returns from the bathroom. He wipes his nose a few times, then takes a sip of his wine, his body and neck stiff as he watches Kate dance.

'It's a wonder you remember university at all!' Kate laughs. 'You were always off your head on something or other.'

Soon everyone is dancing with carefree abandon to the soundtrack of their youth. A flushed and laughing Kate shimmies over to the kitchen and pours a tray of shots, which she offers around. The group gather in a loose circle and, on the count of three, they tip their heads back and chug down the shots.

CHAPTER 17
MAE

It's Saturday morning, and several patients, including Mae, are busy working in the kitchen, preparing pizza dough for the evening's film and pizza night. *Shirley Valentine* is being shown in the cafeteria, and despite the fact that most of the women have seen it before, the mood is high.

'The best bit's when the husband gets fried eggs for dinner on steak night,' someone says.

Others echo their agreement, laughing and chatting amiably. One or two mimic a finger being poked into an imagined plate of eggs.

'He'd have been lucky to get a fried egg off my mam,' a Scottish girl pipes up from the back of the kitchen. 'She only lit the stove to light-up,'

'My mum... now she could cook,' Mal mutters to Mae, both of them standing in the corner of the kitchen, kneading dough in large plastic bowls.

'What was that, then?' the same girl shouts from the back. 'Heroin?

Laughter erupts as Mal twirls round, raising her middle finger systematically to the entire room. Mae smiles to herself and continues to work.

'I'll miss this when I get out,' Mal says, her voice low and thoughtful.

'You can make pizza anywhere,' Mae says stiffly. She flips the dough, refusing to look at Mal, and instead focuses her attention on the task at hand.

'Bitch!' Mal says affectionately. 'Anyway, who in their right mind chooses to make pizza from scratch?'

Mae picks up a small container of flour and adds a little to the bowl; she can feel Mal's eyes watching her every movement, the entire time.

'What's up?' Mal leans in closely. 'You're losing weight and—'

'Nothing,' Mae says sharply. 'Nothing's up.'

'Suit yourself, but it's Saturday, we're having pizza, a movie, and I'm gonna have a good time with or without you.'

Mae sighs as she sprinkles flour on the work surface.

'I reckon it's all that special treatment you're getting from that pisshead psych of yours. It's gone to your head.'

'Mal! I asked you not to—'

'What? I'm only sayin' it to you. Don't be so paranoid, no one's listening.'

Mae stops working and looks directly at Mal, her delicate chin raised in quiet defiance. With a sudden motion, she slams the dough she's been kneading onto the worktop. A few strands of hair fall across her face; she blows them back impatiently, refusing to look up.

'You feelin' low again, is that it?' Mal whispers. 'If the meds aren't working, you gotta tell someone.'

'I haven't been taking any meds… not for months now.'

'What?' Mal stares at her incredulously. 'Well, that's just…' She hesitates, visibly conflicted by Mae's confession. 'Aren't you terrified of losing it again? Of doing something? I know I am.'

'I won't.'

'You don't know that for sure. The thought of not being in control terrifies me. Pile on the stress out there, and you don't know how quickly we might get overwhelmed. I don't want to end up back in here. I want to start living—get a job, make friends… friends that I can go places with, do things with. Then I wanna meet someone, start a family of my own. I want it so fucking much I could scream.'

Mae stops working the dough and watches Mal. Up until then, she hadn't realised how much her friend wanted to get out. It felt like a rejection. Mae's eyes fill and she looks away.

'Talk to me, tell me what's wrong.' She pauses, giving Mae time to answer. When she doesn't, Mal adds, 'Maybe if that psychiatrist of yours would hold off on the whisky she'd spot it.'

'The pills and the therapy don't work for me… nothing's changed.'

'They might if you actually took them. Or if you tried when you're in therapy. Even just a little.'

Mae looks sharply at Mal, her fingers pressing into the dough forcefully. 'They might work if they'd made the right diagnosis in the first place.'

'You don't wanna go round sayin' that, babe. They'll throw away the key.'

'I'm doing what I have to do. What everyone expects me to do. Isn't that enough?'

'Mae, I'm not gonna be here for much longer, so please…' She rolls her eyes. 'Don't have me worrying about you on top of everything else. Look, I'm happy. For the first time in years

I feel like I've got a future, and I thought you'd be happy for me.'

Mae looks at Mal as if she's a stranger, the meaning of her words seeping like radiation into her skin, spreading through muscle and fibre until they settle heavy in her bones.

'I'm not feeling great,' she says, dropping everything and stepping back from the counter. 'My head hurts, I need to go back to my room.'

'Mae, I'm getting out.' Mal shakes her head, frustrated. 'We should be celebrating.'

Mae turns away.

'Unbelievable! You're actually gonna freeze me out? You should be happy for me!'

Mae can hear the anger in Mal's voice, sharp and rising above the background chatter.

'Great friend you turned out to be.'

The room falls silent.

'After everything I've done for you.'

Mae whirls around, her voice cutting through the hush. 'What you've done for me?'

'I don't imagine anyone will be queuing up to be your friend when I'm gone. You don't open up; it's like you've got this great big shield around you, and you don't let anyone in. Your loss though, babe! You're the one who's going to end up fucking lonely.'

All eyes are fixed on the unfolding argument. Staff, guards, and patients alike seem poised, alert to the possibility of a sudden escalation, of threat turning into violence. For the patients, having had all their family relationships and any external friendships curtailed, the real tension lies in the shifting allegiances. In prison, the loss of a friend isn't just about the loss of companionship—it's the loss of emotional support, protection, and, ultimately, power.

Mae ignores Mal. She heads towards a member of staff at the back of the kitchen and whispers something, before being led outside.

†

Closing the door of her room, Mae walks as though in a trance to the sink. There's flour on her hands and up her arm, which she washes off, scrubbing hard at her skin with a nail brush, like doing so will clean off any traces of the rejection she feels. It had never occurred to her until then that her relationship with Mal would come to an end, and that Mal would be okay with it. More than okay. She actually seemed *happy*.

Mae has an uneasy sensation of déjà vu, emptiness clawing at her insides. Catching her reflection in the mirror, she stops and looks at herself.

'You mean nothing to anyone,' she says, and suddenly, without warning, she slams her head into the glass. When she looks up, a mark is already blooming at the centre of her forehead. Her face is pinched and pale, a trickle of blood runs down from her nose. She stares as it drips to the floor—one drop, then another—before the memory takes her.

She is a younger teenager again, dazed and covered in blood, being led out of her kitchen between two policemen. She glances back at her mother, calling out to her again and again, fighting against the strong arms that pull her away, pleading until her voice breaks.

Kate hadn't looked up.

Not once.

Mae feels a familiar explosion of white-hot fear and falls back onto her bed. As she does, her hands reach up to the back of her head, twisting and yanking, until eventually the hair on her scalp gives.

As the pain blossoms, a blissful numbness descends.

CHAPTER 18
CORINE

On her second Sunday in London, Corine suggests a trip to Richmond Park. Lisa agrees immediately—perhaps a little too eagerly, Corine's thinks—but she chalks that up to nurture and a naturally sunny disposition and hopes Lisa won't end up disappointed.

The week had dragged, with little to show for all Corine's efforts with Mae, who seemed to grow more withdrawn and unfamiliar with each interaction. Greenery and fresh air, Corine decides, are what's needed to reset herself—reduce the cortisol streaming through her body, wreaking its invisible havoc.

For the past hour, they've been following the gentle paths around and through the park's wooded areas. Both are pink cheeked and slightly out of breath, but in a satisfying way that comes with movement. The weather helps too: a light breeze cools their faces, and not a raincloud in sight. All around Corine hears the sound of birds calling, dogs barking, and children, liberated by a sense of space, yelling back and forth.

'I love it here,' Lisa says, her eyes fixed somewhere in the distance. 'It feels like we're out in the countryside.' She giggles and turns full circle. 'Wherever you look, there's green space, sky, not a high-rise in sight. Unless you're on that hill over there and look that way.' Lisa points towards the London skyline.

'And it smells so good.' She inhales deeply. 'Unpolluted. I worry about that.' Lisa stops, frowning. 'God, listen to me. What am I turning into?' She clutches her stomach. 'What will I be like when this one's born?'

Corine laughs. 'You should come to the farm—smell real fresh air, feel what it's like to be dwarfed by nature. Everything's so much bigger up there: the sky, the mountains, the beaches, the sea... and emptier, too.' She pauses, then adds, 'I'm not saying it's a bad thing, but people have always worried about one environmental disaster or another. When your mum and I were young, it was nuclear war. Then it was the hole in the ozone. Yesterday's headlines were all about overfishing and climate change. Give it thirty years and there'll be something else worth worrying about. But when you're surrounded by nature, it's easier to get perspective. You're reminded of what will still be here—long after we've gone.'

'I suppose.' Lisa turns to look at Corine. 'You miss Scotland, don't you?'

'More than I imagined I would. Living in a landscape like that—being away from it—makes me realise how lucky I am.' She pictures Mae sitting in the therapy room, staring forlornly at the scenic poster and a sigh escapes. She hears herself repeat words that Joe had said to her whenever she'd questioned their decision to relocate. 'It's a legacy of sorts, and we're tending it for the next generation—whoever they might be.'

'Is that how you feel?'

Corine hesitates. 'I think so. Probably more since I've been away.'

'That's lovely.' Lisa smiles, but Corine can hear the

uncertainty in her voice. Without looking, she can picture a small, pitying smile on her lips. The kind of fleeting smile she had witnessed untold times on the faces of people who were, increasingly over the years, complete strangers.

It was surprising how quickly a conversation about the land or livestock—even leaving the European Union—could snake its way downhill to those painful four words: *do you have children?*

No, Corine didn't.

Then, that smile would appear. A smile that, more than anything, made Corine feel like a failure; that her life had all been for nothing. It said that to be childless was to be lonely and unloved. However well-versed someone was at putting-on a show of false emotions, that hesitant smile always said: *I wouldn't want to be you.*

'I'd never really thought about what we leave behind… not in terms of a legacy. That's a really lovely way of looking at it,' Lisa says after a pause.

When Corine glances sideways, she sees Lisa lost in thought, her expression serious. There's no trace of that dreaded half-smile. She feels suddenly ashamed for having judged her so harshly. *Lisa has a good heart*, she reminds herself. Mary did an incredible job raising her. Corine wishes, and not for the first time, that Mary had lived long enough to hear her say those words. If only she'd offered more praise, less unsolicited advice… words that likely fed Mary's quiet resentment over the years.

She considers mentioning Mary, but instead steers back to safer ground. 'Your legacy will be this little one,' she says gently.

Lisa smooths her stomach. 'Oh, I know I'm not the first woman to have a baby. I just hope I don't mess it all up. People do! I can't say too much to Peter because he worries about me stressing. You know… in case it has an effect on the baby.'

Corine threads her arm through Lisa's and gently guides her along a small narrow, well-worn path that runs beside a partially fenced lake. 'I might not have much experience in raising a child, but if you ever need me—which I doubt you will—I'll be there at the drop of a hat. You can count on that.'

†

'Do you remember you and Mum arguing about that view?' Lisa asks later, as they sit on a bench overlooking Petersham Common. In the distance, the Thames curves and winds its way slowly through London.

'No,' Corine lies.

'I must have been seventeen. You were both getting all heated about my choice of degree. You'd said I should do whatever I enjoyed, and Mum said, *"What, and become a starving painter living in a garret somewhere?"* I remember you sitting back, staring out at the view. It looked like you were ignoring her, but then you said that Turner might have been a bit eccentric, but what a wonderful legacy he left behind. She'd laughed, said, *"He was a mad recluse at the end, wasn't he?"*. You looked furious. I remember you saying, *"Perhaps if he'd had foresight, he might have acknowledged the daughters he'd had illegitimately. They might have looked after him in later life."* Mum more or less told you to shut up at that point. I remember being shocked, hearing her speak to you like that.

I was never sure what you were arguing over.'

'You've got an annoyingly good memory.'

'Well, I was shocked… at Mum. Obviously something had gone on between you two that neither of you were prepared to talk about. Not in front of me, anyway. And it fascinated me, I suppose, how sisters are… so secretive together.'

Corine remains silent, recalling the confrontation all too vividly; how her sister refused to argue, not wanting anything to escalate in front of Lisa. What Lisa didn't know was that, after she had walked off to take a picture of the view, the discussion had taken a different turn.

"The three of us are happy, and I'm not going to apologise for that. If I could change how things turned out for you and Joe, I would. I'm sorry, but your anger… the jealousy… it's too much." Her sister had stood at that point and walked away, refusing to look at her.

Being accused of jealousy had floored Corine. She'd felt hurt, betrayed. That wasn't how she saw herself, her behaviour, the things she said—none of it was motivated by jealousy. It never had been. More a reaction to the growing realisation that she would never have a family of her own. Wounded by her sister's words, Corine had felt something shift deep within herself, and she had known then, no matter how hard she tried, her relationship with Mary would never be the same.

If only her sister had understood the effort it took to face each new day—dreading not just tomorrow, but ten, twenty, thirty years' time. Corine had taken deep breaths, appearing calm on the surface, when inside she'd been a writhing, screaming mess of confusion, anger, and loss.

The accusation had left an invisible wound that had never

healed; a rejection made worse because she hadn't deserved it. It was true, she wanted a child more than anything, but she had never, not for a single moment, wished her own fate upon her sister. And yet... Corine had known the things she'd said would hurt Mary. Hadn't she brought the confrontation on herself? Goading her sister with a power play that, looking back now, seemed warped.

'Anyway, you won the argument at that point; I think Mum thought so too because she shut up. She was always a bit intimidated by her little sister.'

Corine lets out a startled laugh. 'Intimidated? Nonsense! Your mum wasn't intimidated by anything. What I said was glib. She just wanted to smooth your path and make life easy for you. That's what a good mother does.'

Corine's phone rings in her bag. It's Callum. At the sound of his voice, a feeling of dread washes over her. 'Has something happened?'

Callum launches straight into their last conversation, as if no time has passed between then and now. 'It's nothing to alarm yourself with. Your cow has Ketosis, the wasting form. Vet says she's likely had it for a few weeks already, as she's on the turn now and improving. She'll be right as rain in a few days.'

Corine breathes a sigh of relief. 'Thank you, Callum, I really appreciate you letting me know. I can't tell you how thankful I am that you're looking after my place.'

'Och, you know I'd have that land off you at a blink of an eye for my youngest. I'm happy to tend your strip until you can't... or get tired of it... or both.'

She laughs. 'I'll bear that in mind.'

'No need to rush back.'

'Thank you. How's Betty doing?'

'Aye, the dog, well, she's pining alright. Whining to get into the house and over to her spot beside his chair. It's hard to see, so it is. Only to be expected. Dogs are loyal creatures. You know, we were all very fond of Joe, God rest his soul.'

Corine feels tears spring to her eyes, Callum's kindness and imagining Betty beside Joe's empty chair catching her off-guard.

Sometimes she would lay on Joe's side of the bed and imagine his arms around her, tethering her to a world that increasingly offered less and less meaning. These days, she felt like a tuft of sheep wool, being tossed about at the mercy of the wind.

'I'll sit with Betty for a wee while tonight.'

'There's no need to do that, Callum, but thank you.'

'Aye, well, you'll be doing me a favour. It'll get me away from the crowds.'

'Crowds?'

'Indeed, Connor's home for a few days with his new girl. Aye and she blethers so, so she does.'

Corine laughs again, hanging up before slipping the phone back into her bag. *What complicated creatures we are*, she thinks.

CHAPTER 19
MAE

Mae sits crossed-legged on the floor, alongside two other inmates. Judy, their young therapist, pushes a ball to Jess—a pale giraffe of a girl, and the only one making eye contact. Jess embraces the ball enthusiastically, swaddling her arms and legs around it.

'I would say thank you to my nan for looking after my little boy for me. For stepping in and giving me the time to appreciate what I've got waiting for me when I get out. Harry's two now—a real handful. And I know my poor nan is run off her feet with him waking her at six every morning and not always doing as he's told, so I'm really grateful to her. Without her my boy would have been with social services, probably fostered by some fucking rich family, or someone who abuses him.'

'Thanks, Jess! Thanks for sharing,' Judy gently interrupts. 'Let's keep it positive and remember to pass the positivity on, ladies.'

Jess seems reluctant to part with the ball.

'Jess... the ball.'

When she sends it back, the ball rolls slowly towards Judy. There's a haughty expression on Jess's narrow face, a mischievous glint in her eyes.

'What are you thankful for, Judy?' she asks.

There's a titter from Mandy, who lays on the floor, playing with her tight rows of braids. Mae manages a smile and looks up for the first time.

'You don't need to return the ball to me until you've all answered each of the questions, but while I have it, I'm thankful for my job, because I get to work with lots of wonderful people every day.' Judy smiles at each of them.

Mandy raises two fingers to her mouth and pretends to gag.

Judy laughs and pushes the ball to Mae. She sighs, holding the ball at arm's length, as though it might explode.

'I'm thankful... I'm thankful for... for...' Mae looks towards the ceiling as though for inspiration.

'For being blessed with such a sharp mind!' Mandy laughs.

'Exactly! Thanks, Mandy.' She is about to roll the ball to Mandy when Judy stops her.

'No, come on, Mae, you can do better than that.'

Mae's expression hardens. 'I want to thank all those in my life who granted me the power of invisibility, which for some reason doesn't work inside here.' She shrugs. 'They never, not once, actually saw me as a real person. I'd like to thank my father, who may have abused me—if only I could remember the details—and who knows, maybe I initiated it.'

'Mae, please—'

'And my mother, whose nurturing skills ended with a knife—'

'Okay, Mae, let's take this offline and talk about it later. Please pass the ball to Mandy.'

Mae thrusts the ball towards Mandy, who is now sitting up straight, alert and smiling.

'I would also like to thank my mother,' she says, grinning, 'and her very considerate partners, who took it upon themselves to look after me—if you get me—every single time that slag shot up. Sometimes in the very same room, right next to her on the sofa—'

'Okay, ladies, thank you. I think you know this wasn't what I intended, but hey-ho as long as you all got to let off a bit of steam.'

All three girls laugh.

'Remember everyone—you need to have techniques to ease those negative thoughts, and if you don't practice them when you're outside, you will struggle. They're essential tools, ladies, there to help you cope on the outside.'

'I'm all for practicing with essential tools, Judy, but I'm all out of batteries.'

This time, even the therapist laughs.

†

CORINE

Corine and Mae arrive at their one-to-one session at the same time. They nod silent greetings, before taking seats opposite each other.

'You look tired,' Mae says, her eyes widening, as if surprised by her own words.

'I am a little.' Corine touches her forehead, brushing her hair to one side. She wonders whether Mae has noticed the redness of her eyes and the dark circles beneath. 'It's the hotel. Doors slamming at all hours, children running through the corridors, shouting when they should be asleep.' She leans forward and sighs loudly.

Mae flinches, leaning back in her chair.

'What's wrong?'

'Whisky,' Mae replies, scrunching her nose and closing her eyes against the smell.

Corine feels mortified, her mind racing as she tries to come up with a plausible excuse for drinking so early in the day. Cursing herself, she's about to apologise but Mae starts to speak.

'I remember being in bed, I must have been young, maybe nine or ten years old, and a man came into my room late at night, reeking of whisky.' Mae looks upwards, to her left, reliving the painful memory. 'He... he.' She swallows, hard. 'He tried to get in bed next to me, but I screamed and kicked. I was still half asleep... just a child. But I knew it was wrong.'

'What happened then?'

'He left.'

'Did you know the man?' Corine asks, relieved that the focus has shifted.

Mae shakes her head. 'It was dark. My parents had a lot of people over. Lots of parties. It was so dark... I don't know. It's confusing. Maybe it was my dad, maybe it wasn't. I felt so terrified, and I knew... I knew he shouldn't be there. I might have blanked more, who knows.' She sits forward, an earnest expression on her face. 'Could you put me under hypnosis or something?'

'I don't do that kind of therapy, Mae. Besides, memories are unpredictable at the best of times, and it's not unheard of for those retrieved under hypnosis to be false.'

'I don't want to have these thoughts going round and round in my head. Not knowing if Dad abused me or not. Thinking he might have… must have—if Lyndsey claims he did. What do *you* think?'

'I think we often suppress trauma as a way of coping. But you're in a safe space here, Mae, with people around you who care about you, who want what's best for you. We'll support you. If you'll allow us.'

'It's just so difficult to believe that when my own mother never did.'

'I can't speak for your mother,' Corine says gently, 'but she wants to be involved now. She's always supported your release.'

Mae snorts and looks away, folding her arms defensively. 'I'm not even sure I want to be released.'

'I think you're confronting a lot of painful memories as you enter this new phase. And then there's the prospect of release, which can feel like a prison of its own, full of scary possibilities, without instructions or guides on how you're meant to be.'

Mae rolls her eyes, but Corine ignores her.

'Change can be scary,' she continues. 'Just keep taking steps forward—.'

'Most of the women here have family… a parent, sometimes two.' Mae interrupts. 'It's easier for them.'

Corine nods, biting back the urge to repeat that Kate is willing to support her. She understands a little of Mae's trepidation, but not the depth of her resentment towards her mother. Corine knows she has only begun to scratch the surface of that powerful, self-destructive force.

'I get that. It will be a big adjustment, getting out,' she says instead.

Mae looks at her imploringly. 'Do you?'

Corine wants to say that she would understand her better if Mae fully explained what happened the night she attacked Kate, but she knows that Mae will simply retreat into herself if pushed.

'I'm here to support you. To help prepare you for your parole hearing. I'll make sure that the people who need to be in place to support you afterwards are there, ready and waiting.'

'No, I mean… do you understand what it's like to have no one?'

'Oh, Mae, you won't be alone.' Corine feels a fraud just saying those words. She doesn't know how things will turn out for Mae in one, two, ten years down the line, and even if she did, why should Mae trust her? She was someone who needed a drink just to get through the day, who turned up to therapy sessions reeking of booze.

'Will *you* support me after I'm released?'

'I'll support you until the decision is made about your parole. After that, I need to return to my other commitments, I'm afraid. You'll have a probation officer and somewhere to live, work, or continue your education.'

'By commitments you mean family? Children?'

'No. I have a small farm, which a friend is looking after.' Using the word friend felt a little disingenuous, but she liked Callum. He'd been supportive, even if he had other motives.

'What, so, were you married and then divorced or what?'

'Married. Now widowed.'

'I'm sorry.' Mae frowns. 'Do you have children?'

Corine shakes her head. Telling Mae about Michael seems too personal, like she would be unburdening herself in someone else's therapy session.

'You have your sister you could contact when you get out,' she suggests, eager to change the subject.

'Thanks, but no thanks.'

Corine wants to return to the topic of the man in Mae's bedroom, but it's almost the end of their session and she doesn't want to leave Mae too agitated. She makes a note to raise it at their next session.

Mae is already on her feet, ready to go.

'I'm sure you must be desperate to get back to the farm,' she says.

'Wait, Mae, please sit down. Can I ask you one last question for today?'

Mae nods reluctantly but remains standing.

'Why did you insist on me as your psychiatrist?'

'You were nice,' Mae replies without hesitation. 'I remember thinking you were genuinely worried about me. You felt... motherly. And, I suppose, I was lonely.'

'I treated you like the child you were, that's all.'

Mae shrugs. 'What does it matter?'

'You'll have your chance to speak at the multi-disciplinary meeting this afternoon. I spoke to Anne. She's your named nurse, isn't she?'

Mae nods.

'She mentioned you never attend and probably wouldn't go to the next one. That perhaps you felt there were too many people there. Is that right?'

'Yeah, I suppose.'

'They might not feel like it, but these meetings are for your benefit, to make sure that everyone, including you, agrees about plans for your future. They're there to ensure nothing is missed when sorting the best options for your release. It's your chance to say what you want.'

'I want to stay here.'

'I understand your trepidation, but there's a whole world out there.'

Mae ignores Corine. She edges sideways, slipping between the chair and the small table.

'Talk to me, Mae. Tell me about what you're afraid of. You've already let one parole opportunity pass you by. Don't let another. You've served your time.'

The faint scent of her deodorant lingers in the air—fresh, clean, disarmingly innocent. *She's too young to have given up*, Corine thinks.

When the door clicks shut, Corine listens to Mae's footsteps fade down the corridor. Slowly, she sits back in her chair, her gaze falling to a dark stain on her shirt. She curses herself again. She has no idea how to help—and worse, it feels as if Mae still has no interest in helping herself. Or perhaps she can't, Corine thinks. Perhaps she's too vulnerable, too damaged, to see the value of self-preservation?

At that moment, Corine notices the tremor in her left hand has worsened. She holds it out in front of her—only the middle finger and thumb remain stable. It's the same with her right hand.

'You're killing yourself,' she mutters, snatching up her bag and hurrying towards the bathroom.

Inside, she shoves the empty whisky bottle in the bin, covering it with paper towels. Her reflection in the mirror makes her wince. She wipes at the dried stain on her shirt, noting the dark circles under her eyes, the messy hair, the unkempt clothes—and scowls.

'Just do your job,' she says. 'Stop wallowing.'

CHAPTER 20
CORINE

Corine is busy preparing for her second meeting with Mae and Kate when Mae's father calls. Given the way their last meeting ended, she hadn't expected him to get in touch.

Frank speaks quietly, as though he doesn't want someone else nearby to hear their conversation.

'Hello, Frank? Sorry, can you speak up a little?'

'I was, um, I was thinking about the dates Mae gave you.' He coughs. 'You mentioned June twenty-third and, well, I wondered if she'd said anything else about that date? Something that might help me recall what happened. Anything.'

'No, I'm afraid she didn't. I'd hazard a guess that an unpleasant event of some sort took place though.'

'Why would you think that?' Frank sounds defensive.

'Well, judging from what Christmas and Mother's Day meant to Mae, to your family…'

'Could it be a date in the future?'

'I hadn't considered that. I asked Mae to jot down occasions that meant a lot to her and her mum. Just as a conversation starter for their first meeting, and, well, you know the rest. I assumed, like with the other dates she wrote down, that something negative had happened.'

'We split around Christmas, but Mother's Day wasn't ever

a particularly remarkable date, not in terms of Kate's moods, so something must have happened after I'd gone that I don't know about. June twenty-third, though… might it mean something to Kate? Perhaps you should ask her. Or maybe you could force Mae to tell you what the date means?'

Frank ended the call quickly, leaving Corine feeling puzzled. Why had he phoned with nothing to add, only questions? Why was he so keen that she should find out about June twenty-third? He was hiding something, she was sure.

Of course, there was no point asking Mae. That conversation would go nowhere. Depending on how the meeting between mother and daughter went, she might casually mention the date to observe their reactions, but that would be all.

†

A little later, on her way to pick up a sandwich before Kate's arrival, Corine passes Richard's door. On an impulse, she knocks.

'Come in,' he calls sternly. When he sees her, his manner immediately lightens. 'Well, hello there. If this is a social visit, it's perfect timing for a spot of lunch.' There's a pile of manila envelopes on his desk, and a letter he's been reading is spread across his laptop keyboard.

'No, sadly it's not a social visit.' Corine walks past Richard's desk, over to the window, and looks up at the small triangle of grey, cloud-filled sky.

She hears him laugh, and turns to see him smiling at her, his head tilted to the side as if puzzled.

'Missing a view or hoping to find one?'

'Would you leave your children in the care of a sociopath without trying to win custody?' Corine asks, ignoring Richard's question.

'Back up a bit, Corine, you're several steps ahead. I don't have kids, so I'm assuming this is hypothetical. Or perhaps you have a particular sociopath in mind?'

'Remember the list of dates Mae gave me? The final date was June twenty-third.'

Richard shrugs. 'She was trying to get a reaction, goading her mother… making it difficult for you. Whatever the date is, it won't be anything positive, but I think you know that already.'

She nods. 'Something happened on that date, or was meant to happen, and it's likely something that Kate doesn't want to discuss. Mae's dad seems to think so too.'

'So why doesn't she just say it? Don't get tangled up in Mae's games, Corine. You're digging up the worst period in her short life—of course she might conflate things. And it sounds like the mother and father are just as bad. The fruit doesn't fall far from the tree.'

'Maybe Mae doesn't remember.'

'We're here to help reveal memories, not implant them. Mae has to recall experiences, not have them suggested to her.'

'Look, Richard, I don't think Mae's suffering from repressed trauma, I think she remembers every painful detail,' Corine snaps, stung by his comment. 'Why else would she be cutting herself? I think the dates might relate to her parents, not Mae directly. I suspect she's spent the last four years trying to forget whatever happened in that house, and now, seeing her family again is forcing her to face that ugliness. Whatever's stopping her from telling the truth is either too appalling to say out loud, or she's bound by some code of silence that I need to break. I think she's hoping that if I spend enough time with her family, I'll see through their lies and uncover the truth. But Mae isn't going to tell us anything. She doesn't see the point.'

'If she has any evidence that could help her, she would have said so. Be careful of chasing false suggestions here.'

Their eyes lock.

Richard sniffs and rubs his finger along the side of his nose. 'It's easy to read meaning where there isn't any,' he says, pushing the papers on his desk away to one side.

Am I being paranoid, or is Richard referring to our night together? Corine hadn't given any false hope—they'd slept together, no more than that. Besides, he had come to her that night. Questions raced through her mind, sparking a complicated blend of confusion, guilt, and the desire to protect herself.

No, Corine reassured herself, *anything else, any expectations or hopes, are his, not mine.*

'It's just as easy to read nothing into silence,' Corine argues. 'If they'd pushed Mae and her family harder back then—refused to let her hide behind silence—perhaps she would have faced up to what she did, dealt with it, and moved on. She'd almost certainly be released by now.'

'We're taught to resist hubris—the temptation to play saviours, to believe we can fix every broken mind, no matter how damaged they are. We can't expect to uncover some single, tragic event that explains everything. Mae is a young woman with impulse-control problems who attacked her mother with a knife. The evidence supported that. She had her day in court.'

'She was just a child, and a damaged one at that. We both know that evidence can be wrong or missed.'

'Agreed, but I'm not sure where you're going with this. The easiest route for everyone is to get her to say sorry, meet the conditions for her parole, and then we can support her in moving on with her life.' Richard pauses for a moment. 'What time is your meeting with her mother?'

Corine looks at her watch. 'Forty minutes. How did you know?'

'I saw that you'd booked a room. Maybe we could have a quick debrief over a bite to eat?' He sees her hesitate. 'My shout.' Richard ducks under his desk. She hears the rustle of a plastic bag and moments later, he pulls out two Tupperware containers. 'Lasagne or lasagne?'

'Oh, the lasagne, thanks.' Relief spreads through her. Her paranoia had given him an ulterior motive—found him guilty when he was simply doing his job and counselling her. 'Why the two portions?'

'I thought you might appreciate a little home cooking.'

†

On the way back to her office, Corine hears the receptionist from the visitor's desk call out. 'We have a Dr Kate Bailey here. She's insisting on seeing you before your scheduled meeting.'

Corine swipes through the pass-protected door and waits in the reception area, curious to hear what Kate doesn't want to say in front of Mae. When Kate arrives, she is noticeably less chatty with the guards than before. The moment she spots Corine, she gets straight to the point.

'I wanted to talk to you about something that's been bothering me—before my next meeting with Mae.'

On top of Kate insisting they meet, something in her tone irritates Corine. She lifts a hand. 'Let's wait until we're in my office, shall we? For privacy sake.' Then she notices a faint tremor in her fingers. Quickly, she lowers her hands and clenches them into fists, willing them to stop shaking. Her stomach sinks—no time to slip into the bathroom for a little pick-me-up.

Inside her office, Corine gestures for Kate to sit and takes her own seat behind her desk. Kate perches upright at the edge of the chair, as if she might change her mind and bolt at any moment. The window behind her is streaked with dirt, it's semi-opaque surface framing her silhouette against the darkening sky.

'What would you like to discuss, Dr Bailey?'

'Kate… please.'

Corine hears a sharpness to Kate's tone, an impatience that doesn't bode well before their meeting with Mae.

'You've been trying to get hold of Lyndsey to discuss Mae and why she attacked me?'

Corine nods cautiously. The irony of her intentions being questioned doesn't go unmissed. She smiles, but Kate remains sour-faced. She rocks forward in her seat, emitting a nervous energy that's almost audible. It puts Corine on edge.

'I should have been honest with you before, but I wanted to protect my daughter and granddaughters. Lyndsey is staying at The Abbey Clinic—receiving therapy. She had a nervous breakdown. The pressure of having two small children—babies really—and a marriage that's far from strong has taken its toll. I mean, Stuart's okay, but he's hardly her rock. Not the sort you could confide in about sexual abuse at the hands of your own father.'

Kate laughs dismissively to herself, rubbing the index finger of her left hand with her right—her gloved hands, Corine notes, with a touch of sympathy.

'That's why I have the children at the moment. A friend is looking after them for me for a few hours, so I came in to ask you to lay off Lyndsey for a while. She's fragile. Bringing up what her father did to her would tip her over the edge. If you could just leave it for a couple of weeks?'

'I'm sorry to hear that. I completely understand, of course. The hearing is next Monday, so I don't imagine I'll get to speak with Lyndsey before then anyway.'

What must it be like, she wonders, *having one daughter in prison and the other in hospital suffering from a mental health crisis?* Being a mother wasn't a certain path, not by any means, and it didn't always guarantee the happy and fulfilled life she liked to imagine.

'I hope things improve for her,' Corine says.

Kate hesitates. 'Thank you.' She sees Corine looking at her gloved hands and slides them into the pockets of her coat. 'Can I ask you a question before we meet with Mae?'

'Sure.'

'Why do you think she cut me out of her life when it was

her father who molested her sister? I mean, I'm joining the dots here, but given what she did to me…'

'She has never accused her father of doing anything sexual to her.'

'It was me who supported her in court,' Kate says indignantly, ignoring Corine's answer. 'I stuck by her when most mothers would have turned their back.'

It strikes Corine then that it must have been like this for Mae growing up, caught between warring parents. Each voicing their own versions of the truth, demanding to be believed.

'I can't give you an answer, Kate. Like I said, Mae hasn't accused anyone.'

'Maybe she feels guilty?'

'In what way?' Corine tries not to pre-empt what Kate's about to say but imagines it will be self-serving.

'Like Mae led him on in some way.' Kate shifts in her seat. 'I've read about that, about children staying quiet because they think they had something to do with it. Like it was somehow their fault.'

'She was nine or ten years old when this was said to have happened, wasn't she? Lyndsey approaching her teens?'

Kate sniffs. Tilts her head sideways. 'When she was ten, she took to dressing up. You know, the way daughters copy their mothers. I remember she had on a little yellow boob tube of her sisters and a pair of tiny shorts.' She laughs. 'She looked ridiculous—the clothes and badly applied make-up. I laughed and told her to get changed. We had friends over, and I didn't want her parading around in barely anything in front of our guests. Frank said something about our little girl growing up—innocently, mind you—and you'd have thought he'd insulted her the way she looked at him. There was an awareness there—accusatory—if you know what I mean. I often wonder, did she become anorexic around that time too? I mean, she got ridiculously thin, but then I was thin at that age, so…'

Corine waits to be sure Kate has finished. Everything about this conversation feels contrived, as though she is being played. It isn't so much that Kate is planting seeds of doubt—or unfurling threads that will lead, if pulled, to Frank. No, there's nothing subtle about her insinuations. She is practically hitting Corine over the head with them. How gullible must she appear?

'Thank you for sharing that. As for your question about her cutting you out of her life, we often blame those closest to us—a sibling, parent, partner, lover—for the things that have gone wrong in our lives. She may come around in time. Getting released is a major transition for her to cope with, and from what you've said, it sounds like Mae has a lot more going on inside her head than she's let on.'

'Does she still hate me?'

'You feel she hates you?' Corine sounds surprised.

Kate shrugs.

'If you feel Mae's release threatens your safety, this is your chance to speak up.'

'Do you think that?' Kate asks suddenly. She takes a tissue and dabs at the tiny beads of sweat forming a perfect line across her furrowed brow.

'I haven't witnessed any threat from Mae. I think her biggest problem is the threat she poses to herself.'

Kate nods, but she seems distracted. 'I often wonder what would have happened had I gone to the police—reported their father. I was stupid. I gave him a second chance, and now he's the only one getting on with his life, the only one not suffering. Loverboy gets to destroy his family—walk away undamaged—and start afresh. And lucky me! I get to pick up all the damaged pieces. Somehow that doesn't seem fair.'

Kate gives a resigned smile, then, just as quickly, her face resets to neutral. The storm inside her had made its presence felt; shifting back and forth between bitterness and confusion, anger and vulnerability.

'It takes time to get over relationships that have broken down,' Corine concedes.

'Tears fall down Kate's cheeks and remain there, unwiped. 'Especially when the other person seems so bloody happy.' She sits with her hands in her lap, looking every bit the rejected wife.

'Mae mentioned that she'd seen her father with another woman before you'd officially separated. She felt that, by telling you, she had somehow made the affair real. That you blamed her for that.'

'I caught them in our bed in broad fucking daylight,' Kate snaps. 'How much more real do you want?'

'I'm sorry. I imagine that was awful.'

Kate shrugs and wipes her face. 'Look, I'm sorry, but I don't think I'm in the right frame of mind to see Mae today. I don't know how I'll react if she pushes me away again.'

'But, Kate, she's expecting you.'

'Sorry. I just can't.'

†

Mae sits across from Corine, shoulders hunched as she twirls a long strand of hair. Corine wonders how much Mae truly understands the sorrow her mother feels over the breakdown of her marriage. She seems unaware—not only of that sorrow but also that her own withdrawal is likely tied to the collapse of their family unit. Her father's affair shattered their sense of security, pulling away parental love—even if only temporarily—as the adults in her life grappled with their own emotional hurt. Mae had linked her feelings of rejection to telling her mother about the affair—an affair Kate already knew about. In Mae's mind, rejection and truth-telling were inseparably entwined, her own role in the family's breakdown tangled in the mix.

'Can I go now?' Mae asks.

'You do understand that cancelling today's meeting was nothing to do with you?'

'I don't care.' Mae's voice is sullen, dismissive.

'You seem very upset for someone who doesn't care.'

'I can't control what she does. Given our history, expecting anything from her would be pointless.'

This one-sided game of ping-pong is becoming tiresome. 'People change, Mae. You, more than anyone, should know that people deserve a second chance.'

Mae doesn't answer right away. Eventually, she leans forward, her hands clasped loosely between her knees. 'You know, even when I refused to speak to her, I liked to imagine what she'd say if she saw how well I was doing in my studies. When I passed my A-Levels, I offered them up to her. Well, a version of her. The same with all the therapy sessions that went well, every word of praise, every positive interaction… it was all for her.'

'You refused to see or talk to her, Mae.'

'Yes, because the reality—the truth—was that I felt happy, and I wanted to stay that way. My imaginary mum, the one who appreciated me—wanted me to be happy—she wasn't Kate.' Mae looks at Corine, a pained expression on her face. 'There is always more than one truth, Corine. I thought you, with your experience, would know that.'

The comment hurt, as Mae intended it to. Why was she pushing her away? Trying to hurt her when she had Mae's best interest at heart?

CHAPTER 21
FRANK

Frank turns off his mobile and sits back slowly. Looking straight ahead at the white wall in front of him, he rests his hands on the edge of the desk as if to steady himself, his upper body rigid. When he glances down, he sees he's written *June 23rd* on a notepad and underlined it several times in black ink.

'Fuck!' he shouts, screwing up the sheet of paper and throwing it towards the bin.

It misses. Has he made matters worse by calling Corine? Caused the opposite of what he'd intended? If it wasn't already, the date would now be on the psychiatrist's radar and, worse still, on Kate's. Mae hadn't said anything about the significance of the date, so it was possible something had happened that he wasn't aware of, or better still, it didn't involve him. As Frank runs through all the scenarios in his mind, a feeling of dread begins to build in his stomach.

A breeze from the open window blows the curtain inwards, brushing against a photograph of Irene. Frank rises for a closer look. The picture had been taken before she got pregnant—her long hair tumbling over her bare shoulders and down her narrow waist. He'd never felt about Kate the way he felt about Irene. Every day with her filled him with a mix of gratitude and exhilaration, a constant awareness that he had narrowly escaped a loveless marriage—loveless on his side, at any rate.

'The date's a coincidence,' Frank tells himself. 'I left in June, that's all it is.' Try as he might, though, he couldn't recall the exact date that he'd walked out. It was possibly June twenty-third, but he couldn't be certain. All memory of his life back then was blurred. The animosity they felt towards each other had reached boiling point, with every interaction hostile, dangerous. Getting away had been the only thing on his mind—a matter of self-preservation.

The thought of returning to that life with Kate—trapped by obligation and guilt—made him shiver. There had always been an undercurrent of resentment in her, as though the world owed her something, and satisfaction was always just out of reach.

Irene's theory was that Kate had grown up in an unstable home, though she hadn't phrased it quite that way. Only when Frank reminded her of how Kate had turned his daughters against him would Irene flare up, furious on his behalf, calling Kate unhinged and all manner of names. Frank smiled tenderly at the memory of her defending him. It felt good to be loved like that—fiercely, passionately. It made him feel untouchable, as if nothing in the world could bring him down.

It also made Frank question the depth of his own feelings. Was he capable of selfless love? He hadn't been with his daughters; it had been far too easy, choosing to protect himself and his reputation, over his girls. Even now, he felt convinced he'd made the only choice he could. Besides, children grew up all the time without both parents, leading normal lives free of drama. The drama had been created by Kate. She was the eye of any storm, with chaos and misery rotating around her.

Walking away from his home—his girls—hadn't been without sacrifice. He'd been lonely at first, missing his daughters and the routine of being a parent. But the longer he maintained distance, the clearer it became that his life with Kate had been a mistake. No doctor should ever underestimate the therapeutic effect of a little respite. Kate had. She'd expected him to come running back with his tail between his legs, ready to put up with her moods, her joylessness, in order to see his girls. To think he almost had. Only to be accused of the unthinkable.

It seemed to Frank, the more Kate achieved in terms of her career, the more resentful she became. As though success in one area of her life took the shine off another. They'd hired a cleaner to come in one day a week to make things easier but, even then, the house was never clean enough. They argued about childcare—drop-offs and pick-ups at nursery, then school and after-school clubs—the endless round of playdates and parties, end of summer terms, leavers dos. For a social person, Kate could be surprisingly antisocial when it came to the girls. "*They see their friends all day in school, I don't see why they need playdates... Can't you go to the assembly? Lyndsey's a fucking tree, for God's sake... I went to sports day last year, it's your turn.... I can't be expected to take time off whenever a teacher thinks one of them has a sniffle.*"

Things eased a little when they employed a nanny, but nothing got resolved. Once, when Lyndsey had chicken pox and the nanny was running late, Kate had demanded Frank wait at home. When he'd remined her he had his annual appraisal that morning, she was less than sympathetic. "*Why bother? You let Craig walk all over you anyway. No wonder the girls are content to be mediocre, they get it from you."*

Sacrifices counted too. She'd never let him forget that he was "lucky to have her." And if he did forget, even in some trivial way—an offhand compliment to another woman or failing to pour her wine first—she would make his transgression known. *"How do you think I feel when you pay someone else's wife all the attention? Everyone noticed how you snubbed me. No wonder none of our friends like you."*

If someone had asked Frank to describe Kate in a single word, it would be dissatisfied, because nothing and no one was ever good enough. Something had to give, and it was usually him. He'd stopped arguing with her after a while—there'd seemed little point. She'd put herself on such a high pedestal that it was only a matter of time before she fell off without any assistance from him.

It wasn't until he left that he understood how much she controlled him. Only then did he realise how Kate had turned the girls against him, determined to punish him for leaving. *Better to be known as the father who left,* Frank thinks, *than to stay and keep taking her abuse.*

His mind drifts and he shivers inwardly, recalling the night she first accused him of molesting Lyndsey. Even now, the memory could suck the air from his lungs. He'd been out late with work colleagues, celebrating a new appointee to the practice. It was after midnight when he'd returned home, expecting her to be in bed. Instead, she was in the kitchen, tight-lipped, scrolling through her phone. He'd poured himself a glass of water and sipped it, waiting.

It was Kate who spoke first. In a flat, matter-of-fact tone, she told him what Lyndsey had accused him of. She could have been telling him that she'd ordered the weekly shop, for all the emotion in her voice.

At first, he'd thought it was her idea of a sick joke. But then she'd said, *"Perhaps you'd like me to wake her so she can repeat what she told me?"* There'd been a cold slyness, a hint of amusement, in her tone that made his stomach twist.

His head had felt as though something had exploded inside—his thoughts scattering into a million disconnected pieces. He'd asked, *"Why? Why would she say that?"* Then, clinging to certainty, he'd denied it outright. Lyndsey would never say such a thing.

"You crept into her room, unzipped yourself, and climbed into—"

He'd lost it then, screamed at her to shut up. His voice cracked with rage and disbelief. Kate had watched him impassively, saying nothing. Then, in the same cold, measured tone, she'd asked him to leave.

Frank hadn't needed to be asked twice. He'd stuffed a clean shirt into an overnight bag, called a taxi, and somehow managed to give his parents' address. He'd arrived on their doorstep during the early hours, hollow-eyed and badly shaken. His parents, already aware their relationship could be volatile, had assumed it was just another row, expecting a reconciliation in a day or two.

Frank had stood in their bathroom, staring at his own reflection and wept. That's when he noticed it—a smear of red lipstick. Just an innocent peck on the cheek from a colleague.

Or the spark that ignited everything.

Now that he thought about it, if Kate had seen the lipstick all those years ago, there was no way she would have let it pass, not without some kind of retaliation. It hadn't even crossed Frank's mind until now that Lyndsey's accusation might have been Kate's idea of revenge.

An aeroplane passes overhead, and he closes his eyes, listening until the roar fades into uneasy silence. 'Please... please don't let her know about Irene's baby,' he whispers into the empty room. 'She'll make our lives hell.'

Frank leans forwards, resting his forehead against the cool glass, and allows his shoulders to sag.

The sound of the chain flushing reminds him he isn't alone. Today is the first day of Irene's maternity leave. She was the reason he'd lied to Corine, out of a desire to protect her from Kate's poison. Not that Irene couldn't look after herself; she had come to a foreign country alone, found a job, became fluent in the language, and then qualified to become a teacher. She was strong when she needed to be. Never frightened to speak out, to say what was on her mind. Never cruel or dishonest. Not even when tempers flared.

A banging noise startles him. He looks out of the window, but the noise is closer, coming from inside the flat. Frank walks to the door and listens. It's coming from the nursery.

He'd told Irene a version of that night—missing out the accusation of sexual molestation. Her first thoughts had been for the girls. *"Did they hear all the arguments? They were so young; it must have been devastating for them."*

If she only knew, Frank thinks. The girls had always heard—of course they had—but it was never spoken about. Kate had been a firm believer of the old adage: "Children should be seen and not heard." And look how that had turned out.

Frank took no pleasure in the attack—none whatsoever—but Kate had brought it all on herself. No one could live up to her impossible standards. He couldn't change the past, but he would do everything in his power to shield Irene from her unwanted attention.

Frank follows the banging sound to the newly decorated nursery and finds Irene hammering a row of picture hooks into the wall behind the cot.

'I could have helped you with that.'

'Surprise!' she sings, ignoring his comment. There are three picture frames inside the cot, each containing black and white images.

'Oh, sweetheart… you've framed the scans?' Frank reaches into the cot and picks up a frame, his mouth breaking into a wide smile.

'That's the first picture of your baby boy, the dating scan, and this one.' Irene hands him another. 'This is the twenty-one weeks, and I've got the one from a few weeks ago, when we finally got the all-clear. Aren't they precious?'

There had been concerns over the growth of their baby, so Irene had been given a few extra precautionary scans. Thankfully no anomalies had been detected and the baby was following a normal, if smaller than average, growth trajectory.

'They're beautiful.' Frank pulls her to him and brushes her cheek with the back of his hand. 'He's going to be beautiful, inside and out, just like his mama.'

Irene shakes her head. 'I just want everything to be okay with our little one, that's all I pray for right now.'

When she looks up at him, Frank can see she's been crying.

So many raging pregnancy hormones, hopes and fears.

'He'll be perfect,' Frank assures her. 'To think he'll be lying in there in less than a month.'

'June twenty-third, God willing,' Irene says. 'I'm not sure I can wait, and yet I'm as nervous as hell. The closer we get, the more I worry—even after the all-clear. What if the doctors missed something? Oh, God,' Irene groans, holding her hands together in prayer. 'Please let my boy be healthy. That's all I ask. Nothing else—just that. And I will love him no matter what.'

Frank hugs her close, grateful for this second chance.

CHAPTER 22
CORINE

On the way back from the equine centre the next day, Corine receives a text from Richard: Kate had called. She was ready to meet with Mae again, and a room was already booked for the meeting. The news unsettled Corine. Why hadn't Kate called her directly? Such short notice was less than ideal—it gave her no time to prepare Mae.

The equine therapy session had gone well, though, and Mae's mood had lifted somewhat after managing to get an untethered Maisie to follow her into the corralled area. Perhaps she'd take some of the lessons in patience and trust from today's session and apply them to her mother?

Corine and Mae are sitting side by side at the rear of the minibus. The guard is up front, discussing routes with the driver. Traffic slows as cars pass police dealing with a minor collision.

Before Corine can tell her about her mother, Mae turns to her.

'Do you think Fiona was just saying all that stuff to make me feel good?' she asks.

'No, of course not! You've achieved an immense amount in a short space of time—you're a natural. Animals can sense your intentions, and Maisie was comfortable with you. She trusted you. You should be proud of the progress you made,'

Corine assures her. 'They were wise conclusions you drew from the session, and Fiona was genuinely impressed. You should consider working with animals.'

Mae crosses her arms and laughs. It's a self-deprecating one, but Corine can tell she's secretly delighted.

'Who'd give someone like me a chance—an ex-con? I'm tarnished?

'That's an interesting choice of word… tarnished.'

Mae shakes her head. 'Oh no, don't start picking up on every word I say, or I won't say anything.'

'There are people out there willing to give you a chance. You've just got to believe in yourself. Like Fiona said, it's all about trust.'

Mae's face suddenly breaks into a smile. 'Fiona told me about a little girl with autism who came to the centre. Her and her classmates—all from a special school—were asked to get an untethered horse inside a corralled area a few metres from where they were standing. So, they tried all sorts of things, but this one little girl didn't engage at all. She stood to one side, close by, not even looking. Apparently, she rarely engaged and didn't talk much, even though she could.

'But then, as time went on and the other children backed off, this girl walked up to the horse, reached up on her toes, threw her arms around its neck, and started slowly walking backwards towards the corral. She didn't stop until she had the horse inside. Everyone was amazed—including a psychology professor who was there to run a study. They were busy discussing theories about non-verbal communication between humans and animals… or something like that.'

Mae pauses, eyes bright with amusement. 'Anyway, after

a while, the girl's mother came over. She'd been watching from outside the field. When the professor said he'd like her daughter to return, that she clearly had an incredible bond with the horse, the mum looked a bit sheepish. She suggested they try doing the next session earlier. She knew, just from the way her daughter had grabbed the poor pony, that the child just wanted to go home for lunch. That was it. No special bond. She was just hungry.'

Mae laughs, genuinely tickled by the revelation. 'Her actions had nothing to do with empathy or some profound connection with the horse. It was just standing between her and her cheese-and-pickle sandwich.' She laughs again, her whole face momentarily alight.

Corine chuckles. 'Can you imagine their conclusions if the mother hadn't been there? Hilarious.' It feels good to see Mae happy, though she is more than aware that the joke is making fun of her profession and, to a point, Corine herself.

'We're guessing at people's intentions most of the time, though, aren't we?' There's a coolness to Mae's voice as she crosses her arms and looks up at the ceiling, sighing. 'You can't really know anyone.'

'That's where trust and experience come in.' Corine's phone rings and Lisa's number flashes up on the screen. She would call her later when she was alone in her office. 'Listen, Mae, your mum has turned up at The Orchard; she wants to talk when we get back. It might not be a bad idea. Perhaps you can get a few things off your chest before the final meeting. What do you say? Give her another chance?'

'If that's what you think I should do,' Mae replies with a dry smile. 'I'll trust you.'

She turns her attention to the window and remains that way for the rest of the journey.

†

Kate stands when Mae and Corine enter the meeting room. She looks different with make-up on, her hair flatter than usual—presumably the result of the black woollen hat she holds in her hands. A long black coat lays discarded over one of the bucket chairs.

Mae sits opposite without acknowledging her mother.

'Thank you for agreeing to see me. I wasn't sure if, well, at such short notice… but I know how important it is that we speak,' Kate says, looking at Corine. 'Especially as our last meeting is next week—before the parole hearing. These two weeks will fly by and, well, then you'll be out.' She smiles at Mae.

Corine expects Mae to speak; when she doesn't, she finds herself filling in the silence, covering for her. 'That's not a problem, Kate, we know how busy you are with your job and the grandchildren. Take a seat. I'll see if I can get us all a drink. Ruth will be outside—the door stays open—as per the rules.' Corine catches Mae's eye. 'You might want to tell your mum about Maisie; how well you got on today.'

'Oh, is Maisie a friend, darling?' Kate asks, sitting back down.

'Yeah, but she's a bit on the horsey side.' With a sly smile, Mae lowers herself further into the chair, her legs straight, crossed at the ankles. 'Great listener, though.'

'Maisie's a horse, but I'll let Mae explain. I won't be long.'

Corine gives Mae a knowing smile, but she smirks back at her in a way that she knows won't go unnoticed by Kate.

Outside the room, she has a word with Ruth, the guard on duty. 'Be discreet. Watch her, but you don't need to listen to everything.'

This was an exercise in trust, and she hopes Mae will see it that way.

†

MAE

Mae watches as Kate takes off her cardigan, folds it neatly, and places it over her coat. She observes her every move. It seems to Mae that she's buying time, deciding where to start.

Kate smiles across at her daughter, touching the sides and back of her hair. 'I've been worrying about where you'll go after you're granted parole.'

'*If* I'm granted parole. Where I go after I get out isn't something you need to worry about.'

'That's like telling me not to breathe. You're my daughter, of course I'll worry about you. I can't just switch that part of me off.'

Mae sits up, glances towards the open door, then quickly back. 'Oh, come on, Kate, stop playing games, it's just me here. I've apologised in public. You just have to say you're happy with it, after which, we both sign statements to that effect, and we walk away from this and go our separate ways. Four years later for me, but—'

'I'm devastated about those years you lost. Please tell me

you know that. I haven't slept properly since the day you were sentenced.' Her hands are clasped together, like a penitent praying.

Mae looks sceptical. 'It hasn't all been bad in here, I've had some good times. Got my exams, made friends... well, one. She's like family to me—a sister.' Her stomach lurches at the thought of their recent argument and the fact that Mal would, most likely, forget her once she transferred.

Kate leans forward, a shift in her expression. 'Lyndsey can't wait to see you. She talks about you all the time.'

Mae's face hardens. 'I find that difficult to believe since she hasn't stepped foot in here.'

'She had her reasons,' Kate argues, springing to Lyndsey's defence. 'Post-natal depression for one. Both times, and—'

'And so do I,' Mae interrupts. 'I have my reasons for never wanting to see her.'

'What your father did to Lyndsey destroyed her. That evil bastard tore everything apart. Everything has been a struggle for her since then, just trying to function, looking after her two little ones. I can't tell you how hard it's been. Her poor girls...'

'Look, I'm sorry for all that, especially for her daughters, but I sort of don't have the space for Lyndsey right now.' Mae realises what she's said and giggles. 'You know, being here...'

Kate clears her throat, ignoring Mae's comment. 'She asks after you, no matter how ill she is. We both know she's always been the less able one—not academic, not practical, and certainly not resilient. After what your father did, and now this...' Kate gestures towards her face, then stands abruptly and turns away, as though she can't bear for Mae to look at her scars for a moment longer. 'She's not well right now; I'm not even sure you'd recognise her. I've got her in therapy—for all the good that seems to be doing. She's getting worse, not better. Lyndsey needs support… family. And I worry about those babies of hers. If she could get it off her chest—say out loud what he did to her and see him pay—I think she might finally start to heal.'

'I'm sorry for Lyndsey, I really am, and I can't quite believe I'm saying that after everything.' Mae sighs and looks up at the ceiling. 'That desire to always please, it's a design flaw in her. In both of us.'

'Right.' Kate laughs. She flicks her hair behind her ears and walks back to her seat. 'You don't have to tell me about trying to please. I know more about that than anyone, and yet despite always doing my best, bending over backwards for your father, he up and leaves. Commitment, marriage vows, family, none of it meant anything to him. But a mother can't just walk away, not when children are involved. Not like your father did. Yet he's the one who gets to start all over again. New partner, a baby on the way. A boy, for Christ's sake, after all my years of trying.'

'You wanted a boy?' Mae blurts out, incredulous.

Kate gingerly takes hold of Mae's hands and draws them towards her. 'I had you and your sister, but a father always wants a son. Someone in their own likeness to shape and mould. He always joked about being the odd one out—D'Artagnan to the three musketeers—but there was an element of truth in that. My own father was the same.' Kate sighs and leans her head to one side, looking directly at Mae. 'Frank's got what he always wanted now, though, so we won't hear from him again.'

'I didn't think you'd want to hear from him, not after what

Lyndsey accused him of.' Mae frowns, pulling her hands away.

Kate looks into Mae's eyes. 'Darling, if he did do anything to you, please don't keep it secret. It will only come back to haunt you... your sister is proof of that. Whatever you remember, he deserves to be held accountable. I swear, I will see to it that he pays for everything that you've lost. He's the reason our lives turned out this way. I blame him for everything... for this.' She touches her face with both hands.

'I don't remember anything.'

'Don't you?'

'No.' Mae is adamant. She absently pulls at the cuffs of her sweatshirt.

'Not even that time when you were about nine years old, and I took Lyndsey out and left you asleep? You cried and said someone had come into your room.' Kate hesitates. 'Was it him?'

'You didn't listen to me then, so why now?'

'I'm so sorry, I should have listened to you, darling. If I had, maybe none of this would have happened and you'd be living your life.' Kate clasps Mae's hands to her lips, kissing them with the lightest touch. 'Forgive me.'

Mae slowly withdraws her hands, silent. It takes all her effort to control the tiny explosions that her mother's words have triggered in her mind.

†

While most patients are in the TV or games room, enjoying the final hour before lights out, Mae lies on her bed, the door partially open. Every now and again she hears shouts and cheering from an increasingly competitive table tennis match.

The meeting with her mother had started a loop of negative thoughts in her head that wouldn't be silenced. She tries to read, but soon gives up. Not even a new book by her favourite author manages to free her of her mother's words.

She closes her eyes, picturing her hand gliding over Maisie's mane—the short hair along her face, down her neck, and along the length of her strong, muscular back—when a loud knock startles her.

'What's up? You sick or something?' Mal asks as she breezes into the room. They haven't spoken since the pizza night and the atmosphere between them remains tense.

Mal lifts Mae's feet and squeezes onto the end of the bed.

'Just not in the mood,' Mae replies.

'Tell me about it.' Mal picks her nails, waiting for a reply and getting none. 'No, I mean, tell me about it.'

'Oh!' Mae laughs softly. 'There's nothing to tell. Seriously, I'm just tired.'

'Okay.' Mal nods, her eyes and corner of her mouth raised sceptically. 'But the mouth's sayin' one thing and the face another.'

'Didn't you have your big meeting today?' Mae asks, dodging her question. She knew that by avoiding their quarrel, she was merely skirting the obstruction—but there was nothing to be gained from ogling a car wreck. 'Don't suppose they said anything worth hearing? They never do.'

'Wrong,' Mal says and smiles secretively.

Mae knew that if she waited long enough, her friend would talk. Mal never could keep anything quiet.

'I have a transfer date for a low secure unit near home. I'm getting day release!'

Mae sits up. 'No way! When?'

'Day after tomorrow!' Mal squeals and Mae immediately pulls her into a hug. 'I've just come off the phone with Dad. He was crying like a baby. Kept saying all Mum's prayers had been answered.' Mal's eyes sparkle, a smile stretching the width of her face. 'I'm not sure who the fuck she's been praying to, or when she got all religious on me.' She laughs. 'But who cares? I'm out of here!'

'I can't believe it, I mean, I'm so happy for you,' Mae exclaims before they hug again.

Mal jumps around the small room, punching the air in celebration.

Mae watches her, forcing herself to smile. 'God, I wasn't expecting it. Wow! So soon.'

'You'll be out in no time, don't worry. You just focus on that, babe.'

Mae closes her eyes for a moment. They're teary when she opens them. 'I don't want to.' Her voice sounds broken. 'I mean, what's the point of me getting out? I'll always be the girl who knifed her own mother— left her scarred and disfigured—and if it wasn't for my sister's boyfriend calling an ambulance, she would have bled to death. It won't matter to anyone if I never have another psychotic episode again, what matters is that I *could*.' Mae sniffles as Mal puts an arm around her shoulder. 'What I did means I'm capable of doing the unthinkable. I *did* the unthinkable. People will assume the worst of me, and I don't blame them. If you let go once, who's to say you won't again? There're no guarantees, no simple cures for psychopathy.'

'Don't exaggerate, you're no more a psycho than I am.'

Mal's reassurances remind Mae that her friend's mum had always blamed herself for her daughter's situation—for both her children's failings. She had uprooted them, after all, moved them to a foreign country, expected them to fit in to a life that only she had dreamed of.

'I used to be frightened whenever they brought someone new in here. Why should I expect any different on the outside? I'm a risk, no matter how good I've been throughout my sentence. I'm like those notices they put on food: *May contain traces of nuts*. I should come with a warning—danger, could attack when agitated. I should get it tattooed here, in a big red triangle.' Mae thumps her forehead. 'And if my mother goes to the police, which is starting to sound likely, I'll also be someone whose father molested her... not that I remember, but that probably indicates that my brain's not right, or something worse. Oh, and get this, if only I'd been a boy, because apparently that's what my father wanted. That's why it was so easy for him to walk away and disappear from our lives like we'd never existed.'

'Girl, you need to calm the fuck down. You've gone puce, and I don't want you explodin' all over my favourite outfit.' Mal pretends to brush down her standard-wear prison sweatshirt with a flourish.

Mae gives a half-hearted smile and is about to speak, when Mal raises her hands. 'It might have been brought to your attention at some point during your stay in here that I stabbed my dealer, but do you think I'm gonna let a detail—a nano second like that—screw up my entire future? Don't let none of that stuff spoil yours either, or I'll fucking kill you, do you hear me?'

'I hear you,' Mae says, wiping a tear away. 'But mother and dealer… just saying.'

'Meh, they're both just six letter words, hon, that's all.'

Mae laughs. 'God, I really did fool myself that we'd be here forever.'

'Now that *is* crazy!' Mal looks at her steadily, concerned. 'Look, when you catch a sniff of a date, you'll start lookin' forward to your freedom. I can almost taste it—it's sweet and tangy like lemon sorbet with one of those little caramel wafers on the side.'

Mae wrinkles her nose. 'They're about five hundred calories. Careful on the outside, or you'll get fat.'

'Remember what the therapists say about prison being in here.' Mal taps her forehead. 'You need to move on, babe. Start seeing a future.'

It seems unreal to Mae, but in a few short days, Mal won't be in her life anymore. The thought is more than she can bear. Sliding her hands into the pockets of her joggers, she drives her nails hard into her thighs.

'It won't be the same in here without you.'

'I know.'

'I may just have to accelerate my own exit from this place.'

'Now you're talking.' Mal sits forward, her eyes wide. 'Prison break. Two, max three guards each, no problem.' She throws two sharp left hooks and slumps back down, laughing to herself.

I'm nothing to her, Mae thinks. Just as she's about to say something, the first warning for lights out is called. They both groan in unison. Mal heaves herself up and off the bed. With a quick wave of her hand, she leaves.

Fully dressed, Mae slides under the covers and curls into a ball, overwhelmed by a feeling that she doesn't matter to anyone, not even her best friend.

CHAPTER 23
CORINE

Corine's mobile phone buzzes on the bedside table. Barely awake, she reaches out and knocks over an empty wine bottle. It crashes onto the laminate bedside table and lands with a hollow thud on the carpeted floor. Cursing to herself, she grabs her phone and fumbles to unlock it.

'Yes?' she asks, expecting the call to be Callum with more news about the farm. Maybe she should sell it to him after all?

'Sorry to call you at this time, Corine, but Mae's been hospitalised,' Richard says. 'Attempted suicide. She asked for you.'

'Oh God! How bad is it?' Corine sits up. As she does, her head starts to spin, a growing queasiness forming in her stomach.

'She slit both wrists.' Richard hesitates. 'With intent.'

'Jesus... how could I have missed that?' She feels overcome with a sudden hopeless fatigue. *I let her down when she needed me. God, just give me another chance to make this right,* she begs the universe. *Please let her be okay.*

'It's not your fault, Corine, don't start blaming yourself. Besides, Mae's been seen here by the same team of people since she arrived, and no one saw it coming. I don't have enough staff available when two patients are struggling, and right now I have *four* on enhanced observation. If two or three kick off together, you've got a threat to patient care.' He sighs down the line heavily.

'I can't believe it. She seemed to be doing so well, enjoying the horse therapy, and she was just beginning to open up. Fuck!' Corine screws up the bedsheet in her fist.

'Poor kid.' Richard sounds close to tears.

Corine hears him clear his throat before continuing.

'It'll delay her release. Not that she's clinically ready—but when she is, she'll need a carefully planned step-down package. Twenty-four hour supported living is a given now, and there's not much of that around at the moment.'

'Can we talk about this later?' Corine asks. 'I'd like to see her first.'

She knows Richard means well, focusing on what they can do for Mae, but it doesn't stop her feeling sick with guilt. How had she missed the true extent of Mae's vulnerability? Had she asked the wrong questions? Most likely she had been too caught-up in her own problems to notice what was in front of her eyes.

'God, it's been difficult enough trying to get her a properly funded community placement given her history of self-harm,' she murmurs to herself. 'Now it will be even worse.'

'Corine!' Richard's voice is edged with concern. 'It's not your fault. Don't assume the blame or look for it when it's not there. Not everything is within your control.'

'I'm on my way.'

Corine ends the call but remains staring into the blackness beyond the bed, waiting for her eyes to adapt. It takes every ounce of self-control not to scream. She breathes out slowly, deliberately, and forces herself to focus on the sound of a car passing the hotel, its tyres sending out wet spray across the road. A sharp screech, as it rounds a corner too fast.

Then she's aware of someone else in the room—of shallow, laboured breathing. The hairs on the back of her neck bristle. In the darkness, the outline of a man shifts in the corner. Her heart thuds.

'Joe?' Her voice is barely audible.

'You're not her mum.' His voice is strong, undamaged. 'You'll destroy everything if you go to her. How many times do you need to hear that?'

'Not now!' Corine shouts, jumping out of bed. She rushes into the bathroom, banging her shoulder and arm against the door frame. She slams the door, grappling for the light switch.

Corine's eyes close as she clings onto the vanity unit to steady herself, afraid of what she'll see if she opens her eyes. When she does, she lets out a low groan at the sight of her uncombed hair, mascara trailing down beneath her eyes. Retching, Corine sucks her dry lips and swallows hard, trying to stop herself from being sick. It doesn't work. It's nothing but liquid and bile, but it comes up with such force that she feels she might pass out. Turning on the tap, she waits for the water to run cold, then drinks.

Looking at her face in the mirror, she whispers, 'She needs you to step up.'

Corine bites down on her bottom lip and glances back at the door, gripped by an irrational fear of being overheard.

After showering, she does her best to make herself presentable and heads outside, refusing to look at the space where she'd imagined Joe. She tries to focus on Mae, on what she can change. Seeing Joe again is a backwards step; a warning that she needs to address her own grief.

Rushing past reception, she hears someone asking if she slept well, but she's moving too quickly to respond. She hails a cab on the street, and when it pulls up, she is struck once again by the relentless pace of city life.

Her younger self had found living and working in central London exhilarating—an endless rush of adrenaline. The constant forward propulsion felt safe, like a bowling ball rolling down a lane with the bumpers up. Everything had fallen neatly into place: her career, the promotions, her first flat, getting engaged to Joe, their first home together, then marriage.

Until, when she'd least expected it, it all came undone. Suddenly, London—and everything and everyone in it—felt like the wrong choice. Joe used to say, *"Never look back"*, but what if looking back was all Corine had?

Suddenly, Corine feels an overwhelming surge of heat. She reaches to open a window just as her stomach contracts and bile fills her mouth. Pulling a tissue from her jacket pocket, she spits quietly into it. Relieved that the cab driver's eyes remain fixed on the road ahead.

†

The staff are expecting Corine. When she arrives, she is immediately shown to Mae's room. A nurse sits beside the bed as Mae sleeps, her face pale, her wrists wrapped in bandages.

'I'll sit with her until she wakes up,' Corine says.

The nurse nods, squeezing her arm gently. 'I'll keep checking in.'

The simple, comforting gesture touches her. Everyone wants the best for their patients.

Corine stands at the end of the hospital bed, watching the steady rise and fall of Mae's chest. She notices the sharp angles of her cheekbones, the hollowness beneath them, the bluish shadows under both eyes—and the faint, natural upward curve of her lips.

Part of her wants to climb in beside Mae, to offer comfort. The other part wants to shake her awake and demand an explanation. Not just about the suicide attempt, but for the attack on her mother. Why would she try to end her life now, just as it was about to begin?

Even if she didn't get parole, she would be out soon. She was still young enough to make a go of life—meet someone, fall in love, have a family. Mae had so much to live for, and yet she couldn't see it.

Why?

Easing herself into the visitors chair next to the bed, Corine reminds herself to remain professional. Distance was necessary. *You won't be any good to her if you get all emotional*, she warns herself. Her head aches and it's difficult to think straight with the constant throbbing. Reaching into her bag, she takes out two tablets, swallowing them without water. All the while, her eyes remain fixed on her fragile patient.

Mae sleeps for hours, and eventually Corine doses off. She is woken by voices outside at the nurses' station—the morning shift handover, most likely. Cups rattle as the tea trolley is rolled by and the ward slowly awakens.

Mae's eyes flicker open.

'You came,' she says, her voice barely above a whisper.

'Of course.' Corine smiles and takes hold of Mae's delicate hand. A child's hand.

Mae smiles weakly. A little colour has returned to her cheeks, but she's still unnaturally pale.

'Can I get you anything?' Corine asks.

'Some water, please.'

Corine fills the jug with fresh water and pours a small amount into a plastic cup. She helps Mae sit, holding the cup to her lips until she's had enough.

'Are you in any pain?'

Mae shakes her head. 'I don't feel anything,' she says. 'That's the problem.'

'Mae...' Corine whispers.

It's one syllable, but it's imbued with so much emotion that it makes Mae look away. Corine wants to hug her, to say sorry, but aside from being unprofessional, it would be admitting guilt, and she knew Richard would have something to say about that.

'How long have you been thinking about ending things?'

Mae shrugs and looks down at the bed.

Corine sighs quietly. She knows that she hides things from people too—from Lisa, Richard, and herself—so why should Mae be any different? It's like a game of chess, with both players trying to see several moves ahead, expecting a surprise attack, feeling vulnerable.

'We think no one will understand, or that we'll be unfairly judged if we say how we're feeling. But you don't have to carry those feelings alone.'

'I don't know...' Mae turns her head away, not wanting to engage. Outside the barred window, the sky is a dark, graphite grey—not a trace of warmth to be found. 'I don't know how I'm supposed to feel about anything.' Her voice is flat, desolate.

Another rush of guilt hits Corine like a wave. She'd been so preoccupied with the possibility of Mae being a danger to others that she'd missed the danger she posed to herself. She had a job to do, and instead she'd wallowed in her own selfish needs—drinking herself senseless. Last night had been no different; Corine had kept drinking until she'd crashed out. Christ, she was probably still drunk now. What was she thinking?

'I'm so sorry, Mae. I should have seen that things were bad for you.'

'Things weren't… not for a long time. And then… I don't know.' Mae closes her eyes. 'I feel so confused.'

'Are you able to talk about what you were doing or thinking before you did this? Did something… anything happen to upset you?'

'Not really. I saw the hair clip and I… I used it.' After a few moments, she tilts her head sideways and asks, 'Do you love anyone?'

Corine smiles. 'Well, yes, I do, I suppose.'

'Do they love you back?'

Corine watches Mae. 'Is this about your mother?'

'I don't know!' Mae cries. 'I don't know what I thought would change. I hoped things would be different—that she'd finally see me as a person.' She squeezes her eyes shut and shakes her head again. 'I can't believe I was actually excited to tell her about my A-Levels. What an idiot! I could have said I'd earned a first-class degree in biochemistry—it wouldn't have made any difference. She doesn't see me. It's all about *her*. Everything is about Kate.

Her voice cracks. 'She could have divorced Dad years ago. Why now? Why announce it now, just as I'm getting out? That's the only reason she came to see me yesterday. It wasn't about putting things right. She doesn't care.'

'It sounds like you feel she still puts her needs before yours—expects you to take responsibility for how she feels. That's a lot of pressure to put on your children, whatever their age.'

'I remember once—a few days before report cards were due to go home—I was trying to talk to her.' Mae pauses 'I don't know, maybe I wanted to prepare her because I was having trouble concentrating at school? She said, "*Wow, sounds like me. Doctors should be prescribed painkillers just to help them listen to all the bullshit people complain about*".'

'That's harsh. How did she react when you got your report card?'

'She said, "*The one thing you have to do, and you fuck it up.*" She didn't speak to me afterwards, not for a couple of weeks. Didn't prepare meals, do my washing... anything.'

'How did you feel?'

'Confused. Lyndsey never did well at school. She used to say Lyndsey wasn't blessed with brains, but that always felt like a cop out. Like it would have been harder work to challenge her... an effort. It felt like Kate expected nothing from her and everything from me. Or at least no hassle from me whilst she focused on Lyndsey.'

'That's a lot of pressure on you. You were coming up to your GCSE exams when the attack happened. Do you think it was the pressure?'

Mae doesn't answer.

'Exams alone are a lot to deal with.'

'No. It wasn't that.' Mae looks disappointed.

'What, then?'

'She was angry with me before that, my school performance was just an excuse.'

'Why was she angry before?'

'I already told you… I saw Dad with another woman. She resented me for that; telling her, causing all the trouble.'

'Your father's affair did that. Besides, Kate told me she already knew about the relationship.'

Mae looks straight at Corine and her pale cheeks tighten. 'I need to talk to Dad. If he came to visit me, would we be allowed some time alone?'

'I'm not sure that would be a good idea just yet.'

'Please, Corine! It's not as if I'd do anything. Look at me, I haven't got the energy to stand, never mind attack him.'

That wasn't what Corine was worried about. Mae's vulnerability right now was high, and what with the allegations against her father, it could make matters worse. If that were even possible.

'I'll see what I can do. In the meantime, you need to rest. I'll be back in to see you later when your head's a little clearer.' Corine takes Mae's hand and gives it a light squeeze. 'I can sit with you until you fall asleep, if you'd like?'

Mae's eyes finally meet hers. 'I'll be okay. Don't worry about me.' She holds Corine's hand, her grip weak. 'I promise you the risk of me trying to kill myself again is low. About one in ten chance.'

'I'd prefer zero,' Corine says, but smiles. Of course Mae knew the questions Corine would need to ask as her psychiatrist. She'd been a suicide risk since her early teens. 'And where would you say your desire to live was, with one being no desire and ten—'

'About a five, maybe six.'

'Okay.' Corine smiles gently. 'Don't ever feel like that's your only option again, do you hear me?'

'Yeah.' Mae looks down at the bedsheets. 'But haven't you ever thought it would be easier?'

'Once, perhaps. But it's not the answer. If you ever feel like that again, promise me you'll call me.'

Mae nods.

'I'm going to let you rest right now, but we can talk some more later today.' She watches Mae's eyes struggle to stay open. 'Your brain is telling you you're in pain and we need to listen to it.' *Asking the right questions would be a start*, she scolds herself.

Mae doesn't respond. Her eyes close, her breathing slows as she drifts into sleep. Corine backs out of the room quietly. As soon as she's outside, a guard takes her place, sitting on the chair that holds Mae's door open. *Too little, too late*, Corine thinks.

Corine approaches the nurses' station and waits for the nurse to finish her phone call. 'Just a minute, please,' the nurse says to whoever is on the line, glancing up at Corine.

'Don't leave her,' she insists. 'Not for a minute.'

'Yes, of course,' the nurse replies. 'I've got her mother on the phone. She's asking to visit Mae.'

'I don't think that's a good idea just yet, but I'll ask Mae.'

Corine walks back to the room and stands in the doorway. Mae's eyes are still closed.

'Mae… Mae,' she calls gently.

Mae's eyes flicker open.

'Your mum just called, asking to see you.'

'No! No!' she whimpers, shaking her head. 'I don't want to see her.'

'Okay, that's fine, you don't have to. Get some rest and I'll let the nurse know.'

The look of fear on Mae's face bothers Corine. *So much for establishing family ties before release.* What power did Kate hold over her daughter? Parental love could be controlling, she knew that, but neglectful parenting could be poisonous too. Mae's parents seemed to fall into both categories—Frank's non-involvement versus Kate's manipulative behaviour—both damaging, especially in a child's formative years.

Outside the hospital ward, Corine stops at a vending machine and gets herself a black coffee. It's weak, but she sips it gratefully. She sits, staring into space, in need of a minute or two to gather her thoughts; to plan her next steps. Corine looks at her watch, but it's too early to call Richard; she'll see him in an hour or so at work anyway.

Something had destabilised Mae, and in all likelihood, Kate was involved. Letting her speak to Mae alone had been a mistake. Corine feels angry with herself, and Kate. If she wasn't the devastated mother she pretended to be, then it had all been smoke and mirrors, and Corine had fallen for the act.

Was Mae's suicide attempt a cry for attention? Did Kate truly keep one of her daughters at arm's length while focusing on the other? Did she really blame Mae for revealing the cracks in her marriage?

It feels as it everything Corine once took for fact is suddenly uncertain.

She'd always believed that giving birth had changed everything. There was a before Michael and an after. From the moment his tiny body was placed in her arms, he mattered more than anything or anyone else—herself and Joe included. Had he lived, Michael would have had their unconditional love. She had always been sure of that.

She thinks about the dates Mae had given her—the bank of negative memories she drew upon. The only possibilities Mae imagined were awful ones. She had mentioned her mother withholding affection, unfairly criticising her, setting sister against sister. It was no wonder Mae's self-worth had been damaged.

Corine sighs. She must get to the bottom of the sexual allegations against Mae's father, otherwise a huge piece of the jigsaw—possibly the key piece—would be missing.

Poor Mae, growing up without a parent she felt she could trust. Feeling alone.

At that moment, Corine vividly recalled sitting in Michael's bedroom, staring into the empty cot and wishing she could disappear. Joe had entered, his voice edged with irritation as he asked her to come back to bed.

"You need sleep," he'd said.

She had turned abruptly to face him. *"Will it bring Michael back? Because that's the only thing that would make this miserable existence worthwhile. I don't want to be here anymore."*

The look on Joe's face had been like someone forced to relive the worst moments of their life over again. She had been cruel to him.

Corine closes her eyes, steadying herself against the familiar hollowing sensation of shame. She hadn't cared about Joe's pain back then, refusing to share her loss with him, denying his feelings as though she were the only one that mattered. Worse still, she had repeated that behaviour, and not just in the early months, but on and off for years. It was remarkable Joe had stood by her, shouldering her abuse, her anger and grief, as his burden. She had carried her anger and sadness around, nurturing it like a phantom pregnancy.

'You never gave up on me,' she whispers.

She thinks of Mae. Imagines trying to start a young life devoid of hope—with no one having your back. The very definition of alone.

CHAPTER 24
CORINE

Corine returns to the hotel to freshen up before heading to The Orchard. As she enters the room, she sniffs the stale air. Glancing at her watch, she feels relieved—it's still early, too early for housekeeping. Her eyes skim across the devastated room, as though seeing the mess for the first time. She unlocks a window, but it barely makes a difference; the small opening lets in a flood of noxious petrol fumes and smoke.

A siren screams somewhere down below, setting Corine's pulse racing, as though someone had jumped out and surprised her. *Mary would do that*, she recalls. Right up until Corine escaped to university, leaving her sister to look after their father alone.

The realisation about what her sister had taken on—the complete responsibility for their father's depression—hits Corine like a blow to her chest.

'I was ungrateful,' she mutters to herself.

She takes a plastic laundry sack from the wardrobe, snatches up her dirty clothes, and stuffs them inside. Next, she empties the miniature bottles from the fridge into a separate plastic bag and places them beside the laundry bag near the front door. She will ask the hotel staff not to restock her fridge.

As she clears away a pizza box and other debris littering

the bed, the hotel phone rings.

'I have a friend of yours in reception, a Kate Bailey here to see you. Shall I send her up?'

'What? No, I'll come down.'

She wonders how Kate knew about the hotel. Had she let slip where she was staying? Perhaps she'd mentioned it to Mae, and she'd said something to Kate? Whichever way she'd found out, it was highly irregular.

Kate is waiting for her outside the lift. She doesn't bother with a greeting.

'Why is Mae refusing to see me? I went to the hospital, but I was asked to leave.'

The receptionist glances up and away quickly.

'Let's talk outside.'

Corine leads the way out of the hotel and towards a small park to the left of the building. She crosses her arms tight across her chest, bracing against the cold.

'I'm sorry, this must be an awful shock for you. Mae's okay, though. She's on twenty-four-hour watch.'

'I heard you when I called the hospital. You were with her.' Kate's tone is accusatory.

'Yes. As her psychiatrist, I was asked to assess—'

'I'm her mother, for fuck's sake. My child just tried to end her life and I was turned away. As her mother, don't I deserve to know what's going on?'

'I understand how you feel, Kate,' Corine tries to reassure her.

'You do? Really? You don't have children, *Dr Alexander*. I don't expect you to understand what it feels like to be told you can't see your own child.'

'It's Mae's choice who she sees. She's eighteen.' Corine sighs, waiting for the high-pitched beep of a truck reversing somewhere close by to stop. When it does, she continues. 'She's weak right now and needs rest. All she'll be doing is sleeping for the next twenty-four hours, by which time she may have changed her mind and agree to see you.'

'Did she say why she did it?' Kate stares at Corine intently, her mouth pinched, angry.

'That might take time, I'm afraid.'

'She seemed perfectly okay when she spoke to me, but something must have triggered it.'

It sounds to Corine as though Kate is deflecting blame. *Perhaps she's more concerned about how this appears: Mae committing suicide immediately after speaking to her?*

'I'll talk to her when the time is right. Rest assured, she's safe and you'll be kept informed. I'm really sorry, but I've got to go. I have an appointment.' Corine smiles flatly at her.

'If your appointment is anything to do with my daughter, I should be told about it. I don't appreciate being pushed out.'

Corine frowns. 'I'll call you,' she says simply, but as she turns to walk off, Kate grabs her wrist.

'I heard you stepped out of retirement to help Mae. That she'd asked for you.'

Corine pulls her wrist free. 'That's right.'

'Mae doesn't always make the right decisions, that much should be obvious. Though perhaps if you'd been more attentive—less distracted by other things—she might not be in hospital with slit wrists.' Disgust is written all over Kate's face.

'As I said, I'll call you and we can arrange a time to meet

in my office.' Corine turns away and heads towards the hotel without looking back. She can feel Kate watching her. *Blame is what we do*, she tells herself. *It's a natural response to anger.*

Back inside her room, Corine checks her notebook, stopping at Frank's phone number. Her hands shake as she taps his number into her mobile and waits. He answers immediately.

'Hello?' his voice booms out.

Corine realises she must have accidentally tapped the microphone symbol. She quickly adjusts her phone. *Don't let Kate derail you*, she tells herself. But the accusation of neglect has already lodged itself under her skin.

'Hello, Frank, it's Corine, Mae's psychiatrist. I'm sorry to have to call with this news: Mae's okay, but she attempted to take her own life last night.'

'Oh my God!' Corine hears the words catch in his throat. 'Is she okay?'

'She's fine, being watched twenty-four-seven. She wants to see you.'

'She does?' Frank sounds surprised. 'Of course, yes, I'll come straight away. Where is she?'

'No, not right now. She's sedated, so she'll sleep for most of today. I'll see how she is tomorrow, but perhaps I could meet with you first? It's important we talk before you see her if that's okay? I could come to you today… if that works?'

'Sure. I've got the day off.'

'What about your partner?'

'She'll be fine, we've talked. How… what did Mae do to herself?' he adds softly.

'I'm afraid she cut both wrists.'

†

Corine regrets not taking the train. The cab journey south of the river is intense, with heavy traffic punctuated by sporadic bursts of bone-rattling speed. The driver seems intent on driving inches away from the cars in front, personally offended each time he's forced to brake. A few times, Corine is thrown forward. When the cabbie notices, he manages a vague apology.

'Uber drivers!' he mutters.

When they pull up outside the block of flats, Corine sees Frank arguing with the elderly gentleman she'd spoken to on her previous visit. The man turns his back on Frank—it's a slow manoeuvre, like a badly executed three-point turn—then limps away unsteadily, mumbling something under his breath.

Corine pays her fare but doesn't tip. 'I'll get an Uber next time,' she says pointedly and slams the door, not waiting to hear the driver's response. 'Trouble?' she asks Frank as she approaches the flat.

She needn't have asked. Someone had smeared black paint across the front door to his flat. It looks fresh, and thickly applied, with paint dripping down like rivulets of blood. There's a bowl of soapy water sitting on the welcome mat.

'That guy's demented.'

'Gosh, did *he* do that to the door?'

'No, it wasn't him. He wouldn't have the nerve. He's all mouth, that one, but it did seem to please him. You know the type… gets off on the misfortune of others.'

'Kids, do you think?'

Frank shrugs. 'Who knows.'

'What is it? X marks the spot?'

Frank steps aside to let her in. 'It's a cross… a plague cross, I think.'

'A what?'

'During the plague, they would paint black crosses on the doors of those who were infected as a warning.'

Now she was closer, Corine could see that it *was* a cross. Still, Frank's theory seemed rather far-fetched. 'Who'd do a thing like that these days?'

'Someone not right in the head. Someone like Kate. It's the kind of thing she would do to pay me back for the divorce. Her idea of revenge. I just hope she doesn't know about Irene's pregnancy.'

Revenge was something Corine hadn't considered. Kate had calmly announced the end of their marriage in one of their meetings and hadn't seemed especially upset by it. Surely a new baby on the way wouldn't change that?

'How can you be so sure? I mean, that she'd do something like this?'

'I know her. Though, I doubt this is about the baby… it's too subtle. If Kate knew I was having another child, she would have confronted me by now. There's no way she'd let that go.'

He sounds overly paranoid to her. Kate had moved on. By agreeing to a divorce, hadn't she shown a willingness to move on with her life? Most likely this was the work of a bored teenager.

'Perhaps other doors have been sprayed,' she suggests.

'No, it's a warning,' Frank replies. 'Please don't bring this up with Irene, I don't want to frighten her.'

Corine nods, not wanting to dwell on the topic further. It's surprisingly bright and airy inside the flat, with light floors and walls. She takes a seat on a small velvet sofa; Frank sits in a chair opposite. He offers her tea as an afterthought, but she declines.

'How's Mae?' he asks. He fidgets with a cloth he's used to wipe his hands, rolling it into a tighter and tighter tube.

'She's safe... and as good as can be expected, given everything. Her body's still recovering, but she's being looked after and is out of any immediate danger.' Corine pauses. 'No one saw this coming.'

Frank nods as he unravels the cloth.

Corine waits patiently for his questions, expecting confusion, anger, blame.

'I want to help. I've not been a part of her life for years; even before I left, I wasn't a good dad. Absent, usually... hiding from Kate. That wasn't fair to the girls.' Frank hesitates. 'I didn't do what Lyndsey said I did, and like I've told you before, I suspect Kate had something to do with that lie, but I can't prove anything. I should have stood up to the accusations, fought for my girls, but I ran away. They've suffered. Both of them. I only hope it's repairable.'

'You know about Lyndsey?'

'Her husband, Stuart, called me out of the blue a couple of days ago. She had a relapse, he said. He wanted to meet, to talk, but wouldn't say why.'

'Will you meet him?'

'He may just want to punch me in the face, but yeah, I

will. He seemed angry, with Kate mostly, so I suppose I'm a bit intrigued.'

'How is Mae?' a heavily accented voice asks from across the room.

Corine looks up as Irene enters. Her hair is loosely coiled in a bun, and the leggings and T-shirt she's wearing reveal a definite bump. Five or six months, Corine guesses, maybe more.

'Weak, but she'll be okay,' Frank tells her.

'Why did she do it?' Irene asks, addressing the question to Corine.

'I need to talk to her about that.'

'You must have an idea,' Frank asks.

'This is a period of enormous change for Mae. I think she's afraid of resuming life outside of prison, not knowing anyone or where she'll be living. Going through the trauma of the attack all over again in preparation for parole has obviously had a bigger impact than anyone imagined.'

Corine expects Frank to accuse her, but he doesn't. Instead, he looks across at her, surprised.

'She isn't going to live with Kate?' he asks.

'No. Mae was adamant about that.'

'I'm sorry, I know she's having a terrible time, but she can't come and live here,' Irene says adamantly. 'Not with our baby.'

'Irene…' Frank sounds more disappointed than annoyed. He stretches his hand out to Irene's, as if to reassure her. Turning to Corine, he says, 'I told her everything.'

She nods in acknowledgment.

'Who will punch you in the face?' Irene asks. She must

have been listening all along.

'I was talking about Stuart, Lyndsey's husband.'

Irene frowns and looks from Frank to Corine and back again. 'I'll come with you. He won't punch you in front of me.'

Frank laughs and smiles lovingly at Irene. 'I need to clear my name. I don't want the accusation hanging over me. Over us… our family.'

'Understandable,' Corine says, then turns to address Irene. 'And congratulations.' The word sounds inappropriate—out of place—given the circumstances. She turns back to Frank. 'Mae wants to see you, and I expect she'll want to talk about the accusations. She's fragile, just remember that. Take things slowly. She might appear confident, but she isn't.'

'Is she dangerous?'

'Irene!' This time Frank looks offended.

'No, it's a reasonable question given what Mae's serving time for. Mae is complex, but I don't think she would hurt anyone.'

'Besides herself,' Frank mumbles.

They continue to discuss Mae's condition, her recent state of mind, how she tended to internalize her emotions even as a small child, but with Irene coming and going, Frank grows evasive; quick to direct the conversation onto easier topics.

'Is there any history of mental illness in your family?' Corine asks.

Frank shakes his head. 'Not my family, no, certainly not.'

He asks about the likelihood of Mae's psychosis recurring, and in the split second before Corine answers, she is left feeling shame at humanity's wordless impulse to always place the blame on someone or something other than themselves.

'It's always a possibility. Stress can bring it on, but it's treatable and outcomes can be excellent.'

'Irene worries.'

'I understand, she's going to be a parent. It changes everything.'

They talk for a short while longer before Frank sees Corine out. She takes the opportunity to speak with him alone.

'If you did cross any boundaries with your children, you shouldn't go to see her tomorrow,' she warns, her instinct to protect Mae surfacing. 'Mae's too fragile right now. You can always talk to her later. Do the right thing, Mr Bailey, for all your children.'

'I am doing the right thing,' he snaps. 'Finally.'

'Good. I'll let you know what time tomorrow. Come find me and we'll speak beforehand… if you like.'

She steps away, and Frank returns to the task of cleaning the front door.

The air feels chilly after the warmth of the flat. Corine fastens her jacket, wishing she'd put on a warmer coat. She edges around the tightly parked cars in the driveway, the strap of her bag catching on a wing mirror. She unhooks it, hearing as she does, her name being called.

'You forgot your scarf!'

Corine retraces her steps and takes the scarf, thanking Irene. Outside, with the breeze whipping Irene's clothes, Corine can see she's further along in her pregnancy than she first thought.

'It's a beautiful scarf.'

'Thank you, my husband bought it for me years ago.'

Irene looks like she wants to talk, but something is stopping her.

'Everything okay?' Corine asks.

'Yes, but it's all very confusing and scary, what happened to Frank's family. I don't know Kate, but how bad must your relationship be to have a daughter cut you like this?'

Corine nods. 'I've asked myself the same question. None of it makes much sense. If you hear anything, please call me.' She hands Irene a business card. 'And take care,' she adds, smiling down at Irene's stomach.

Irene's hands cup her stomach protectively. 'Yes, I will.' She smiles and backs away, tripping slightly.

Corine winces. *Anything can happen*, she thinks. In just one moment, a person's entire life can be altered—destroyed forever. Once again, she is forced to confront her own trauma. This constant game of hide and seek that she plays with negative intrusive thoughts has gone on for far too long. If Corine were diagnosing herself, she might say she had classic signs of PTSD.

You have a choice, she tells herself. *Be consumed by grief or confront it and move on.*

The moment she is out of sight, Corine stops to get her bearings. She hears the sound of a car breaking heavily. A man gets out of a Mercedes shouting at the driver of a grey Range Rover. It looks like the driver of the Range Rover pulled out without looking, forcing the other vehicle to break hard. Immediately, Corine thinks of Kate. Was she following her?

No sooner had the thought occurred, when Corine hears a man's voice drifting through the open roof light. 'For Christ's sake, Sledge, watch what you're doing.'

Sledge didn't sound like the kind of person she wanted to confront.

CHAPTER 25
CORINE

The train pulls into Waterloo Station just after midday. The concourse is crowded, a maze of obstacles, both moving and otherwise. Corine weaves around people, dodging suitcases being dragged absentmindedly behind their owners. A window display in a bookshop catches her eye and she stops to look. Pink-nosed bunnies, lemon-coloured chicks, and fluffy lambs frolic over brightly coloured children's books. Not a single bible story in sight.

Sensibilities were changing, Corine knew that. But ageing without children felt like swimming at sea with the shoreline drifting further away. Children were a parent's fixed point; they anchored the adults in their lives, gave them a reason to stay afloat—even the undeserving ones.

Had she been undeserving? Maybe her parents had deserved better? She hadn't spoken to her mother during the last year of her life and her father had practically forced her to attend the funeral. That sad little gathering—with the new family up front, comforted by relatives—herself, Mary, and their father sitting at the rear of the church, barely acknowledged.

She had thought her father weak then. Now, she shuddered at her own naivety. He had risen above his own anger, hurt and loss, putting his children first, paying his last respects to a woman he still loved—the mother of his children.

Corine stops herself. Why was she thinking about this now?

There was, of course, always a reason. Certain clients, their situations, they got to her. Even if, as with Mae's case, she wasn't seeing the full picture.

Inside the bookshop, Corine can't decide between the stuffed bunny and fluffy lamb, so grabs both. She spots a matching story book and puts it her basket. She would give them to Lisa when she next saw her.

'Someone's going to be happy,' the young man at the till says as he scans the book.

'Beats a plate of boiled fish, I suppose.' He seems confused by her reply and smiles vacantly. 'It was always fish on Good Friday when I was a child.' The cashier still looks vacant.

'Ah, yes. Any excuse to spoil them. And why not!' His voice is loud, superficial. He looks relieved when she leaves.

Corine walks away feeling out of sync with the world. Maybe she'd always been that way? The memory of cautioning Mary for spoiling Lisa makes her cringe. In truth, if she were a mother herself now, she'd probably do the same. Her child would know that they were the centre of her world—that she had their back, no matter what.

Before Michael, she'd been naïve, inexperienced, yet absolutely certain that raising a child would come easily. Forget the pointless balloons and endless stuffed toys that Mary indulged Lisa with. Education, experiences—that was what truly mattered. Corine had taken Lisa to art galleries, libraries, and theatres—places to spark her imagination and nurture her passions.

They had been *her* passions, though… not Lisa's. Corine feels her stomach churn. She was lucky to still have Lisa in her life. In her head, she hears Joe's voice as clear as day.

"Don't mess it up."

The tube to Embankment is crammed with people—like a scene from a disaster movie. Corine decides to walk, cutting across Waterloo Bridge, hoping to clear her head before meeting with Mae. In the forty minutes it takes to reach The Orchard, a clear conclusion settles in her mind: guilt was destroying her. It felts as though every role Corine had played in life—daughter, sister, wife, mother, friend—she had somehow fucked up. Being a psychiatrist was all she had left, though a voice in her head warns her she is fucking that up too.

She takes a deep breath and attempts to silence the crippling negativity. It's clear what *her* kryptonite is, but what's Mae's, if it isn't guilt? What had destroyed her hope? Mae's lack of remorse worries Corine, as does the claimed impulsivity and the strained ties with family members. She is bright enough to hide things; to manipulate facts and swap lies for truths; to present the manipulated as manipulators. Based on the evidence alone, Mae could be diagnosed as a sociopath. Worse still, a psychopath.

But was she?

By the time Corine arrives at the hospital wing of The Orchard, she is determined to confront Mae and get her to open up. As she swipes past the ward's security door, she catches sight of a framed ink sketch. The artist has drawn a version of Little Red Riding Hood, with the wolf's mouth dripping honey. It gives Corine an idea. If Mae won't reveal the truth, then perhaps she might expose the lies.

Corine passes through security and strides down the long corridor towards the hospital wing. Inside, she checks in with Mae's nurse and gets an update.

When she enters the room, Mae appears to be sleeping, though her eyes open immediately. Her body looks tiny and fragile in the bed. The mere sight of her triggers an emotional response in Corine.

'Sorry, did I wake you?'

'No, I can't sleep.'

'I can get you something for that, if you want?'

'No, it's okay. I've slept—just not in the last five minutes.'

Corine puts her bags down and sits in the chair beside the bed.

Mae's eyes slide sideways towards the bags. 'Been shopping?'

'Oh, not really. I just couldn't resist an early Easter present for my niece's baby. It's due soon.'

'Nice.' Mae looks tired. Someone well-meaning has tucked the sheets in tightly around her.

'How're you feeling?' Corine asks as she loosens the bedsheets.

'Like I've just run a marathon. My heads a little foggy.'

That'll be the drugs, Corine thinks. 'You'll feel that way for a while. Shock, loss of blood… it takes time to recover.'

'Recover.' Mae laughs. 'What do I have to recover?' She laughs again, a slurred, slow laugh. In that moment, her face looks older, and weary; the face of someone used to carrying the weight of disappointment with them. 'Last time I looked, I didn't have anything of value to lose.'

'You've served your sentence, Mae. It's time to forgive yourself, to make a new life outside this place. It's scary, but you'll have support. I promise you that.'

'But that's just it. I don't want to get out.'

'I hear you.' Corine hesitates. 'There will be a delay to your parole hearing now, but I think you know that. You have to be fully okay before…' She stops short, not wanting to upset her. Watches the delicate skin of Mae's eyelids wrinkle as she blinks.

They sit in silence for a while, Mae rubbing the skin between her thumb and index finger. It reminds Corine of their first meeting together. She feels as though she's messed everything up. She wants desperately to make things right.

'I spoke to your father. He's keen to meet with you,' Corine says, watching how Mae responds to the news.

'When?' she asks sleepily. 'Today?'

Her meds need adjusting, Corine thinks. *I'll get the paroxetine lowered.*

'You're still weak,' she warns Mae. 'My concern is that it may dredge up some difficult memories you're not ready to deal with right now.'

Mae rises up, agitated. 'I need to see him. Please, Corine, can I?'

'Okay, don't stress, I'll sort it. You need to rest.'

'Alone… I'd like to see him alone.'

That wasn't really an option now, but Corine could explain that when Mae was less fragile. 'I'll sort the meeting,' she replies, dodging the request.

'Thank you.' Mae smiles softly, her shoulders dropping as the tension in her face falls away.

Her gratitude breaks Corine's heart. She doesn't deserve it. 'Before I do that, do you think you could tell me about how you were feeling, just before you cut yourself?'

'I don't know.'

'Come on, Mae, this works both ways. I need you to help me understand.'

Mae hesitates. 'Hopeless. I was feeling hopeless and anxious.'

'How long have you been feeling like that?'

'Months now. I haven't been able to sleep or eat properly.'

Corine frowns. 'You didn't say anything.'

She shrugs. 'You'd have just prescribed me more meds. Besides, it might have looked like an excuse to stay.'

'Did anything happen that particularly upset you on that day or during the days before?' Mae looks down at the bedsheet. 'Did your mum, or anyone else, say anything?'

Mae shakes her head.

She doesn't trust me, Corine berates herself. 'You were upset when your mum told you about the divorce. Did it make you feel like she was focusing on herself again? Pushing your needs to the periphery?'

Mae shrugs again. 'Yeah, I suppose. I know it sounds selfish of me, but it's what she does. She has to be the focus of everything.'

'Do you feel loved by your parents?'

'Not really.' Her expression shifts, her eyes thoughtful; soft. 'Though they might say different. Who knows. Maybe I have unrealistic expectations. What do *you* think a good parent should be like?' Her eyes flick up to Corine's eyes and she holds her gaze.

'Well, a good parent tries to be kind, loving, supportive, a good role-model, I suppose. They set clear, reasonable boundaries.' Mae was eighteen now, though. Legally, her parents didn't owe her anything.

'Should they love you more than anything? More than each other?'

'Are we talking about excessive love? Parental attachment can be too much. Is your mother too demanding or too dependent upon you?' It crosses Corine's mind that she had devoted all the love she had to a dead son, neglecting Joe. 'Or are you referring to the wrong type of love?'

Mae doesn't reply.

'If your father molested you, it wasn't your fault. Talking about it will help.'

'I have no real memory of that—just what I told you already. I can't say the same for Lyndsey. Maybe he molested her, maybe he didn't. They were both preoccupied parents, though, but I suppose that's just the luck of the draw, isn't it? Just before I did this.' Mae lifts up her bandaged hands and drops them down again. 'I felt like no one cared. Not genuinely. It sounds stupid to me now; maybe I read too much into things, but I always believed there was some grand plan, that things would end up okay in the end. But that's just being a child, right? Relinquishing responsibility, allowing someone else, something else, control your life.'

Corine sees her own feelings echoed in Mae's words. She nods. 'Go on.'

'Kate came in playing her old fucking games and it threw me.' She lifts her wrists and turns them over, as though examining them. 'I felt abandoned all over again.'

At last, Corine thinks, *something I can work with*. 'I can see why you would interpret—'

'Then I thought, grow the fuck up! Not everyone lives in an Austen novel. There's no preordained plan controlling my life, it's just me. I have a selfish mother and a selfish father who left. He may tell me otherwise, but I'm not going to hold my breath. I'm okay with most of that now. It is what it is.' Mae lifts her chin and looks at Corine. 'I survived them. I survived all of this.' She looks about the room until her eyes come to rest back on Corine. 'You said you'd help me sort things out, for when I get out of here.'

Corine reaches over and holds Mae's arm. 'Of course. And I appreciate your honesty.'

Was it honesty, or was Mae playing a role, saying what she knew Corine wanted to hear? She needed to speak to Richard, share her fears. Hopefully that would allow her to think straight.

Corine feels her phone vibrate. She has two missed calls from Lisa and Callum; she'll call them later. Mae's eyes are beginning to close again. She watches the rise and fall of her chest slowing and waits for her to fall asleep.

Corine places the small cuddly lamb on Mae's bedside table. It looks out of place in the sterile grey room. Silently, she tiptoes out, leaving the door open. One of the nurses instantly resumes her watch. Before she leaves, Corine re-writes Mae's prescription and discusses it with the nurse in charge.

She asks to be called as soon as Mae wakes up.

CHAPTER 26
CORINE

Not wanting to put Lisa out, Corine suggests they meet at a café close to her. The place is part art gallery, part factory, with exposed brick walls, pipework, and large colourful canvases that Corine thinks look more like the work of a local pre-school rather than a serious artist. The artist's details and prices are listed below each piece, but before she can get her glasses out to have a look, a waitress ushers them to a small empty table at the back. They order immediately on Lisa's advice—poached eggs and spinach on sourdough toast. Corine refrains from commenting at the caviar prices, but only just. *This is progress*, she tells herself. *Get with it or be left behind.*

After a while, their conversation becomes stilted. Mae's suicide weighs heavily on Corine's mind, but it isn't a topic easily dropped into conversation. Not without seriously affecting the mood, anyway, and she wants to keep things positive, if only for Lisa's sake. Thankfully, her niece either fails to notice Corine's subdued mood or tactfully doesn't mention it, lurching instead from one baby-related anecdote to another.

She is positively bursting to get on with being a mother but is worried about the effect her leaving part way through term-time will have on her students.

'They grow so attached at that age,' Lisa tells Corine.

She feels overwhelmed by the presents she's received from parents and staff. She describes a beautiful baby shawl, hand-knitted by the grandma of one of her favourite students—Harvey, a little boy with Downs Syndrome—before switching topics and telling Corine she's adamant not to waste a moment of her maternity leave. That started yesterday and, apparently, Lisa had already installed childproof locks on all the cupboards in the house. Corine can't help but laugh—it would be months before they had to worry about that. Still, her happiness is infectious.

The food, when it comes, is good—so good, they order a second pot of peppermint tea and a slice of spiced apple cake each. Corine's real motivation for the cake, though, is less about appetite and more about supporting Lisa. No one likes eating cake alone.

'I want another baby straight away,' Lisa announces as she tucks into her cake.

Corine laughs, wiping a crumb off her lower lip. 'While I can see the appeal of a large family, all those years of nappies, vomit, tantrums…'

Lisa's lips thin, her expression suddenly serious.

Lighten-up, Corine reprimands herself. *Stop with the unsolicited advice.*

'… might as well be continuous.' Corine says the exact opposite of what she really thinks. 'Why not get it all over with at once, if that's what you both want.'

'I know it's not the trend these days, but I can't think of anything better than a large family.' Lisa pauses, looking down at the table. 'Like you say, I mean, I might as well get it all over at once. Assuming it happens that way.'

Corine nods vigorously in agreement, willing Lisa to feel comfortable again; wishing she could tell her the truth but knowing it would be going against what Mary had wanted. Still, Lisa's sensitivity touches her—after years spent listening to others, family and friends included, endlessly banging on about their children, even when Corine had dropped in subtle hints about her own childlessness. It wasn't that she didn't want to hear about their kids; she just wished they had some sense of when to stop. Surprisingly, many didn't.

'Your mum and I wanted a brood when we were younger too. Shame neither of us found it easy to get pregnant.'

Lisa puts her fork down and frowns at her cup of peppermint tea. 'Mum never mentioned having problems conceiving. She just decided not to have any more because she enjoyed work so much.'

'I meant me,' Corine interjects.

'What was the problem, if you don't mind me asking?' Lisa bites down on her lower lip and toys with her teacup.

'Oh, just not meant to be, or bad luck, I suppose.'

'So there weren't any genetic issues? I mean, that could run in the family?' Lisa glances down at her empty plate, looking nervous.

'No, no,' Corine tries to reassure her.

There may well have been genetic reasons behind why she'd lost so many babies, but medicine hadn't been advanced enough then to explain why. At least, that's what a very kind geneticist had told them a lifetime ago.

Corine sips at her tea, hoping her face won't give her away. There was no point worrying Lisa unnecessarily.

'Do you think you'll ever do anything with your psychology degree?' Corine asks, changing the subject.

'Teaching was only ever supposed to be temporary; to get some experience with children. I'd have to do three years of postgraduate training to get a doctorate in clinical psychology. It's just not an option right now. I almost don't know where the last four years have gone.' Lisa shrugs.

'Life goes too quickly. And before you know it, you're old.'

'Actually, that reminds me, I got talking to a woman at the school gate the other day. She stopped to ask about the school for her grandchildren. One must have mental health problems because she was interested in whether the school offered counselling or therapy services. I told her we tended to refer to professional services for assessments, though I warned her that it could take months to get assessed. She asked if I knew a good psychiatrist and, somehow, we ended up talking about you.'

'You realise I'm heading straight back to Scotland after this, don't you? I've a farm to run, I don't have time to run a clinic on top of everything else.'

'I told her as much, but she was a bit pushy... asked a lot of questions. I felt a little sad for her. She looked like she'd been in an accident... lots of scars.'

Corine's stomach flips. 'Where?'

'She didn't say—'

'No, I mean where were her scars?'

'Well, I only saw her face. She had clothes on.' Lisa laughs. 'Thankfully.'

'What about her hands?'

'What about them?'

'Were they scarred too?'

'No, I don't think so. I would have noticed. Why all the questions?'

'Oh, nothing. Ignore me. It's sleeping in that bloody hotel bed, my mind's all over the place.' *There are women other than Kate Bailey with scars on their faces*, Corine reminds herself.

'So come stay at mine! Please, Aunty Corine, I insist. You know, you were quite the hit with Peter.'

'No,' she chuckles, 'I'm messy, you'd both hate me within a day. And I keep terrible hours. Don't you remember your mum saying how her half of the room was all neat and orderly when we were growing up and my side looked like it had been ransacked? I'm still the same. People don't change much.'

They both laugh, but it occurs to Corine that if people don't change much, there had to be a clear reason why Mae acted so completely out of character four years ago. Kate must have done or said *something* to infuriate her. But what? What would cause a normally placid child to snap? Corine didn't buy the story she'd been told by Kate. Was it possible she was defending herself?

If Mae and Kate weren't prepared to talk, Corine had no alternative but to try and contact Lyndsey again, despite Kate's pleas to keep her out of the situation.

†

Back in the hotel room, Corine empties her bag and realises she forgot to give Lisa her presents. She places the paper bag, holding the story book and bunny, on the desk and pours herself a glass of water. Sitting on the bed, she takes out her notebook and writes the heading: *Conclusive*. Beneath it, she lists four points:

1. *Deep-rooted anger towards mother and sister.*
2. *Anxiety around release, linked to refusal to return to family home or rebuild familial relationships.*
3. *Confused but reaching out to father.*
4. *History of self-harm culminating in a suicide attempt. Still signs of anorexia—nothing in hospital records from last eighteen months.*

Corine stares out of the window for a few moments, tapping her pen against the page. Then she writes another heading: *Inconclusive*. Beneath it, she writes:

1. *No evidence of psychosis or indication of complex psychiatric disorder. Patients often have complete amnesia after violent episodes—Mae recalls details.*
2. *Claims impulsivity but no signs in the two years prior to recent suicide attempt. Highly probable mother said or did something during her last visit—no other changes in Mae's life?*

When she finishes writing, Corine sits back and stares at her notes. If Kate *did* say something that drove Mae over the edge, she was unlikely, given her track record, to admit it. Most probably, Mae feels she has never been heard by anyone, least of all the people who should typically value her the most. As her therapist, Corine had failed to make it any easier. Asking Mae to elaborate on her suicidal thoughts was like forcing her to eat a five-course meal.

'Where to begin without completely overwhelming Mae?' Corine sighs heavily.

After a while, she writes:

> *Mae doesn't feel she has a future. She feels neither safe nor valued.*

She stares at the sentences she has written, then closes the book. The habit of not seeing the value in one's own feelings starts in childhood. Moments later, she thinks of something Kate had said and opens the book again. She writes: *Talk to Lyndsey*.

CHAPTER 27
KATE

The taxi turns into the entrance of The Abbey Clinic and drives slowly along the gravel path, pulling to a stop in front of the large Georgian mansion. Kate steps out of the passenger side. She waves as the taxi pulls away and mouths, "Thank you." The crunch of gravel beneath wheels and outbursts of angry birdcall break the silence. Two crows fight over the viscous remains of something flesh coloured and bloody.

Kate turns away in disgust.

Staring up at the building, she sighs heavily and strides up the steps two at a time. The receptionist greets her warmly before calling through to a different section of the building, making the staff aware that Lyndsey has a visitor.

'She's in her room. Been there all morning, from what I hear. Refused to leave.'

'Oh dear, I'll see what I can do about that,' Kate replies, heading down a number of corridors into another reception area.

The second receptionist presses a button, and Kate pushes her way through a large door into a small waiting area where piano music plays. She's met at the second door by a female staff member, who hugs Kate, talking to her in hushed tones.

Kate nods solemnly.

'She's refusing to attend classes, or her one-to-one therapy, and she threw her breakfast tray this morning in the dining hall. We're not sure why.'

'I'm so sorry, I'll speak to her. She's missing her girls. Thanks, Pat, I know you look after her like she's one of your own.' Kate gives a tired smile and heads down a long corridor with several rooms on either side. She stops at the final room and knocks.

No one answers.

'Lyndsey, darling?'

Silence.

Kate sighs and pushes the door open. It's dark and airless inside. The curtains are still drawn, but Kate can make out Lyndsey's shape beneath the bedcovers. She opens one of the curtains, just enough to see without straining her eyes, and walks over to the chair beside the bed. Kate lifts an armful of clothing and places it on the back of the chair. The room is a mess.

'What's wrong, Lyndsey?' Kate's question is met by silence. 'Why are you refusing treatment? Darling, speak to me.'

There's no reply.

'Do you have any idea how much this place is costing us?' she snaps, growing impatient.

Lyndsey sits up. Straggly hair falls about her tear-stained face. Her eyes are swollen and red from crying. 'Who was the man in the room with my babies?'

'I have no idea what you're talking about.'

'There was a man,' Lyndsey snaps, agitated.

'Don't be ridiculous. You sound crazy. You must be confused, it's—'

Lyndsey bunches her hands into fists. 'Beth told Stuart

that a man came into the bedroom when she stayed at yours. You had friends over, music on. Who was it?'

'She probably had a nightmare. You know what children are like at that age—overactive imaginations. Don't tell me that's why you're refusing to get up?'

'You always have an answer, don't you? You know better than everyone else. She's *my* daughter and *I* know her. She doesn't make things like this up.'

'I'm not saying she made things up—'

'No, just that she *imagined* everything.'

'That's very different.'

'Is it? Is it really, Mother? That's the fucking problem in this family. No one knows what's the truth from a pack of lies. I'm not sure I've ever been able to tell the difference.' Tears fall freely down Lyndsey's cheeks. She throws herself back and pulls the covers up under her chin. 'I feel so guilty all the time. I'm a shitty mother; I mess everything up. They're going to hate me when they grow up, it's only a matter of time. Dad already hates me, and Mae too.'

Kate watches as Lyndsey pauses.

'Why is Mae's psychiatrist asking to see me?' She blinks rapidly and wipes her face. 'I wouldn't blame Mae if she never wanted to talk to any of us ever again. I should have gone to see her, but I couldn't... I just couldn't.'

Kate smiles indulgently and moves a section of hair from Lyndsey's face. 'I wouldn't worry about Mae or her so-called psychiatrist. I'll sort all that. My love... talking of sisters, and liars... Mae's asked to see your father, too.'

Lyndsey's expression changes immediately. She shrinks further back into the covers. 'Why? Why would she want to see him? Mae hates him, doesn't she? After everything?'

Kate shrugs. 'Who knows. Prison changes people, hardens them. Mae's complicated, she always was. She's prepared to see him, that monster, and yet she's refusing to see her own mother when I've always stood by her, by both of you, no matter what. He's not satisfied with abandoning his family. He's determined to bloody ruin us, the heartless prick.' Kate leans forward and strokes Lyndsey's arm. 'You know what he'll do to her. What he'll get her to say.'

Lyndsey shakes her head. 'I don't understand. Why now? Why wait until she's getting out to speak to him?'

'He's having another child with that baby-teacher of his. She's not much older than you, the fucking cradle-snatcher. He can have a family and cast it aside, no consequences. Then he replaces us, just like that.' Kate clicks her fingers. 'Your father's got away with every sick thing he's ever done and now he's sinking his claws into Mae again. He'll manipulate her, just like he always has. Who knows what he'll get her to say.' Tears fall down Kate's face. 'I don't think I can handle all this, not again.'

'Don't cry, Mum, please don't cry.' Lyndsey sits forward and hugs Kate. 'Everything will be fine, you'll see.'

'Oh, baby, I don't know what I'd do without you. Promise me you'll pull yourself together and come out of here my happy girl again.'

Lyndsey grips Kate's hand and nods.

'You're a good girl. I knew I could rely on you, darling.'

Kate jumps up and throws open the windows, leaving Lyndsey wincing from the sunlight. Her face is pale, exhausted.

'I'll go and talk to Dr Tyler, see what he's prescribing you.

You've been so calm until recently.'

'Someone told you about breakfast?'

'You know people open up to me in here. It's being a doctor all these years. I'm trusted, you know that.' She smiles and heads out of the room. As she leaves, she looks back at her daughter. 'Therapy helps. Talking to someone helps.'

'Not when you can't tell the truth,' Lyndsey whispers, but Kate is too far down the corridor to hear.

†

Kate knocks on a door with a brass nameplate that reads, Dr Theodore Tyler. A man's voice calls to her to come in. Inside, a large, balding man with an Old Testament beard sits behind a highly polished wooden desk.

'Ah, Kate, always good to see you.' He rises to shake hands, towering above her.

'Lyndsey isn't herself, Ted. It's knowing Mae is going to be released soon and her father being on the scene again, bringing all those traumatic memories back… flashbacks. Her anxiety is through the roof, she's just confessed as much in her room.'

'She still hasn't said anything in her one-to-one sessions.' Dr Tyler indicates for her to sit and perches himself on the edge of his desk. 'She finds it difficult to verbalise her anxieties, and if you hadn't told me what happened to her, well, I'd be none the wiser.'

'I'd hoped that would change,' Kate replies, slumping down in a chair and crossing her legs. She looks beyond Ted. A clock ticks loudly on the mantle behind him; above that, a cracked oil painting of a pompous looking middle-aged man in eighteenth-century clothing looms down in judgement. She stands. 'Mind if I open this window?'

Dr Tyler shrugs. 'She's very dependent on you. She needs to learn to express and regulate her emotions herself. It's not healthy.'

'In the meantime, she's in acute distress and it would be remiss of me if I didn't flag this with you. Perhaps you could up her diazepam for a few days? It might help her symptoms… stabilise her mood. I'd hate for anything to happen to her on your watch, Ted, I really would.'

'I'll look into it.' He smiles stiffly. 'Perhaps you'd reconsider family therapy? Since Lyndsey seems to respond so well when you're around. This is her third time here; we need to do something different.'

'Ha, well, maybe.' Kate matches his stiff smile. 'People make life choices like they're picking a sandwich at a fucking service station and then wonder why their life didn't turn out as they expected.' She laughs. 'I know I've said this before, but she should never have had a baby at eighteen. She isn't suited to motherhood.' Kate turns her back on Dr Tyler and looks out of the window. 'Some women just aren't.'

†

It's getting dark outside, and Kate is sitting in the empty dining room with Lyndsey. A plate of cottage pie and grey looking vegetables lies barely eaten in front of her.

'Try a little more, darling, it'll help you sleep through the night.' Kate points at the pie.

'Stuart will be coming soon with the girls.' Lyndsey is barely awake, inhaling in shuddering bursts.

'Oh, didn't I tell you, darling? I called him, told him to have a night off. The girls need a little break. They'll come in with him tomorrow.'

Lyndsey nods, but her eyes are glassy, vacant. 'I miss them. I miss my babies.'

'I know you do, darling.' Kate lifts a spoonful of food to Lyndsey's mouth. She takes a small bite and eats slowly. 'Better?'

Lyndsey nods.

'Okay, well, I'm going to see you back to your bed and get you all tucked up nice and snug. Tomorrow, when you have therapy, you can tell Dr Tyler all about what your father did to you. Okay?'

Lyndsey nods, her eyes half closed.

'You've got to promise me, darling. I'm depending upon you. Your girls are too.'

CHAPTER 28
CORINE

Frank sits outside Mae's hospital room, waiting to be summoned. *He looks nervous*, Corine thinks.

'Good to see you here, Mr Bailey.' She gives him what she hopes is a reassuring smile. 'Come on in.'

Frank nods and shakes her hand.

As she steps aside, he hesitates at the door. Corine isn't exactly surprised. It's been years since he's seen his daughter, and she knows Mae looks unwell to say the least.

'Mae,' he says softly, his voice thick with grief.

'Dad.'

It takes less than a second for her to pronounce those three letters, a single syllable, but the effect on Frank is obvious. His face breaks out into a smile, his shoulders dropping as he relaxes, presumably at the knowledge his daughter still considers him a parent.

'Mr Bailey, why don't you sit there next to Mae, and I'll give you both some time to talk. I'll be just outside if you need me. For anything,' Corine says, directing her final comment at Mae.

Frank moves into the room, sitting in the empty chair beside his daughter, his hands perched nervously on his lap as Mae nods to Corine.

She leaves, making sure to position herself out of sight so

she can watch them from the open doorway.

Frank clears his throat. 'How are you feeling... now, I mean... after?' He shakes his head. 'Lame question, sorry.'

'I feel stupid for doing what I did. I regret it, I really do. It was another moment of temporary insanity.' Mae smiles. 'Which I'm prone to, as you know.'

'You must have had your reasons.'

Mae shrugs.

They take each other in, presumably noticing the subtle changes wrought by time.

'Please don't ever do anything like that again,' Frank blurts out. 'I just... thank God you're okay. If you ever feel that way again, please, please let me or someone... anyone... tell anyone. I can promise you things will always get better.'

'You sound like a mindfulness ad,' Mae chuckles.

He looks at her blankly.

'They put posters up on the walls here,' she explains, 'to encourage positive thinking.'

'Do they? I mean, encourage positive thinking?'

'You can't just tell someone to be happy.'

He nods and rubs his hands together nervously. 'If it's okay with you, I want to help.'

'You'd have to be available for that,' Mae replies flatly.

Frank shrinks back. 'I will be... if you'll allow me. In whatever capacity.'

'By whatever capacity you mean besides being a parent?' Mae gives a nervous laugh, looking down at her hands. 'I'd have thought that was a big enough job. Easy to mess up, though. Some of the stories I hear in here. You'd be surprised how many cases of substance abuse starts with the parents.

That and other things.' She pauses, then looks him straight in the eyes. 'Anyway, why wouldn't I have you?'

Frank rocks forward, the tension in his upper body showing. 'I never should have left you, but I had no choice. I put my needs before yours and Lyndsey's, and for that, I'm sorry, I truly am. You both deserved a better father than me, a braver one.' Frank sighs and sits back in his chair.

'You had no choice? Really?'

'I had to get away from your mother. What happened with Lyndsey... the accusations... I should have faced up to them. I realise that now. If I had, you might not be here... in this situation. If I couldn't cope with Kate, what chance did you have?' Frank leans towards her. 'We were always close, you and me, and I keep thinking if only... if only I'd stood up to her. Me instead of you. I'm sorry I wasn't around.' Frank says, his voice gentle, lulling. 'I regret that.'

Mae nods and looks back at her hands, his comment clearly bothering her.

'What did you think, when you first heard I'd stabbed her?' she asks.

'That she probably deserved it,' Frank replies without hesitation.

Mae fires him a look that Corine can't gauge. The room suddenly darkens as clouds shift in the sky outside, casting shadows across Mae's face. 'We've all got regrets. But can you live with them? I suppose that's the game changer.'

'I didn't do anything to Lyndsey,' Frank says defensively. 'I promise you, Mae. I don't know why she said that. How anyone could do that to their own daughter... it's repulsive.'

'Sometimes the truth is too painful to face.' Mae's voice

sounds mechanical now, disconnected.

'I swear to you, I never touched your sister. The idea of it disgusts me… makes me feel physically sick.'

'What they said you did, it was…' Mae winces and looks away.

'I know, I know, but I didn't do it. Please, Mae, please listen to me. Your mother denies it, but she obviously manipulated Lyndsey, twisted her against me, used her to destroy my life. I thought that leaving her, severing all ties, would solve things, but Kate won't give up. I'm going to fight this battle once and for all and finally put it all behind me, so that I can move on with my life. The fact that Kate didn't go to the police speaks volumes.'

'What changed? Why are you prepared to say all this now?' Mae asks, after an uncomfortably long silence.

Frank shuffles forward in his seat and turns to the window. 'I know what Kate's like. When I heard what you'd done, that you'd attacked your—'

'It wasn't just that, though, was it?' Mae interrupts him. 'You say you know what she's like, but you must have thought I had a reason to do it.'

'Yes… yes, of course.'

For a moment, Mae seems unable to speak. 'That's interesting,' she finally says, 'because even back then, I knew it was wrong. It *is* wrong to stab your own mother, isn't it? Even if she's a total fucking psycho, it's still wrong to take a knife to her.' She doesn't wait for Frank to reply. 'Unless it was self-defence, and, well, it wasn't. She didn't deserve that, no one does…' Mae looks him in the eye, as though she's trying to read his mind. 'I didn't ask you here to talk about that. I was curious why you're suddenly so keen to clear your name, four years down the line. What's changed, Dad? Will you at least be honest about that?'

Frank looks down at the ground and shifts nervously in his seat, struggling to speak. It would be almost amusing, were it not so pitiful, how the roles had been reversed. 'No. Well, yes, I suppose I... I met someone. Just over a year ago now. Irene. She's Spanish... a teacher.'

Frank pauses, but Mae waits for him to continue. He looks nervous. *Perhaps he's afraid of his own daughter after all? Corine muses. Afraid of her interrupting his new life with Irene?*

'I need to be honest with her.' Frank swallows hard, his throat dry. 'Starting a relationship with secrets is a recipe for disaster, and Irene's a lovely lady, inside and out. You'd like her, she's—'

'Have I got this right?' Mae interrupts suddenly. 'You want to clear everything up so that you can start afresh with a new partner? I mean, you've been with her for over a year and not told her yet. Something must be different to make you want to *now*.'

'Well, you see, that's... I... we...'

'Oh, the baby. Yes, I know,' Mae says, her voice sharp with venom. 'Congratulations, Dad. Brave of you to pass on such fucked up DNA.'

'How do you know?' Frank asks. 'Who told you?'

'It doesn't matter. What's important is that you found a reason to change your life, to make it better. I'm happy for you.' She looks up at him. 'It's a reason you didn't have before. Good for you!'

Frank doesn't register the emotion in Mae's words, too

caught up in his own head to notice her pained expression, her glistening eyes.

'Does your mother know?' he asks pointedly, his face turning pale. 'Christ, we've been so careful.' Frank gets up and walks towards the door. 'I warned Irene that if Kate ever found out she was pregnant, she'd make our lives a living hell. Fuck!' He paces up and down and suddenly turns to Mae. 'Did you tell her? Did your psychiatrist?'

Corine considers breaking up their meeting, but something stops her; makes her wait just a little longer.

Mae's voice sounds broken. 'It was always about the two of you, wasn't it? Me and Lyndsey… we didn't matter. We were only ever minor characters in the story of your lives.'

'Oh, come on, that's not true, Mae.' Frank sits, reaches for her hand, but Mae withdraws immediately.

'Please, Dad, just listen. I never want to ask this again.'

Her voice is barely above a whisper and Corine has to lean in slightly to catch her words.

'You can tell me about Lyndsey,' she continues softly. 'Was it to get back at Mum because she had you by the balls for having an affair?'

Frank stares at his daughter in disbelief. 'Mae, I'm not the monster your mother and Lyndsey accuse me of being. I'm the victim here. Driven from my life, from everything I worked for.'

'I remember someone coming into my room once. Someone who shouldn't have been there.'

The last bit of blood drains from Frank's face. He stands slowly, staring at her. 'No… no. Not you too?'

'I can see this is stressful for you to talk about but be the parent for once. None of this makes any sense to me either. You're a GP with access to all sorts of drugs. Rohypnol can be bought like sweets. Why would your victim even have to know?'

Frank looks horrified. 'I'm sorry. I know I've been… that I'm a selfish bastard. But I am *not* a monster.' He swallows hard. 'I'll go, I can see that this was a mistake. Your mind is made up and I'm not going to change that.'

'That's it?' Mae laughs. 'That's your defence?'

'Take care of yourself,' Frank spits, walking towards the door.

Corine quickly sits down, looking up as Frank storms past.

'Everything alright?' she asks.

'No. Can I have a word?'

She signals to one of the nurses to keep an eye on Mae and follows him down the corridor. 'Go ahead,' she says, once they're far enough away.

Frank looks around, checking no one can hear. 'Did you tell Kate about Irene's pregnancy?'

'No, of course not. That's none of my business.'

'Well someone has.' He's almost growling now, leaning towards her, his face inches away, menacing. 'If Kate says or does anything, I'll—'

'Careful, Mr Bailey, I'm not some vulnerable teenage girl you can threaten.'

Frank stares at her, his eyes full of rage. Then without saying anything more, he storms off.

Corine runs after him, unwilling to let him go without saying her piece. 'You should be doing everything possible to stop your daughter from hurting herself again.'

'She's damaged and I am not equipped to fix her. That's your job,' Frank says, his voice edged with fury.

'What happened to clearing your name?'

'Lies have a way of morphing into the truth in people's minds if they hear them often enough. Mae's been around Kate for too long. I don't want any of her poison near Irene, she's fragile right now. Anyway, it's clearly too late.' He glances back at Mae's room. 'She as good as said I'm the bad guy. I don't have the energy to change that, or the money to fight it in court. Irene will understand.'

'But will she trust you? Will you feel comfortable putting your child to bed, giving him a cuddle, knowing—'

'For fuck's sake, leave me alone!' Frank turns and stomps past the reception desk towards the exit.

Sighing, Corine returns to Mae's room.

The last thing she expects to hear is laughter.

'Moira thinks my dad's a ride,' Mae explains as Corine enters.

'I didn't say it like that.' Moira blushes. 'He's well put together is all I said. Slim, like.' She refills Mae's water jug, without looking at anyone.

'Do I take after him, do you think, Moira?' Mae asks, laughing.

Before Moira can answer, Corine interrupts. 'Thank you, Moira, I'd like to talk to Mae alone please.' Moira looks grateful for an excuse to leave. As soon as she's gone, Corine turns to Mae. 'What just happened?'

'Nothing.' Mae rubs at the skin in between thumb and forefinger.

It's what she does when she lies, Corine realises.

'He was clearly upset.'

'Oh, and that's no doubt my fault, is it?' Mae puts her hands to her temple as though her head aches, or she can't quite believe what Corine is saying.

'Don't put words into my mouth. Of course I want to know what was said to upset… to anger him. But, more importantly, I want to know that you're okay. You are all that matters right now.'

Mae looks at her blankly for a moment, as if startled by Corine's words. 'He's a selfish prick, but he says he wants to put things right, so I suppose I can't knock that, can I?'

'And do you trust him?'

Mae shrugs. 'It's his word against theirs.'

'You don't remember anything?'

'Like I said, I have a vague memory of a man coming into my room, but nothing else. Probably just a dream. I can't say for certain it was my dad or that he did anything, just that whoever it was shouldn't have been there. I think I said that to him. Or I might have just imagined or dreamed it.'

'Do you recall anything else about the memory, any detail, however small?'

Mae shakes her head.

'It could be tactile, or a sound… a smell?'

Mae sits forward. 'The smell of whisky.'

Corine's phone rings. She turns it off.

'Go on.'

Mae frowns. 'It's probably unrelated memories that I've spliced together.' Mae's eyes look heavy, watery. 'Nothing's clear. I think I'm in bed… it's dark. Something woke me up, but… ugh, it feels like a dream. Disjointed. Surreal.' Mae shakes her head again. 'That's all. Nothing else, nothing at all.'

Corine squeezes her hand. 'Don't stress. Get some rest and we'll talk about it tomorrow; you'll feel a little stronger then. I'll check in later.'

'You don't have to keep checking me, I'm not going to do anything.'

'I know. I trust you'll talk to me if you need to.' Corine shivers inwardly at her own words, knowing that anyone who commits suicide is most at risk of relapse for the first three months to a year following an attempt. Mae will have to be monitored for a long time.

The fact that her father had just stormed off meant that the last of her post-prison family options had gone.

'Do you think I'm mad for doing what I did? Attempting to end things?'

'No, of course not.'

'Weak, then?'

'No. You're not weak, Mae. I think you felt like you were out of options, and I know what that's like.'

'I just wanted to stop the pain.' Mae's face crumples, and her tears fall freely for the first time. 'This constant feeling of emptiness.' She forces a smile. 'I mean, I wouldn't want to be around me if I had a choice. I have nothing to offer.'

There was so much to unpack in her words, such suffering, such a deeply embedded lack of self-esteem.

'Can we talk about why you feel so empty?' Corine asks, handing Mae a tissue.

Mae wipes her eyes, visibly exhausted. 'Not right now. I can't.'

Once again, Corine couldn't help noticing that she shared the same mindset. It was vital that Mae could see a future for herself—vital for both of them.

Kneeling beside her, Corine whispers, 'I promise you you'll feel your life's worth living again, that you have value. You have so much to offer, my darling. The way you felt… feel, it's temporary. It will change. There are good people out there who want to help you.'

†

As Corine leaves Mae's room, she spots Richard waiting for her. She smiles, surprised to see him.

'I overheard what you said. Promise me you aren't getting too close.'

'She's vulnerable and I'm trying to make her less so. Isn't that what you'd expect from her psychiatrist?'

'I don't want to see you get hurt.'

'I'm just doing my job. I should have been more involved four years ago.' A nurse approaches and Corine breaks off their conversation, asking her to keep a close watch on Mae. 'Don't leave her on her own. Someone needs to be with her at all times. I'll be back in an hour or so.'

The nurse nods and heads straight to Mae's room.

'We should catch up,' Richard suggests.

'That would be good, but I need to make an urgent call first.'

'Anything I should know about?'

'Know anything about farming?' She smiles and goes to walk away, then spins to face him again. 'Wait! Do the patients ever access the internet? Social media?'

'A few have privileges when they're getting out, but it's all closely monitored. They can't comment on anything, there are blocks. Why?'

'Oh, I was just wondering. I wasn't sure whether Mae had been accessing information from her mother or using social media to find things out about her father's new partner.'

'Mae's close to Malika… she's leaving tomorrow. That might be the connection.'

Corine's insides flip. 'Why did no one tell me? Malika's leaving will have a *huge* impact on Mae. She's her only real friend! Christ, does no one talk to each other in this place?'

'The placement only came up a couple of days ago. Someone would have talked to Mae, of course they would, and you would have found out at the last meeting, had you attended it.'

Corine nods, hearing the reprimand, but she is already walking away. 'I'll catch you later,' she calls over her shoulder.

Once she is out of earshot, she calls Callum.

'Hello? Hello?' From the way he's yelling, and the difficulty he has hearing her, it sounds as though he's caught in a storm. The forecast for Scotland had been for unpredictable weather for the next few days.

'Callum? It's Corine. Can you hear me? Is everything okay?'

Cows moo in the background, muffled by Callum's heavy breathing and the sound of metal on metal. Probably a gate being closed.

'Aye, I can hear you. I'm truly sorry to have tae say this, but I cannae believe you would do it to me, Corine.'

'What are you talking about?'

'I'm looking aftae your farm like it was my own and...'

The line crackles with static. She hears only the words "selling" and "behind my back".

'Wait, let me go to my office and I'll call you back.' Corine listens to Callum ranting as she leaves the ward. 'Callum, please listen. I have not sold the farm and I have no intention of doing so. I don't know who it was who called you, but it's someone chancing their arm.' She listens. 'Callum, Callum?'

Nothing but static.

CHAPTER 29
CORINE

Corine leans against the windowsill in Richard's office, drinking coffee from a takeaway cup. The feeling of the warm sun on her back does little to relax her. Richard has his feet up on the desk, revealing red socks that perfectly match his red tie. He'd always taken good care of himself, his appearance. Corine wonders why he'd never married.

'Have you considered the fact that Callum may be acting out of self-interest?'

'That's too Machiavellian for my wee corner of Scotland. No, Callum wouldn't make something like that up, he's painfully truthful. That's what I love and fear about him.' Corine would kill for a cigarette right now, a temporary surge of dopamine to help propel her forward.

'He wants the land, doesn't he? For his offspring? His heirs.'

'Christ, it's not the sixteenth century and I'm not some marauding Brit.'

'Okay, so he claims someone called and said they'd bought the farm, which conveniently brings the subject to a head. He implies you've used him, denied him the opportunity to buy the land. You deny, but feel guilty, make promises, at the very least feel that you are on the back foot with him. You owe him. Twice now.'

Richard's enjoying this far too much, Corine thinks. People loved to imagine other people's lives; she was no stranger to that indulgence. But it always ended with someone's glass half full. Usually hers.

'Richard, if I didn't know you better, I'd say you've turned into a bit of a cynic. Or drama queen.'

'Cynic? Me? Never.' Richard grins. 'But I suppose in a world without drama, we'd be out of a job.'

She laughs. 'My personal life has been dramatic enough, thank you very much.' She glances out of the window. 'I want a peaceful future—just the sky, some space, my depressed dog, and straightforward people who live far enough away that I'm genuinely pleased when I see them.'

'Nothing else? Really?'

Corine thinks about Mae, confined to her hospital room; trying to end her life when it was just about to restart. She thinks of Lisa, her happiness soon to be increased exponentially.

'No,' she replies, smiling wistfully. 'But seriously, thanks for always seeing my side.'

'Ah, well, that leads me nicely to the fact that Mae's mother has requested a meeting,'

'When?' Corine takes out her phone. 'What day?'

'With me.'

'Oh.' She raises her eyebrows.

'Don't worry, she probably just wants to let off steam. I'll try to put her off. Direct her back to you. I take it Mae still doesn't want to see her?'

Corine nods.

'Legally there's nothing Kate can do about it. There's a

provisional date for Mae's parole set for next month, and it's looking like she will need to go to a therapeutic setting upon release, so…' Richard trails off, but he holds Corine's gaze.

'I'd like to help with an appropriate placement. What's been proposed isn't suitable. Mae wants to get away from London, and places are difficult to secure.' Corine stands, already feeling stress settle across her shoulders, weighing her down. 'Thanks for the coffee, I owe you.'

Richard smiles, and Corine can tell he knows the debt will never be repaid; each time he's mentioned lunch or drinks recently, she has made excuses—keeping their meetings professional and firmly in the office.

'You know, you remind me of Joe sometimes.' The statement is unexpected, even to her.

Richard gives a shy smile. 'How's that?'

'You're generous,' she elaborates.

'Thank you, I think. But I must confess, I got your coffee free with my rewards points, if that's what you're referring to?'

Corine laughs heartily as she leaves the room.

†

Back in her office, Corine sees the bag containing the book and toy she'd bought for Lisa on the chair by her desk. She picks up the phone and dials Lisa's number.

Peter answers, sounding surprised to hear Corine's voice.

'I thought she was meeting you?'

'What? No.' She panics. Had she forgotten about an arrangement? No, Lisa mattered too much for her to forget. 'She's probably meeting up with a friend and said my name by mistake.'

'Maybe.' Peter doesn't sound convinced. 'If you hear from her, ask her to call me, would you? Her waters could break any time.' He pauses. 'Don't say I was fussing, she'll go mad.'

'She'll be fine. I'll ring, don't worry,' Corine reassures him, hearing the concern in his voice.

As soon as she puts the phone down, she starts calling round about possible placements for Mae. Corine knows it's not her job, but she wants everything to go as smoothly as possible. The next time she looks up, it's two o'clock and she's not yet had lunch. She decides to step outside for some fresh air and grab a sandwich from the deli across the street.

It's darker than it should be outside. The sun has disappeared, black clouds hanging overhead, threatening and ominous. As Corine steps off the pavement to cross the road, she sees a grey Land Rover with tinted windows.

Her heart rate accelerates. Is Kate following her? Corine wouldn't put it past her.

Someone in bright clothing zips past on a moped, an orange scarf floating behind them like the feathers on the underside of a red kite. Corine watches them disappear out of sight, the pop of colour waking her out of her paranoid state. Don't jump to conclusions. Kate is probably here to meet with Richard.

Inside the deli, Corine orders a cream cheese and smoked salmon bagel and stands aside to check her phone. She has one missed call from Peter and a voicemail from a number she doesn't recognize.

The message is from a very irate-sounding Kate.

"I don't know what ideas you're putting into Mae's head,

but you need to stop confusing her. Can't you see what your meddling has done? It has to stop. I forgave my daughter for what she did to me because I know what she suffered—what both my girls suffered at the hands of their so-called father. That man gets to see Mae, gets to move on with his life, as if nothing ever happened. But you'll see. It will all come out. And then you can take that smug, professional, fucking smile off your useless, fucking face!"

A deli worker shouts out her order, and Corine, slightly dazed, takes the bagel without saying thanks. Her mind is fixed on the voicemail as she crosses the road towards the office. The Land Rover is still parked up. Without thinking, Corine strides across, heart thudding in her chest, and hammers on the window. She will give Kate a dose of reality. How dare she say such things to her?

Slowly, the window lowers, revealing a well-dressed man in his forties, a perplexed expression on his face. An elderly gentleman with rheumy eyes sits in the passenger seat beside him.

Corine scans the back seats. No sign of Kate. Her heart drops. 'Forgive me, I thought you were someone else.'

She turns away without waiting for either man to respond.

†

Sitting at her desk, Corine stares at the bagel in front of her, her appetite gone. She wraps it back up and pushes it to one side. A shot of something strong would help settle her nerves. She roots through her bag but doesn't find anything.

'If you can't go longer than a few days without a drink,

you're in trouble,' she chides herself.

Sighing, she picks up her phone as a distraction. There are two voicemails. The first, she deletes—it's from Callum, and she'd listened to it already. The second is from Lisa.

"Hey, it's me. Where are you? Call me. I have something for you."

Corine saves the message and digs deep inside her bag again, pulling out a large leather wallet. It's empty, aside from two yellowed baby scans and an adoption certificate. She pulls the certificate out gingerly, looking at the three names on the document: Mr Theodore Malone, Mrs Mary Malone, and Lisa.

She puts it back hastily and closes the wallet.

'She doesn't need to know that.' There's a distinctive rasp to Joe's voice, though he sounds younger. 'You're better than that.'

Corine shakes her head and closes her eyes, trying to free herself of her husband's apparition.

'And you're dead, my love,' she whispers.

CHAPTER 30
FRANK

Frank is prepping dinner when Irene walks into the kitchen. He smiles as he watches her inhale the citrusy smell in the room. 'You look good enough to eat.'

'Thank you.' Irene moves from one side of the room to the other, placing her keys and wallet in her bag. She turns on the lights. 'Do I look *very* pregnant?'

Frank laughs. In the last fortnight, her stomach seems to have doubled in size. 'Turn sideways.'

She laughs and does as he asks, her hands held stiffly at her side like an obedient schoolgirl.

'Magnificently so.'

Satisfied, Irene walks over to a cupboard and looks inside. 'Have you seen my purple water bottle?'

'In the fridge,' he replies as he chops a courgette into small squares.

'You're so thoughtful.' She retrieves the bottle and places it in her bag, before looking at him expectantly.

'You're not going yet, are you? The flight isn't due to arrive until five. You'll be waiting around for hours.'

'I'm excited. This is her first grandchild. Her first trip to London.' She stands close to him; takes a piece of red pepper, and bites.

'Are you sure you don't want me to go with you?'

'I want her all to myself,' she says, then pouts. 'Sorry, I should have asked. How did it go today?'

Frank stops chopping and shrugs. He doesn't want to ruin Irene's excitement. Though she spoke with her mother daily, they hadn't seen each other in a year. She'd been counting down the days.

'What did you talk about? Come on, I want details!'

He might ask Irene the same question but knew she wouldn't appreciate it. 'Everything and nothing,' Frank says, as he drizzles olive oil over a tray of vegetables.

'Oh, come on!' she groans.

Frank couldn't pretend to understand the relationship Irene had with her mother. Though he loved his, they rarely spoke on the phone, and months could go by without him thinking about her. She had her own life.

'It was the first meeting. She'll be out soon, so we'll have plenty of time to talk then. There's no use rushing things.'

'Frank, you know we can't have her here. Not with the baby.'

'Can you stop saying that!' Frank snaps.

Irene looks hurt and he instantly regrets shouting. Perhaps she will understand when she has her own child, but right now, it's all about her baby.

'I let her down,' he explains calmly. 'I need to put things right, but it'll take time. Mae's got to trust me again.'

'Did she say anything about her sister and the horrible lies she told about you?'

'We didn't discuss it.' He turns his back on her and opens the fridge, rooting about. 'I could have sworn I bought parsley. Damn, we're out of lemons, too, I should go get some.' He gathers his keys and wallet and rushes out of the door. 'Back in five. Wait for me!'

†

Standing outside the corner shop, Frank takes his phone and calls The Abbey Clinic. He's greeted by the same snippy receptionist who spoke to him last time.

'No, Mr Bailey, I'm afraid Lyndsey is still not available to talk. Perhaps you might call her mother or husband, they both visit regularly.'

Frank ends the call, frustrated, and sets off back to the flat. As he turns the corner and enters the busy front drive, he notices a car he doesn't recognise. A middle-aged man and woman, both dressed in grey suits, approach him.

'We're looking for a Mr Frank Bailey,' the woman says.

'That's me.' Frank sees she's holding something up to him, a badge of some sort, and his heart sinks.

'It's your partner, Mrs Bailey.' For a moment Frank pictures Irene and his legs wobble. 'Dr Kate Bailey. She's made an official complaint about you, with regards to your daughters Lyndsey and Mae Bailey. Is there somewhere we can talk?'

†

IRENE

Irene has spent the last two hours reading pregnancy magazines in a crowded Heathrow lounge. The articles are virtually identical, yet they fascinate her. She wants to know every detail of her baby's development—from kidney bean, to watermelon, to actual, non-food-related baby facts. She stretches out her legs and slips the magazines into her bag. It's almost five o'clock. Time to walk to the arrivals gate.

The desire to see her mama pulses through her, alive and vital. Besides Frank, her mama is the only person in the world she truly loves—and who loves her back entirely. Always has, always would.

Irene makes her way to the front of the barriers, eyes fixed on the arrivals doorway. Her phone bleeps in her bag. Then again. And again. She pulls it out and flicks open the screen. A torrent of text messages fill the screen, all from an unknown number, all saying the same thing:

"*You don't deserve that child.*"

Irene looks around, panicked. A sea of faces suddenly engulf her. One or two return her gaze. No one she recognizes. She feels her heart quicken, her head spin.

'Irene! Irene!' Her mama's voice calls. 'Hola, cariño!'

The familiar tone soothes Irene like a blanket wrapping itself around her, protecting her.

'Hola, Mama!' Irene unhooks the barrier strap, and the two women embrace. A smaller, older version of Irene clings on to her daughter, refusing to let go as the crowds spill out behind them. Eventually, Irene eases back, and her mother cups her stomach, as though holding a rare and precious gift.

With her mother beside her, Irene feels invincible. She knows the text messages are likely from Frank's ex—or one, maybe both, of his daughters—but she won't let anyone ruin this moment. They stroll back through the bustling airport concourse, and head towards the train station, chatting at hyperspeed.

CHAPTER 31
CORINE

Corine is in the bathroom at work, vigorously brushing her teeth. She cups her hands over her mouth and exhales. Satisfied that any trace of alcohol has gone, she rinses and spits. There's no one else in the bathroom, yet she still checks over her shoulder before pulling two empty miniature vodka bottles from her bag and burying them in the bin. She avoids her reflection in the mirror, ashamed at how easily her willpower had crumbled.

Being alone in the hotel room last night had been hard; sleep impossible. Joe's warning had unsettled her more than she cared to admit, leaving her tossing and turning well into the early hours. Her mind jumping back and forth, skimming and then diving deep into memories that were further muddled by fatigue. Things were said. Promises made and, worst of all, broken. Joe accusing her of sabotaging her own life, blurring into memories of her accusing her mother of the same self-centred destructiveness.

"You're better than that," he'd said.

Corine forces herself to look at her reflection in the mirror: taupe silk blouse, hair pulled neatly back, lipstick. All of it a façade. An attempt to appear fully functioning, when inside, she is an empty husk, held together by secrets and longing for what could have been.

Would she ever live in the moment again? Corine suspects not. She'd always be overwhelmed, ruled by her past. Once again, she feels the familiar cloying pain of unattainable loss. Was this a fate worse than death?

'I'm sorry, I have to tell Lisa the truth. If I don't…' Corine closes her eyes. In her mind, a dark-haired Joe stands beside her, his face moving and shifting, his mouth silently forming the word, *"No"*. 'No one wants to be alone. Isn't that why you went out on the quadbike in a storm? You thought I'd left you.'

Corine exits the bathroom abruptly and heads back to her office, closing the door behind her. At her desk, she takes out the brown leather wallet and places it in front of her before picking up her mobile. She swipes the screen, her finger hovering over Lisa's number—hesitating. Then she slams the phone down and slumps back in her chair, staring out of the window at the sliver of dusty sky.

Her phone rings. It's Peter.

'Have you heard from Lisa?' he asks, a note of urgency in his voice.

'No.' Corine glances at her watch.

'I'm worried. She hasn't been in touch all day.'

Corine tries to sound upbeat. 'She's probably on her way home as we speak.'

'She always calls. Something's not right. What if she's gone into labour somewhere?'

'We're in London, Peter. It's not as if people wouldn't notice a woman in labour.'

Peter laughs, but it sounds forced.

'I'll keep calling her,' she assures him.

'I've tried that, she's not answering.'

'Perhaps she left her phone somewhere, or ran out of battery?' Corine was beginning to worry herself. Lisa was organised, meticulous. Her phone always charged. Several scenarios played out in her mind, all ending in Peter missing the birth. 'I'll keep trying.'

'Okay, thanks.' He sounds distracted. 'I'll call you if I hear anything.' He ends the call without saying goodbye.

Corine takes the leather wallet off her desk. Now was not the time. Finding Lisa was her priority. She picks up her coat and bag and leaves the office, intending to make her way to Lisa's house. As she is leaving, she hears Richard's voice calling her name. She hesitates for a moment, then relents.

'Yes?' Corine stands in the doorway of his office, her face expressionless.

'Mae's brother-in-law has turned up at the hospital. He's asking to visit Mae.'

'I'm not sure that's a good idea. She's never mentioned him.'

'He has Mae's nieces with him. He's being quite insistent.'

'Is he?' Corine folds her arms.

'That's not all. I received a call today from a detective asking if Mae could be interviewed regarding allegations of sexual abuse. Dr Bailey and the older sister filed a complaint with the police.'

'Oh God! Mae's not up to that. Can you look after things with the police, stall everyone a bit? Just a day or two? My niece is about to have a baby any time now and no one can reach her. She's not answering her phone.'

'Go,' Richard replies. 'Family comes first. I'll deal with this.'

Just like that, Corine understands why they are still friends. Despite not having a wife or children of his own, or ever mentioning a wider family, Richard cares. He gets it. She could learn a thing or two from him.

'Thank you,' she whispers, fleeing the clinic and heading to the main street, where she stands on the edge of the curb waiting to hail a cab.

A double-decker bus roars by too close, forcing her to step back. An advert on its side catches her eye—personal health insurance. A forlorn looking young girl stands alone, holding a bike still fitted with stabilisers, while her friends cycle away on theirs without support. *Make Sure You're Around for the Important Things,* the advert reads.

Corine tells herself to get a grip. Lisa will be fine, she's a grown woman with a full life, a doting husband, and a family of her own very soon. Most likely she's enjoying her last few days of freedom before the chaos of motherhood begins.

Turning back, she walks towards the hospital. What matters now is reaching Mae before anyone else does—helping her prepare for what's to come. Reassuring her that she'll be there for her for as long as she's needed. And maybe seeing her young nieces will lift her spirits, help her realise she isn't alone—that she has family.

As Corine retraces her steps, there's a niggle in her stomach, a restlessness that remains. She calls Lisa. When the voicemail kicks in, she attempts to sound jovial.

'Aunty Corine here, my love. Can you just put us all out of our misery and call? How can anyone be at the birth if no one knows where you are? Please, darling… call back.'

CHAPTER 32
LISA

Despite promising Peter she would rest all morning, Lisa had been out of bed and in the shower the moment he left for work. That was the second lie she had told him that day. The first was claiming she was meeting Corine for lunch. Peter hadn't questioned it, which was a relief. The thought of having to elaborate—adding facts and tiny details—would have felt like an even deeper betrayal.

She had blow-dried her hair and tied it back with a scarf. After wrestling with the buttons on her favourite dress, she had opted instead for a loose-fitting tan sweater, and a long stretchy maternity skirt. The real battle was putting on her trainers, her arms straining to reach around the curve of her belly, aiming blindly for her feet.

She had more than enough time to get to the café in Richmond, where she was meeting Anita, a counsellor from The Angel Trust—a charity supporting newly bereaved parents. She wasn't entirely sure why, but her recent conversation with Corine had unsettled her. It felt as though her aunt was holding something back.

The feelings stirred old memories—of her mum and Corine whispering together, always changing the subject whenever Lisa came within earshot. She couldn't have been more than sixteen when she overheard her mother telling

Corine she'd had too much to drink, that she should stop talking before she said something she'd regret.'

"Then get her tested," Corine had said. *"While she's young. It's better she knows her options if she ever wants a family of her own."*

Her mother's response had been angrier than Lisa had ever heard. She had shouted at Uncle Joe, ordering him to take Corine home. Lisa had loved her mum dearly, but she could be sharp—cruel, even—especially when wounded. Baby Michael hadn't been gone long, and Lisa had felt her aunt deserved a little more compassion.

She had called the charity on an impulse, asking about the likelihood of Sudden Infant Death Syndrome running in families. Before long, she had found herself confessing a morbid fear of things going wrong—either during the birth or in the months that followed—just as it had with Corine.

Lisa rarely dwelled on Corine's son, but he was always there, quietly present in the back of her mind. The cousin who had died. Seeing Corine again, hearing her talk about her pregnancy, about Michael, had brought those fears into sharper focus.

The counsellor she spoke to, Anita, had explained that while genetics could be a factor in a small number of SIDS cases, the risk remained low. Even so, the thought of any risk terrified Lisa. She had broken down on the phone, and before the end of the call, Anita had offered to meet her in person.

She offered to visit Lisa at home, but the thought of Peter finding out had filled her with shame and made her feel hysterical. Since the charity was based in Richmond, they had agreed to meet there instead.

The trains were busy, but Lisa arrived at the café early and had been shown to a table by a large bay window overlooking a patio. The two interconnected rooms were packed, the air buzzing with conversation.

Lisa had asked the waitress for water and the woman had nodded towards an old-fashioned sideboard with jugs of iced water. She picked up one of the jugs and brought it back to the table, just as her phone bleeped—her friend, Dana.

There had been a sudden commotion outside as two pigeons fought over leftovers on one of the empty tables. As Lisa watched, she noticed the patio door had been left open by one of the waitresses. She pulled her jacket tight and listened to Dana's voicemail.

"I have the most gorgeous photos of your baby shower! I'll ping them across, call me later!"

Lisa poured a glass of water, but just as she had been about to drink, a dark shape appeared in her peripheral vision, flapping. She yelped and jolted backwards, splashing water all over her face and flinging her phone into the air. It landed with a dull thud in the water jug.

When she looked up, something—a bird most likely—was flying in the opposite direction, out through the open patio doors.

A woman had appeared behind her and plunged hand into the jug of water, retrieving Lisa's phone. 'Are you okay, hen? That pigeon came straight at you. Either that or the mangy thing was blind.'

'I'm fine, thank you.' Lisa had said, grabbing at a pile of paper napkins to wipe her eyes. 'Well, I will be when I fix my contact lenses.'

'I'll get you some more napkins. I'm Anita, by the way, from The Angel Trust.'

'Thank you.' Lisa had sat down, blinking myopically at the hazy, retreating figure of a woman dressed head-to-toe in black.

CHAPTER 33
CORINE

It's Beth's small, serious face that Corine recognises first. She is staring ahead, her knees pulled up to her chest, oblivious of her surroundings. Stuart, Lyndsey's husband, pushes a sleeping Zizi back and forth in her buggy. A pale face and tuft of damp curls protrude above a crocheted blanket. Corine slips past them and heads towards Richard's office. The door is open. He's alone, with papers spread out in front of him.

Corine gives a small cough. 'They're still here, I see. Has anything been agreed or discussed before I go out there?'

Richard shakes his head. 'I thought you had a family emergency?'

'Seems not.'

'I was just going to speak with him. He's keen to talk to Mae… keeps saying he wants to speak privately, but it's your call. She's your patient. Is Mae up to it?'

'I think she'd like to see her nieces. Kate went to great pains to point out that the eldest, Beth, is like Mae.'

Corine's phone bleeps—a new text from Peter, asking if she's heard from Lisa. Her stomach tightens. *Where is she? Why did she say we were meeting today?* All of a sudden, Corine is sick of the suspicion and the lies. How can she ever expect Mae to be honest about her life when Corine's own life is steeped in deception?

Richard pushes the papers he's reading aside. 'Everything okay? You look worried. Look, if it's your niece—'

'It's fine,' Corine snaps, cutting him off—and instantly regretting the sharpness in her voice. It reminds her of the way she speaks to her dog, Betty: commanding, often unnecessarily so. 'I'll speak to Mae. This could be just the tonic she needs. Her nieces are little sweethearts.'

'Oh, I might not have said, but Mae's being moved from the hospital back to her room at The Orchard.' Richard raises his hand as though to silence her. 'But don't worry, she'll remain on constant watch. I'm sorry, her bed was needed.'

Corine can't think of what to say for a moment, feeling suddenly tired and lacking the energy to complain. *No point making Richard's life any more difficult than it already is.*

'Can you get someone to bring them over in ten minutes?' Corine asks. 'I want to speak with Mae first. See if she's up to it.'

'Sure.' Richard frowns. 'You feeling okay? You seem a bit low.'

Corine shrugs. 'Nothing that a bit of zolpidem or benzodiazepine wouldn't cure.'

Richard laughs and appears to mull over her possible insomnia treatments. 'Can I cook for you one night?' he asks as she turns to leave.

Her eyes widen in surprise. 'Do you have a particular night in mind?'

'No, not really. I'll hedge my bets and say whichever night you can make this week.' They stay looking at each other for a while. 'Come on,' Richard cajoles. 'I promise there won't be anything pre-cooked, no reheated single frozen portions or—'

'Have you been spying on me?' Corine laughs. 'I'd like that, thank you. Tomorrow?'

'Fantastic.' Richard beams at her as she lowers her eyes and walks away, touching her hair.

As soon as Corine is back in her office, she calls Lisa again. The phone rings, unanswered. She waits a few minutes and tries again. Nothing. Lisa's phone was probably switched off. *Everything will be okay*, she tells herself. But the problem with having lived through unexpected trauma, Corine knows, is that she will never fully believe that again. Bad things happen, and to those she loves. She remembers telling Joe the same thing. He'd told her to look at the upside: they were unlikely ever to be caught off guard again.

†

Mae looks surprised when Corine tells her she has visitors, but pleased when she finds out who they are. She fiddles nervously with her hair, pushing it behind her ears in readiness to meet her family. Her face is pale still, but there's a touch of colour about her cheeks that puts Corine in mind of a Bouguereau painting.

'I'm here if you need me,' Corine reassures her. 'I'll keep the children busy, so you have time to talk.'

They're in the same therapy room where Corine first spoke with Mae, and she feels a distinct impulse to throw open the window and rip the pictures off the walls.

'I'm surprised Stuart brought them,' Mae tells her. 'It must be frightening in here... seeing me.'

'You've a point there, crazy old you,' Corine jokes, trying to ease Mae's worries, though the thought had occurred to her the moment she saw Beth's anxious little face. A prison was no place for children, and that included the ones who needed to be contained for the good of society. 'He's reaching out to you, Mae. Give him a chance. Believe me, you'll want to see your nieces.'

Mae looks up. 'Why?'

'Because they're adorable.'

Mae purses her lips, suppressing a smile.

†

MAE

Once Corine has welcomed her family inside, and assured Mae that she'll be "just outside if needed", Mae finds herself suddenly alone with Stuart and two small children.

He leaves the pushchair, with a sleeping Zizi in it, in the corner of the room and walks forward, one hand guiding Beth, the other stretched out to greet Mae.

'Mae,' he says in a shaky voice.

'You've changed,' she replies truthfully. He looks so different to how she remembered him. 'No nose-ring?'

'Had to grow up pretty quick for the girls.' Stuart nods towards his two small daughters, then shakes Mae's hand awkwardly. 'Thanks for meeting me. I... well, I need to talk to you, about... about—'

'Need?' Mae frowns. She isn't sure she has the energy for a

serious conversation right now. Shifting her focus to Beth, she decides to change the subject. 'And who is this?'

The little girl looks sideways at her. 'I'm Beth.'

Mae gets down to her level and kneels in front of her timid niece, trying to remember how to talk to small children. 'Lovely to meet you, Beth. How old are you? Ten? Eleven?'

'I'm four,' Beth says proudly, standing a little taller.

Mae sees her own eyes staring back at her. 'Wow, you're so grown up!'

Beth giggles and relaxes a little. Mae observes her quickness to laugh and wonders if it's accompanied by a keenness to please. She hopes not. As an obedient child herself, she instantly recognises in her niece a disposition that could be exploited in thoughtless hands. Mae offers her hand. Beth shakes it, clearly tickled by the adult formality directed at her.

'Are you my mummy's baby sister, like Zizi is my baby sister?'

'I suppose I am.' Mae wants to say in years only but stops herself.

Beth smiles and twists the end of one of her plaits into her mouth without taking her eyes off Mae. The sound of movement, snuffling, can be heard from the pushchair in the corner of the room. Stuart glances over, looking worried. He has a stooped way of holding himself, as though apologetic about his height.

'She's due another bottle soon. We should have dropped it by now, but with Lyndsey being in hospital, it's comforting for her.'

'Don't apologise,' Mae says.

'Would you like me to take her?' Corine asks from the

doorway. 'Beth, perhaps you can show me what to do? It's been a long time since I've looked after a small person like Zizi.'

Stuart nods gratefully and Beth skips over to the pushchair. With a little help from Corine, she guides it towards the door.

'We'll be just outside. Call if you need anything,' Corine tells them, glancing at Mae.

She resists the urge to roll her eyes. *So overprotective.*

Stuart stands there, looking at her. Mae isn't sure where to begin.

'It's good to see you,' he says eventually. 'How are you? I mean, really? I can't imagine what it's been like for you in here.'

Mae squeezes both hands, her eyes moving about the room. What does he expect her to say? Of course she's not okay. 'The girls. They're so sweet,' she says instead.

Stuart's whole face lights up. 'Yeah, we've been lucky. They're very different kids, but they're easy, and Beth's as bright as… well, Lyndsey says she's as bright as you. Zizi's into everything. Except sleep.'

Impatience gets the better of her. 'Why are you here?' she blurts out. 'Why now, I mean?' Mae watches as he walks over to the chair and sits, not looking at her. 'Dr Alexander won't stay out there for long. If you've got something you want to say, now is your chance.'

Stuart rubs his knees and takes a deep breath. 'Okay, did your father sexually abuse Lyndsey?'

'What does Lyndsey say?'

'Right now, she's saying he did. That he molested her over a number of years.'

Mae shrugs. 'Well then.'

'That's it?' The look on his face is desperate. 'That's all you have to say? *Well then?*'

'I don't know what you expect from me. I don't owe you, or anyone, anything.' She strides across the room and back again, her bandaged wrists held in front of her.

'Please, Mae, tell me the truth. Did he ever do anything to you? Touch you inappropriately?'

'Not that I remember.'

'It's not exactly something you'd forget.' Stuart's large bony hands grip his knees, his knuckles turning white, bloodless. 'Something like that… it's traumatic, life-changing, not to mention the fact that it leads to the total destruction of everyone involved. Do you get what I'm saying?'

'You're trying to find an excuse for why Lyndsey's so fucked up.' Mae stares at him defiantly, but he can't hold her gaze and looks away. 'Can you imagine if it was all just fucking fiction?' She starts to laugh. 'You'd have to be mad to make up something like that, don't you think?'

†

CORINE

Outside in the corridor, Corine listens to Mae laughing when two tiny plump hands reach out impatiently. Corine can't open the straps of the pushchair fast enough. As she struggles to unclip her, Zizi's cries become more and more fraught, revving up to a full-on meltdown. Corine puts on her glasses but still can't work out the clasp. Zizi throws herself backwards, face red, her eyes two tiny folds in her face, just as Beth steps forward and unclips her.

'You have to pinch and pull at the same time,' the little girl explains.

Zizi howls.

Corine lifts her, feeling actual fear. She rocks the furious child, ignoring the waves of heat coursing through her entire body. 'There, there, sweetie-pie, you want your milk, don't you?'

The mention of milk and the sight of her bottle in Beth's hand has an instant soothing effect on Zizi. Corine sits down cautiously, taking the bottle with shaking hands and plugging it straight into the baby's open mouth. Zizi sucks loudly, takes a few shuddering breaths, then nestles against Corine's chest.

Corine winks at Beth. 'Thank you. I think someone's happy now.'

She carefully removes Zizi's hat and smooths down her hair. The action triggers a memory of her creeping into Michael's nursery, dressed for an early start at work. She had been off for almost a year by then. At first on maternity leave, then, when she couldn't bear to leave him at the end of six months, she'd taken a further five months as unpaid leave. It had been a big financial readjustment, but her and Joe had both wanted to give their son the best start in life.

Corine pictures herself tiptoeing over to Michael's cot. She'd expected him to be asleep, but he'd turned his head to face her. She'd whispered to him, imploring him to sleep, as she backed out of the room. A quick check of her watch told her it was five-fifteen in the morning; Joe would be up in an hour. Picking Michael up would have made her late for work, and she'd wanted to make a good impression. She'd listened in at the door, heard Michael snuffling, coughing a little, and then silence. Thinking nothing of it, she'd left for work.

Two hours later, Joe called. His voice broke as he tried to tell her. Then a paramedic came on the line and said the words that shattered her world—Michael had passed away.

'You should have picked him up,' Corine hisses. Tears spilling from her eyes.

'Zizi's a girl,' Beth tells her. 'I'm not supposed to pick her up unless Mummy or Daddy is with me.'

†

MAE

Zizi starts to cry again, Beth's high-pitched voice trying to console her little sister the way she must have heard adults doing.

'There, there, Zizi, baby, it's okay now sweetie-pie.'

Such reassurances sound wrong to Mae, coming from the mouth of a child with an awareness of responsibilities well beyond her years.

Zizi's cries escalate.

Stuart looks to the door, then back at Mae, as if torn by a terrible choice: his daughter, or the truth. He sits forward in his seat. 'I know what you did, what you sacrificed to—'

'You should ask your wife to be honest with you,' Mae interrupts. 'I'm about to get out.'

Standing abruptly, she walks over to the picture of the beach and runs her finger along the shoreline.

'Your father's been arrested. Lyndsey accused him of sexual abuse during one of her therapy sessions. The police interviewed her.'

Mae turns sharply to face him. 'They have evidence? Credible evidence, I mean?'

Stuart glances at the door. 'A few years back, when Lyndsey was pregnant with Beth, she told me she'd made it all up. You must know that?'

'It sounds like you don't trust her… your wife… the mother of your two children. I'm assuming they both weren't mistakes, Stuart.' Mae watches for a reaction, her head tilted to one side, but he gives none. She nods slowly and leans closer towards him. 'Oh, I see, yeah. So, if she's prepared to falsely accuse her own father? What would she do to you if you ever crossed her—or decided to leave. Or, God forbid, had an affair? That's a scary thought.'

'I didn't say I didn't trust her. Anyway, Lyndsey's not herself right now. She's getting therapy.'

'Right, so that's why you're here, bringing your two little girls to see their psycho Aunty Mae. You want me to offer you some sort of reassurance? Bit late to remember me when I'm getting out.'

'They would need corroborative evidence to prosecute.'

'I don't owe anyone anything.'

'He's still your father.'

'And I'm his daughter. He hates Kate, but he still left us with her.'

Stuart nods. 'I wanted to visit, Lyndsey did too, but she gets so upset and we didn't think it would be the right place—'

'We?' Mae looks at him quizzically. 'Who is we?'

'Me and your mother.'

'Ah.' Mae laughs. 'I should have known a twisted allegiance would develop between you three. You know, Lyndsey and I never really got on, not just after the attack, but before too. She was like a cuckoo in the nest, getting bigger and fatter, taking up all the space.' She chuckles bitterly. 'I think it disappointed Mum at first, Lyndsey being so big and dumb, but then Kate realised she could use it to her advantage.'

'Mae, please.' Stuart's chin falls to his chest. 'Who is this helping?'

She ignores him. 'Oh, don't get me wrong, I was dumb too. But at least being in here—away from her—I could see how she used us. How she manipulated us to be and do and say whatever the *fuck* she wanted. We were her front line of defence, besotted little minions prepared to sacrifice our own lives to gain her attention. Her approval. All of this was about her getting back at Dad. She would happily sacrifice her own flesh and blood to get back at him for leaving.'

'Lyndsey's changed,' Stuart replies softly. 'Beth and Zizi mean everything to her; she always puts them first. Isn't that how all this started?'

'*All this*? You mean the loss of my life, my freedom, being branded a psychopath? Not a single person in the entire fucking world to rely on. Do you have any idea what that's like?'

Zizi's cries resume, and they both look towards the door.

'If you do anything with your life, make sure you have their back. No matter what.'

'Please… I don't want the girls dragged into this,' Stuart whispers.

Mae wonders if he's frightened Corine will hear. 'Then why did Lyndsey go to the police? What was she thinking?'

'She's drugged up to the eyeballs on antidepressants, sleeping tablets, and fuck knows what else. She hadn't mentioned anything to me, and then suddenly…' Stuart shakes his head. 'Your mum had been in with her the day before she spoke to staff about your father.' He hesitates. 'About what he did.'

Mae sighs heavily. 'Dad's new partner's having a baby. His, by all accounts.'

'You heard, then?'

Mae nods.

'I've looked into it. Even if there isn't enough evidence to convict him, he could still end up with a Sexual Risk Order against him. Bye-bye, second chance.'

Mae fiddles with her bandages. A thin brown line runs the length of the bandage on her left wrist. She sees Stuart notice. He smiles sympathetically.

'You were always the strong one,' he adds.

'This…' She folds her arms defensively. 'It's what we do in here to kill time. A means to an end, that's all.'

'Still, I'm sorry.'

'What do you want from me, Stuart? Talk to Lyndsey, it's her mess, and I don't owe Dad anything. I've been used enough. Now please leave so I can get on with my so-called life. I really just need all this to be over.'

There's a bang and the door springs opens. Beth leads with the pushchair. Corine has hold of Zizi, whose cries fill the room. Stuart rises wearily, his arms outstretched. Beth is part way through a nursery rhyme, her voice so flat and monotone it breaks Mae's heart.

'I'm afraid I'll have to take her home, get her fed.' Stuart takes hold of Zizi and bounces her up and down on his hip.

Corine is all smiles, her voice breathy. 'Beth has been an absolute star singing songs for her little sister. That kept her happy for a short while, didn't it, Beth?'

'Sometimes she cries no matter what I sing. Grandma says singing lessons might help.'

'You tell your grandma that your voice is perfect just the way it is,' Mae says, smiling at Beth. She bends down, takes hold of her tiny hands. 'That was a nice thing you did, singing for your sister like that, but she isn't your responsibility. Mummies and daddies are the ones who are supposed to look after their babies. You're meant to have fun.' She reaches over and tickles her.

Beth flays about, laughing, enjoying the attention.

As Stuart leaves, he looks back at Mae. 'I'm sorry, Mae. It was wrong to ask you… to expect anything more from you.' He stops, seemingly lost for words. 'We are the ones who owe you.'

Mae glares at him. She can feel Corine looking at her from the other side of the room.

'Stuart,' she calls after him.

He looks back.

'Give me one good reason to care.'

'Can I come and see you again, Aunty Mae?' Beth asks, her innocent eyes gazing up at Mae.

'Oh, I'd like that.' She raises her hands level with her face and waves, until Stuart and the girls disappear from sight.

CHAPTER 34
CORINE

Back in her office, Corine can't get Stuart's words out of her mind: *"We are the ones who owe you."* What had he meant by that? She would raise it in their session tomorrow. But it was Mae's expression that lingered, unsettling her the most.

Corine sighs. If everything had gone according to plan, this would have been their final session. By next week, she would have been on the train back to Scotland. At the start of it all, she'd imagined the ending would come with clarity. Instead—perhaps truer to form—she suspects it will sputter and crackle, then peter out with no crescendo, no revelations, no truth at all.

She has already cleared her desk for the evening, filed away all her notes and observations, and left Mae's casefile in order. As she drops her notebook and pen into her bag, her phone bleeps. It's Peter.

He launches straight in, his voice taught with worry. 'Lisa's still not home. Or answering her phone.'

'Have you tried ringing her friends?'

'No one has heard from her.'

'I'm sure she's okay. If she'd gone into labour, someone would have called by now. She's probably shopping, getting a few last-minute things. Once the baby's here, then—'

'Wait a minute,' Peter interrupts. 'I can see the impression of an address on this notepad. I'll get a pencil.'

Corine hears drawers being pulled open and closed.

'She's written a number on the notepad, and three o'clock, Crowthorne Lodge. I think it says Anita? I don't even know where that is, or anyone called Anita... Anita Angel? Do you know anyone by that name?'

'No—but that's in Richmond Park.' The woman's name sounds fake, like a drag queen persona. 'She must have met a friend for lunch. Keep calling the number. I'm on my way to yours.'

It doesn't makes any sense, Corine thinks. She throws everything into her bag and grabs her jacket, a heavy feeling settling in her stomach. Why go that far, this late in her pregnancy, without telling anyone? And who was this woman? Was she the same woman who'd—coincidently—bumped into Lisa at the school gates? The one who'd asked about a therapist for her grandchild?

Suddenly, nothing feels like a coincidence anymore. Too many things have happened without good reason, and none of them sit comfortably with Corine. What if the woman Lisa was meeting was the same one who had called Callum about buying the farm?

Outside, Corine hails a cab and gives the driver Lisa's address. But as the car pulls away, she changes her mind. 'Actually—take me to Richmond Park instead. The café just inside the grounds.'

'Opposite the main car park?'

'That's right, and can you try to hurry? It's important.'

Once the cab starts moving, she calls Peter. 'I'm on my way to Richmond; I'll see if Lisa's still there.'

'Why would she still be there, it's six-thirty? She'd be on her way home by now. I don't want you to waste your time just because I'm worrying.'

'You're not wasting my time. If she isn't there, I can stretch my legs—get some fresh air. Besides, I'm craving space and a little greenery. Call if you hear anything.'

She ends the call and immediately dials Mae's father, Frank. He picks up at once, as though he's been waiting.

'Hi Frank, it's Corine Alexander.'

'I can't speak,' he says brusquely. 'Is Mae okay?'

'Yes, yes, she is.'

'Look, if this is about… Well, I'm sure you're aware I've been accused?'

'I just heard. Do you think Kate is behind all of this, the accusations?'

'Perhaps you could tell me? Did she and Mae get together and—'

'Mae has nothing to do with this as far as I'm aware. She's never said anything to me about you specifically.' Corine thinks for a moment. 'This may sound like an odd question, but are you a whisky drinker, by any chance?'

'I don't touch the stuff. Beer and the occasional glass of wine, maybe. Why?'

'Oh, it's nothing.'

'In answer to your first question, I *know* Kate is behind this.'

'She would use her own daughter to get back at you?'

'She already has.' Frank hesitates. 'Look, I need to go.'

'Frank, wait! Can we talk tomorrow?'

'That might be difficult. Irene's mum just flew in from

Madrid. They'll be back soon, and I'm fucked if I know what to tell them.'

'I'll speak with Mae again tomorrow. Call me when you have a moment.' Corine pauses, thinking. 'If it helps… Mae never actually accused you of anything.'

Corine ends the call and turns to face the window. The whole situation is a mess—an enormous, tangled mess. As the streets of London slip by, her thoughts drift to Joe. She had always felt he was making her choose: between him and Lisa, between their marriage and the role she'd stepped into after Mary died.

She stares blankly through the glass, barley registering the shifting scenery. Her mind is caught, replaying a moment she knows she can't change.

"She's my flesh and blood, and I have a chance to build a relationship with her. She thinks she's alone!"

"Tomorrow isn't the time, Corine. Not at Mary's funeral. With emotions so high, who knows what might be said."

"You don't trust me."

"Let things settle. Tell Lisa you're busy on the farm, that you can't leave," he'd replied, ignoring her. *"She'll come to terms with it, given time."*

"What—like we did?" she'd shot back, bitter.

"It's different for a parent and you know it."

The sky above their new kitchen extension had been dramatic, with dense black clouds that reflected her mood. She'd turned away from him, fists clenched.

Joe had taken a long breath before speaking.

"You did a good thing all those years ago." He'd sounded worn down by the weight of the same argument, the endless

ache of unresolved grief. *"And then life dealt us a cruel hand. It wasn't fair or just—it just was. But please, my love… honour the promise you made your sister. Mary had another surrogate, but you were the one who insisted. Don't allow grief to define you. You're more than that. And no one—not even Lisa—will ever replace our son."*

Those had been the last clear words he ever said to her.

Corine had walked out and boarded a train to London, intending to go straight to Lisa's place. But delays meant she arrived late and tired. Not wanting to put Lisa out, she'd called Richard instead, hoping to stay at his flat. He hadn't picked up.

In some ways, she'd been relieved. Their friendship had always felt slightly unbalanced—knowing Richard cared for her more deeply than she did for him.

Standing in the middle of Euston Station, unsure where to go, she had called Joe. His voice had sounded slurred from drinking. He yelled at her to stop being a selfish idiot and to get the next train home.

Corine had wanted to scream—to release all the years of silent hurt she'd swallowed in the name of other people's happiness or comfort. Instead, in her best therapist voice, she'd replied, *"Thank you for your honesty. I'll be staying at Richard's for now. After Mary's funeral, I'm going to do what I should have done years ago. If it goes the way I hope it does, I may not come back."*

Joe had left her four unanswered messages after that. Four missed opportunities to alter the course of his life, to save him from his drunken recklessness. Corine had ignored them all. Had she stayed with him—called him back—the accident, and his eventual death, might never have happened.

'Don't let grief control you,' she whispers, just as the cab pulls up at Crowthorne Lodge.

She pays quickly and runs up the path between sedate, manicured lawns to the white Edwardian building that houses the café. She pushes the door—it doesn't budge. It's locked. Corine hurries to the rear of the building, where tables stand empty, chairs stacked and chained. The sun sits lower in the sky, but the garden is still alive with people enjoying the lighter nights and mild weather. She scans the area—no sign of Lisa.

She stands for a moment, staring at the painterly view.

'Come on… think.'

CHAPTER 35
IRENE

It's peak time on the London underground. Commuters spill off station platforms into the maze of underground tunnels like ants, pulled along by the vibration of trains. Irene's mama stops suddenly, her hand on her daughter's arm. People tut as she urges Irene to slow down in softly spoken Spanish.

'I'm fine, *Mama. Estoy emocionada de que conozcas a Frank.* You will love him!'

Helena smiles, grabbing her small suitcase from her daughter's hands. 'I pull, *sin argumentos.*'

'Okay, boss, but stop worrying.'

Irene walks ahead, leading the way, unable to stop smiling. She's happy her mama is with her again, sharing the same space and breathing the same air—however fusty it smells. It feels like she can finally relax and look forward to the birth, knowing nothing bad will happen with her mama by her side. God forbid anything did happen during the birth, her mama would care for her grandchild with all the same love and devotion that she gave her own four children.

Irene drops back, linking her arm through Helena's, and they resume their conversation, barely pausing for breath until they reach Waterloo Station.

There's a blast of air through the tunnel as a train approaches, followed by a screeching of breaks. An announcement sounds, doors slide open, and the train empties. Immediately, those waiting stream on board, and the train carriage fills in seconds—every seat taken.

Irene and Helena move away from the door, leaning against the platform wall to allow the last determined few to contort their bodies into the train. Another warning sounds, urging passengers to stand clear, and they watch as the train pulls away. Theirs is due in two minutes.

People hustle past, jostling for space further down the platform. Someone bumps against Helena's suitcase, sending it into the back of her leg. At her mama's soft cry, Irene turns just as another blast of warm air signals the approaching train—this one moving faster, at a high speed.

That's when it happens.

Irene experiences everything in slow motion—the train pulling in, a sudden shove, her mama's hand grabbing her jacket and yanking her back with all her strength.

In the chaos that follows, Helena holds on tightly, drawing her daughter to her, away from the platform edge and towards the relative safety of a bench. Too shocked to speak, Irene allows herself to be guided, her eyes darting frantically over the bustling platform.

A train guard arrives first, and minutes later, two police officers appear. They offer to get Irene checked over, but she refuses.

'I just want to go home,' she whispers.

The police press for information—a description of the assailant. Irene shakes her head; she saw nothing. But Helena explodes into an outpouring of Spanish, which Irene hurriedly translates.

'It was a woman. Tall, thin. She was wearing a long black coat, with a hooded top underneath. The hood was up, covering her face. It all happened so quickly—Mama didn't get a clear look.'

'Did you see anything else? Any distinguishing features that could help us identify her?'

Again, Irene translates. 'Her hands were scarred. Terrible scars.' Irene mimics her mama's gestures, indicating, 'Here and here.'

One of the officers relays the description over his radio.

Irene closes her eyes, drawing in a sharp intake of breath. 'Oh my God. It's my husband's ex. She did this. She has scars on her hands…'

'Do you have her name? An address?'

'Yes, Kate Bailey. My partner, Frank, can tell you where she lives.' Irene gives the officer Frank's number, leaving him to call while she quickly fills her mama in on what she's just told the police.

'Thank you,' the officer says a short while later. 'And thank your mother. We've got people looking for her. Someone's analysing the security footage as we speak, so we should get ID confirmation soon.' He looks at Irene and hesitates. 'Is there any reason why she might want to harm you?'

†

KATE

Kate is sitting in the front carriage when she spots the police officers on the platform. She slips off her coat and stares down at her phone, pretending to scroll—but it's too late. Two young female officers have already clocked her.

'Mrs Kate Bailey?'

'Excuse me?' she asks, looking confused.

'Are you Kate Bailey?'

'Yes. Dr Kate Bailey. Please don't tell me something's happened to one of my daughters? Granddaughters?'

'I'm going to have to ask you to come with us, Dr Bailey. We need you to answer a few questions at the police station.'

'Why? I haven't done anything!'

'We have CCTV footage of you pushing your estranged husband's partner in front of a moving train. You do not have to say anything—'

'Don't be ridiculous, I'm a doctor! I look after people. I don't harm them.'

'As I was saying, Dr Bailey, you do not have to say anything, but it may harm your defence if you do not mention, when questioned, something which you later rely on in court.'

CHAPTER 36
CORINE

Corine approaches her sister's empty house with a heavy heart. They hadn't spoken in the months leading up to Mary's death. Even before that, their relationship had been strained for several years, marred by resentments, both real and imagined. Then came the unexpected: Mary's heart attack, putting an end to any sort of reconciliation between them. Not that a reconciliation would have been any more than a quiet conversation, but for them, it would have been enough—a signal to move on. Before that, a few days had been the longest they'd ever gone without speaking. The longer they'd left it, the less likely it had seemed they would find a way back to each other—even a begrudging, fragile one.

Something about the large 1940's semi—with its lead windows and huge sloping roof—reminds Corine of Mary: solid and practical. When had she stopped seeing her that way? What had prevented them from finding that inevitable path back to each other? A sinking feeling coils in her stomach, hollow and gnawing. The overwhelming desire to knock and see her sister open the door tells Corine what she needs to know. She would give anything for that chance—to see Mary again. To apologize. To be forgiven. To forgive.

Now, standing in front of her sister's modest family

home, Corine finally sees things from Mary's point of view. Lisa has always come first. Always. Telling her that she was Corine's biological daughter—after a lifetime of believing that Mary was her natural mother—now felt heartless. It altered nothing. It only muddied the waters of what had been a perfectly happy family.

Michael's death—and with it, her chance of motherhood—had been devastating, but it hadn't given Corine the right to go back on her word. To claim Lisa as her own.

Before Corine had offered to be a surrogate, Mary had planned to use someone unrelated and an anonymously donated egg—minimising the risk of the surrogate mother deciding to keep the baby. That had been Mary's biggest fear. At the time, Corine had believed she would never feel anything other than altruism towards her sister. Her only priority had been to deliver Mary a healthy baby. But grief over Michael's death had changed everything—altered her thoughts, her feelings, even her dreams. It had driven her to act in unexpected ways. Ways she was now deeply ashamed of.

She had wanted to be a mother—at any cost.

Perhaps Mary had stopped calling because she'd been afraid of her? That, in her reduced state, Corine might take her much longed for family life and tear it to shreds. She almost had. If it hadn't been for Joe—his quiet reminders that she was still a good, decent person—she might have destroyed everything. Mary's life. Ted's. Lisa's.

Corine knocks on the front door, but no one answers. The dark, heavily curtained windows are impossible to see through, even with her nose pressed to the glass. No sign of Lisa. She moves along the side of the house and runs her hand down the back of a small woodshed until she finds the hidden key. Her chest tightens as she unhooks it and lets herself inside.

'Hello... Lisa?' Her calls are met with silence. A shiver passes through her.

The vibration of her phone makes Corine jump. It's an unknown number. She doesn't answer. Two missed calls from Frank blink on the screen. She'll call him back tomorrow—after speaking to Mae.

Out of habit, she slips her shoes off and steps into the dark-panelled hallway, sniffing at the musty air. The lounge door creaks as she pushes it opens. Inside, pieces of her parent's furniture draw her attention—a chintzy floral chair her mother loved; a crystal vase that had belonged to her great-grandmother; an assortment of ornaments and photographs capturing family moments, precious to no one but them.

How long before they were all forgotten? One generation? Two?

Every milestone of Lisa's life had been captured and framed by Mary. Every birthday, holiday, prize-giving, lost tooth, and bout of measles. Corine was surprised she hadn't noticed before, but she was in a fair few of those photos. In the background. *As it should be*, she tells herself.

Someone has placed an open cardboard box filled with photographs on the sideboard, and Corine picks up a picture of herself sitting on a garden bench, holding a baby in her arms. Her face and stomach are still swollen from giving birth.

'I love that photo.'

Corine startles, almost dropping the frame. 'Lisa,' she

gasps, feeling shocked and relieved at the same time.

Lisa stands at the door, wearing an old chunky cardigan of Mary's. Her eyes look tired, and puffy from sleep.

She joins Corine next to the sideboard and takes hold of the picture. 'You look so young, it's unbelievable to think you were in your thirties then. You look like a baby.' Lisa peers closer. 'You were obviously expecting a girl with that pink shawl.'

Corine takes the photo from Lisa and pretends to study it closely. 'People passed down lots of things back then. In fact, I think that was probably one of your blankets.' The lie comes easily. She had been almost twenty-six when she gave birth.

Michael hadn't come along until twelve long, difficult years later—years spent trying to conceive, struggling to carry a baby to full term.

The bench she was sitting on in the photograph was long gone, but the memory of that day remained as vivid as ever. Joe driving her from the hospital to this house. Sitting in the garden, cradling the baby girl she had just given birth to. She hadn't wanted to release her—but handed her over anyway, casually asking Mary if she'd decided on a name. Lisa had seemed like a plain name to Corine, unsuitable for such a precious little darling, but she hadn't said anything. It was Ted's sister's name, after all, and she had been taken in a car accident when Ted was a boy.

"You did a wonderful, selfless thing, my love, but she's their baby," Joe had said later, when she'd questioned their choice of name.

Corine had looked away, hiding the tears that streamed down her face. She hadn't expected the grief—the aching longing to hold the baby girl she'd carried for nine months. Joe had comforted her, reassuring her they would have a baby of their own soon enough. Little had they known the years of sorrow that lay ahead. After Michael's death, that selfless act had started to feel like her biggest mistake.

Lisa replaces the picture and picks up another, this time of her mother and father sitting on a rock, a backdrop of blue skies.

Corine watches her, noticing the ruffled hair and the vertical creases on her face—clear signs of sleep. 'We've all been wondering where you'd disappeared to.'

'I just got off the phone to Peter. I'm so sorry—he said you were in Richmond Park looking for me. I was about to call you.'

Corine's shakes her head and sighs. 'We were worried something had happened to you… that you'd gone into labour.'

'I had an urge to be here…'

'It's okay, you don't have to explain.'

'I must have fallen asleep.' Lisa shakes her head, embarrassed. 'I'm sorry for worrying everyone.'

'I'm just relieved that we didn't miss the birth.'

'We?' A smile blossoms across Lisa's face. 'You've changed your mind? You'll do that for me?'

'For you, and your mum. If you still want me?'

'Yes, yes, of course I do!' Lisa throws her arms around Corine. They stand, embracing—a new generation nestled between them.

'Mary would have loved to hold your hand through this. What mother wouldn't?'

Lisa sighs and steps to one side, her gaze drifting to the sideboard. She lifts a photograph of her parents on their wedding day, brushing the dust away with the sleeve of her cardigan. 'That last week, before the heart attack, Mum talked about calling you. She said you were always there for her when things got tough. I think she felt she had let you down—that losing a child was the greatest loss imaginable, and you had every reason to react the way you did… isolating yourself.'

She pauses, her thumb tracing the edge of the frame. 'She never told me what you argued about that last time you visited, but I heard her telling you not to come round. I told her I couldn't believe she'd spoken to you like that. I'm not sure if you remember?' Lisa hesitates, her voice softening. 'I think you'd been drinking heavily.'

Corine sinks into her mother's old chair, rubbing her hand along the soft fabric of the arm—comforted by a sense of the past, of easier times. 'The drinking… I mean serious drinking… it started before that. Not long after your wedding. Seeing you getting married… it made me think of Michael—how things might have been.' She exhales slowly. 'Drink was always my weakness. Then the arguments started. Joe wanted me to get help, but I wouldn't listen. I refused to see reason.' Corine turns the gold wedding band on her finger, the metal worn from years of wear. It had been Joe's mother's ring before hers, and all the more precious for it.

'I'm so sorry. Mum was upset, she wanted to put things right, but then she…'

'I know, love, I know. I'm so terribly sorry.'

'I barely remember the funeral, but you were there and

that was a real comfort. I didn't expect you to go back that same afternoon and then to not see you… and poor Joe.'

'I saw how devastated you were about your mum, and I should have known what to do or say, but…' Corine pauses. 'I stopped drinking for a while after that. I needed my head clear, to look after Joe. But then, months later, he… he died.'

'What? Months? But you only got in touch two months ago! That's why I sent baby-shower invite—I didn't want you to feel alone. You were there for me when I needed you… and I wanted to be there for you.'

Corine smiles, fighting back the urge to cry. 'I appreciate that. But it took me a while to get my head together. It was a simple burial, in a small graveyard close to the croft, overlooking the sea. He wanted me to scatter his ashes where we scattered Michael's, but… I couldn't. I wanted him closer. Somewhere tangible. Somewhere I could visit.'

'Why didn't you tell me sooner?'

They stare at one another for a moment.

'You had your own grief to deal with and I didn't want to make things worse. Besides, I had Betty and the farm to keep me busy, and the storms this year have been relentless. Then I got the call about Mae…'

'Your former patient?'

Corine nods. 'I'd never met anyone so utterly alone before.' Tears fall freely down her cheeks now. She wipes them away and smiles apologetically.

'You've got me. You'll always have me,' Lisa says, settling on the arm of the chair and leaning down to hug her. 'What was it you wanted to tell me the other night? You said you had something to give me.'

Corine's hand drifts toward her bag, acutely aware of the brown leather wallet inside—the documents that could change everything between them. But she knows, with a sudden clarity, that she will never give it to Lisa. Being a mother takes more than a title, more than a name printed on a legal deed.

'I can't remember,' she lies. 'Nothing important, anyway.' Corine picks up the picture of her and Lisa as a baby. 'Can I keep this one?'

'Of course, we should both choose the ones we want to keep.' Lisa gazes at a photograph of her mother and father. 'I've decided to put the house on the market. It's been sat empty for long enough. I've got my memories, they're all I need.'

'Keep some of their things, love. It helps with the grieving process, and later… the memories.' Corine smiles. 'In fact, if you don't mind, I'd like this chair.'

Lisa looks surprised. 'But that was Grandma's chair. I didn't think you'd want it.'

'She was still my mum,' Corine acknowledges, giving her a half-smile. 'She wasn't all bad.'

CHAPTER 37
CORINE

The morning after Kate's arrest, Corine sits opposite Mae in a small therapy room, its bland walls doing little to bridge the distance between them. Frank had called first thing, his voice strained with exhaustion, and told her everything about Irene's ordeal. Corine studies Mae's face, unsure how she will react to the news, but certain it's better that she gets the truth from her, from someone who cares.

'They have video evidence,' Corine says, 'and an eyewitness. In all likelihood… she'll be convicted.'

Mae doesn't speak. Her pale face stares blanky across the room, her eyes fixed and unseeing. She rubs the soft skin between her thumb and forefinger—an old, self-soothing habit.

Corine waits, giving her time to process what she's just heard.

'Like mother, like daughter,' Mae says eventually, with a shrug so flippant it makes Corine's chest tighten. As though none of it—Kate, the attack, the arrest—really mattered.

Corine feels a sudden impatience kick in. Lacing her hands together, she forces herself to take a deep breath. 'You,' she begins, pointedly. 'Need to think about yourself, young lady.'

Mae laughs. 'Young lady? You sound ancient.'

'I feel ancient,' Corine says, her voice rising despite herself. 'Ancient, chasing around London trying to find the truth—trying to stop your life from catching fire. Lyndsey has confessed to everything. She lied about your father, and she lied about your mother's attack.'

Mae blinks repeatedly, her whole demeanour changing. For the first time since their therapy sessions began, she looks genuinely thrown. 'Lyndsey isn't well.' She shifts nervously in her seat, her eyes narrowing. 'She doesn't know what she's saying.'

'Your father wouldn't agree. Nor Stuart. Yes, your sister has issues, but they're not all of her own making.'

Mae doesn't respond. Her face is closed-off, sullen.

It's a look that Corine has come to recognise as defensive; an unwillingness to take a chance or to trust another person. Who could blame her, given everything that had happened in her young life.

'Lyndsey's trying to put things right, Mae'

'Bit late for that,' she sneers. She sits up and smooths the creases in her sweatpants, chewing her bottom lip nervously. Her eyes track around the room before coming to a stop.

Corine follows her gaze to a picture of a mountain scene. 'It reminds me of my farm.' Corine says, closing her eyes. 'Long horizons, dramatic storms, and clouds so big and black you can imagine it's the end of everything.' She opens her eyes. 'Yet on a calm day... well, it's as close to perfection as you could wish for.'

'It sounds beautiful.'

'It is.' She smiles, quickly adding, 'You should come.'

Mae stares, again visibly surprised. The edges of her lips

start to curl upwards but something stops her.

Corine needed to find a way of connecting—that one thread that might make Mae finally open up.

'I couldn't see the beauty in anything for a while,' Corine says. 'I lost my way on more than one occasion. Many years ago... and recently—when my husband died. I was devastated and so, so angry with him for leaving me alone.' She smiles sadly and taps her head. 'Things got a bit crazy in here and I almost did a terrible, selfish thing—something I would have deeply regretted.'

'I don't know about crazy, but you always seemed sad. Even when I first met you.'

'I was. And I suppose a part of me always will be. Grief, trauma, loss... they're complicated. It takes time to adjust, to learn how to live with them and still go on with your life.'

Normally, Corine would have stopped there. Professional boundaries existed for a reason, and she had already said more than she should. But Mae was looking for someone to trust, and Corine knew that if no one ever put Mae's needs first, she might never risk it herself—never learn that she was worthy of love.

'I lost my little boy, Michael, eighteen years ago. He was three days away from his first birthday. I'd just started back at work. That morning, I peeked in on him, then slipped out to work, relieved to be off the hook. God, I hated myself for that. I kept thinking—if I'd stayed a bit longer, if I'd picked him up, if I'd made a different choice in that split second... Maybe... But it didn't make any sense. Some things just don't.'

'I'm sorry.'

Corine nods. 'Sudden Infant Death Syndrome, they call it.'

'That's horrible.'

'My poor husband, Joe… he got the backlash of my grief. I drank. I threw myself into work. Then I drank some more. It's easy to be consumed by loss—by everything you don't have—until you lose sight of what you have. As a psychiatrist, I was supposed to know better. I was supposed to use the tools I gave to my patients—therapy, supervision, support—but I didn't even know where to start. And then the shame sets in. It makes you doubt yourself. It silences you.'

There's a pause while Mae's eyes scan Corine's face. 'You left your job so suddenly back then that I thought maybe I'd had something to do with it. That you thought I was so terrible that you couldn't stand to work with me.'

'What? Oh God, Mae, no! None of it was your fault. You know, so often in my career, I'd hear it all, *"My parents hated me… my life is hopeless… I was abused by a family member… forced to take drugs… no one understands me… I want to throw myself in front of a car… off a building… I want to kill you…"*' Corine raises a hand to her temple. 'It gets noisy in here. But you—your silence… it was deafening. You, Mae Bailey, were a first for me.' She gives a small shrug. 'You were right about me being sad though. Joe and I both were. And if I'm being honest, it didn't help that you were the same age my son would have been. But that's not why I left.'

Mae nods, her eyes locking with Corine's.

'We decided to move to Scotland years before I was given your file. It was to be a fresh start, somewhere we both loved. The goal was self-sufficiency—and it worked too, for a time.

Then my sister died unexpectedly, and I came to London. And... that's when my husband had his accident.' Her eyes fill with tears, and she wipes them quickly. 'I can't believe how selfish I was, blaming him. For a moment there, I even felt like he'd come off his quad bike on purpose.'

Mae listens intently, her beautiful green eyes wide with sympathy.

Neither of them speak. The quiet stretching, heavy and unbroken.

Mae sighs. 'I felt like Mal was abandoning me. I barely spoke to her the day she was transferred. Like she was responsible for it.' She gives a breathy laugh. 'Totally crazy.'

Corine studies her, knowing the reasons for Mae's attempted suicide were tangled and deep. Her best friend leaving might have tipped her anguished mind over the edge—but Mae's pain had roots far older, and far darker.

'You know you can keep in touch with Mal, right?'

'I know. We spoke on the phone last night. Her mum isn't doing so good.' Mae hesitates. 'Could we talk about her some other time?'

'Sure,' Corine says, and smiles. 'But can I just ask—was it Mal who told you about Irene's baby? The date of birth, June twenty-third?'

Mae shakes her head. 'No. Irene wrote me a card months ago. Just a few lines, saying they were having a baby. She gave the due date. She begged me to tell her why I wouldn't speak to Frank.'

'So, you wanted to see if your mum knew about the baby?'

'No, I knew she did. I just thought it would make her reveal her true self sooner. I didn't realise how angry she'd be, though. I underestimated that.'

Corine waits for her to continue, but Mae's gaze drifts, her thoughts clearly elsewhere. 'You know,' Corine says gently, 'if you hadn't pointed out that my shirt was buttoned all skew-whiff, or winced at my boozy breath, I would have gone on lying to myself—wallowing, drinking myself to death. I owe you, Mae Bailey. And I'm here for you, whenever you're ready to talk.'

'When will you go back to Scotland?' Mae's voice is quiet, barely a whisper.

'I've decided to stay for a while. Until my niece has her baby, and we get your release sorted.' Corine smiles, reaching out for Mae's hand. 'The rest is up to you. You just need to trust a little.'

A shy smile spreads across Mae's face. 'What about your farm?'

'A friend is taking care of it. Better than I ever did. I've other plans brewing... of a therapeutic nature. Would be a good place for people to get some head space.'

'What, like a retreat?'

'I'm not sure I'd call it that. Besides, words can infer too much—'

'Like "mother," for instance,' Mae interrupts.

Corine nods slowly. 'You're not wrong there.' She chuckles, looking around the therapy room. 'These pictures served a purpose in the end. They reminded me that some places are easier to get perspective. These bland rooms.' She kicks the table. 'With everything nailed down and no views or windows to speak of... they damn well clog the arteries. If I'm going to test my ideas, though, I'll be needing a guinea pig.'

A smile flickers across Mae's mouth. She glances sideways at Corine, then lets her gaze drift towards the barred window. Outside, sunlight bathes the building in a pale, yellow glow. A wind builds suddenly, rattling the glass, and just as quickly falls away. Between the gusts, the room settles into a heavy, expectant silence.

Mae is stubborn, that much Corine knows. But something else is holding her back. Some unspoken burden.

Mae stares out of the window, she flexes and straightens her slender, white fingers and swallows hard. Without a word, Corine fills a plastic cup with water and slides it across the table. Mae takes it, gulps it back.

'You've stopped biting your nails!' Corine exclaims. 'That's fantastic!'

Mae smiles broadly, clearly surprised at Corine's delighted outburst.

'A little bit of cheeky pink on those nails would look good. I'll see what I can do,' she says, and winks.

'One of the girl's has a varnish called "In the Buff" and another called "Copper-Feel",' Mae says, giggling.

She's still just a child. 'Kate doesn't deserve your loyalty, Mae,' Corine tells her. 'Nothing you or your sister did would have been enough. Your mother only really cares about herself—and about what affects her. She would have found fault no matter what you did or said.'

Mae's lips curve into a tight smile, but she says nothing.

Corine lifts her notepad and flips it open to the page with her notes from that morning's call with Frank. 'Do you remember telling me to watch your mother? To really see what you see?'

Mae nods, her eyes still fixed on the table.

'I should have seen someone self-obsessed, narcissistic, and destructive. A pathological liar. But I believed her. When Kate told me she'd gone part-time at work to help Lyndsey out, to look after her grandchildren, I bought into it completely. Later, when I questioned Stuart about it, he said she'd practically demanded to have the children a couple of times recently, but otherwise she'd been strictly unavailable on the grandparent front.'

Mae nods, her arms folded, fingers softly tugging at the skin on her elbows. 'That sounds like Kate.'

'Now I know Kate spent most of her free time spying on people and trying to infiltrate their lives, causing disruption.' Corine thinks of Kate phoning Callum, claiming she'd bought the croft, deliberately stirring up trouble between them. And poor Lisa, cornered at the school gates, oblivious to Kate's deception. But Mae didn't need to hear any of that. It wouldn't bring her any closer to sharing the truth about her own family.

'Welcome to my world,' Mae says sullenly.

It was hard to imagine Mae opening up, but Corine presses on. 'Kate was spying on your father and his new partner,' she says. 'She even totalled her car doing it. That's why she was being driven around in her old university friend's Land Rover. Your father saw the crash—but Irene was in the car, and he didn't want to frighten her.' Corine leans forward. 'Did you know your mother's nickname at university was Sledge?'

Mae shakes her head. 'She hated the snow.'

Corine smiles faintly. 'Not that type of sledge, I'm afraid. More of a sledgehammer. She was known for being forthright, outspoken. She hated losing in an argument.'

'I can see that.' Mae hesitates, her brow furrowing. 'Dad knew what she was like… he could have acted sooner.'

Her eyes flash, and Corine recognises the destructive anger that she herself battles with.

'We could all be accused of that,' she concedes. 'I'm sorry, Mae, I believe I failed you.'

Mae looks around, her eyes catching anywhere but Corine's expectant face. *If she is angry with me, she has every right to be.* She suddenly realises Mae's lip is trembling, and once again that urge to scoop her up, to protect her, kicks in.

Just as Corine is about to end to their session, Mae starts to speak.

'Mum said it would be our secret—that the only thing I had to do was stay quiet. It wasn't lying, just omitting the truth. But things didn't go to plan. I mean, Mum didn't press any charges or anything, but I was considered dangerous and charged anyway. That's when she started asking me to make false statements—to cover things up, to protect Lyndsey.'

Mae hesitates, and Corine smiles warmly at her—compassionate and encouraging. 'Tell me about that day. Start anywhere.'

'It was Sunday, early evening, and I was in the kitchen, helping Mum serve a roast. I spooned the last of the roasted vegetables onto the plates. Mum was moving about behind me—slamming cupboard doors and throwing dirty pans into the sink. I don't know why she bothered preparing a roast; it always ended in recriminations. But Stuart, Lyndsey's new boyfriend, was around, and she was probably just putting on a show for his sake.

'She told me to get Lyndsey and Stuart from upstairs. I remember her voice was sharp—a warning. She'd been on a short fuse since finding out about Dad's new girlfriend, and I'd already been screeched at about schoolwork she thought I hadn't spent enough time on. Partway up the stairs, I called out to Lyndsey, but as I got closer to her bedroom, I could hear her sobbing. I paused at the door, listening, but couldn't make out what was being said—just Stuart's steady voice alongside her tears, probably trying to reassure her. Pandering to my sister, like everyone did…'

'Your doing so well,' Corine encourages, her expression supportive.

'"*Dinner!*" I shouted, hammering on the door with my fist to shock them. Lyndsey told me to fuck off. Back downstairs, when Mum asked where they were, I was half tempted to repeat Lyndsey's words. Instead, I said they were on their way and sat down, waiting for the signal to start eating.

'Fortunately, for Stuart's sake, Mum didn't know him well enough to lose it in front of him. But by the time they took their seats at the table, everything was cold. Mum was quietly furious. Lyndsey looked a mess—she hadn't tried to hide the fact she'd been crying. Her nose and eyes were red, with big clumps of mascara pooled beneath like Halloween makeup.

'Mum didn't seem to notice; she was all smiles, wishing everyone *"Bon appetite!"* before gulping down a glass of wine and pouring herself another. I pretended not to notice, kept my head down and ate. Eventually, Mum said something to Stuart about him toying with the food on his plate. She asked him if he was hungry. Then she turned on me. *"Take your elbows off the table, eat up! I haven't spent all morning cooking for you to make patterns on your plate.'"*

'That sounds intense.'

Mae nods, finding it hard.

'Keep going, you're doing great.'

'Lyndsey threw Stuart a look,' Mae continues. 'Then she said he had something he wanted to discuss. Stuart had a coughing fit, stuttered... then denied he had anything to say. Lyndsey looked as though she wanted to kill him. Then she turned to Mum. *"What would you do if I said I was pregnant?"* she asked. The air in the room was sucked in, like a vacuum. My whole body tensed, expecting Mum to explode. I couldn't tell if it was Lyndsey's ploy for attention or an actual possibility. Either way, I braced myself.'

'And what did your mum say?' Corine asks.

'She said she'd kill her.' Mae looks up at Corine. 'She didn't explode the way I'd expected her to, but her voice was threatening—cold. All the while, she kept smiling. *"Are you?"* she asked. Lyndsey looked at Stuart. He put his head down and stared nervously at his plate. I think seeing Stuart's response—the fact he didn't deny any of it—was what made Mum lose it. *"You're fucking kidding me. How the hell do you and stud-muffin over there think you're going to look after a baby? Neither of you work!"* she screeched at them.

'Lyndsey kept repeating she was sorry, but Mum was all fired up by then. *"It's the ABC of fucking,"* she'd said. *"If you're gonna screw around, wear a condom. Are you a Catholic, or just a fucking idiot, Stuart? Looking at you, I'm guessing both."* Lyndsey got all defensive of Stuart. I honestly thought he was going to faint. He comes from a nice family, so all that aggression... shouting in front of guests... they probably weren't things he was used to.'

Mae let out a long sigh, taking a moment to steel herself for what was coming.

'Then she told them they weren't to worry—that she would "sort the mess out". Lyndsey had stopped crying; suddenly got all serious. She asked Mum what she meant. *"Oh, I don't know, Lyndsey. I'll buy you a pushchair and a cot and some pretty little romper suits until you stop wanting to play mummies and daddies—and then I'll look after the mistake for the rest of my life. Or I could arrange a termination and make sure your simple little life is kept on track. Just keep your fucking legs shut in the future."*

'Lyndsey screamed that she was having the baby and there was nothing Mum could do about it. Mum threatened to throw her out. She asked if Stuart's family would have them both and their screaming baby. That's when Stuart said he hadn't told them. He kept stuttering. Mum mimicked him and said she hoped his fucking was a little more fluid than his speech. Lyndsey called Mum a bitch and knocked her plate off the table. *"No wonder Dad left you!"* she screamed. *"You're a total fucking bitch! I hate you!"*.'

Again, Mae pauses.

'It's okay,' Corine reassures her.

'Mum laughed. Then the real twisted stuff poured out. She said Lyndsey could always go and ask her father to support her. The same man she accused of molesting her. *"How will that look? Christ, some might even suspect he's the father. He's not the father, is he?"*.'

Corine shudders.

'Lyndsey screamed that Mum had made her say that about

Dad. That's when Mum slapped her.'

'How did you feel about the accusations?'

'I remember asking what was going on, what did Lyndsey mean, but neither of them answered. Instead, Mum continued to yell at Lyndsey: *"You're not right in the head, Lyndsey. You fuck things up and you keep fucking everything up, and that's why you're getting an abortion."* Lyndsey screamed that it was all Mum's fault, that she'd only said those things because Mum had asked her to. She just laughed in Lyndsey's face. I remember Stuart got up and walked out of the kitchen. Mum wafted her hand towards the door—she had a drink in the other. *"You gave him what he wanted and now he's gone. A baby won't change anything, you idiot."*

'It happened in seconds. Lyndsey grabbed a knife from the table and lashed out, slashing wildly at Mum. I screamed, terrified. Mum backed away and tried to defend herself, pleading with Lyndsey to stop. It all happened so quickly. I didn't know what to do. I just froze. Pathetic, I know, but…'

'That must have been beyond awful for you, Mae.'

Mae leans forward, her hand shaking as she rubs it across her mouth and chin. She nods. 'Then Stuart was there, screaming at her to stop. She did, thank God. Hearing his voice seemed to bring Lyndsey to her senses and she dropped the knife. Luckily it was a table knife, sharp, but it could have been so much worse. She sat there on the floor, clutching her knees, sobbing. I could see she was in shock.'

'What happened next?' Corine whispers.

'Mum's face and clothes were covered in blood. I ran over to her, distraught, thinking she might die of her injuries, from the blood loss. There was so much blood.'

Mae shifted in her seat, exhaling slowly.

Corine could see how difficult it was for her, especially after keeping quiet for so long.

'Weirdly… Mum seemed unnaturally calm. She sounded out of breath but kept reassuring everyone that she'd be okay, that the cuts were superficial. She asked me to get towels. I remember hearing Stuart call for an ambulance as I ran upstairs. When I got back with the towels, Mum and Stuart had been talking, but they fell silent. Lyndsey had curled into a ball and lay moaning to herself.

'Then Mum took hold of my hand—that's when she told me she was going to say it was me. Lyndsey was eighteen and would go to prison, but I wouldn't because of my age. She said if they asked, she would say I flipped because of exam stress. If she didn't press charges, I'd be home in a few days. At worst, I'd have to see a psychiatrist and she'd sort that. *"Just don't say anything. If you do, you'll make matters worse. Tell them it's a blur, you don't remember. Better still, say nothing."*…' Mae hesitates for a moment, then lifts both hands to her face, tears falling thick and fast.

'Oh, Mae.' There it was—the reason for Mae's silence: loyalty to a selfish, unstable mother who, seeing an opportunity for a more convenient outcome, took it. Better risk Mae spending a short spell in a psychiatric ward than have Lyndsey and any grandchild end up in a prison cell.

Corine pictures a trusting, obedient, fourteen-year-old Mae in an impossible predicament, and her heart breaks.

'I remember Mum stroking my hands and face, kissing me. I had her blood all over me. Probably intentional.' Mae shudders. 'She picked up the knife and gave it to me to hold.'

Mae stares across at the barred window, as though in a trance. Corine wonders if she's finished. She'd been through so much—this tiny, delicate, warrior of a girl.

'Thank you, Mae, that can't have been—'

Mae cuts her off. Corine imagines she's back in her childhood home, reliving those awful events, determined to get to the end.

'Lyndsey showered with Stuart's help, and I put on her clothes. The ambulance came first. The police arrived a little later. Mum refused to sit in a wheelchair or get on a stretcher, but I could tell she was in pain. I really did think she might die. I was terrified… numb. As the police were taking me away, she shouted, *"No matter what, I'm your mum."*'

'She should have protected you.'

'Even then, I heard an accusation in her words—like she was tying us together forever with an invisible noose.'

CHAPTER 38
CORINE

SIX MONTHS LATER

Corine sits at the kitchen table, an open laptop in front of her, a file and papers spread to one side. She smiles as she talks to Richard on the phone. He's about to go into a meeting but has insisted on taking her call.

'Thank you for going to the hearing tomorrow. I want to shield Mae for a while longer. Lyndsey has Stuart, and he's positive it'll be a quick sentencing for Martin. Kate, though… her lawyers are saying she has significant mental health issues.'

'She'll be claiming early-onset dementia next,' he says, laughing.

Corine chuckles. 'She should be more like her old university chum, who, by all accounts was also her part-time chauffeur and recreational substance supplier. Good old Martin made it easier by confessing. Two of his students complained about him, but it was all hushed up. You know how these expensive private schools are—they've got to maintain their cleaner-than-thou reputations. He tried to buy the boys off with gifts. In fact, Mae only recently remembered the tutu he bought her just after he'd come into her room. Kate even showed me a video of her wearing it. Now I know why she looked so unhappy and wanted the damn thing off. She was lucky he didn't do anything else, given what he did to poor Lyndsey.' Corine sighs. She can hear the distant sound of chatter through the earpiece.

'I should probably go,' Richard says.

'Yeah, call some order to that meeting. I look forward to seeing you here at the farm, sharing my plans.'

'Did I hear that right? Sharing your plans.'

Corine laughs and hangs up. She walks to the sink and fills a glass with water. As she sips, she notices the fine day beyond her window—the sun shining brightly between rolling cotton-ball clouds.

She walks into the new extension to get a better view outside. Betty lies fast asleep, curled up on Joe's chair. Corine doesn't have the heart to shoo her off; instead, she gently strokes the soft fur behind her ears.

'You still miss him, hey, Betty?' Corine whispers.

Betty looks towards the view, as if expecting to see Joe outside.

'You and me both, girl. Did you hear that, Joe? We miss you.'

At the sound of Joe's name, Betty sits bolt upright—ears pricked, head turning, eyes bright and expectant.

'Go back to sleep, you big softie,' Corine says, stroking her head. 'He's not coming back anytime soon.'

Betty jumps down from the chair and heads for her bowl. It's empty. She sniffs at it, nudges it forwards with her nose, then looks back at Corine.

'Oh, you've got into very bad habits, dog.'

Betty whines and steps backwards, head lowered.

'Trying to make me feel guilty, are you? Okay, okay, I'm getting you something to eat.' She picks up the dog bowl and heads to the hallway, returning moments later with it filled. 'Wait!'

Betty sits and offers her paw.

Corine pets and fusses the top of the dog's head. 'Go on, eat. And don't be getting a mess over my clean floor, you wee pest.'

Corine returns to the kitchen table, puts on her glasses, and presses her mousepad. The text document she's working on reopens and she scrolls back a page earlier to a section titled: *Families and Reintegration*. After a moment, Corine breaks off from reading and rolls her hair, clipping it up with a tortoiseshell clasp. She takes a deep breath and begins to type.

> *From a youth and criminal justice perspective, the role of the family in reducing recidivism and supporting successful reintegration into society is well documented. But what if a family support network is absent, or not ideal? What if a significant relationship, such as one with a mother or father, is broken, or worse still, toxic? How then do you successfully re-integrate young offenders in the absence of parental support?*

Corine sits back and glances to the side, then scrolls to another section and begins to type.

> *Studies within the area of false confessions suggest that the urge to confess stems from a high receptiveness to stress in response to perceived pressure. For some*

> *individuals, being easily influenced may help to 'keep the peace' and avoid conflict, but it also makes them extremely vulnerable.*

The sound of voices and laughter from outside distracts Corine, and she stops to listen. Moments later, the porch door creaks open and the voices grow louder. She hears coats and boots being pulled off and dropped on the floor, before Connor, Callum's son, walks into the room. Even wind-swept, he is handsome, with his dark hair and pale complexion.

Connor pulls off his wool hat and grins at Corine.

Mae appears behind him moments later. She doesn't look anything like the Mae from six months earlier—her face seems lit from within, animated; even her body-language is more expressive. Her jumper is covered in mud, bits of grass, and hay.

'You're meant to feed it to the cows, not roll in it!' It was out of Corine's mouth before she could stop herself. Immediately, her face flushes hot. 'Oh, no, I didn't mean that!'

Mae laughs, her eyes wide but exaggeratedly so.

'I'll have you know I'm not that sort of man,' Connor exclaims, feigning shock, though the pools of red on his cheeks betray his embarrassment. Betty offers a welcome distraction as he crouches down to stoke her.

Mae laughs again.

'What happened to you?' Corine asks.

'Och, well, Mae seems to think the new goats are her pals. I told her, never turn your back on them, especially Myrtle, she's a demon when she's in with her kids.'

'Lesson learnt.' Mae chuckles and rubs her left hip. She walks to the sink and pours herself and Connor a glass of water.

'You staying for a spot of lunch, Connor? I've made fish pie.'

'Can you please save me a wee bit for tomorrow? Sorry, but I promised I'd help Dad with the tractor. Did I tell you?' He hesitates and looks at Mae. 'Dad's livestreaming feeding the cows this afternoon for a special school in Peterhead, all being well. He wants me as technical support.'

'You see, you *can* influence him! Good for your dad, he's got a big heart. Can you tell him thanks for everything? Especially freeing you up to continue helping around here. I really appreciate everything you've both done.'

'Aye, it's no bother. I'll be free full-time in a few weeks. Just as soon as I've finished my dissertation. Then I can take on the full load, as agreed. I'll get a chance to see if it's really for me, without the father breathing over my shoulder.'

Corine frowns. 'Do you feel pressured, Connor?'

'Corine!' Mae groans.

'What?' she exclaims.

'God, no,' Connor assures her, shaking his head. 'I'm so grateful to the old man for looking out for me. Farming is in my blood, so it is, and he knows me better than anyone.'

'You looking after the farm has allowed me to focus on setting up my new practice. And for that, I'm eternally grateful.'

Connor beams at her, and Corine can't help but smile.

As she listens to Connor and Mae laughing and teasing

each other, it strikes her once again that Mae, like Connor, had faith in her parents. She trusted her mother to do right by her—not to encourage her to take the blame for a crime she didn't commit and throw her life away.

By the time Mae had realised what she had been asked to sacrifice—and to keep sacrificing—her fragile sense of self-worth was gone. Her value, by being sacrificed, had been called into question by the one person who should have valued her the most. Indeed, if a mother doesn't place any value on her child's life, it should be no surprise when the child doesn't either.

'I suppose that makes me your first patient. Corine? Corine?'

'Sorry, what?' Corine asks, shaking her head.

'I said, I'm your first patient,' Mae repeats.

'Oh, come on, you know you are much, much more than that.'

'Yeah,' Mae replies, smiling impishly. 'I do.'

†

Later, when Mae is washing dishes at the sink and Corine wipes the table, the phone rings.

'Hello?' Corine answers. Immediately, her face lights up. 'How is my little darling?' Looking up, she waves to Mae, putting her hand over the phone. 'Quickly, come and listen, Mary's trying to talk!'

Mae swipes her hands on a tea towel and rushes over. 'She's five months old, there's no way she's talking yet.'

'Och, she's trying, though, bless her.' Corine holds the phone up for her to listen.

'Put the speaker on,' Mae says. Leaning over Corine, she taps the speaker button, and the room fills with the sound of gurgling. 'Hello, Mary, hello there,' she whispers.

A gargling sound, like spittle caught at the back of a throat, breaks the silence—and both women laugh.

'Did you hear that?' Lisa's voice echoes from the phone. 'Isn't she amazing, trying to talk? She is, yes she is. Whose Mummy's clever girl?'

'Ah, ya ya, da da,' Mary babbles.

Corine and Mae look at each other and laugh.

Their conversation centres around baby Mary—her appetite, sleep patterns, and how excited she gets when Peter comes home from work. Lisa tells them about a visit to the health centre earlier that day for a weigh-in. They both laugh when Lisa says Mary was the heaviest baby there, and no one could believe she was breastfed.

'Ooh, what a little porker!' Mae laughs. She looks at Corine, expecting her to say something, but sees that her mind has wandered off.

'Sorry, gotta go—my right boob's about to explode—Mary's not latching on properly,' Lisa announces. 'I'll call tomorrow. We can't wait to see you in July!'

'Us too,' says Corine.

'Bye, Lisa. Bye, bye, Mary-boo, see you soon!' Mae coos.

Once Lisa ends the call, Mae watches Corine moving about the kitchen as though in a trance. It isn't like her to be so quiet, not after a phone call with Lisa.

'Shall we go for a walk on the beach whilst it's still light?'

'Sure,' Corine answers, but she makes no attempt to move. Mae walks to the hall, puts on her coat and shoes, and waits.

†

Corine finds herself standing at the kitchen sink, gripping its edge tightly, acutely aware of the urge to open a bottle of wine—and drink glass after glass. Would this battle in her mind be a constant one? On the surface, she was the happiest she had been for a long time, yet even now, her loss and guilt threatened to sabotage that fragile peace.

When Lisa mentioned feeding Mary, Corine felt a stirring within—a haunting recollection of let-down, her body instinctively readying to feed her baby. Every three hours with Michael, like clockwork, and for months after.

'Are you ready, it'll be dark in an hour,' Mae asks, bringing Corine back into the present.

'Sorry,' Corine murmurs. 'I was… Oh, it's nothing.' Walking past Mae, she sits on the bench in the hallway, ready to pull on her boots.

†

The long curve down to the beach is sheltered by tall white sand dunes, some up to fifteen metres high, dotted with clumps of wild grass and bursts of yellow gorse. When the dunes end and the vista opens, the view in all directions is breathtaking. Before them stretches a long sweep of empty, white sand, lapped by clear, blue water. Cliffs rise sharply and jut out on either side before plunging dramatically into the sea. A handful of rocks stand proud of the water, providing resting places for seals—though none are visible today. Birds call out above their heads—terns, black guillemots, and the occasional cormorant swooping and gliding on the westerly winds.

Betty moves freely, stopping to sniff seaweed or to check they've not gone too far. Mae bends down, picking up a shell here and there, then something bigger. She turns it around in her hand, holding it up for Corine to see. It's a piece of driftwood, sun-bleached and twisted into an unusual shape.

'Someone would pay for this if I varnished and mounted it. I'll call it *twisted*... no, *shaped by... nature*,' Mae suggests.

'Ha! You might be onto a winner there.'

'Can I ask you something?' Mae says as she pockets another shell.

'Sure.'

'Back then, when you finished talking to Lisa, you seemed a little sad. I thought you'd... well, you'd seemed happier recently.'

Corine smiles at her. 'I am happier, and that's thanks to you—and this.' She gestures to their surroundings. 'It's beautiful here, and I can see the good it's done you. You're happier, aren't you?'

Mae nods.

'And Connor, bless him—that boy's got a mighty crush on you.'

She giggles. 'No, he's here because you pay him to look

after the farm.'

'That too, but Callum told me he'd split up with his girlfriend.' Corine winks knowingly. 'I wonder why?'

Mae laughs sheepishly. 'That was over a month ago. Anyway, stop dodging my question. Why did you look so sad?'

'It was just a moment. They're happening less often, which is a huge improvement for me.' Corine pauses. 'I wasn't quite prepared for this one.'

'I'm sorry.' Mae studies her thoughtfully. 'Michael?'

Corine meets her gaze but can't bring herself to speak. Words lodge in her throat, heavy and immovable.

'You know, even if you had picked him up before you went to work, he still would have…' She hesitates. 'You can't blame yourself.'

Corine nods and quickens her pace, as if trying to outrun her thoughts. 'I know, I know. Will you stop worrying? It's not in your job description. A few months ago, I would have blotted everything out with drink from the moment I woke up.'

Corine stops suddenly and sweeps her hand towards the horizon. 'Just look at this place. Joe was right—we're lucky. You helped me see that again.'

Mae threads her arm through Corine's, and they walk in companionable silence. Betty darts past them, nose to the sand, having caught the scent of something. After a while, they pause. Corine points out to sea and pulls a pair of binoculars from her pocket, handing them to Mae. In the distance, black heads surface in the water—seals, bobbing and diving like a huddle of open-sea swimmers in wetsuits.

'There's two... no three... crikey, there's four of them!' Mae laughs, pointing out to sea. 'A whole family.'

Corine slips an arm around Mae's shoulders and looks, but not in the direction that Mae points. Her eyes rest on the figures standing to their side. A husband and son, as familiar to her as the beat of her baby's heart.

THE END

THIRD